FUGITIVES *of*

Chaos

FUGITIVES *of*

Chaos

John C. Wright

TOR®

A TOM DOHERTY ASSOCIATES BOOK

New York ·

FUGITIVES OF CHAOS

Copyright © 2006 by John C. Wright

This book is printed on acid-free paper.

Edited by David G. Hartwell

A Tor Book
Published by Tom Doherty Associates, LLC
175 Fifth Avenue
New York, NY 10010

www.tor.com

Tor® is a registered trademark of Tom Doherty Associates, LLC.

Library of Congress Cataloging-in-Publication Data

Wright, John C. (John Charles), 1961–
    Fugitives of chaos / John C. Wright.—1st ed.
        p.   cm.
    "A Tom Doherty Associates book."
    ISBN-13: 978-0-765-31496-3 (acid-free paper)
    ISBN-10: 0-765-31496-7 (acid-free paper)
    1. Orphans—Fiction.   2. Boarding schools—Fiction.   3. Kidnapping victims—Fiction.
    4. Immortalism—Fiction.   5. Great Britain—Fiction.   1. Title.
    PS3623.R54F84   2006
    813'.6—dc22
                                                                                2006005721

First Edition: November 2006

Printed in the United States of America

0 9 8 7 6 5 4 3 2 1

For my mother,
in memory of all the chaos
I created in my youth

CONTENTS

Acknowledgments   9

Dramatis Personae   11

1
Interlude with Amelia   15

2
Paper, Scissors, Rock   29

3
Circuitous Acts   41

4
Blackmail   61

5
The Cold Stars Turn   75

6
The Barrow Mound   91

7
The Kissing Well   107

8
Talismans of Chaos   *121*

9
Wings   *135*

10
Waters   *147*

11
Talon, Tooth, and Nail   *167*

12
North by Northwest   *179*

13
Freedom and Flight   *195*

14
The Crossing   *211*

15
Blind Spots   *229*

16
Remember Next Time Not to Look   *243*

17
The Ire of the Heavens   *255*

18
Festive Days on the Slopes of Vesuvius   *269*

19
The Fury of the Deep   *289*

20
Dies Not, Nor Grows Old All Her Days   *311*

ACKNOWLEDGMENTS

The translations of Herodotus used herein are based on the work of G. C. Macaulay, J. C. Wright, S. Felberbaum, and G. Rawlinson. Any errors or omissions are strictly the author's. The translation of Hesiod is taken from H. G. Evelyn-White.

DRAMATIS PERSONAE

The Students

(Primus) Victor Invictus Triumph ❖ Damnameneus of the Telchine

(Secunda) Amelia Armstrong Windrose ❖ Phaethusa, Daughter of
Helius and Neaera of Myriagon

(Tertia) Vanity Bonfire Fair ❖ Nausicaa, Daughter of Alcinuous and Arete

(Quartinus) Colin Iblis mac FirBolg ❖ Phobetor, son of Morpheus and
Nepenthe

Quentin Nemo ❖ Eidotheia, child of Proteus and the Graeae

The Staff

Headmaster Reginald Boggin ❖ Boreas, of the North Wind

Dr. Ananias Fell ❖ Telemus, Cyclopes

Mrs. Jenny Wren ❖ Erichtho the Witch

Miss Christabel Daw ❖ Thelxiepia the Siren

Grendel Glum ❖ Grendel, son of Echidna

Dr. Miles Drinkwater ❖ Mestor of Atlantis

Taffy ap Cymru ❖ Laverna, Lady of Fraud

The Olympians

Lord Terminus ❖ Zeus

The Great Queen, Lady Basilissa ❖ Hera

Lord Pelagaeus, also called the Earthshaker ❖ Poseidon
The Grain Mother ❖ Demeter
Lord Dis, also called the Unseen One ❖ Hades
The Maiden, also called Kore ❖ Proserpine
Phoebus the Bright God, also called the Destroyer ❖ Apollo
Phoebe, also called the Huntress ❖ Artemis
Lord Mavors ❖ Ares
Lady Cyprian ❖ Aphrodite
Trismegistus ❖ Hermes
Tritogenia, also called Lady Wisdom ❖ Athena
Mulciber ❖ Hephaestus
Lady Hestia
Lord Anacreon, also called Lord Vintner and the Vine God ❖ Dionysus

FUGITIVES *of*

Chaos

1

INTERLUDE WITH AMELIA

1.

I was dead for about half a day.

There was still a "me," a girl who woke up in the infirmary, but she only had my memories dated earlier than a fortnight ago. She was a suspicious girl, yes, and she knew her elders were up to something, and she was pretty sure she was not a human being.

But the last two weeks had never been, so she had never crawled through impossible secret passages with Vanity, never flown with Quentin, never seen the Old Gods sitting at their revelry at the meeting of the Board of Visitors and Governors, or learned the horrid tale of the Lamia. She never heard the ringing in a locked safe of the hypersphere shaking from the shock of the music of a siren. She never had a pancake fight with Colin on a morning when all the staff slept, the first day we ever made our own food for ourselves; she never followed Victor into the woods, walked across a snowy landscape that could not be the Gower Peninsula, and never saw a white ship from beyond the edge of the world.

I do not know what it was that happened during those events or during the imprisonment that followed. I cannot point to the moment.

But something had changed me. Amelia was a girl involved in playing an elaborate prank on her elders, keeping secrets from them, trying to find out about her past; serious, yes, but still a prank. She was doing it more to please Victor than for herself. Amelia occupied only the three normal dimensions, like everyone else.

Phaethusa was a woman involved in a war.

It was Amelia who woke up in the infirmary.

2.

Amelia spent about an hour simply lying in her bed in the infirmary while a thin and severe Doctor Fell and an equally severe Sister Twitchett fretted over her, took her temperature, bent their heads together over charts.

Finally Dr. Fell said, "The medications I have been giving you once a month are for some reason ineffective. Are you certain you have been taking the doses as prescribed?"

Amelia tried to hide her dread. Of course she had not been taking those damned medications. Victor did not want her to.

She said, "But, of course, Doctor. You know what's best."

"Znf! I also know you do not believe that. You have reached that unfortunate age where you have all of life's answers and you know everything more perfectly and more profoundly than your elders. But you are a bright girl; you get good marks in math. If I am 3.4375 times your age, and not cognitively deficient, surely I have 3.4375 times your experience and knowledge?"

She blinked up at him. "I am sure I don't know, Doctor. How old am I?"

"Sixteen. Now get up. The Sister will bring you your clothes. Obey instructions in the future or you will find yourself in this place again, or perhaps in someplace worse."

3.

Amelia saw two things that struck her as slightly peculiar and "sensed" one thing that was so very peculiar as to be without any sane explanation. Did she ask questions? Did she ask Dr. Fell for help? She did not. Amelia might have been a child, but she was not a stupid one.

The first odd thing she saw, through the disinfectant plastic drapes hanging around her bed, and through a crack in the open door to the waiting room, was Sister Twitchett, carefully examining the pockets and inner lining of the skirt and blouse she had gotten from Amelia's room. She had an instrument shaped like a horseshoe (a metal detector?), and she was rubbing it slowly up and down the seams. With her other hand, the Sister was feeling every inch of seam with her fingers, looking for irregularities in texture.

While Amelia watched, Sister Twitchett pulled a lump of fabric about the size of a walnut out of Amelia's skirt pocket. It looked like a ribbon or sash that had been knotted and reknotted into a snarl. Twitchett picked at it disinterestedly and, when she could not get it open, shrugged and replaced it in the pocket.

Amelia wondered, Why are they searching my clothes? Nosy grown-ups.

Amelia hurriedly lay down and composed her best innocent face as Twitchett came bustling through the door with the school uniform draped over one arm.

"And remember to put on the necktie!" ordered the Sister.

Amelia grimaced.

4.

The other patient in the infirmary had his hand wrapped in a bandage, and his little finger was clamped in a tiny banana-shaped tube of metal. He was a dark-haired man with sad, tired eyes. The second odd thing Amelia saw was that the man hesitated before introducing himself, as if he had forgotten his own name for a moment. His name was Miles Drinkwater, the new civics teacher. In the spring, he would serve as a coach for a swimming team to be formed. He had hurt himself, naturally enough, swimming.

"I was out of my depth, Miss Windrose," he said.

Amelia thought she detected a slight accent in his voice, as if he perhaps were Italian or Greek, despite his English up-country name.

But what was that look of fear in his eye? Teenagers can sense fear like dogs, and Amelia somehow knew that she intimidated Mr. Drinkwater.

She thought she knew why. Amelia, it must be recalled, was a little proud about her good looks, which she had wished upon herself in youth by staring into a mirror. So Amelia made a point of holding his hand a bit too long when shaking hands, and standing half a step too close, and dropping her eyelids shyly, toying with her richly hated necktie, and doing the little bits of stage business she thought of as "Vanity stuff."

Mr. Drinkwater did seem mildly taken aback, puzzled, and then amused. As if he had been locked in a cage with a raging lioness, only to discover her to be a circus animal, quite tame, doing gentle children's tricks, balancing on balls or leaping hoops or something. He visibly relaxed.

It was the opposite of the expected reaction. Amelia did not know what she did wrong, but she knew she did not do "Vanity stuff" as well as Vanity did. Vamping takes practice, and Amelia (usually) thought such tricks were beneath her.

Humiliating.

Amelia thanked the new teacher, was excused, and walked down the corridor away from the infirmary. She did not bother swaying her hips or darting coy glances over her shoulder back at him. She knew already that she had endangered her grade from Mr. Drinkwater for that quarter, and she had not attended a single lecture yet. Great, just great.

It was just one of the little arbitrary things that can ruin a young girl's morning. Adults forget what it is like not to be able just to shrug things off, not to have any of the important things in your life under your own control.

5.

Outside, Amelia leaned against one of the leafless trees lining the carriage circle before the main house. It was a spot she liked, out of direct line of sight of any windows either from the Manor House or the Great Hall.

She shrugged one shoulder out of her coat, rolled up her sleeve. Amelia rubbed her upper arm and stared at it. She saw nothing out of the ordinary.

And yet, clear and persistent, there was a sensation coming from her upper arm. Not just a sensation, but an emotion. Her arm liked her. Her arm was friendly. A warm, tail-wagging, puppy-like, unabashed friendliness radiated from one motionless spot above her elbow.

6.

Vanity was overjoyed to see her; the two girls met with hugs and little hopping dances of joy. "I didn't have anyone to talk to for a week! It gave me the screaming meemies!"

Vanity had apparently suffered a bout of pneumonia, as well, but recovered four days ago. The only odd thing about her recovery was that Dr. Fell had prescribed "alternative medicine" for her. Instead of just being injected with some drug, Vanity had spent a day drinking odd herbal tea and sniffing candles of incenses concocted by Mrs. Wren ("aromatherapy") and listening to Miss Daw play her wonderful lilting violin ("music therapy"). It was odd, but it seemed to work, for Vanity felt refreshed and content afterwards.

"I think it was just that I got out of classes for a day! Of course I felt better!" Vanity exclaimed, giggling.

Amelia said, "Have you ever had a body part of yours feel . . . well . . . friendly?"

Vanity's huge green eyes glittered. "Colin has. Let me tell you the filthy thing he said about his you-know-what. We're sitting in seminar, and he's holding his pencil in his pocket, and poking up the front of his trousers every time Miss Daw walks by. You know. So his zipper is like . . . You know! Looks like it's throbbing. I couldn't keep from giggling. So Miss Daw spots him. He says, bold as brass, 'Why, Miss Daw, I find lectures about high-energy physics to be most exciting! And my fellow student, Mr. Lovejoy . . .' "

Amelia stood up and stared out the window. Outside, moving with slow, painful hops among the dry bushes and the leafless trees, trying to push a wheelbarrow, was Mr. Glum, the groundskeeper.

"What happened to the groundskeeper . . . ?" asked Amelia in a voice of horror.

Vanity said, "Chopped his own foot off with an axe or something. Pretty clumsy, if you ask me. I say he deserves it. Filthy old man. He's always giving me such looks!"

Amelia said quietly, "You're a horrible person, Vanity. Pitiless and cruel. Go away and leave me alone."

"Well, what's wrong with you? He *is* a dirty old man! Is something wrong with you?"

"I suppose there is. I don't want to talk to you just now. Go away."

Vanity's lip trembled, and she ran off, tears in her eyes. It was just one of the little arbitrary things that can ruin a young girl's morning.

7.

Amelia had Miss Daw for astronomy that morning. She could not shake the feeling that there was something odd about Miss Daw. Every now and again she was staring at Amelia, and her normally cool, china-doll-perfect looks were shadowed with a hint of emotion. Sorrow? Fear? Amelia did not know what to make of that; perhaps Miss Daw was afraid of catching pneumonia.

Later, in second-period language tutorial, Mrs. Wren had them translating passages from Book IV of Herodotus, the one called *Melpomene.*

Vanity read: *"Many battles were fought, and the Scythians gained no advantage, until at last one of them thus addressed the remainder:"*

Amelia read: *"What a thing is this that we are doing, Scythian men! We are fighting against our own slaves, and we are not only becoming fewer in number ourselves by falling in battle, but also we are killing them, and so we shall have fewer to rule over in future."*

Colin read slowly: *"Now therefore to me best it seems spears on the one hand and bows to drop; to take, on the other hand, everyone the horse the whip,* sorry Headmaster, I mean his horsewhip, and to go near self? Um, Himself to go near? Lemme try again, Teacher: *It seems best to drop the spears and bows and take up every man his horsewhip, and go near the foe and get like right up in his face, and open up an industrial-strength can of whup—"*

Mrs. Wren said, "A little less license with the translation, please, Mr. mac FirBolg."

Victor also read slowly, puzzling out the Greek declensions. Or perhaps he was interested in what the passage said: *"For, while they were seeing we had arms, then they considered they were similar to us, and born of similars, but whenever they see for themselves we have whips instead of arms, having learned that they are our bondsmen and admitted that, they will not abide our onset."*

"On the other hand, Mr. Triumph, you need to take more license. The thought in the original Greek is fluid and logical: the language in many ways superior to our English. Try to capture some of that elusive grace. For example, *not born of equals* would have been better than *born of similars.*"

Quentin, the best student in Greek, sight-translated without sparing a glance at his lexicon: "*The Scythians followed this counsel, and the slaves were so astounded that they forgot to fight, and immediately ran away.*"

In the seminar discussion afterwards, Amelia made good points, for which the teacher praised her. "The decision of the Scythians was not based on morality; it was economic. No matter what his values or his philosophy, a man who fights his own slaves during a rebellion suffers an economic loss. Whichever slave owner damages his slaves the least gains the advantage."

It was Quentin who said, "Notice that the bonds involved were not physical, but spiritual."

For third period, they had to don cap and gown to attend Headmaster Boggin's philosophy lecture.

The Headmaster was in a more relaxed mood than was his wont, and he plied his lecture on Kant's *Prolegomena* with many digressions; and he darted sudden questions to the startled students. One question led to another, and eventually Boggin left the lectern, drew up a chair, and turned the class into a round-table seminar. He seemed particularly gracious, almost charming, whenever he spoke to Vanity or Amelia.

"Mr. Triumph, you seem, may I say, unduly critical of the Great Father of Modern Philosophy! What in general seems so to annoy you?"

Victor answered, unabashed, "If you will forgive me, Headmaster, I prefer our own English philosophers to these German metaphysicians. Hobbes spent his first sixteen chapters defining his terms. In Kant, I do not see one single definition at any point. Kant speaks of moral imperatives so abstract that a man is defined as 'immoral' if he takes any pleasure or gets any reward for following moral law; Hobbes speaks of the fear of violent death at the hands of others, and recommends a very logical strategy for avoiding that danger, i.e., combination with those in like danger with yourself. The rewards he offers are immediate and practical: peace; commerce by land and sea; letters; mechanics; agriculture; and the prospect of living a life which is rich, companionable, refined, civil, and long."

"Mr. Triumph, some would say these German metaphysicians offer an almost religious motive to fight on at any cost. If you seek no reward and fear no loss, nothing can deter you. Whereas the cynical common sense of our English Mr. Hobbes would have us submit to any form of tyrant, rather than risk anarchy."

"Who fights more wisely, Headmaster? The zealot who fights without knowing or caring what he stands to gain or lose, or the free man who knows his home and property and personal safety are at stake? Which wars did more damage to the country and the common people, the cynical Wars of the Roses, or the idealistic Thirty Years' War? Forgive me if I prefer the practical to the . . ."

"To the impractical, Mr. Triumph . . . ?"

"No, Headmaster. I was going to say, to the nonsensical."

The Headmaster laughed out loud and, for some reason, seemed so pleased with this answer, or with the class, or perhaps with life in general, that he dismissed his students with ten minutes to go before next period.

8.

Amelia and the other students used the ten minutes to have a quick powwow.

There was a little semicircular courtyard tucked between two wings of the Manor House, set (during the summer) with a little herb garden. An oak had once grown up through the middle of a circular bench; now the stump made a nice footstool. The students all sat there, facing each other and watching over each other's shoulders, watching in every direction for any sign of grown-ups.

Victor put out his hand: "All for one."

Quentin said, "And one for all."

The girls chimed in: "One for all—one for all."

Colin waited until Vanity and Amelia put their hands in the circle, and he plopped his hand down on Amelia's, caressing her knuckles with his finger in an oily fashion; and he said, "And all the girls for me!"

Then he said, "Ow!" when Amelia, without removing her hand from the circle, elbowed him in the ribs.

Victor slapped his neck. That was the sign that everyone should assume the conversation was being bugged.

Then Victor said, "What's your favorite color, Amelia?"

Yellow was her favorite color. Everyone sighed, except Colin, who groaned. Yellow Alert meant no unsecured communications, even when alone, and everyone was to wake up at midnight to participate in a conference (by tap code) through the dormitory walls.

Quentin said, "I'm curious as to why you're curious about her favorite color, Victor." (Translation: *Why the alert?*)

Victor said, "I see a squirrel. Rare this time of year." *(Girls, start chattering.)*

Amelia was annoyed. Not only had she and Vanity just had an argument that morning, but it was something of a stereotype, if not an outright insult, to assume that girls could just blather on and on about nothing on demand.

Vanity did not help matters by living up to the stereotype. She apparently had forgiven Amelia, and now wanted to chat about Mr. Drinkwater, the handsome new teacher.

Amelia tried to follow the conversation of the boys (the "Macho Patriarchy," as she called them) while they coughed and tapped the benches in code or made innocuous-sounding comments with double meanings.

Victor said, "The weather is getting warmer." (This comment was hard to translate, because the weather actually was getting warmer. In code, it was supposed to mean that things were heating up; that is, the grown-ups were up to something.)

Quentin: "Seems cool enough to me, except for one thing."

Colin said, "Rum luck that we all came down with Doctorfellitis at the same time. Missing the big meeting, whatever that was. But won't it get colder as the week goes on?"

Victor had been writing a note in his notebook. He passed it around the circle. Unfortunately, he passed it to his left, so that Quentin saw it first and Amelia saw it last.

Never so much drugs before. Never knocked us out for days at a time.

Vanity (still chattering away like a stereotype) took out her pink pen and circled the *s* in the plural "days" and put a question mark by it. Amelia passed the note back to Victor.

Victor took an almanac out of his coat pocket, opened it to a page he had dog-eared, and passed it to Vanity. Amelia peered over her shoulder. It was a chart listing the predicted times of the rising and the setting of the moon and certain major stars, cross-referenced by latitude and time of year.

Colin said, "Hey, look what I found!" (Translation: *I stole this.*) And he pulled out a folded back-page from a newspaper, one of the several that arrived daily in the large mailbox, surrounded by stone like a pillbox, at the far end of the drive. He had circled the times given for sunrise and sunset, moonrise and moonset for today.

The two figures agreed that today was Monday, December 18. But the school calendar and the class schedule for today indicated that it was supposed to be Wednesday the thirteenth.

Vanity turned away from Amelia and said to Victor, "Remember what they taught us in science class?" (Translation: *Always seek independent confirmation.*)

Quentin said, "This may not interest anyone but me . . ." *(This may not convince anyone but me.)* ". . . but who wants to see a card trick?"

Quentin took his Rider-Waite deck of tarot cards out from a cedar box he kept in an inner pocket. He shuffled, cut the deck into three piles. He said, "Pick a card, any card."

Vanity leaned across the circle and picked one of the cards, turned it faceup. It was Key Eighteen: the Moon.

Quentin said, "That's been happening all day."

Colin said, "Good job in language tutorial today. Not everyone speaks Greek as well as you do, pal." He passed him Victor's notebook. "Why don't you write out that passage for me we were looking at."

Quentin wrote in his small precise hand:

—*2day* clearly *Monday, not Wednesday. Monday is assoc w/ Moon (obvsly!) but also w/ White Roses, silver, Willow trees. All signs v. obvious. Saw Owl by day, flew widdershins thrice around clock tower: Warning of Danger! Key XVIII = deception.*

Colin rolled his eyes and sighed. "Look, the big meeting is over and we missed it. The weather is turning colder again. We all got sick, but we're all better now, so . . . so what is all this? My favorite color is Irish green. Why don't we all just relax?"

Victor leaned over and pointed to what he had previously written in the notebook:

Never knocked us out for days at a time.

Colin turned to the rest of us. "What's that you've got in your hand?" (*Let's see a show of hands.*)

This comment was also hard for Amelia to translate because, at that moment, she had pulled the lump of fabric out from her skirt pocket. She was staring at it in confusion, utterly confounded.

It was a knot. A knot with no beginning and no end. It looked like it was made out of an apron sash.

Amelia looked up to see that everyone else was voting.

Vanity was usually impatient with Yellow Alert restrictions. She held out her mittened fist, thumbs-down.

Colin said, "Caesar says, 'Kill the Christians!'" and showed his thumbs-down.

Quentin and Victor both gave a thumbs-up. Quentin said softly, "Spare the gladiator, who fought well, and the plebes will thank you next games, despite that they presently howl and yell."

A tie. Everyone turned and looked at Amelia.

She was staring at the impossible knot of fabric in her hands. She looked up, tears in her eyes. She raised her hand, thumb up. She whispered, "Vanity, what's your favorite color?"

Vanity raised an uncertain hand to stroke her red hair.

Colin made an impatient noise. "Oh, you are kidding. If things are that bad, what about plan C?"

(Plan C was "Call the cops.")

Amelia shook her head. "The sun has come out." *(It was getting a lot warmer; danger was growing.)*

Colin said, "Plan C is a great plan."

Victor said, "What do we say? That they overmedicate us here? I understand that happens in a lot of schools."

Colin snorted. "We'll think of something. We'll say Vanity is being sexually molested by the teachers. Heck, I'll sexually molest her my own self. At least I'll get put in a nice prison colony, and I won't be here any longer!"

Vanity smirked at him, saying, "Why don't you go sexually molest yourself, Colin? Oh, wait! You might catch a social disease from yourself! You don't know where you've been. Bleh!"

Vanity stuck out her tongue, and Colin smiled and pantomimed pulling down his zipper, with exaggerated welcoming gestures toward her tongue.

Amelia looked back and forth at this. Childish. So childish. But we are not children anymore. We cannot afford to be.

Quentin said to Amelia, "How hot do you think the weather will turn? Like spring?"

Amelia shook her head.

"Like summer? Tropic summer?"

Amelia shook her head.

"How hot?"

She whispered, "Do you remember the myth of Phaëthon?"

Victor passed the notebook to her.

I wrote quickly:

They erased our brains, all of us. Me, they slipped. There is a creature in my bloodstream. Sympathetic. This knot reminded me that I had amnesia. I tried to remember. Creature felt, wants to help. The creature is an amnesia-inducing drug. Knows how brain works. Helped. Starting to open brain block.

   I know who we are. I know who they are. They can hear whatever we say; listen on the wind. No talking!

Victor leaned over and pointed to the sentence, "I know who they are." I wrote:

Boggin = Boreas, North Wind; Fell = Telemus, a cyclopes; Wren = Erichtho, witch; Glum = Grendel, sea monster; Daw = Thelxiepia, siren. Drinkwater from Atlantis.

Vanity, giving Victor a look of impatience, leaned in with her pink pen, and circled one sentence over and over. "I know who we are." She started sketching big question marks and exclamation points. I wrote:

I am a Greek goddess from hyperspace. Quentin from underworld; Colin from dreamland; Victor from outer space; Vanity is from Homer. We all have magic powers.

   Names: Phaethusa; Eidotheia; Phobetor; Damnameneus; Nausicaa

And, because I did not know whether I would have the chance, I wrote the secret out quickly:

Victor has power over Wren; Quentin over Glum; me, Fell; Colin, Daw.

Boggin unkn ???? V. Dangerous! Flies! Bends space! Curses! Spanks!

Also reverse. Watch out!!! Glum stops me; Wren stops C; Daw stops Vic; Fell stops Q. Boggin (?) stops Vanity?

If catch us, erase memory for good, no slip-ups.

Victor looked around at the others. He said, "Vanity's favorite color."

No one doubted me. No one called me crazy. It was the proudest moment of my life. All my friends trusted me.

All four of them held out their hands, thumbs-up. Unanimous. Red Alert.

Red Alert was the code for maximum security and greatest care.

It was the code for the escape attempt.

Colin leaned over the note. "Half a mo'. What's that word there?" He was pointing at "Spanks!"

But by then, the ten minutes were up, and the bell was ringing. I had the excuse of gathering books. We all hurried off to next period.

Less than six hours, I was the girl I used to be less than ten days ago. One would think there could not be much difference.

Now as I walked to the library with Victor, all the clichés that you hear about in old songs, but which never appear in real life, applied to me. There was a spring in my step and a song in my heart. I stood straight and proud and tall, and my face almost hurt from how wide and bright my smile was.

I could not figure it out, and I did not really know why. There is nothing to show it in anything I did that morning, during those six hours when I was just Amelia, but take my word for it: My life was tepid. The girl from ten days ago felt dull, harassed, and joyless, all the time, and she never noticed it, any more than a fish notices being wet.

But before ten days ago, I had never matched wits with Grendel and, to save my soul, outsmarted him. I had not talked Thelxiepia into standing aside silently while I undid Dr. Fell's foul potion. Ten days ago, I did not have two gods, Trismegistus and Mulciber, both vying for my favor. Ten days ago, I had not been the one brighter than the others. Ten days ago, I had not been the dangerous one.

Even if I failed and ditched now—and the chances of failure were higher than the chances of success—at least it would be my hands on the controls of the crashing airplane.

I resolved, as I walked, to be the most dangerous one I could be. And in my mind, that meant one thing: thought. Think things through; then act. First be patient; then be brave.

My smile faltered and my footstep got heavy.

"What is it?" said Victor.

I shook my head. I could not answer aloud, not while the wind might be listening, but a poignant thought had pierced my heart like a needle.

They had stolen Quentin's first kiss.

Again.

2

PAPER, SCISSORS, ROCK

1.

Headmaster Boggin and Lord Mulciber were standing on the steps of the library, talking in low tones. There was no way to avoid walking past them without being tardy for our study period.

I now wished I had taken my Dramatics lessons more seriously two years ago, when Miss Daw had insisted we attempt to put on a Shakespeare play with just five students to play all the roles.

I tried to recall what my first impression had been upon seeing Lord Mulciber, who now to me seemed kindly and funny, if gruff. I remembered he had looked like Quasimodo from *Notre Dame,* all humpback and twisted leg and crooked shoulders broader than a yard across. I tried to get a look of pity or disgust or something on my face, but I was not doing it. In the end, I just decided it was cold enough to allow me to put my scarf over my mouth and nose.

Lord Mulciber was standing on the upper step, but his head was still only about level with Boggin's breast pocket. Victor stepped past the two with a brisk nod, but Mulciber put his thick steel walking stick in my way and said, "Reginald, you must introduce us."

Victor turned and looked back down. His face was expressionless; he had one foot higher than the other; his hands were relaxed and by his side. But I had never seen him look more dangerous.

Boggin said uncomfortably, "Carry on, Triumph. Tell the librarian that

Miss Windrose is excused with my permission for a moment or two, there's a good lad."

Victor turned like a soldier and continued on in.

"What do we have here, an Arab girl from a harem?" said Mulciber. "Show us your face, girl."

That made me blush. Maybe I would have blushed more if I had actually been Amelia with no notion of who this was. But maybe not.

Boggin cleared his throat. "Miss Windrose, this is His Lordship, Weyland Talbot. It is his family which owns the estate on which we stand; it is his generosity which houses and sustains us. Please treat him with all due courtesy."

"How do you do, Your Lordship," I said, putting my left foot back and sketching the briefest possible curtsy.

Here was what was so strange. I could not remember what I was like. Would I have been more shy? Less? Maybe a little rude? Or fascinated or repelled? I have never actually studied myself before. I did not know what to act like.

Boggin said, "His Lordship expressed the desire to see your face, Miss Windrose. I hope you will not continue this conversation all muffled and, ah, obscured."

Mulciber said, "Reggie. You like the sound of your voice. Only you. Got me? Let me talk to the girl. And you! Windrose, is it? What about that face of yours, eh?"

I leaned forward and presented my cheek to him. Boggin raised both eyebrows. Mulciber squinted (and scowled) a moment, not understanding my gesture. Then he snorted loudly and squinted (and grinned), raised his huge thick-fingered hand, and plucked the veil away from my face.

The folds of the scarf fell lightly down across the bosom of my jacket.

"Very nice," said Mulciber.

"I thank Your Lordship," I said coolly, straightening a bit.

"Don't get vain. I've seen better. I have better at home," he said, scowling (or maybe he was still grinning).

"I am sure Your Lordship's daughters are very beautiful, sir," I said. (I thought myself terribly clever for this comment, clever enough to remember that I was not supposed to remember who his wife was.)

He scratched the stubble of his skull with a finger as thick as a sausage.

"No. I got no little ones. None that are any damn good, anyhow." He looked rather sad for a moment, and there was real pain in his eyes. "No, I guess you could say I married young. A showgirl, actually. Gold digger, just like everyone warned me against. She run off with a soldier boy. Serves me right, I guess."

I was actually past embarrassment and well on my way to pity at this point. I said, "Your Lordship—? I mean, please don't tell me your . . . not that I don't want to hear, but . . ."

"But I shouldn't be telling a stranger, right? You see, your face fooled me, Miss Windrose. Ever get the feeling you met someone before?"

"Well, Your Lordship, I get that feeling when I see Vanity. It is quite an eerie sensation. She is my roommate, you see, so I actually have seen her before. Every day, actually. But the sensation is still quite eerie."

"Heh. Heyah. Funny one, aren't we. Listen, Windrose! I was asking Boggin here who his best and brightest student is. Your name came up. I want you to send me your résumé when you graduate. I have a large industrial concern on the Continent, and I can always use new folk."

I turned to Boggin. "Headmaster, when exactly is the date of graduation?"

He said coldly, "When you turn twenty-one, the institution can release you."

"And when is that date, sir?" I said brightly, "I'd like to mark it on my calendar. I am sure His Lordship would, too, wouldn't you, Your Lordship?"

Boggin looked at Mulciber. Mulciber just smiled, obviously relishing Boggin's discomfort.

Boggin turned back to me abruptly, saying, "Since you are presently sixteen, that would make it five years hence. We do not know the date of your birth with any precision. January first may be assumed to be the date."

I said to Mulciber, "I understand, Your Lordship, that sixteen-year-olds are sometimes legally allowed to work, at summer jobs if nothing else. Your Lordship would need to acquire Headmaster Boggin's permission, as he is my legal guardian, of course, but considering the great debt he no doubt feels in his heart toward Your Lordship for this wonderful estate. . . . Well, he would not do anything to obstruct Your Lordship's plans, may I assume that?"

Mulciber grimaced. "Stop with that 'Lordship' stuff. I bought my title, and I did it only to make it easier to do business in England. You're a sweet girl, but you've studied how to annoy people, haven't you? Well, don't annoy me."

I said, "Sir . . . ? What may I call you?"

He opened his mouth to say "Stumpy" . . . I could almost see he was thinking it. . . . But then he changed his mind and said, "Mr. Talbot will do for now."

He reached into a breast pocket of his finely tailored suit and pulled out a business card, which he proffered to me. I took it with thanks, looking confused. "I do not have phone privileges," I said.

Mulciber looked at Boggin. "Oh, Reggie here will fall over himself to make things smooth for you, Windrose. He just tried to bollix up what I was working on, and he did a damn fine job of it, too. He doesn't want to bollix up any more of my things, or it will go bad for him. I think he understands that. Don't you, Reggie!" And he poked the Headmaster in the chest with his metal cane.

"Of course, Your Lordship . . . ," said Boggin, looking angry and ashamed. It was his pride, you see. English gentlemen never called each other out in front of lower orders, servants, or children.

"See that you do!" snarled Mulciber.

"Mr. Talbot," I said.

"What is it, girl?"

"Are you and the Headmaster—? I mean, are you in some sort of financial trouble with him or something? I realize it is not my place to ask, but you seem so angry. . . ."

Mulciber smiled. "I had some friends in Herculaneum. They saw me angry. This isn't angry. Reginald and I are not competitors. We are enemies, and I may have to kill him someday. I hope not, though. Bad for business.

"Good day to you, miss. Reggie, I'll see myself off the property. I know the way. 'Tis my damn property anyway."

And with a rolling gait, clashing his steel cane at every other step, Mulciber stomped away.

I actually felt sorry for Boggin. I don't know why I did, because I knew what he had done and how he brought it on himself. But I said, "I am sorry I had to see that, Headmaster. I am really sorry."

Boggin drew himself up and glared down at me. For a moment, I could see peeking through his expression that masculine pride and almost sexual power he had shown in dealing with me before. But it did not come to the fore. He wanted just to order me to forget it, to sponge away his humiliation in my eyes.

But he thought I had forgotten he was a god, one of several involved in some sort of deadly struggle, between factions vying for control of the throne of heaven. He thought I did not remember being carried through the air in his strong, strong arms. He thought that I did not remember being spanked by him.

So he couldn't say whatever he wanted to say. He couldn't erase his shame by reminding me of his power and pride. He was supposed to be just the headmaster of a school.

"Let us not speak of this again, Miss Windrose. Perhaps His Lordship is aching in his joints, and the pain has distracted him. We cannot be too quick to judge those whom fate has condemned to being grossly crippled, can we? That will be all. You may go."

And since I was pretending just to be a schoolgirl under his command, I went.

I looked back through the panes of glass of the library door. Boggin was facing away from me, but he had his hands to his face, as if he were wiping away tears of rage.

Victor would not have felt sorry for the Bad Guys, I thought. He would have noted, in a precise and dispassionate voice, that emotion was a weakness, and any sign of weakness on the part of the enemy is a potential advantage for us.

I fall short of the Victor standard.

2.

Victor and I had study hall that period, and we sat in the library, facing each other, our books and notes spread out, looking as if we were studying.

In fact, I had my eyes half-closed, and the words of the textbook into which I stared seemed to swim and grow flat in my vision. I was seeing the words on pages that were not open under my left hand and right hand; I was seeing the internal texture of the paper and bindings.

I began to see its internal nature (dry and patient), moral relation (textbooks were required to be honest and candid), and utility (the gleaming nonlight of the usefulness to me of the text was fading dimmer and dimmer as I thought less about classes and grades, and more about escape). Oddly enough, the histories and philosophy works from second and third period, lying unopened on the table, shone very brightly (except for Kant, who was black as pitch). It was by this light that I could see other objects around me in hyperspace.

Because hyperspace was dark. There was no sun nor stars here, and the objects that had shed light for me before—Miss Daw's concentric wheels, or the chiming of the hypersphere—were absent.

Also, there seemed to be more layers of substance, a heavier medium, than had been here before, as if the whole school, and a wide area of time-space before and after, had a new energy-structure imposed on them.

I did not have the ringing hypersphere to stimulate me; I did not have Vanity and the magic green table to allow the native laws of nature to leak in here from Myriagon.

Basically, I was stuck.

Don't get me wrong: I could see things around me in four-space, but even the little things I used to be able to do (such as the trick of making heavy objects less massive) simply were not working. I could see world-lines and probability paths, but I could not deflect them anymore.

I could see the various limbs and energy-extensions of my 4-D "body" lined up "next" to me in hyperspace, neatly folded like nested spoons or the segments of a Japanese fan.

Let me see if I can explain this without it sounding gross. Imagine my body was a geometric shape like, say, a pyramid. When it is base down, the flatlanders living in the plane on which it rests see it as a square; when it has one side down, they see a triangle. To them, it looks like the square body changes shape and loses one angle.

A more feminine example might be conic sections. Base-down, a cone forms a circle (my normal girl body), but as the cone axis tilts, one generates ovals of various eccentricity, parabolas, or hyperbolae (my other bodies that looked more deerlike or swanlike or dolphinlike). In the limiting case, when the plane is tangential to the cone's side, one generates a line, which has very different properties from other conic sections. (I had shapes or limbs that "looked" like strands of energy, or music.) If the plane goes through the origin, one generates a point. (In effect, I could turn insubstantial.)

The trick I did to look like a centaur was to rotate in a deerlike body from the waist down, while keeping my face and upper body "flat" in the plane.

At the moment, I was unable to wiggle left or right, which meant I could not manifest any manipulator constructs (i.e., limbs) into this time-space.

So I could see the dark parts of Victor's nervous system, and I could see how small an adjustment I would have to make to the tilt of his governing monad to bring the meaning axis back to bear. . . . But it was out of reach. His memory was out of reach.

3.

My plan was to spend the whole period writing in my notebook, to give a report to Victor of the events and discoveries of the last ten days. I swear, I sat paralyzed for about two minutes, just trying to think of how to boil it down or what to put first.

The period was half over, and I had covered about four sheets in tiny writing, on both sides, and I had not even hit all the main points I wanted to cover. It was like trying to walk up a mudslide; every paragraph I wrote seemed more inexplicable than the previous paragraph, further down the slope of confusion. There simply wasn't enough time to fill Victor in on all the background, and details I thought I could skip kept cropping up as important. Soon my margins were covered with little arrows pointing back to previous paragraphs I was trying to clarify.

To hide what I was doing, I wrote on the back pages in the notebook whose first few sheets contained the real report I was supposed to be working on for organic chemistry. If the librarian, Miss Flinders, got up from her desk to look over my shoulder, she would see nothing suspicious.

But Miss Flinders did not move from her post behind her desk, where she was wrapped in a heavy quilt with her jacket and hat still on, her feet propped on a little cherry-red electric space heater she had smuggled in. The library was an old building, not connected to the central heat, and there were no fireplaces in the main room, where so many old, dry books were kept.

The fifth page was the beginning of my questions and recommendations for what to do next. Since Miss Flinders was so far away, and not looking, I thought it safe to tear the five pages from my notebook and pass them to Victor under the table.

4.

Here is an excerpt:

Paper scissors rock. Can't restore your memory because Glum wished off my powers. I can see, but cannot touch, the 4-D world. Colin could wish back on; but Wren stops wish power w/ curse. Q could lift curse, but Fell anesthetized his magic w/ chemical dose (affects nervous system? suppress REM sleep? spirits think he's unclean?). Your cells could construct antidote, but Daw shifted your monad in 4-D to block your molecule control. I could realign your monad, but Glum negates me. Round and round.

Powers need two things to work (1) subj must be healthy, un-cursed, un-negated, un-drugged. (2) Permission from Head of Bran to let laws of nature (?) come into this dimension from our homes. Boggin or Vanity (!) can ask Bran to grant permission. Special green table acts as radio to Bran. One in Boggin's waiting room; another in warehouse (Drinkwater knows where). Boggin has toe-ring made of same green, portable version (?).

IMPORTANT Even w/o permission, some home laws of nature "leak through" at the boundaries surrounding the estate. Get partial results. Quentin went north to the Barrows to cast his flying charm.

BUT!!! Boggin has things (talismans?) in safe in Gr Hall that wake up our powers. 2nd fl. SW corner office. If yr magnetic psychokinetics working, could zap safe open, get stuff to turn on PK, then open safe. If my pw'r working, reach through safe wall, get talisman to turn on power. Round and round.

5.

I ended the fifth page with a question: *Where were you standing when you first PK'd a metal object? Colin's letters to Hollywood had real magic in them. Where did he write them, in the dorm or somewhere else?*

Victor was writing out the answers. I could see, over the top of his book, his pencil eraser wagging back and forth in short, crisp motions. Then something happened.

I saw an object. It was not in this continuum. Like the beam of a light-house, turning toward me. . . .

6.

I saw Miss Daw. She was sitting rather stiffly on the couch in Boggin's waiting room, her knees pressed together, a thin briefcase balanced atop them, both gloved hands on the handle of her briefcase.

She was also Thelxiepia. The fourth-dimensional extensions of her body, however, her wheels within wheels of musical energies, had other substances affixed, or attached, or oriented along their hypersurfaces. Unlike me, her 4-D body was dressed, armored, equipped.

One instrument that orbited her outer wheel structure was something like a lens, a device that amplified the massive hyperlight of overspace. There were other instruments for sending and recording signals, measuring tiny variants of the utilities of objects, introducing fluxes into the webwork of moral strands that ran from object to object to examine the moral implications of hypotheticals. I could tell what these instruments were for, because they were so useful to Miss Daw they practically blazed with the whatever-it-was that my utility-detectors picked up.

Miss Daw rotated two of her outermost wheel-structures and imprinted a cluster of meanings on a thread of energy running from where she was through my area of time-space. This imprinting was similar to what I had done to give Dr. Fell's molecule-size memory-erasing engines within my body their own free will.

When the energy flux passed through my body, a new sense, or perhaps it was an overlap of the utility and morality senses, translated the flow into words:

"Miss Windrose, I am obligated to Boreas to reveal any plans and schemes of yours discovered to have an adverse effect on his interests. As you pointed out in an earlier discussion, I am not *necessarily* obligated to be prompt or zealous in reporting my findings, particularly in cases where (as here) your intent is not entirely clear.

"In which case, for your own sake, if not for mine, would you at least try the tiniest bit not to be so blatant about your little schemes? If you leave notes lying around under desks or in books, where anyone glancing in through the fourth dimension can plainly see them, I cannot for long continue to pretend to be oblivious.

"Do try to exercise a modicum of caution. Briareus and Cottus are not blind. Erichtho has a seeing glass; Grendel feels troubled in his heart when his desires are frustrated, as, no doubt, a successful escape on your part would do."

7.

Thelxiepia rotated something like a mirror or an echo-dish into my view; and I saw the pages in Victor's hands, shimmering with utility (because I needed so badly to talk with Victor) but also snarled with a huge and attention-getting warp in their moral nature. Apparently, the universe considered my word I had given to Boggin, that I would do nothing he would regret, to still be binding me, and to be violated by passing notes to Victor.

She rotated her lens away from me; the searchlight beam failed. Hyperspace was dark once more. But now I knew that, just because it seemed dark to me, did not mean it was dark to everyone or everything that might be there.

I remembered how, less than an hour ago, I had vowed to myself how elusive and clever I would be. A sensation of dread trickled into my chest, drop by drop.

8.

Victor meanwhile, passed a note back to me. *Colin at Kissing Well when wrote letters, Apr 22, 24, May 1, May 25. Magnetic control centers in my brain activated during bad rock climbing accident last year, east slope of Kerrugan's Rock, 3:04 PM Feb 17. Tumbled 30 m, reinserted metal pitons into rock face at remote distance.*

I looked Victor in the eye and gently slapped my neck. Bugs. I pointed to the notebook I was writing. He very casually leaned back and yawned, his gaze traveling quickly over the ceiling. He was looking for cameras or something in the light fixtures.

Victor brought his gaze back down to me. He casually raised his hand as if to run his fingers through his hair, but instead tapped himself twice on the head and pointed at me.

You are the head. Take the lead.

CIRCUITOUS ACTS

1.

It made a certain amount of sense that I should be leader. I was the only one who knew the information, and, apparently, we were being watched much more closely than any of us would have guessed, so closely that even passing under-the-table notes in an empty room was fraught with risk.

But the prospect of being leader scared me.

Every time we found out more about the situation, it seemed increasingly complex. In stifling our powers, for example, they had used not one but two or maybe three methods, each from a different paradigm, each operating by its own rules. Our enemies had factions, and each faction had factions in it, and even within a single person, such as Thelxiepia or Grendel, there were opposing impulses and imperatives.

And how safe were we? Mavors said he would kill anyone who killed us, but whoever sent Lamia had not cared about that. Someone wanted to start a war. The quickest way to do that was to kill the hostages. Us.

And what did they have on their side? Even if our powers turned on tomorrow and operated at full strength, we were still amateurs at their use, fighting experts. For example, how had the school staff found us during our last escape? Had they seen the boat Vanity summoned and set a guard around it? Possibly.

But what if my escape had snarled the morality strand representing my promise to Boreas, giving Thelxiepia or Erichtho the Witch some ability to trace us down through the fourth dimension? Or what if Dr. Fell merely implanted a radio transmitter in our clothing, or in our flesh?

So that was my task, as leader. Escape from a situation that was complex, dangerous, and littered with unknowns. Get out of the burning labyrinth without stepping on the buried land mines.

If I made a mistake, it was Vanity and the boys who would pay for it. And if I let my fear of making a mistake paralyze me, we would be unprepared and helpless when the time came.

And the time was coming. As long as it seemed to me, ten days is not a long time. Negotiations between Mavors and Mulciber and whoever else was involved might be far from over.

But once the factions came to an agreement as to what was to be done with us, it would be done. Boreas was playing a game of delays, pretending we were younger and less powerful than we really were. There was a hint that he intended to use and keep us for himself. I saw how shamed he was when it was his turn to be spanked, so to speak, by Mulciber, who stood above him as Headmaster Boggin stood above me. If the five of us could serve as the key to elevate Boreas above his peers, would he let that key pass out from his grasp?

Well, the first step of my master plan was this: Go to history class, and pretend I had read up on what Gibbon said about the life of Imperator Julian the Apostate. It was now fourth period.

2.

I spent the whole day, lunch, afternoon classes, sports, supper, evening lecture, and retirement doing nothing a schoolgirl would not do. I did not talk, I hardly even thought, about what to do. The information that I was in charge of the group trickled from Victor to Colin to Quentin, and at some point the next day, was leaked to Vanity, who was watching me anxiously at breakfast, seeing how I would bear up under the pressure. Colin took to saluting me with a Nazi "Sieg Heil!" when he passed me in the hall.

But I said nothing and did nothing related to the escape plan. Patience, patience was my motto: patient as the mouse who watches the cat watching the mousehole.

I spent breakfast staring at a fork. I thought about picking it up to stab

Colin in the hand. I thought about trying to eat my soup with it. I thought about using it to eat my omelet. The fork grew brighter and dimmer in my higher vision. It had to do, not with how well I imagined doing the act, but how serious I actually was in my will.

Interesting. The amount of "usefulness" given off by an object could be changed. I think the thing I was picking up with the sense I called "utility" was really something related to time; how many changes in the number of possible futures issuing from the object depending on my relation to it.

Time passed. First period, second period . . .

I had to wait for a time when I knew both Miss Daw and Mrs. Wren were occupied. The others had other ways of spying on us, I am sure. But I feared Thelxiepia's amplifying apparatus, and whatever looking glass or crystal ball Erichtho might have.

After music and before chemistry was the moment: Miss Daw was collecting the sheet music we had written, while Mrs. Wren was (I could see through the walls) setting up the beakers and retorts in the lab for her lecture.

I made a quick scan of the fourth dimension. No one seemed to be looking. Miss Daw was on the other side of the room. At my desk, I doodled on a piece of paper, writing words, letters, and phrases here and there across the top, middle, and sides.

I wrote the alphabet in two-letter grouping: *AB CD EF GH,* and so on. I wrote: *Head, lips, breasts, arms, back, behind, calves, feet, toes.* I wrote numbers, *1 2 3 4 5 6.* I wrote a little rhyme: *This building has stairs; that building puts on airs; the other building has rooms to let; the last building has bushes to get.*

I took the paper, folding in eighths and sixteenths, so that each little phrase was in its own separate square of paper, and pushed it into my skirt pocket.

I looked into my own pocket with my higher senses. The paper was dim and useless in its present form. It was not something that broke my oath to Boggin. Its internal nature was papery, and slightly playful.

I waited through fourth period, fifth. Dinner. Lecture. Sleep. Another day.

Two days, three. Vanity and Colin at breakfast on Friday had relapsed into their old, cheerful, talkative selves. It was not until then that I realized the Red Alert status we were under made us stiff and nervous. I was not the only unconvincing actress in the group. But since I, the leader, had done nothing for a week, those two probably figured all bets were off, why worry?

Victor, of course, seemed the same as usual. Time and danger did not flap his unflappable nature. Only Quentin was pensive.

On Friday, when we had lab, I leaned over to Quentin's ear and said, "Spirit one." If the wind could hear my words, it could not "hear" what I was pointing at. And I pointed at the rack of hypodermic needles in a cabinet behind Dr. Fell. "Spirit," as in "spirit away," meant *Steal one and palm it.*

I did not even see him do it, and I was watching for it. Quentin stepped up to the front of the room to give his lab demonstration. He asked Vanity to come up and assist him. Somehow, her hair got lit on fire by one of the Bunsen burners, and she ran in a circle, screaming, until a bored-looking Dr. Fell took her by the shoulders and patted her head with a wet paper towel.

I looked with my higher senses and saw, there in Quentin's pocket, inside a false bottom in his pen case, the hypo. It was of no particular use to me while it was in Quentin's pocket; he, of course, had no use for it.

Smoothly done.

Of course, I also started blushing red as a beet. Glowing like gold next to his inner pants pocket was Quentin's masculine member, which was apparently very useful to him, or useful to me, or something. I wondered how Miss Daw kept her composure, seeing what we all looked like under our clothing.

I was not the sleight-of-hand artist that Quentin was, but I took the opportunity to pick up some paper towels and filter paper and slide them into my notebook.

3.

Patience, patience. On Saturday night, Vanity and I sat in the Common Room and talked about boys. Chattering, Victor would call it. I am sure real girls who live normal lives talk about real boys that they know, or film stars. We either talked about Victor, Colin, and Quentin, or we talked in theoretical terms about characters from books we'd read. I don't know what other girls read. We discussed whether, if you had to marry a sea captain, Ahab would make a better husband than Odysseus; of kings, whether Marcus Aurelius was better than Arthur Pendragon; on a related topic, whether Mordred was worse than Commodus; whether El Cid was braver than Saladin; whether Socrates was wiser than Aristotle, considering that Socrates let the Athenians kill him and Aristotle didn't.

It was eerie and uncomfortable talk, for me, since Vanity did not recall that Odysseus might have been (and might still be) her husband; and when she spoke about how unusually kind and charming Colin had been this week, I remembered that she did not remember Quentin's (twice now) first kiss.

She had a little napkin in her hands, which she tore into shreds absentmindedly when she spoke about matters too near her heart. Impersonating her, I pulled the piece of paper I had been carrying for four days in my pocket. Every day I had transferred it into a new skirt, unfolding it and refolding it along the same seams. Having been folded and refolded, it came apart neatly at these seams, and I had thirty-two random little notes, some with only one word or two on them, or a pair of letters. I swept the litter back into my pocket. Certain of the notes began to become more useful to me than the others, and to glow a bit in my higher perceptions. But if Miss Daw could decipher my intent from those scattered notes, well . . . then she was more clever and better equipped than anything we children could overcome.

Which I feared might be the case.

4.

That night, as I lay in bed, looking around me in the fourth dimension, I saw motion. Squinting, I saw the Manor House laid out around me, like a 3-D man staring at a blueprint.

I saw a cone-shaped object in hyperspace, made of writhing arms, hands, fingers, like a frozen tornado of worms. It was only a cone in the fourth dimension, however. In three dimensions, each cross section formed one of many increasingly large and heavy bodies.

The tip of the cone, the smallest body, intruded into our continuum. Boggin was talking to that body. It was dressed in a well-cut blue pinstripe suit, and wore a heavy gold watch on its wrist. He was one of the giants who had been at the meeting of the Board of Visitors and Governors, or one of his race. He and Boggin were entering a room just off the dayroom they used as a faculty lounge. They both had cups of coffee in their hands, and Boggin was pulling a bottle of whiskey from a locked cabinet, to spike the coffee and "Irish" it up, so to speak.

The part of the giant's body that looked like a six-foot-tall man had something, some apparatus, to convey the words he spoke and heard to the main bulk of the real giant, three hundred feet tall, that was wading through the thick gelatin of hyperspace. I could hear his half of the conversation.

"Is it true that you keep your girl prisoners all nude and chained up at night on feather beds?"

In my imagination, I filled in a possible answer from Boggin: *No, I am impotent, but I get my jollies by spanking the blonde.*

The giant laughed. "Very funny. And where do you get these bunny costumes, eh?"

Hugh Hefner is my homosexual lover; he sends me gifts.

"Well, I suppose I know you too well to expect a straight answer from you, Boreas. Of course, there is what the Hindoos would call a karmic symmetry here. You are not going to get a clear answer from the Unseen One until He hears what Mavors and Mulciber have decided between them. What did you do to upset Mulciber?"

He wanted to spank the blonde, but I wouldn't let him.

"Oh, really? But I think you do know. In any case, Mavors is not going to give you a final decision about the Uranians until after his people talk to the Destroyer and the Huntress. And, well, you know how everything slows down around the holidays. The Destroyer doesn't like to grant audiences in midwinter, when his influence is weakest."

Only Miss Daw knows what my buttocks tattoo says.

"I have been told that we will have definite action by the New Year. The Unseen One will act unilaterally, whether or not Mavors and Mulciber agree. Some recent event—I know not what—has convinced the Lord of the House of Silence that the Uranians are a danger."

5.

Saturday was terribly boring for me. For the life of me, I couldn't remember what it was I did, back when I was merely Amelia, to entertain myself during my time off.

Eventually, I went to the gym and put on my tights and a sweatshirt, a leather jacket atop that, earmuffs. Then I laced up my running shoes and began jogging the grounds. I was a little too undressed for that chill weather, but I thought my exertions would keep me warm.

I jogged. The snow had fallen a bit on Wednesday, but Thursday had been bright and fair, the temperature hovering around the melting point. Now, the snow had a slight crust of ice, soft and feathery beneath a fragile shell.

It was not the best surface for jogging. I plunged through with every step, and had to yank my unbooted and besneakered foot out of an icy mouth with every step.

I ran the mile to Arthur's Mound, which is a wide and flattened dome of raised earth, heaped up by some ancient and forgotten peoples. Over and down the other side I went, crunching through paper-thin ice with each footfall.

The trees, first one, then several, rose singly or in stands here and there along the snowy south lawn. A little farther on, the stands were thicker and more numerous, and I was not sure if it was the outlier of the forest I was in, or not.

Where was the South boundary? Colin and Quentin, Victor and Vanity, each had their separate ideas. What was my idea?

My thoughts were loose and free at that time, since the cold wind was coursing through my lungs, and the muscle burn was beginning to make me unaware of my body. Ideas rippled like clear water through my fancy, making white ripples here and there, as other thoughts, fishlike, darted from their shining surfaces.

A big whale-type thought stirred up my mental waters. If the South boundary had not been mapped in all these years, it must be innately un-mappable. A thing is innately unmappable when the act of mapping the thing changes its ability to be mapped.

Think, for example, of Heisenberg uncertainty of mass and position. You can see a target particle only by rebounding a photon or some other particle from it. If the photon is more massive than the target, you lose the position information, because the target is struck forcefully enough to move. If less massive, the photon rebounds, but you know nothing about the mass of the target except that it was large enough to stop the photon.

I wondered if the Southern boundary, all these years, was a probability wave, a zone or clouds of possible locations, which collapse into certainty when looked for.

I turned on my higher senses and looked. I was assuming the "boundary" would have a moral significance to me, since I had, in effect, promised not to cross it. It might also be very useful to know where it was. The nature of the estate ground might be different than the outside ground, since there was some evidence that Lord Terminus had established this place in its own pocket universe, only tangentially related to the surface of the time-space occupied by southern Wales.

And I saw it collapse into existence not a hundred yards away from me. To one side was the estate ground. To the other were not one but four versions of the forest, each one at right angles to the other.

To my eye, the versions were identical. Each tree and snowflake was in the same location. But my other senses could detect differences.

In the first, each tree and rock brimmed with shining usefulness. No object was any more useful than any other object: as if any thing could be used for any purpose, without being restricted by what its actual properties were. A stone or a patch of snow was just as useful for lighting a fire as a stick of wood.

In the second, each tree had a moral nature. It was intelligent, or it housed an intelligence. Or was it intelligence? A dog is not intelligent, but it is still wrong to be cruel to an animal who loves you. There was something august in the trees, something that must be treated with a certain dignity and respect.

In the third, each object had a definite internal nature, set and defined, but no moral nature whatsoever, and no innate utility. In this version, things were what they were without any reference to whether they helped human beings or not.

And the fourth was bright, shining, beautiful, as every rock and tree and patch of snow was controlled by its own governing monad, its own bit of free energy, which made the other factors—utility, morality, and even inner nature—uncertain things, rich with possibility. I saw the other factors like pearly gray clouds of luminous mist, spread in wings and streams from every object, heavy with wonder. If a symphony were made into matter, it would look as that version of the forest did.

And I was on the far side of the boundary.

The boundary had collapsed into existence about a hundred yards to my right. I was off the estate grounds, but, interestingly enough, the universe was not snarling my morality in sign that I had violated my agreement with Boggin. Why? I am not sure why. Maybe it had to do with intent. I had not been trying to cross the boundary; I wasn't trying to escape. Instead, the boundary had sneaked up and jumped into being behind me when I looked for it.

Of course, now that I knew I was breaking a rule (what is the opposite of trespassing, anyway?), I sprinted back along the snow surface to get back onto school grounds.

On the other hand, maybe I should not be running. The 3-D version of me, Amelia, was not supposed to know where the boundary was.

I slowed. There was a moment of pressure ... of increased potential ... when I passed the actual definite line of the boundary. As if my body, and every atom in it, had to decide which version it belonged in, as if there was a moment of uncertainty.

Did I get a vote? I decided I did. I voted myself to be Phaethusa, the multidimensional native of Myriagon, daughter of Helion and Neaera. . . .

It was like pushing through the surface of a bubble. For a moment, my higher senses went blind.

I kept up the sprint, feeling that warm light-headedness and sense of tireless strength that come from a really good run.

When I looked again, the boundary was a field of uncertainty, and my act of looking collapsed it again. This time, it was thirty yards behind me. And . . .

I stumbled. My feet fell through the surface of the ice coating the snow.

I looked back. No footprints. For the last thirty yards, between the two positions where the boundary had manifested itself, the paper-thin layer of ice on the snow was unbroken.

During that time, I had, unconsciously, made myself lighter. It was my old trick, my ability to bend world-lines. It was back.

I went to go look for some heavy rock to lift.

6.

My ebullience faded, fortunately, before I found any good-size rock. Patience, patience, remember that motto. If Erichtho or Thelxiepia had seen me running along the top of the ice, the bad guys at least knew that my powers were beginning to return. However, since Boggin had not erased years and decades of memory, they must have known that we knew we could do odd things that other human beings couldn't do.

Assume they saw it. What would they think? That I knew what the phenomenon was, why it was caused, what had happened? No.

I went to the gym and stretched out, cooled down.

And afterwards? What would Amelia have done?

That night, in bed with Vanity (do I need to mention that our room was cold again, and we had no fire lit, because the conversation where Boggin had agreed that we could have a fire was one of the things erased from the "present" story-continuity?), I told her about my ability to walk on top of the ice.

She must have known from Colin where he wrote his love letters, because she said, "East, the sea, is Colin's direction. Yours is South. The other two boundaries are the graveyard and the rocky, lifeless hills. Well, it's obvious who goes where. How come I don't have a direction?"

Of course, she did not recall that she was not one of us chaoticists at all. I could not remember if I had told her at the powwow; maybe I had and she'd forgotten.

Or maybe she knew I was putting on an act for the benefit of unseen listeners. Vanity is insightful, and I am not the world's best actress.

To let the unseen listeners believe that we girls were on the wrong track, I said, "You're thinking three-dimensionally. What if the other boundary is in time? At the moment this estate is sold to a new owner, will be your time."

I did not tell her (or the listeners) about the four versions I saw.

As I lay, slowly falling asleep, I kept thinking about the four versions.

At some point, I must have truly been asleep, because it was Lord Morpheus, robed in starless midnight skies, his hair dark like moon-smothering clouds tinged silvery at the edges, who sat on my windowsill, a hooded black owl in jesses on his wrist, and said, "The first you saw was my son's version. In dream, any object can be made to perform any task. The second belonged to the Graeae boy, the son of Proteus; his people see dryads. The third was Telchine, a world of blind and careless atoms. Why do you think your people developed the senses you did? Of course your world was the bright version, daughter of Helion; your name means 'radiance.' "

"Why are you here?" I said, or seemed to say.

"I have come to warn you that the Psychopompos, the son of Maia, is your enemy; he has appeared at my house and urged my vassals to disobey me, to raise the comet-streaming banners of Chaos and Old Night to war, and press the infinite armies of phantasy and dream into attack. My son would die, he said, but high honors would bury him, and he be treated as worthily as any of the fallen in war. The Father of Lies spread the rumor that secretly I wished for my son to be sacrificed in our noble cause, I, who have, across many wasted eons, commemorated the undying enmity with cosmos with the death rites of many brave knights fallen in my service.

"I have kept my wife in an enchanted sleep since the day young Phobetor was kidnapped, that she would not weary out her eyes with weeping, which, in our world, is the only cause of death. Will you tell him we still love him so?"

I said, "I cannot speak while enemy ears hear. As soon as I may, I will tell him."

"The Emperor of Dreams grants you a boon. Of what would you care to dream this night? I can make phantasms of Boreas or Damnameneus to wait upon the secret and voluptuous desires burning in your loins. I should warn you, however, that it will be my son Phantasmos whom your arms will clasp and your lips caress, should you choose this form of boon."

"I want to dream about escaping."

"Then dream of flight. The walls and windows of the Great Hall are set with spells and wires of cunning make, to set alarms to blow should any forbidden hand intrude. Only the heavy door through which you first entered is unwatched. I grant you shall recall this when you wake."

7.

That Sunday we had chapel.

At breakfast, I began sniffing and snuffling and wiping my nose with a handkerchief. Mrs. Wren made a comment that I should not have been out yesterday so lightly dressed, and handed me a packet of paper tissues.

Mrs. Wren was hungover, the first time (so far as I could tell) this week. Was this a sign that they were relaxing their guard?

They did not know I knew they were watching me, and so this might be a slip-up on Mrs. Wren's part. Unless, on the other hand, this was deliberate, not a slip-up at all, in which case her comment was meant to tell me that they knew I knew they were watching, and now they wanted me to know that they knew I knew.

In the first case, I should continue to act as if I did not know I was being watched, because she might not realize that she just let slip that they were watching. But if the other case were the case, I should either act like I knew they knew, but did not know that they knew I knew, or else just act like I knew and I knew that they knew.

Of course, on the third hand, I had been running over snowy lawns where anyone looking out a window could see, and left footprints that would last till the next snowfall. Maybe Mrs. Wren was just making the comment any adult would make talking to a child with the sniffles.

Comedy is easy. Intrigue is hard.

As we were queued up outside the chapel to go in, I put my hankie in my pocket, which still held my many little notes. Certain of them suddenly grew brighter in the utility aspect, and I was able to snatch them with my fingertips and fold them into the hankie.

I drew the hankie out again, sniffed, and dropped it at Quentin's feet.

Quentin stooped, gentleman-like, and made a show of returning my hankie to me. When I got it back, the slips of paper were gone.

I said, "I am ever so grateful when a kind gentleman returns something I have dropped."

He said, bowing, "Always at your service."

The ones I had passed him read, in no particular order, "Behind," "this building," "CD," "Bushes," "6," "feet," "stairs."

It is possible that Quentin would look for six stairs or six bushes, rather than in the bushes six feet away from the stairs behind this building. He might not know what I meant.

But I submit that it was impossible for anyone reading the notes in my pocket to know what I meant until I stood in front of the chapel and passed the note. The same words would have had a different meaning ten minutes ago, while I was in front of the main Manor House.

And he could not know, Quentin had no need to know, the CD contained Miss Daw's Fourth Dimensional music, which had been used, while I was imprisoned, to nullify my powers. It was useless to him.

I do not know what sign Quentin passed to Colin, but Colin gave one of the most memorable performances of his career, and probably got in as much trouble as a kid can get in without being sent to reform school.

In the middle of the service, Colin leaped atop the back of the pew, flung out his arms, and shouted, *"I'm converted! I've seen the light! Jesus save me! Amen, brothers!"*

And as Boggin and Fell rose up to get their hands on him, Colin skipped and jumped from pew to pew, shouting and carrying on, *"Servants of dat ol' Debbil, youse betta jus' b'ware! Judgment Day is a-coming! The Great Star Wormwood falleth from the Heavens, and one third of the seas shall be as blood! And, lo, I beheldeth a great serpent with seven heads, probably the same one Hercules killed earlier, and I wonderedeth if he woreth seven hats when it raineth!"*

He jumped from the altar to the font, to the rail, kissed the statue of the Madonna, slapped the baby she held, and made a break for the front door.

He went out the door, Boggin and Fell went out after him, Miss Daw rose to her feet, her pretty face scarlet with indignation, Mrs. Wren got out her hip flask and sneaked a drink while no one was looking, and Mr. Drinkwater also walked out the front door, covering his smile with his unwounded hand. Dr. Foster, at the lectern, sighed, turned the page, and continued reading from Ecclesiastes, mumbling slightly, too dignified, really, to notice the interruption.

Quentin and Vanity got up and walked outside to watch the chase scene. I stayed dutifully at my prayers, while Victor leaned over and looked at the workbook where Dr. Fell had been doing sums.

From outside, Colin pounced on a coiled green garden hose and wiggled it around his head, screaming, *"And behold he that worketh wonders in my name shall pick up snakes and receive no hurt from them. Watch this! Ow! Fuck! That goddamn bloody snake just bit me! What kind of piss-ant religion is this, making promises to a child!"* He pantomimed being attacked by the garden hose. It really was quite funny, and I had to stifle a laugh, or give away the fact that I could see through walls.

"Come along, Mr. mac FirBolg. We have all had just about enough," I heard Boggin saying.

"Stand back! I am about to start speaking in tongues! Rafel mahee amek zabi almit! Papa Satan! Papa Satan aleppe!"

Of all things, it was Mr. Glum, tottering and unsteady on his peg leg, who hobbled up in the slippery snow behind Colin and fell on him with a tackle. Colin writhed and screamed and frothed, calling them all sinners and condemning them to damnation and hellfire.

This time I was watching Quentin, through the wall. He did not retrieve the CD. I saw him walk back to the bushes behind the chapel, kick around in the snow until he found the disc, and then kick the snow back over it. He broke off two twigs from the bushes and laid them across the spot to form an X.

Since we were the only ones in our particular pew in the chapel, I leaned over and whispered to Victor: "Can you make something to play a compact disc?"

Victor smiled. "Build? No. Too complex. Get? Yes. Take time."

"When?"

"Christmas. Have to go into town."

It was December sixteenth. Christmas was eight days away.

Of course, if Quentin crept out one evening, the CD without a player would be no use to him; if Victor got a disc player, the player without a disc would be no use to him; neither of them had sworn any particular oaths not to do these things.

Do I need to mention that Victor always smelled nice? When I leaned forward to whisper in his ear, I could scent the scent from his hair. He shaved, and used aftershave, but even without that, there was always a healthy, clean, out-of-doors kind of smell to him. I really wanted to kiss his nicely shaped ear while I had my lips right there, but I didn't. I was the leader, after all, and leaders cannot fraternize with their troopers, or show favorites.

8.

I was tempted to do everything myself, since I could look around in the fourth dimension and see if anyone was coming, and I took a risk any time I communicated to someone; words could be heard by Boggin; notes could be seen by Miss Daw, and maybe by Erichtho.

Boggin, dragging Colin by the ear, stepped back to the chapel door and called out in a loud voice, politely asking Mrs. Wren to accompany him.

I decided to try to kill two birds with one stone. Maybe Colin's distraction was big enough to hide more than one message.

Victor got up and walked out when Wren did. Miss Daw and I were the only two people left in the chapel. Dr. Foster continued to mutter and mumble, something about whether the Second Person of the Trinity had two natures or one nature, and whether that nature was shared with the Father or issued from the Father.

I heard Victor, outside, say to Dr. Fell, "Sir, why must we waste our time with this superstitious nonsense? The concept of an infinite being is self-contradictory."

Fell said, "Quite right. And any such being who craves adoration from people like me is hardly worth adoring, if I understand what that word means. Well, Boggin does not seem to be about. Still, we mustn't have you running around unsupervised."

"Sir, we could go to the lab. There is a variation on the Millikan experiment I would like to try. May I use the apparatus? You could supervise me there."

"Very good. Come along."

Vanity and Quentin did not escape so easily. They were herded back into the chapel. Vanity was seated next to me, then Quentin, then Miss Daw.

Without moving from my position or raising my head, I used a higher sense to stare at Vanity.

Immediately, she looked over her shoulder.

Vanity had not been imagining it. She really could tell when people were looking at her.

I looked away, looked back, looked away, looked back. . . .

Every conspirator under the age of majority should learn Morse code. It would save a great deal of time and trouble. Under my breath, so low that only Vanity could hear it, I hummed the tune to *Baa-baa black sheep, have you any wool?*

With each note, I looked at her with either one, two, three, or four of my higher senses, either from her left or right, front or back, from above or below. I had to run through the little song once or twice till she caught on.

Dr. Foster forgot where he was in the service, and went back to the beginning again. So we had plenty of time. Miss Daw may have been irked that I was humming to myself during the service, but, on the other hand, we had both heard this part before, not half an hour ago.

9.

Sunday afternoon: Colin was in detention for the rest of that Sunday, and apparently, for the rest of his life; I went to the library; Victor was in the schoolroom lab, apparently having just a fine time with Dr. Fell, frowning over experiment results. Vanity and Quentin sat in the Common Room doing math homework.

Vanity made a little chart, a four-by-six matrix, and put the first twenty-four letters in the alphabet in it. Then, while I looked at her first through one sense then another, at different angles and directions, she wrote out: *Write names of staff teachers hide in var cache when not watched a ap cymru b boggin c sprat d daw e wren f fell etc. . . .*

Immediately after, Vanity wrote out a dozen names on little slips of paper while Quentin rummaged up a number of small watertight containers from his room: a pop bottle, some plastic baggies, a little soapdish with a snap-shut lid.

Then they dressed up in their snow things, filled their pockets with this litter, and went outside to play a combination of soccer and snowball fighting, with just a little bit of hide-and-seek.

Even had Miss Daw been watching Vanity cipher, the note would have appeared to be of very little use to Vanity, or to me, and the act of hiding the names of various staff members in various places around the grounds would seem meaningless. I do not know if even Miss Daw knew that we had assigned letters to our various cache spots. For example, spot A was the little courtyard where the bench circled the stump of an oak. There was a hollow spot between two roots.

I did not see Vanity hide any of the notes. She could tell when people were watching, and she waited till no one was.

But seeing Quentin pelt Vanity with snow, so that she was breathless with cold and laughter, and watching the somewhat playful grabbing and tackling and tickling they imposed on each other during their hide-and-seek made me sure Quentin was going to try to steal a kiss. As far as he could remember, his first.

Once or twice it looked like he was building up the nerve to do it. But Vanity looked a little worried, and kept glancing at the upper windows of the north wing, where Colin was in detention, as if she were thinking of him.

10.

The library had a typewriter. From the tongue-clucking comments I had overheard from the cleaning staff (some of whom were Cornishwomen from across the Bristol Channel), this was certainly the last typewriter in the British Isles, maybe in the world. Everybody else, everywhere else, used computer word processors.

I had permission from Mrs. Flinders, the librarian, to use it, and I typed up what I am sure was the worst résumé of all time. I had no idea what was supposed to go into a résumé, or what one looked like.

I was sure that some book in the library might have the information on how to write such a thing, so I spent at least an hour combing through *Middlemarch* and *Emma* and *War and Peace,* looking for scenes where characters went to find jobs. Unfortunately, most of them seemed to be aristocrats, who did not seem to have to work for a living, or else got a job (as Pierre did) through knowing the Freemasons. *Great Expectations* was no help; neither was *A Christmas Carol.* Nor was Plutarch's *Lives,* nor any of the histories of saints. Apparently none of these famous people in their famous lives ever had to get a job.

On the theory that résumés had only been invented after the French Revolution, I went to the books in the modern section. I spent half an hour looking over *Ulysses* by James Joyce, and certain books by T. S. Eliot and E. E. Cummings. Our copy of the first book must have contained printer's errors, and a lot of them. There were nonsense words and run-on sentences on every page. In one of the chapters, the printer had left out all the punctuation. I am certain the author must have sued the printing company for putting such a thing out on the bookshelves with his name on it.

The other two books were not anything I could make sense of. The Dewey decimal number indicated that they were poetry, but I knew what poetry was. Poetry was Milton; poetry was Keats. This was goofy rubbish. I assumed such books had gotten into our library by mistake, perhaps as a prank.

In any case, I found nothing in the modern works that told me how to write a résumé. I asked Mrs. Flinders for help, but she had only the vaguest notions.

A résumé was supposed to boil down your life experience to one sheet of paper. My sheet was blank.

A résumé was supposed to list your experiences. What experiences was I supposed to have, at my age, me, a young girl who had never worked a day in her life? With a student body of only five students, there were not any clubs or intramural sport teams I could boast of leading.

If my résumé had been entirely honest, I am sure some of the entries would have been eye openers:

- First woman explorer in hyperspace
- Participated in failed escape attempt from your institution
- Discovered your true identity
- Escaped with my brain intact after your people tried to erase my memory
- Eroded Grendel's desire to blot out my memory by batting eye-lashes
- Object of lust and unlawful desire by many men, including Boreas, Grendel, and maybe even Colin
- Cooked my own breakfast, once. Burnt eggs.

So, in case you are wondering; no, my résumé was not honest. It contained some tepid information about my grades and did not fill up even half a page. Looking at it, I wondered how anyone my age ever got a job. I certainly would not let someone with no experience near any heavy machinery, mine, factory, or office. Small wonder half of England was on the dole.

And in case the context doesn't make it clear, I was writing it for Mulciber aka Lord Talbot, the man who owned the estate I lived on.

I wondered how a person who makes a mistake on a computer erases it. Erases the magnetic tape it is written on, I suppose. I have also heard certain computers correct one's spelling as one types. That sounds like utter magic to me; I would have to see it to believe it.

But I wished for such magic that Sunday afternoon as I sat typing. I was using carbon copy paper, and my fingers were all stained blue from the ink. Every misspelled word required me to throw the whole sheet out, and the carbon, as well. This was particularly annoying when the last word on the page was the misspelled one.

I also did not know how to close a résumé. I put *Sincerely Yours, Amelia Windrose* at the bottom, as one would in a letter. I am sure that was wrong, but I did not know what was right, and neither did Mrs. Flinders.

11.

Patience or no patience, there were some risks I could not avoid. I thought that the risk was now as low as it was going to get. Anyone watching me type endless copies of the same wretched résumé over and over again no doubt fell asleep long ago, or hanged himself in despair.

I typed this note: *There is one who has betrayed you. The name is in a bottle buried beneath the roots of an oak stump in the small courtyard between the N and E wings of the main Manor House.*

I took out the carbon copy and the original. Since the inky carbon paper contained a slight imprint of the words, I tore the carbon paper into shreds.

I was relying now almost entirely on Miss Daw's reluctance to turn me in. I had no doubt that Miss Daw might have seen the notes. She could easily have seen what Vanity had been doing all afternoon. But I had little to lose; she knew already that my memory was back.

I went to the Headmaster's office to get some stamps. We needed the Headmaster's permission to send out letters.

Boggin (I saw through the wall as I walked past the north wing) was still patiently lecturing Colin, while Colin (no doubt) was saying nothing but, "Go on."

No one was in the office but Taffy ap Cymru. He was seated at a desk smaller than Mr. Sprat's, with his feet on the table.

I showed him my résumé, and the business card from Lord Talbot aka Mulciber, and explained I had a legitimate reason for sending out a letter.

I gave him my brightest smile and tried to look as innocuous as possible.

He frowned, looked amused and annoyed at the same time, and slowly climbed to his feet, then sauntered over to a locked drawer, where he took out a book of stamps. He actually had to sign a little book saying who was getting the stamp and why.

I also asked for a second stamp to place on a second envelope, this one addressed to the school, which I wanted to place inside the first envelope, to speed Lord Talbot's answer.

4

BLACKMAIL

1.

I was back less than ten minutes later.

"What is it now?" asked Mr. ap Cymru.

"I have a question about the mail," I said. "May we talk privately? I mean, really and truly privately?"

He glanced left and right at the empty office. "This is not private enough for you, Miss Windburn, or whatever your name is?"

I said, "I was thinking of changing my name to Laverna. I understand that a person can legally change his name as often as he likes, provided he is not doing it for the purpose of perpetrating a Fraud."

With a sigh, he heaved his boots off the desk again, and said, "Come along."

He led me down a short corridor past rich wall hangings and mannequins in chain mail, past fans of swords and crossed pikes, to a narrow door paneled to look like the wainscoting. Beyond that door was a corridor, much narrower, which was boarded with unpainted wood, and walls of dirty white plaster. A crooked stair led up around a bend, to another door, also unpainted. Here was a small attic room beneath a slanted roof. A single dormer window shed gray light on a cot, a dressing table, a wardrobe. There was a single wooden chair with no cushion.

He closed the door behind me, moved a candlestick over in front of the mirror that was affixed to the back of the door. There was a second mirror affixed to the wardrobe door; when the wardrobe door was opened, the two mirrors were parallel. He lit the candle with a cigarette lighter.

The reflection in the mirror was not that of a man, but of a woman. When ap Cymru turned to face me again, he was no longer a man. She was a woman.

She was shorter in her woman shape, though her hair was the same color, cut now into a pageboy bob. Her features were rather Italian, hook-nosed and red-lipped, with eyes large and dark and soulful in a way Northern people's rarely look. I do not know if a boy would have found her face handsome; she seemed a little too strong-featured for that. But I thought she was striking-looking.

The man's shirt seemed suddenly too baggy on her, except that it was tight around her chest. She hiked her pants up to her waist, and tightened the belt. They were loose around her legs, but tight at the hips.

She sat down in the chair and gestured to the bed. "I don't have many guests. Welcome to the servants' quarters. I suppose this is a part of the world you've never seen."

I did not sit. It seemed hot and close indoors after my little expedition to the post box. I rummaged in my skirt pocket and took a step toward her.

She must have thought I was much more dangerous than I thought I was, because she reached into the cigarette box next to her, opened a false bottom, and pulled out a revolver.

She pointed it at me.

I raised my hands. I said, "Don't shoot! I only want to show you the piece of paper in my pocket!"

She said, "Sit down on the floor. Take this paper out of your pocket with the first two fingers of your left hand and toss it to me."

I knelt down on the floor and drew out the paper with my fingertips. I tossed it into her lap.

She opened it up with her left hand. The letters were slightly smeared in the way that carbon copies are, so she could tell it was not the original. *There is one who has betrayed you. . . .*

She said, "Mind if I smoke?"

"Well, you've got me at gunpoint, so I guess I am not going to object," I said.

"Don't be smart. D'you want one?"

"A cigarette?"

"Do you smoke?"

"I don't know. I never have, so I suppose that means I don't."

"You really do have a smart mouth, don't you, blondie?"

"I wasn't trying to be rude!" I said. "I was just answering the question. I don't smoke."

"Of course, Little Miss Perfect wouldn't smoke." Without taking her eyes from me, or lowering the gun, she put a cigarette between her lips, lit it left-handed.

I said, "You have no cause to talk that way to me. What have I ever done to you?"

"Fold your hands in your lap. Keep them where I can see them. For one thing, you're blackmailing me, or trying to."

I folded my hands in my lap. I noticed that being held at gunpoint was a lot like being in chapel, or a classroom, with people telling you how to sit and when to speak, and so on.

She put her elbow on the desk surface next to her, and leaned sideways to put her chin on her palm, with the cigarette held lightly between the first two fingers of her hand. It looked like the kind of pose a Hollywood model would strike, bonelessly elegant, and at ease. She studied the note, looking down through her long black lashes.

She looked up. She said, "Are you actually blackmailing me? Is that what this is about?"

I said, "We want passports and visas, and five tickets on an airplane out of England. I don't really care where. Rome would be fine. New York would be nice, too."

"Yeah, New York is nice come springtime. All the muggers bloom in Central Park." She drew another languid puff on the cigarette. She seemed to be waiting for me to say something.

I said, "Is that thing really loaded? You're making me nervous."

That made her laugh aloud. "Me? *I* am making *you* nervous?"

A very slow moment of silence crept by.

She said, "Since when do peasants make royalty nervous?"

I said, "When they demanded the right to bear arms. About since the French Revolution, I'd say."

"You're still being smart-mouthed with me."

I said wretchedly, "I never blackmailed anyone before! I don't know what I am supposed to say!"

She made a small wave with her cigarette, leaving a little irregular circle of smoke in the air. "You are supposed to threaten me till I feel nervous enough to give in to your demands, I guess."

I shook my head. "I don't need to threaten you, and I don't really know how to do it. Besides, you're already nervous. You said so. Can you do it? Get us five passports and tickets out of England? We need them by Christmas."

"You're being ridiculous, little princess. It would take me six months to get any sort of paperwork made for you. Have you ever dealt with the English civil service?"

"Maybe you could get them illegally . . . ?"

"Do you think I just have friends who are forgery artists, or that I know some sort of smuggling crime lords?" she scoffed.

"Actually, well, yes. You are the goddess of smugglers, after all. Cornwall is right across the water."

She took a puff on her cigarette. She tilted her head sideways and narrowed her eyes. "What happens if I shoot you through the head, instead? Not that I'm planning to, but it is traditional in situations like this to ask that question."

"Mavors kills you and your family. If I am dead, the original of that letter reaches Boggin; he finds your name hidden in the spot designated; you get caught."

"But you foolishly handed me a copy of the letter. I can go to the spot right now and dig up the bottle, or put someone else's name in."

You probably will not believe that I did not think of that till then. My oh-so-clever plan, my oh-so-subtle plan had a hole in it large enough for an elephant to walk through.

I am sure I am the worst actress ever, as well as being the stupidest person on Earth. But since I had nothing to lose, I tried to hide the feeling of utter self-contempt that was boiling up in my breast, and I lied. "That's not the letter I sent. That is just an example."

"You went to the trouble of typing out a carbon copy of . . . an example?"

I said, "I didn't think you would believe me, otherwise!"

She laughed and put the gun back in its little secret hatch beneath the cigarettes. "Okay, I'm not nervous anymore. Fine. Get up. Dust yourself off. Go out and play."

I got up slowly. "I really am going to turn you in. The letter is already in the mail. I couldn't stop it if I wanted to."

"Listen, blondie, Boggin knows who I am. He is a past master at the type of cloak-and-dagger stuff you botched here today. The witch and the siren know all the secrets here on the estate. I was careful, but I got caught.

"Boggin, he's got evidence that I am working for Trismegistus all set to land in the lap of Mavors if anything happens to him. Trismegistus knows it. Boggin knows Trismegistus knows. Each one knows I am a double agent working for the other one, but each one thinks the other one is going to kill me if the other one finds out.

"Now, I have letters of my own, in the hands of people I trust, set to go find Mavors if anything happens to me, with evidence that Boggin knew I was a traitor and that he didn't turn me in. That makes Boggin a traitor. So he and I sort of cancel each other out, leaving me, more or less, under the control of Trismegistus, who will turn me in to Mavors if I don't let myself get blackmailed by Boggin to make Boggin think I work for him. Do you get all that? I can draw you a chart if you didn't follow all the steps."

I said, blinking, "So whom do you really work for?"

She mashed out the cigarette. "They had you in a cell with a collar and a leash around your neck. I've got one, too, only mine is invisible, and I was dumb enough to put mine on with my own hands. At the moment, Trismegistus is holding the other end. You didn't need to go through all this whoop-de-do to get me to help you. Lord Trismegistus wants you guys out, and free. He wants peace between Cosmos and Chaos. You four are the only possibility to making that peace."

I said, "Who would you help if you were free to do what you wanted?"

She smiled and stood up, tugging at her belt buckle. Her bosom flattened like balloons with the air let out, her hair crinkled and got short, her hips slimmed.

A man again, he said, "Are you blind? I am a shape-changer. I am one of the daughters of the Old Man of the Sea. If there was peace between Cosmos and Chaos, I could go home and see my folks again. I'll get you your passports and stuff by Christmas. Here."

He tossed me a small key on a chain.

"This opens a bus locker on Waterside Street in Abertwyi. There is only one bus station in the village. The locker number is on the key. It's no

bigger than the size of a phone booth, and only three rows of lockers, but the village is so small that even you couldn't miss it, blond brain.

"I'll clear my stuff out before Christmas and leave you children a nice stocking present there. I cannot promise the siren won't find out, or the witch. I'll even give you some spending money, which you weren't smart enough to ask for.

"Rome is cheaper than New York by a long shot, so it will be Rome. The air tickets will be third class, and you will have to find your own bumbling, bungling way to get to the airport at Bristol. You may have to change planes at London Heathrow. It's a big airport, so don't get lost.

"I'll leave some sightseeing maps and instructions on how to buy fish and chips from a street vendor. When you get caught, and brought back here, I'll tell you how to contact Lord Trismegistus, and he can set you up with a real escape."

"When . . . ?" I said.

"When. Not if."

Ap Cymru paused to let that comment sink in.

Then: "You want to save time and have me leave the contact instructions in my stocking gift?"

I nodded.

He laughed harshly, walked over, snuffed the candle out with his fingers, and held open the narrow door for me, bowing and smirking.

He swatted me on the bottom on the way out. I turned around, my hands doubled into fists, but he just laughed and wiggled his finger at me. "Temper, temper, little blackmailer!" And he closed the door.

I rubbed the seat of my skirt with my hand, pouting. Colin and Boggin and now ap Cymru. Did everyone want to swat my bottom? I thought it was a guy thing, but ap Cymru was a girl.

That thought made me queasy, so I skipped away downstairs before I had another one.

2.

Days went by. Finally, it was Christmas Eve. Collin was let out of confinement for carols.

At dusk we all trooped the two miles along the road to Abertwyi. There

was snow on the ground, but the air was chill without being unpleasant. Picture-postcard weather. Miss Daw passed around a lighter, and we lit long white candles we held.

We walked from house to house, singing songs of joy, peace on Earth, and goodwill to men. Miss Daw led us; her voice was like an angel's, clear as crystal, strong and fair. The rest of us did not do badly, considering we have had music classes since as far back as memory goes. Boggin had a voice that was loud and deep without being overly tuneful; he joined in once or twice for some of the songs. Mrs. Wren did not sing, but daubed her eyes with a hankie, overcome by sentiment. Or perhaps Christmas carols wounded her ears. I mean, she was a witch, after all.

The decorations that the villagers hung on their houses transformed them into fairy palaces. Light shimmered on the eaves, little toy Santas in sleighs were arranged among lawn gnomes, divine babies in mangers were watched over by shepherds and kneeling farm animals. The lampposts in the town square each had wreaths upon them, and red bunting ran from pole to pole.

Some of the houses we sang before invited us in for a moment of warmth and a cup of hot cider. Several of these houses were undecorated and somewhat shabby-looking. Often, no one lived there but one old lady, by herself or with a clowder of cats. Boggin made a point of handing over a small wrapped present or an envelope. I assumed from the grateful re-actions that these presents were expensive indeed, and that the envelopes contained money.

We were also invited up to some of the finer houses, large ones set well back from the lanes, some with gates and stone fences of their own. One was owned by Sir Rice Mansel, others by families called Penrice, Myrick, or Lucas. Old money, long established in the parish. But there were also new houses, well built, with all the walls and gates and ornaments of the old money. New money. The Lilac family was one such.

Since we tramped back and forth across the village following no partic-ular straight lines, I assumed our visits and their timing were controlled by some unspoken protocol as rigid as the exchange of salutes during the changing of the guard at Buckingham Palace. The Lilac family were the last on the list, perhaps because they had the most money or had earned it by doing something useful, like running a cannery. That put them at the bottom of the social totem pole, it seemed.

We had been invited only into the foyer of Sir Rice, but Mr. and Mrs. Lilac invited us into their drawing room.

The drawing room was paved with stone for half its length, but had a split-level made of polished wood overlooking it, with a short little balcony rail separating the two. Pushed up against this rail was a long table set with food. Here was a steaming crystal bowl of cider, a second of eggnog, and a third for the adults, spiked with alcohol. Other trays of food arranged in cunning decorations were spread across the table.

Here was a Christmas tree of splendid size, every branch, practically every needle, hung with lights and decorations and gifts. In a fireplace, a Yule log was burning.

Mr. Lilac insisted that we taste some hors d'oeuvres, which apparently was a deviation from strict protocol, because Boggin rather sharply told him we could not accept so much generosity. But Colin made the question academic by taking one sliver of peppered meat out from an otherwise perfectly symmetrical wheel of finger foods and wolfing it down.

The unspoken rules apparently did not allow Boggin to hurry us away after we had, so to speak, broken bread with the Lilacs.

We spent about half an hour there, holding little paper plates covered with truly good food, including slices of warm apple pie à la mode with scoops of homemade vanilla ice cream sprinkled over with cinnamon.

The adults, I am sure, talked about whatever it is adults talk about in situations like this. Sports, I suppose, or complaints about politicians or foreigners. Mrs. Lilac spent some time complimenting Miss Daw, who received the comments with gracious humility.

The two Lilac twins, a pair of straw-headed tall fellows named Jack and Edmund, stood awkwardly near Vanity and me, while a third boy, named Clive, even blonder than his brothers, sat a little ways away, watching in sullen silence. Quentin did not even try to appear sociable. He stared into the crackling fire, as if seeing meaningful shapes in the flames.

Only Colin was at ease, asking the twins about their favorite (you guessed it) sport teams, telling them that, tall as they were, they would do well at snooferball, or some other made-up sport; he talked to them about evil tricks one could play on neighborhood dogs; he described his conversion to Christianity during the sermon last week. This thawed the ice a bit; the twins were laughing and shaking their heads in disbelief, while the youngest one, Clive, looked more and more offended with every passing moment. The ice froze over again when Colin told the twins that Vanity and I were lesbian lovers. They gave us looks of mingled shock and admiration.

Vanity and I were holding hands at that moment, and she was whispering in my ear, "Do you know what happened to Quentin's walking stick? He really misses it. He says he can still hear the spirits, but they can't hear him anymore."

I glanced over at Miss Daw, who seemed occupied at the moment. I whispered back, "It was shattered during a duel of magic with Mrs. Wren. He should not accept any gifts from her."

Vanity shrugged up her shoulders and gave a little squealing grin. "He had a duel of magic, and he missed it! That's terrible! He'll be crushed! What did Colin do? Was there a fight?"

I said, "You don't remember this, but you actually like Quentin."

She gave Quentin a look. He was sitting by himself, morose and dull. Colin was telling a joke in a lively fashion, his face full of fun, and had the shocked twins laughing again.

Vanity said, "Where's Victor?"

Good question. Where was Victor?

3.

Victor appeared at that moment in a doorway leading to the back of the house. I may have been the only one looking in that direction at that moment. Lily Lilac was leading him by the hand, smiling, her eyes sparkling. Her parents allowed her to wear makeup, on holidays, at least, and her eyes were painted with green shade, and her lips were pastel pink. Except the pink was smudged.

4.

I saw too much. I saw more than I wanted to. Like a glimmering gold thread, there was a strand of moral energy between them. Promises of some sort had been exchanged between them. They had obligations running to each other.

I am glad my paradigm did not operate on pure emotion, like Colin's, or Grendel's, or else the Lilac girl would have been reduced to ashes on the spot, her silly, vacant look of pride, her thickly made-up face, her grasping hands and haughty, paint-smeared eyes, all blasted to nothing in an instant.

I told myself I was older than this; too mature for jealousy. I did not believe myself, however. Myself knows a bald-faced lie when she hears it.

Vanity saw the look on my face. "What's wrong?" She looked sidelong at Victor and Lilac. From the blank look on her face, I could tell she was not seeing what I was.

I saw a young demigod, pure and handsome, and an oozy, giggling little presumptuous harlot touching him with her monkey-paws. I saw something sacred being blasphemed. I saw degradation. Grendel had spoken of his feeling that he dare not touch me for fear of leaving a dirty fingerprint. I did not know what he meant, then. I knew now.

5.

And I saw, as if my life flashed before my eyes, pictures of Victor as he was now, as he had been last year, five years ago, ten. Victor was brave the way a fish is wet; it was so much a part of him that he was unaware of it. He was unable to imagine living any other way. As far back as I could remember, he had been the leader, the strong one, and the one who never doubted, never gave up hope, never knew fear. He never cried, even as a child.

He was the one, back when we were small children, when we were Primus and Secunda, who held my hand and told me the secret, the secret too enormous and wonderful to be true.

He told me that this world was not our home; that these people were not our people; that our real parents were still alive; that somewhere, someday in the shining future, we all would escape, and find the place where we were meant to be. Someday, we would find our home. Someday, we would be happy.

We had been sitting on the brink of the Kissing Well when he had told me that, looking out over the sea. It was raining, rain coming down in silver sheets, beating the grass into mud, and the little peaked roof of the well, like a witch's hat, was drumming with rain, and the noise echoed from the well.

I had been crying about something. I do not recall what. Quentin being given the strap because he would not eat meat, perhaps, or Tertia (as Vanity was called then) being forced to spend the night in another room, because we whispered too much at night.

Primus took my hand and told me the secret. And I put my head on his shoulder, because it was so strong. I stopped crying, because Primus was there.

And I thought he meant we would be happy together. I thought he meant we would make a home together.

I suppose I had the vague idea that him and me, the older ones, would be taking care of the three little kids. Together, a family. Us.

Husband and wife.

6.

When he picked his name, I thought he was picking it for me: Victor Invictus, Victor the Unconquerable, Mr. Triumph. It was a promise that we would prevail, a promise that we, together, would overcome our enemies. When I picked my name, I thought about how good "Amelia Triumph" sounded, and I thought he had selected his name with an ear to how mine would sound alongside.

And, as he spent every day with me, every afternoon, every hour, I knew that we were the ones meant for each other. We were the special people, the Uranians, the children of Chaos. Everyone else was the enemy. Even Vanity might not be fertile with him. I was the one, the only one.

And it took only one lipstick-smudged smile from Lily Lilac, daughter of a fish cannery man, to show me I was not the one. I was not anything.

7.

Vanity steered me by the elbow over to the punch bowl and got me a ladleful of eggnog. I think she sneaked me a cup from the adults' bowl; it tasted bitter and filled my head with a warm lightness. I coughed, and she patted my back.

Boggin must have noticed something, for his eyes traveled between where I gagged on a stolen drink and where Victor was arm in arm with a girl propriety would forbid him to be alone with, for he cleared his throat and said with gentle firmness to our host, "Why, Mr. Lilac, I fear my charges may be growing somewhat beyond control, perhaps a bit too, ah, jolly, there is the right word, too jolly, even in a season as holy as this one. I must wish you a most Merry Christmas, sir, and the happiest of New Years, and we must be on our way. Long walk back through the snow!"

Boggin smiled and Mr. Lilac shivered.

8.

It was a two-mile hike back; neither the longest walk, nor the coldest, but I thought it the dreariest of my life. Mrs. Wren had been given a ride back in the new car Mr. Lilac was so proud of. The rest of us walked, following the bobbing light of Miss Daw's electric torch.

I will not bore you by reciting my circling thoughts. If you have ever had your heart broken and your dearest hopes betrayed, you know. If not, you no doubt imagine you would handle the matter with a stiffer upper lip than poor Amelia Windrose. For all I know, you might very well handle it better than me. I doubt you could handle it worse. At least I did not cry out loud, and the cold helped me keep all expression from my face.

The line of us spread out a bit as we marched.

I suppose, as the fearless leader of a bold band of escape artists, I should have been examining the situation for possible escape routes. I did notice Colin glancing at the deserted woods left and right and looking at me impatiently, as if I were any moment about to give the signal to club Boggin over the head with a rock and skip away laughing over the snowy hillocks. Colin may have somehow sensed what he did not consciously remember: that Mrs. Wren was the one who countered his power, and she was absent. But I had had bad experiences braining Boggin, and I was in no mood to skip.

Once only, Vanity tried to cheer me up. She put her hand on my arm and leaned close to whisper. Her breath made a white plume in the cold night air. "You can't have ever been serious about Victor! Not in that way. He thinks of us as his sisters. His little sisters. Can't you tell?"

This was not exactly what I wanted to hear. I shrugged her off my arm without answering, and trudged onward, watching my boots make one mushy step after another in the gloomy snow.

I saw the lights of the main house in the distance, rising above the stony walls that paralleled the road, when Victor fell into step behind me. He said only, "Done."

I turned my head to glance at him, but he had already slowed his gait, and so was a pace or two behind me.

Opening one of my higher senses, I saw something in his coat pocket; a slim plastic case with earphones and control buttons, one door for the battery, the other for the discs. It was a compact disc player.

THE COLD STARS TURN

1.

I lay awake that night, watching the stars moving through the northern window. Charles' Wain circled the polestar like a cycle, moving against the little etched lines and dots of the star-dial Victor had made for us. The Septentrion, they called those stars in ancient days, and they said the wheel they made, which neither rose nor set, was the Table Round which Arthur kept in heaven, till the time, in England's hour of need, when he and the sleeping champions shall wake from where they slumber in Avalon.

I recited their names to myself as they turned, the seven who never set: Dubhe, Merak, Phad, Megrez, Alioth, Mizar, Alkaid, and Alcor.

No names in Greek or Latin. They come from a time when the Arab astronomers, sitting by starlight atop minarets tall above the hushed desert, counted and watched the stars, noting them with an advanced mathematics, of which the West knew nothing, perhaps with the *De Caelo* of Aristotle or the *Almagest* of Ptolemy open on their laps. Eternal names, written in the sky, to remind the proud Western peoples, and perhaps those in the East as well, that no victory, no supremacy, endures.

Nothing lasts forever. But when you are waiting for hours to pass, waiting for the stars to turn, everything seems to.

Vanity (snuggled up in my bed, for warmth) I had hoped would keep me awake, talking. But she did not know tonight was the night, and I dared not tell her.

Also, she was not kept in doubt, tormented by hopes, and by fears that those hopes were false. Victor had only kissed that horrible Lilac girl to get her disc player, right? He didn't really like her. But on the other hand, what kind of coldhearted cad would toy with a girl like that? I knew how she would feel if she learned he had played her false; it was how I felt now.

Vanity slept soundly, little sighs from pleasant dreams escaping her soft lips.

I also thought of things I might have done, or done better. I did not know for sure that Mrs. Wren was curled up around a bottle of booze, singing Christmas carols, and love songs popular fifty years ago, while she huddled beneath three quilt blankets in her rocking chair, rocking herself to sleep and oblivion. I wished I had been able to get a bottle of something strong into her hands.

I did not know whether Miss Daw, seeing us all, plain as paper cutouts on a chessboard, move and leave our rooms, would turn in the alarm. I wished I had spoken to her again, to stiffen her resolve, if not to betray Boggin, then, at least, not to aid him.

I was not sure where Grendel Glum was tonight. I wished I had made a point of checking. I could have spoken to Lelaps the dog, who seemed friendly, and arranged some sort of signal-bark when his master slept.

And I wished I had checked more clearly which windows were where. Through the wall, through my higher senses, I could see a splash of light from the window of another building reflected from a snowy oak tree. But the building itself was too far away (through the murk and heaviness of higher space) for me to see whose window it was. Was Boggin up late? Was ap Cymru?

At one o'clock, the light was still on. It might have been the porch light I was seeing.

At two o'clock, it was still on. I was not willing to wait longer. Boggin, no matter how fine his hearing, no matter what alarms and charms of watching he had on us, still must sleep. Two in the morning on Christmas Day was one time he certainly must be asleep, unless he was still trimming the tree, which I doubt.

I shook Vanity by the shoulder to wake her. She mumbled and tried to turn over. I shook her more and whispered in her ear: "Merry Christmas! Today is the day! The day we escape and get away!"

She raised her sleepy head, her red hair all tousled, her sleepy eyes half-lidded. "Sun's not up yet. . . ." And she flopped back down onto the pillow.

I yanked the covers off her, exposing her to the cold air. She curled up slightly, sticking her bottom in the air, but pouted and did not open her eyes or stir.

I then saw what the appeal was for Boggin and Colin and so on. I put one hand over her mouth so she wouldn't yelp, and swatted her bottom with the other.

She jumped, and tried to bite my hand, but did not make noise beyond a shrill *mmph* through her nose. It makes you feel like you're in charge, when you can spank someone.

I hissed, "It's time! Time! D-Day! Zero hour!"

In my mind's eye, I pictured a stopwatch beginning to tick. I had spoken the words aloud. If there was a mechanism, a spirit or a spell listening to us, it had heard. It was only a matter of time till pursuit came.

"You didn't have to hit me! This leader stuff has gone to your head, Melly."

"By dawn we'll be aboard your silver boat. By dusk we'll be anywhere in the world we like! Will you get up?"

"Okay, I'm up. I'm up! But I still say you've gone mad with power."

"I'll retire in an hour, and go join Cincinnatus on his farm, okay? I want you to touch the door and see if you can feel anything odd about it."

"You woke me up to feel a door?" But she padded over to the dark iron-bound panels.

"Well?"

"I feel something!"

"What?"

"The door is really damn cold, Amelia."

"Come on! Be serious!"

"What if I don't feel serious?"

"Dictatrix Amelia knows how to deal with recalcitrant subjects. I'll get Colin to spank you."

"Hmm. I might like that."

"Vanity! You like Quentin!"

"Quentin the Quiet . . . ? Mr. Ignore-me, you mean. I'd like him fine if he'd grow up and do something. He's never done anything like the act Colin pulled in church. Colin is annoying, but that took guts." Vanity closed her eyes and listened at the door.

I thought to myself that it was true. No matter what they had erased out of Colin's conscious mind, a certain strength of character was present that had not been there before. He no longer feared them. For a grown man, the penalties that can be inflicted on a boy at school are not really that frightening.

But it seemed grotesquely unfair. Quentin had faced the Lamia, and even under threat of immediate and bloody death, he had not flinched. He did not remember that trial; did that mean he lost the virtue that harsh tempering had given him? Or was it merely hidden, quietly beneath his mild surface, where Vanity did not see?

Vanity opened her eyes. "There is something watching the door. It doesn't blink or get distracted, so it is not a living thing. It doesn't listen when we talk, so it is deaf, or looking through a camera, or something. It is also paying attention to you, but sort of in a remote way. It is checking your location."

Checking my location. I did not like the sound of that.

I said, "It's a promise I made Boggin. I said he would not regret leaving my door unlocked, so I could use the bathroom."

She put her hand on the door again. "But the door is locked. I get that not-this-way feeling."

I blinked. "What 'not-this-way' feeling? What is a 'not-this-way' feeling?"

Vanity said, "I thought everyone got them. In the Gothic romances they do. You know when the heroine is the only one awake at night, and she is only wearing a filmy, flimsy nightshirt, and she is standing at the top of a dark, deserted stair, which leads into the one cellar her mysterious husband warned her not to go into, and all she has is one stub of a candle that is sure to go out? She puts her foot on the top stair, and all of a sudden she shivers . . . ? You know. Not this way."

I pointed to the wall beneath the seventh goblin face. "Try over there."

She did. Vanity walked over and pressed her cheek against the stones. Her eyes popped open. "Hey. This way. But it's a brick wall."

"Secret passage. Don't you read the Gothics?"

And I handed her the candle snuffer and told her about the switch in the mouth of the goblin on the wall.

Vanity poked the hook into the wall ornament. It clicked. The panel in the wall slid open. "Oh my gosh!" exclaimed Vanity. "That is *sooo* cool! How did you find out about this?"

"You found it."

"Gosh!" she said, shaking her head in delight. "I can't wait to get my memory back. It sounds like I am a really cool person."

2.

We dressed quickly. The fabric of our blouses and slacks was ice-cold from the drawer. I had not thought of Vanity's trick of sleeping with our clothes in the bed; even if I had, I might not have done it, for fear of alerting the watchers to our plans.

In a minute or two, we were in the tunnels, crawling. I had her go first, since she was the one (I thought) who might be bending time and space to make these corridors possible. I also wanted her to give me a signal if she got the not-this-way feeling, or the being-watched feeling.

But this time, I was looking out through the walls at the surrounding rooms. I was expecting to see the space-time sharply curved in the fourth dimension, perhaps in a toroid.

3.

Some of the walls had the rooms and chambers of the Manor House behind them, much as you'd expect. But other walls had strange things behind them. Strange beyond description.

Odd things. Spiderwebs with mushrooms growing under them; tiny men armed with stings from bees and wearing acorn caps for helmets; grinning gnome faces hanging in midair who winked at me; women made of smoke, whose hair streamed in swirls behind them, looking over their shoulders as I passed.

Other walls had forests beyond them, or starry night skies of alien constellations, mountains with carved faces rising from the sea, or fields of flowers luminous with moths and fireflies. Here were windowless domed houses, inhabited by squat, sluglike creatures, blind and slow, who oozed gelatinously across a landscape of gray ash and silent craters of black oil. There were forests thick with hanging orchids, flowers larger than parasols, and troops of albino elephants trooping through the moss.

I saw squat trolls dancing waltzes with fairy maidens with wings of ice; I saw myself and Colin and Quentin, dressed as lords and ladies, crowned with flowers and candles, riding winged horses; I saw a city of basalt towers, above which coffins as large as church steeples loomed, as if a race of pygmies had erected their town at the feet of monuments in the mausoleum for giants. I saw a dark place from which the sound of bones rustling against bones issued, and horror, and fear, and panic seeped from that darkness like a colorless light.

I saw a Lady, huge and very fair, like a mother might seem when seen from a child's eye. Her eyes were kind and her hands were soft. To either side of her sat a metal hound, one of silver and one of gold.

I saw a man with red hair; he was very thick through the chest and broad at the shoulder, and a sly half-smile played at the corner of his mouth. He was dressed in beggar's rags, but beneath the rags came a glint of rich armor, such as a warrior-prince might wear. In his hands was a bow made of rhino horn.

Dreams. I was seeing Vanity's dreams. And what I saw was affecting me: Fear and longing, touches, soft sounds, memories, were floating through my brain.

I closed two or three of my higher senses and just kept an eye on Vanity. I could not see her, but she was my guide, and she was the person I needed most in all the world, at the moment. In my usefulness-detector, she glowed like a star.

4.

There was no reason not to talk while we crawled.

I whispered, "Do you actually like Colin?"

She said, "He's a fathead. I might like the man he'll grow up into. If he loses his baby-fat-headed-ness."

"When did you stop liking Quentin?"

"I am just getting tired of waiting for him to make up his mind. There is such a thing as too quiet, you know. What has he ever done?"

"Quentin discovered how to fly! He broke into the meeting of the Board of Visitors and Governors, discovered who the enemy was, and was almost killed for his trouble. You'll remember everything in a little while . . . I hope."

I did not know whether my hope had any justice to it. I knew, among the staff, whose powers canceled out whose among the Uranians. But Vanity? She was a Phaeacian. Both Boggin and Mestor seemed to have the same space-distorting powers she did. But who had worked on her to blank her memory?

Maybe—and this was just a guess—it was a combination of two powers, and both were needed to stop her. Who had promised Vanity to Glum? He had mentioned more than once that she was "promised" to him. If that promise had been made by Boggin, for the purpose of inflaming Grendel's desire to keep her here, then maybe Grendel was one of the two powers needed to suppress her power.

Who was the other? Mrs. Wren, I assume. Why else have her be the one to lead us in nighttime prayers for so many years? Unless it was Fell, who gave us injections once a month. Or Boggin? The Board had said explicitly that he was here to stop Vanity. Was that merely because of the green ring, or did he have an anti-Phaeacian power?

Maybe. I was speculating in midair at the moment.

But I did know that I could still use my sight powers, and had regained the limited ability to affect weight when I walked along the South boundary. Quentin complained that spirits could not hear him, i.e., he could not affect them, even though he could still see things in tarot cards; his version, so to speak, of my "higher senses." If I got Quentin to the North boundary, when the barrows pushed up their cold mounds, his ability to fly might come back. If he could fly without his walking stick. If, if, if . . .

We crawled in silence for a while. I took the risk of glancing through the walls again.

5.

I saw a long manlike shape in the waters. Its third eye rolled and shimmered in its forehead like an orb of metal. Telemus held me around the waist, high above the frothing wild waves, and driving rain formed black sheets, beating the water white. Waves like sudden mountains rose and fell to every side.

Telemus held a knife to my throat. "Tell him to quell the storm."

The sea giant—he looked like Victor—turned his head toward me, his eyes shining like lamps. "I am embedding this message by means of cryptognosis into a preconsciousness level of your nervous system. The paradigms of Chaos have agreed only on this one point. We will wait for you to free yourselves. Once we have regained contact with you, we will descend down into the Cosmos and destroy its foundations. All biochemical-based life shall cease operation. Communicate on this frequency, by means of focused thought-energy signals directed at our outposts in the Hyades cluster. Longitude and Right Ascension notation follows. . . ." There followed degrees, minutes, and seconds of arc.

An invisible signal—somehow in the dream, I was aware of it—sprang from the sea giant.

The clouds parted. Here and there, stars appeared in the gaps.

There were beings above the clouds. Far, far above. Their bodies looked like statues, hanging without weight, and coated with a gold metallic surface instead of skin. Only the smallest, little specks, were man-like; their faces were the faces of statues, stern and kingly.

Ten and one hundred times their size were a second group. These others were oval, like seeds from a metal tree.

One thousand to ten thousand times their size were even larger beings. This third group were shaped like serpents, mile upon mile of golden armor.

This third group were very large, and very high up indeed. Sunlight, harsh and unfiltered from any atmosphere, glinted like solidified fire off their starboard sides. Their port sides were black with unsoftened shadow.

The giant in the water was not a giant; he was microscopic. He was a Telchine, a servant of much vaster beings. The Fallen were not fallen at all, but orbiting. I kept revising my estimate of how far away they must be, how large they were. . . .

My dreams. We were crawling through my dreams now.

What sort of power did Vanity have? What were the Phaeacians?

6.

I saw two dreams up ahead. One showed a red lake, steaming beneath a desert sky. From the lake came a naked figure, rising, and a sensation of voluptuous passion and luxurious demand radiated from the figure. The sensation was so strong that it took my breath away. I could not see, in the dream, if the figure was male or female. As the figure rose, the blood-red fluid streamed down arms spread wide. From it came a sound like a drumbeat, beats so loud that they seemed like gunshots, pounding, maddening.

The second dream showed a handsome old man seated on a crocodile. His beard and hair were white, and his expression was benevolent. On his wrist he carried a goshawk, hooded and in jesses. Next to him was a donkey, which, even as I watched, stood and became a donkey-headed man, and then a bearded man with a hoarse and coughing voice, who said, "One comes, and, with her, another!"

A third figure was there, a bull with a man's face, and between his hooves were circles and epicycles drawn in the ground, and signs of the zodiac written around the edges. "Sisters fair, yet sharing nor sire nor mother."

The old man on the crocodile replied, "Not hither crawls that which we stand to ward away; yet sound alarm, for so strict duties say. Wake, young Master, wake! Of liberal arts and sciences you shall dream more anon; but in no wise may we touch the world, now that your wand, our bridge, is gone."

The second dream flared up and faded like a candle being snuffed.

7.

I whispered to Vanity, "Quentin just woke up. He knows we're coming."

"How do you know?"

"I can see through the walls. The tunnel runs out of normal space-time through a dreamscape and back in at another point. The distances are skewed."

"This is just a great tunnel, isn't it! Are you sure I found it?"

I said, "Found it? I think you made it. How can you not remember? Two weeks ago you told me you had been having dreams about this secret panel every night for months. That was before the segment of memory they erased. How come you don't remember this?"

She shook her head. "Memory works by association, not by chronological order. Maybe they just ordered me to forget my magic powers."

I said, "I have a theory that your powers are based on states of consciousness. That you enter types of awareness below dreams and above normal alpha wave states that other people cannot reach. If that is so, I do not see how they could have erased your consciousness. Your unconscious memories should be open to you, at some level. If you can reach that level. Do you see what I mean?"

"They could do it in two steps. First, change my nature so that all my memories were stored mechanically, then, physically invade the brain to interfere with the storage mechanism."

Grendel and Fell. They had used a very similar combination of powers on me. It made my nape hairs stand up to hear her talk so calmly, and say aloud almost exactly what I had been thinking.

Vanity said, "Which way was the dream coming from? I've reached a fork."

"Left. Look for a peephole."

8.

All three boys were awake when we reached their dormitory. Quentin and Colin were still pulling on clothes, staring at the main door leading into the dorm, obviously expecting us to appear there. Both of them jumped slightly when Vanity and I came out of a hatch in the wall. Quentin sat on the floor, his trousers around his ankles. Colin hopped and hopped, looking puzzled and annoyed.

"How'd you do that?" he demanded.

Vanity put her hands on her hips and tossed her head, her green eyes alight. "Magic!" she said loftily.

Victor was over by the window, throwing a rope down. The bend went twice around the bedpost, and both ends trailed out the window. One end was a bowline with a loop, so we could lower ourselves down by letting out the other rope. The last man down could draw the rope out, and leave nothing but an open window to show the way we went.

I said, "We may only have minutes. Please assume the alarm has already been given. No talking! Out the window, double-time. Dressed people first."

I went first, and practically just let the rope slide through my fingers, regardless of the speed of my descent. Near the bottom, I made the Earth less attractive to me by spreading or spraying my bundle of world-lines outward at a sharp angle. For a moment, I was weightless. I put my feet on the ground, and weight returned with a jolt.

Victor, Vanity came next. Then Colin.

He said, "So what is the plan, Dark Mistress?"

"North," I said.

Quentin landed, yanked the rope down after him.

Quentin said, "Are we each going to go to one boundary of the estate, and regroup at the Great Hall?"

I was surprised. "How did you figure that out?"

Colin said, "We saw the notes you wrote Victor. Quentin's tarot cards figured out the rest of it."

I said, "That's bad. If Quentin knows, Wren knows. You guys did not talk about this, did you? The wind can hear us; Daw can see through walls and around corners."

Victor shook his head brusquely; Colin looked a little guilty. Quentin said, "Your note said Boggin can listen along the wind. Colin and I talked. I thought indoors was safe. No wind."

"It's my fault," I said. "I should have had Victor destroy those notes immediately."

Victor said, "You didn't tell me Miss Daw could see through walls."

Another big mistake from Leader Amelia. Keep the troops informed of security risks. I tried to throw off a sense of rising despair. I said bravely, "Spilt milk. Assume the enemy knows our plan. What are they doing?"

Victor said, "You tell us. Only you remember seeing them in action."

"Well, they must be taking their own sweet time getting here. Since Boggin can fly, I don't know what is keeping them."

Victor said, "Fear. They don't know what we can do, how much we re-membered."

Quentin said, "They would not come for us here. Right now, we are five kids standing outside a dorm window. They're at the boundaries, waiting. The boundaries are where our power is."

Colin said, "Assume they moved the safe."

I said, "If our powers were working, they have to split us up to defeat us. They'd be posted around the boundaries."

Colin said, "But? Dark Mistress, our powers are not working."

"They don't know that. I am afraid of splitting up. They can crush us singly."

Colin said, "Dark Mistress, hello? Hello? Earth to Amelia! If none of our super-duper powers are operating, they can crush us anyway, singly or as a group."

I said, "I want to see if I can turn Victor on."

I turned toward Victor.

Colin said, "I could make the obvious joke at this point. . . ."

I said to Quentin, "Give me the hypo."

He passed over the syringe he'd stolen from Dr. Fell.

Colin muttered, "Quick, Watson, the needle!"

I took out some of the filter paper I had filched, made a crude funnel, held my hand over it.

My palm and fingertips turned red. Vanity crinkled up her nose in a silent *Eyew, gross* expression as blood dripped into the filter.

I said, "This is a creature that exists on a molecular level. It knows how the brain is put together. I have asked it to unblock Victor. It might work; it might not. Miss Daw is the one who knocked his memory askew, by manipulating the fourth dimension; but if Dr. Fell tried to erase any brain segments by purely mechanical means, this might undo the damage. There is a risk of—"

Victor yanked his sleeve back and thrust out his arm.

I thought about Lily Lilac. That made it easy to thrust the needle in.

Everyone stood waiting to see if Victor would keel over or something.

I said, "A brisk jog will get your blood moving. And we don't have time to wait."

Vanity and Colin were giving Victor worried looks. Nonetheless, we set off at a brisk trot to the North.

9.

I spoke in white, puffing whispers as we ran. "Three stages to powers. First. Vision powers. ESP. Tarot cards. They can't stop at all. Second. Little powers. Make things light, heavy. Fly. TK. Jump long ways. Can stop for a while. Boundaries turned on before. Why not again? Third stage. Talismans. Kept in safe. Change shape, walk through walls, talk to molecules. Goal: get to safe. Need little powers on to get into Great Hall. Wired."

Quentin puffed, "Why me first? No staff. Need wand."

I shook my head. I was out of breath to explain my plan. I looked at Victor. He was trotting along, his feet moving up and down in the snow like pistons, his expression calm, smooth, unafraid. To him I said, "Anything? Remember?"

He said, "Not yet. If I understand the table of opposition, of who stops whom, you should have given the injection to Quentin, not to me. Quentin is trumped by Fell, who used materialistic science to banish his alchemy. I was trumped by Daw, who uses the fourth dimension to neutralize three-dimensional science, right?"

It was actually the relativistic and quantum-statistical worldview overcoming the limitations of the absolutist Newtonian atomistic-mechanistic model, but I was too out of breath to say.

Maybe he was right. One more bad decision from Leader Amelia. Dear God in Heaven, but I hated the job of leader.

10.

Tattered clouds like ghost ships were being blown along the starry sky, and a pale moon, now here, now hidden, shone on the bright and silent hillocks of snow. The barrows were in a hilly place, far from anything, and bits of broken wall, or standing stones erected by ancient peoples, stood here and there among the widely spaced mounds.

We had stopped jogging. Everyone looked at me.

I said to Quentin, "What did you do last time?"

He said, "If I could remember, I would not need to do it. But I had my walking stick. Apsu. Where is he? I miss him."

I said, "He was a gift from Mrs. Wren . . ."

When I spoke, a rustle of cold wind started from the north, and blew across us. I tucked my cold hands into my armpits and turned my back to it. Vanity was tugging at her muffler; Colin and Quentin squinted and hunched their shoulders. Only Victor, who stood without scarf or hat or gloves, seemed unaffected, and his gaze traveled left to right, as if he were watching some unseen thing move quickly past us.

The wind gust died down. I heard the sound of snow slithering and hissing, windblown, moving away to the south, and diminish.

To Victor, I said, "What is it?"

He said, "Magnetic anomaly. Interesting."

Quentin said, "What about the staff?"

I continued, "The staff. When you used it against her, it shattered in your hand."

Quentin looked stricken.

I said, "What's wrong?"

"You are thinking of these things as super-powers, aren't you?" he said, a trace of bitterness in his voice. "Like a mechanism you turn on and turn off. I do not think it works that way. I think it is like being a Roman Catholic priest. If you get married and break your vow of chastity, I don't think you can just get divorced and become a priest again. If my staff was broken, my power is broken. It's over. Let's go on to another boundary."

Another failure for Leader Amelia. Maybe this one wasn't my fault. But on the other hand, I remember Quentin telling me the spirits were shy. He could not even fly when people were watching. Nothing would happen while there was a big group here.

Even if he had a staff.

Vanity said, "What causes magnetic anomalies?"

Colin and I stared at her curiously. It seemed an odd question. I said, "What do you . . . ?"

Victor said, "Any electromagnetic power of sufficient magnitude to—"

Colin interrupted sharply, "Hey! Stupid people! It was a demon! A thing! It went to get help! Time to run away! Which direction? Give the order, Dark Mistress!"

I said, "East. Run. Hold on to each other! Last time they used a magic spell to split us up!"

It is really not that easy to run holding hands, and I am sure it looks quite silly. The hilly terrain did not make things any easier, and the hills were getting steeper as we pulled to the East.

Ahead of us in the moonlight, I could see the cliffs of the Downs, treeless and barren, raising sides of chalk and limestone, pale as cloud, against the stars.

I was doing fine for a long, long stretch. Vanity was soon out of breath, and Quentin was not doing much better. Colin was gritting his teeth and puffing like a steam engine, but seemed to be keeping up the pace by sheer willpower. Victor did not seem tired at all.

We were all pelting down a snowy slope, which did not seem steep at all, when suddenly (to me, it seemed sudden) the slope was much sharper than it had first appeared, and I was sliding. When I fell, I pulled down Vanity with me; she let go of Quentin's hand.

THE BARROW MOUND

1.

We two slid and slithered down the hillside, and when Quentin tried to jump after us to get us, he tried to yank out of Colin's hand, who was apparently unwilling to let go. Their feet went out from under them.

It would have been funny if it weren't so dangerous. I fell and slid about fifty yards, and Vanity skidded to a slow halt a few yards beyond me.

We were still among the barrows. There was a huge mound, larger than the others we had seen, in the dead center of a smooth and perfectly round depression like a crater. It was down those crater sides we had just fallen, as if pulled inward toward the barrow.

This mound had a stone doorway, half the height of a man, set with pillars and lintels of unfinished stone: a half-buried henge.

It would have seemed eerie and unearthly, except that there was evidence of modern man here. There were tarps and crates off to one side. Lights had been rigged around the stone door. There was a small diesel-powered generator under an ice-coated tarp. Nothing was on; nothing was lit. It looked as if the archeologist and his assistants had packed things for the holidays, and expected to be back here digging in a week. There was even a flatbed truck with wide, oversize off-road tires parked not far away.

I climbed to my feet. "Vanity—!"

She stood, slid another few feet downslope, stood again. "Fun. Let's do that again. Kidding! Just kidding!"

"A spell made us rash and stupid last time. Tell me if you can feel if we are being watched."

She looked left and right. "Where are the boys . . . ?"

They had fallen farther down the slope. Indeed, they were almost at the stone entrance to the barrow.

I did not like the look of that. Like the tumble that had split us up when we approached the seashore, this had all the markings of a trap being sprung. I did not want to shout, but I saw Colin get to his feet, and without bothering to look back to see if the rest of us were hurt, he started to walk slowly and stiffly toward the black square entrance to the mound.

His motion was stiff, doll-like. Quentin was rising to his feet also, walking with sleepwalker steps after him.

I bit my lip. No shouting. I stooped, gathered a snowball, and let it fly at Colin. I have a good throwing arm, and managed to knock off his hat with a plop of snow. Colin shook himself and turned around, angered and startled.

I pointed furiously to where Quentin was walking stiff-legged toward the waiting stone door. Colin squinted at him, looking angry. He jumped forward in three long strides, put out his hand and yanked Quentin roughly; the younger boy stumbled and went to one knee.

I said, "Vanity! Report!"

She closed her eyes, raised her hand, pointed upward. Her other hand lifted and pointed down.

Her eyes snapped open. "Overhead and underfoot. Two of them."

I looked back up the slope. I could see Victor's slender silhouette in the moonlight, a shadow against the brighter snow behind him. He was stepping sideways down the slope, carefully and quickly placing one foot after another.

A shadow passed across the face of the moon. I looked up.

It was Dr. Fell, levitating.

The tails of his white lab coat floated and flapped around his legs. He had neither hat nor overcoat, as if cold meant nothing to him. Like a shark diving through cold, black waters, he dropped feetfirst out of the night sky, heading toward Colin and Quentin.

He was a hundred feet up. I saw a blue spark appear on his brow. He had opened his third eye.

An azure beam darted from the eye, stabbing down. Somehow,

impossibly, Colin moved faster, and threw Quentin down with himself atop. The beam struck Colin. I was expecting, I do not know what, an explosion or something, but the beam seemed to do Colin no more hurt than a flashlight.

On my table of opposites, I wasn't sure how Colin's paradigm matched up against Dr. Fell. Neither one trumped the other. Where they roughly equal? Or were they both immune to each other? I didn't know.

Dr. Fell hovered lower. I could see, under his lab coat, he was wearing a jacket of chain mail. I had seen those chain-mail jerkins every day of my life. It never occurred to me that anyone except the mannequins in the corridors could wear them.

He shouted down, "Mr. mac FirBolg! Move aside, or I will be forced to deal with you!"

Colin answered him by holding up two fingers. Not a victory sign. *Fuck you with horns on, buddy.*

Dr. Fell took a syringe out of his jacket pocket, filled it from a vein in his arm. He held the syringe for a moment before his face; an azure spark flickered between his metal eye and the tube.

He closed his third eye, and he opened his hand. The syringe hung in the air a moment, unsupported. Then it turned end over end and darted toward Colin.

Colin slapped the speeding thing out of midair just before it touched him, clapping his hands together like a man swatting a wasp. His clasped hands jerked back and forth for a moment, as if the wasp were still alive. Then, with a funny look on his face, Colin slumped over in a faint.

"Well, that was not difficult, was it?" Dr. Fell asked himself.

Vanity and I were simply too far away to do anything. I was not sure if I should call out. Neither of us, apparently, had been seen yet. But I was stepping quickly down the slope, and Vanity followed me. What was I supposed to do once I got closer? Maybe I could make Fell weigh more, and drag him down out of the air.

Quentin was on his back, awkwardly holding Colin's body between himself and Fell.

Fell looked at a coil of electrical cable that was resting next to the diesel generator; then he looked at where Colin was slumped over atop Quentin. The cables unwound and reached across the snow like arms of an octopus. The cables must have had copper cores he was manipulating magnetically.

Loops of cable snaked around Colin's shoulders and legs, and yanked him to one side.

"Now, then," said Dr. Fell. He opened his third eye again.

The battery of lights atop the stone door swiveled around in their brackets, and turned on, a silent explosion, dazzling. Dr. Fell did not blink, but he jerked his hand up to guard his forehead, where the metal eye—his real eye—was.

I saw Victor, now far below me, not twenty yards from the entrance to the howe. He was covered from head to foot in snow. Behind him, in a straight line reaching back up the slope, was a crease of snow where he had (evidently) flung himself headfirst down the side of the crater, using his stomach as a toboggan. He was not ten yards from the empty truck and the other crates and equipment of the archeologist's camp.

Dr. Fell's head swiveled like a gun turret toward Victor, and his third eye gleamed with blue light. Firefly dots of azure blue streamed out along the beam.

Victor raised his head; the flesh along his forehead creased and puckered and opened. A metal eye appeared on Victor's head. His eye was a deeper, purple color, and streaks and sparks of gold flickered through the beam that issued from it.

The beams did not pass through each other, as light would have done. Instead, where they met in midair, the tiny motes of gold and azure canceled each other out with a flash like heat lightning.

Dr. Fell called down in a dispassionate voice: "I ask you to surrender."

Victor called back in a voice also calm and matter-of-fact: "Impossible. I can be killed, but I cannot be defeated without some act of consent on my part. I do not consent."

Dr. Fell said, "That strategy limits your available range of options. You lose the opportunity to minimize unfavorable outcomes and maximize favorable ones."

Victor replied, "Only in the short term. Over the span of all possible future interactions, positive as well as negative, a declared policy of no-surrender lowers transaction costs by deterring zero-sum situations."

Fell: "Your policy renders the present interaction negative-sum."

Victor: "I am taking that into account."

"The cost to you will be higher than to me."

"My cost-benefit calculation also includes my companions, who may survive whether or not I die, into the satisfactory outcome definition. Your satisfactory outcome range is more limited."

"But my strategic options are far greater to begin," said Dr. Fell, and he raised his hand.

Again, both their metal eyes lit up. There was an exchange of lances of fire, a strike and a parry.

I could see the internal nature of the charged particle packages being sent out.

Dr. Fell had emitted molecular engines designed to enter Victor's body, find his nervous system, and send a shutdown command to his motor centers. He had ionized the particles and accelerated them by means of a magnetic monopole he had generated in certain specialized centers of his nervous system.

Victor's response was to ionize the air in the beam path, so the molecular engines lost their charge. Neutral, they could not be accelerated. They were still dangerous, but now they were drifting quite slowly, like a little cloud of dust motes, down, up, whichever way the Brownian motions of the air carried them, a spreading vapor of fine ink.

Victor's metal eye flashed fire; this time it was Dr. Fell, still standing in midair high as a treetop, who ionized the space around him. A counterthrust and counterparry. Nothing done. Neither man was vulnerable to attack at that level.

Vanity put her hand out to stop me. "What are we going to do when we get there?" she said.

I slowed down. It was a good question.

Victor pointed at the cables still wound around the motionless Colin. Colin spun over in the snow, a human yo-yo. The cables jumped off Colin and snaked up into the air, lassoing Dr. Fell.

Two of the four arc lights went dark as the cables from the generator jumped skyward at Victor's gesture. The generator cables fused (in little hissing flares of acetylene light) to the dangling ends of the cables winding around Dr. Fell.

Meanwhile, Dr. Fell's metal eye dilated. A shower of motes flickered across the snow to every side of Victor. I saw the meaning of what was happening. The internal nature of the snow—cold and noninflammable— was being disintegrated into hydrogen and oxygen—flammable. It was chemically impossible; the energy of the reaction needed to split a water molecule into atoms and recombine them into O_2 and H_4 was not present. . . .

The snow at Victor's feet glowed red, writhed like a living thing, and then exploded. The flame was not red; it was blue-white, and an outer, hotter flame rushed over it, and popped like a balloon.

Fell lowered his head, and the blue beam narrowed like the cutting torch. I saw motes stream out from his pupil, molecular machines programmed to break apart the chemical bonds of anything they touched. It was a disintegration ray. His chin touched his breastbone.

With a screaming hiss, the ray began cutting through the cords wrapping his arms.

I saw Victor, coated in flames, step forward out of the globe of pale fire. His skin had been replaced by a diamond crust, which he had collected out of the atmospheric carbon. He raised one diamond-gleaming hand. The diesel generator's switches flipped. The turbine turned on.

Fell had cut through the insulation, but had not yet severed the copper core of the cable. The voltage arched between the bare copper and his coat of ringmail. There was a flash like a photographer's bulb going off, and a smell of ozone permeated the air.

The dazzling afterimage in my eyes showed a purple banner of smoke, thin as cigarette smoke, hanging between the spot where Dr. Fell had just been hovering, and the wreckage of the truck, struck in two by the impact, with a crater of splashed snow in a wide circle around it.

The remaining two arc lights failed. I heard the diesel engine whine and splutter into silence. I could smell burnt insulation.

The white fire surrounding Victor fluttered and was gone. My eyes were blind. I waited for them to re-adapt to the starlight.

In the darkness, Vanity cheered and clapped. "Fell fell!" She cheered. "Hurrah for our team! Go, Victor! Victor, go!"

I said, "Fell is not hurt."

"How far was that? That was at least as tall as a ten-story building!"

"He altered the internal character of his muscles and bones into something like wood. He splintered, but the pieces are regathering. His nervous system was not harmed. . . ."

She said, "Can you see? I can't see a thing."

"Vanity, I don't know what to do. Should we run up and try to help?"

"Help with what? Help how?" she said. "I don't even have a baseball bat . . ."

The headlights of the truck turned on. The bulbs, trailing wires like the eyestalks of a crab, rose up out from the grille, and turned toward the wrecked truck body.

Dr. Fell stood up out of the wreck. He did not stand up the way a man would, bending his legs, squatting, putting a hand on the ground. No. Stiff as a corpse, as if pulled upright by invisible wire, he went from being prone to being upright. Imagine a man stepping on the tines of a rake, and seeing the handle lift suddenly upright, and you will know what it looked like.

The prosthetic he wore for a face was torn and burnt. An impatient hand pulled at the tattered mask and threw it away. The integument underneath it looked as hard as bone. The mouthparts looked like the mandibles of an insect. There were no eyeholes, only one central orb, gleaming and turning, in the forehead, like the headlamp of an oncoming train.

The two exchanged radio signals. I do not know what higher sense of mine detected and interpreted the rapid pulse of meaning between them, but I heard it, somehow:

Fell: "If defeat-conditions cannot be reached, then the core value for our interaction matrix is null."

Victor: "I am treating this as a single instance of an infinitely repeatable set."

"A child cannot harm me, but I can deliver any harm up to but less than death, which will involve unacceptable repercussions."

"I am no longer a child, Dr. Fell. I am Damnameneus of the Telchine."

"I am Telemus, one of the Cyclopean Archons. Our race defeated yours in times past; that instance has application here."

"There is still an information cost associated with determining the truth-value of your assertion of invulnerability."

"Let us proceed to the demonstration. . . ."

The hood of the engine flew open, and the engine block, pistons, cylinders, battery, and shaft rose up into the air and spread apart, as if being laid out on the three-dimensional blueprint. Then wires and parts of the engine began reconstructing themselves, as if evolving into some new machine.

Where the diamond statue of Victor stood, a greenish smoke began bubbling up out of pockmarks in the snow. Fell was gathering and recombining the chlorophyll traces in the winter grass beneath the snow to make chlorine gas. I could sense Victor altering his body chemistry to compensate, shifting into a nonbreathing form.

Vanity could see Fell, illuminated by the spotlights of the truck headlamps, but Victor and the poisonous gas were invisible to her.

The petrol tank crumbled suddenly, and gasoline drenched Dr. Fell.

Fans of molecular machines spread out from Fell in each direction, reaching under the ground. I saw where nitrates, like bubbles forming in lava, were being drawn out of the soil to combine and create explosives.

I said, "We better get farther away. Colin and Quentin . . ."

Colin lay on a heap, motionless, limp as a rag doll. Quentin was gone. Gone.

The lights from the truck splashed enough illumination to show me the dimple shadows of one set of footprints, leading directly into the burial mound.

I said, "Look to Colin! See if he is alive!"

And I ran.

2.

I do not know if Vanity was trying to disobey me, or if I was no longer leader, or if she was just scared, but she ran after me for about half the distance between me and the stone door, farther behind with every step.

The stone door loomed before me, a cold mouth, gaping. I bent double and began slithering, crawling, and duck-walking as fast as I could into the mound. To me, it was not as dark as a natural mound would have been. The original purpose of these prehistoric mounds was to bury dead kings. It was still carrying out that function; to my eyes that could see the utility of objects, it seemed to have a faint glow.

Vanity, behind me, stopped at the stone door. "Amelia . . . ?" she called in a quavering voice.

I put a point of view behind her, and looked at her. She turned, and in the light of the gasoline explosions coming from the direction of the truck, she could see Colin's motionless body. Vanity went toward him.

I could see through the wall of the mound. There was a spiral crawlway, lined with massive blocks, leading to a domed chamber in the center. I could see a strand of moral force running from my heart to a silhouette lying prone. It was my moral obligation to help Quentin.

There was a tangle of other strands and lines of moral order, or disorder, strung throughout and past the chamber walls, like a spider's web, twisting and twisting.

I reached the inner door. The chamber inside was dark to my eyes. But the utility . . .

No. The chamber here was not useful to the long-dead kings. It was useful, very useful, to someone else. Someone here.

One moment, she was invisible. The next, I could see her bent silhouette, her pointed hood and shapeless cloak, as a group of moral force-lines issued from the distaff she held in her hands.

She said, "High diddle doubt, my candle's out, my little maid's not at home; saddle my hog and bridle my dog, and fetch my little maid home. Why are you so far from home, my little maid?"

The voice was so strange, I almost didn't recognize it. Perhaps what I thought was her normal voice was merely a put-on, an act. "Is that you, Mrs. Wren?"

A dry laugh. "There was an old woman dwelt under a hill; and if she's not gone, she dwelleth there still."

I said, "Not Mrs. Wren, then. You are Erichtho."

No laughter, this time.

She said, "You cannot take my name from me. That art you do not know. You do not name me, little girl. You know not whence I came or whither I go."

The darkness was silent for a moment, as if she were waiting for a response from me, some sort of verbal parry. I could think of nothing to say.

She laughed again, a noise like dry leaves crumpling. She said, "There was an old woman tossed in a basket seventeen times as high as the moon, but where she was going no mortal could tell, for under her arm she carried a broom. . . ."

I said, "Undo what you've done to Quentin!"

"Or else, what, my little maid? Will you send young Colin in to chop me with a great sharp axe?"

I said, "I didn't say that!"

I could see the strands looping and weaving back and forth in the chamber.

"No word of greeting, no kiss on the cheek, for the old nurse, the old granny, who raised you from a kitten? The hands I taught how to play pat-a-cake are raised now to strike me, is it? The feet I taught their first steps to, are raised high to kick and run away? The food I fed, the strength I gave you, now is turned against me, eh?"

As if they were fibers of wire or rope, I saw the strands loop around my arms and legs like nooses. One went into my heart. One went into my stomach. I felt nothing, but a cold sensation passed over my limbs.

She said, "Woe is me! Oh arms, oh legs, oh strength! Hear me!"

I ran forward at her, thinking I could knock her down or stop her mouth before she spoke her spell. The silhouette I thought was her crumbled in my hands when I touched it, and something, rings or a crown or something, slid off the disintegrating skull and bounced away.

An illusion. Even my senses could be tricked by witchcraft.

Her voice was behind me: "Here's Sulky Sue. What shall we do? Turn her face to the wall till she comes to."

The cold force wrapping my limbs threw me facedown on the floor of the burial chamber.

I could see her silhouette again, now stooping over me. "Is this the sweet voice I taught to sing, to say her prayers at bedtime, and is it now raised up to curse and revile me . . . ? Oh, tongue, hear me!"

I had only a moment to say one thing. While she talked, I also talked. I said quickly, "Is this the witch who kidnapped me as a babe, to be raised as a captive in an alien land, surrounded by those who hate me? Is this the witch who stole my childhood and life, so that I never will know my mother's smile? Is this the witch who gave me nothing freely, but all her gifts were poisons, meant to trap us? Fire! Hear me! Burn this witch!"

She stopped in the midst of her spell, hissing. For a moment, it was as if I could feel the fear radiating from her, as if she expected a fire to come burn her.

I heard a little quivering sigh come from her. "That spell might have worked, oh my clever girl, if you had any of the True Art in you. But you are a Helionide, aren't you? A daughter of the Nameless Ones? Your power works another way, with crooked angles and tangles of geometry, and stepping sideways into higher worlds. Well, there is no higher world for you, my kitten. Tomorrow you shall be back in your cell, and the day after, this will be a dream, and all your clever tricks and clever escapades will be blotted out. We'll know what to look for, next time round, and we'll flush more of you into oblivion. Years more. We'll induce the shape-change, if Grendel will do his work. How'd you like to be a seven-year-old, eh? Oh, to be young again!"

I said, "Thief of my life, thief of my soul; I call upon the lordly dead whose house you desecrate to avenge me."

She struck me in the head with the handle of the distaff she carried. *Thunk.* My face was driven against the stone. I bit my lip and tasted blood.

I spat the blood onto the floor.

She said, "There are none to hear your prayers, little maid. I am old and wise in the ways of my art; this place is mine."

I said, "I ask the Lord God of Israel, the God of Jacob, and of Isaac, and of Abraham, to save my friends from bondage and oppression. Of all the gods of all the tales told in ancient times, only He upheld the weak."

She cackled. "And of all the tales, tales of that one are the most false! I knew Abraham! He was a liar and a child-murderer! If—"

A shadow stood up out of the spot of blood I had spat on the floor. I could not see it with my eyes—during this whole time, I saw nothing with my eyes, as the tomb was dark—but the strands of moral force woven in and around her distaff all curled and fled away from him, revealing the negative outline of a tall shape.

She began to scream, a high, thin, shrill noise like an animal might make. The shadow moved. I don't know what it did, but her voice diminished, and went mute.

I wondered if I had gone deaf. But no, I could hear her rattling breath hissing through her teeth. I heard her feet rustle as she took a step back, then two. I heard the tap of her distaff on the stones of the chamber floor, and the hiss of her skirts.

A cold voice spoke. In speaking, it did not breathe or pause for breath: "In life, I was Romus, son of Odysseus by Circe, set to watch the Lady Nausicaa. In that duty I failed, and was slain by cruel treason. For many seasons the evil of Boreas kept me locked in a coffin, unable to rest, and my watchfulness was turned against my mistress, and used, not to protect, but to enslave her.

"Here is the witch who cast the spell on me, to confound my shade, and turn my fate awry.

"Now, witch, I embrace you. Feel my cold dead arm clasp about you, closer than the lover whom you poisoned. When the Dog comes, we shall both be dragged down together. Hell awaits us."

I heard a rustling noise in the chamber, a hiss of muffled horror, but I could see nothing.

The cold voice issued forth from the darkness again, like icicles shaped into words: "There is my aunt, the sister of Circe, Phaethusa, who is of my house and blood; and there is the man who set my shade to rest, and paid, of his own hand, my toll to cross the hateful Styx. Rise ye both! And speak. What is in my power to grant, although I am but a handful of wind and dust, I shall perform."

I got shakily to my feet. My head bumped stone. I could not see where I was. Maybe it was near the center of the chamber, at the dome's highest point. If so, the highest point was not very high.

Quentin said softly, quickly, "Denizen of night, can you grant me my powers again?"

The ghost said, "Not I. Only the hand that dealt the wound can cure it."

Quentin said, "Granny, I will forgive your crime against me, if you will return my staff and swear to forgive all crimes I have ever done against you, and release me from all debts, past, present, and future. Furthermore, I want you to swear to . . ."

I put my hand on his arm. He could not see the strands, but I could. If he asked for too much, it would go against him. If he asked her to forswear her oath to Boggin, for example, he would be doing something that would provoke a bad reaction.

Romus said, "Speak, witch, and swear."

Mrs. Wren's cracked voice trembled. "Thy staff and wand of office I make whole, and I forgive ye all crimes and ills you have ever done me, and release you from all debts, past, present, and owing."

I saw the strands shift and sway.

I said, "I will forgive you for kidnapping me, if you will release me from any obligations of fealty, thanks, or gratitude. I am no longer your child, or anyone's. Say it."

She said, "I release you. You are free and independent. I accept your forgiveness. In addition, I will give you this gift . . ."

I saw the strands twitch and begin to weave together. . . .

"No!" I said. "You are most kind, but I fear I cannot accept."

The strands parted. The web that had snared us fell away and was gone. The witch's power over the two of us had failed. I felt joy, don't doubt it; but when the strands faded, I also lost the only guide that allowed me to "see" in this utter blackness. The usefulness of this burial mound to Erichtho had also faded. The place was dark to all my senses.

Romus said, "I go now into the dreamless sleep of Elysium, where a fair white table had been spread for me. This last gift I grant. Witch: I give to you your life. Aunt Phaethusa: I grant you that you shall never be in darkness, wherever you go. Man of the Graeae: I grant you that your wand will come to your hand upon your call. Its dead spirit I breathe now back to life. It will inhabit any stalk or wand or spear or stick you shall hold in your hand, and it shall never be taken from you again, until the world ends. Anubis. Go into the stick."

I saw the shadow move, and the utility-light, the usefulness to Quentin, of the distaff Mrs. Wren was carrying brightened a hundredfold. She screamed and threw down her staff, as if it had burned her.

Quentin reached down in the dark and picked it up.

I saw the shadow vanish.

I said, "Well, this seems pretty dark to me right now. Quentin, is she in the boat you were in? She can't cast spells without her wand?"

"I think so."

"Mrs. Wren? How about a truce, long enough to get us all out of this burial mound . . . ?"

No answer. I heard motion.

Quentin tapped his staff on the ground. A pearly radiance issued from the top, where a hank of yarn was wound round and round it. There were shallow shelves to either side, where bones and dust gathered mold. Gold rings lay on the floor.

The place seemed much, much smaller in the light. The door was mouse-hole-shaped, and hardly had room to crawl into.

Quentin said, "She's making a break for it."

"Let's crawl. How fast can she go?"

So we both crawled.

When we came out into the snow again, there were columns of fire burning near the truck, which was scattered all across the slope behind.

A complex-looking machine, blocky and square, made of engine parts, lenses, wires, lay on its side in a puddle of flickering gasoline. It had a big tube issuing from one end like a gun barrel, but I think that was only from the muffler.

There were craters pockmarking the snow here and there, and fantastic bubbles of oily-colored ice, like half-buried skulls, protruding from the snow.

Victor was standing on bare earth. He was wearing the chain-mail jerkin.

There was a wide ring of steaming snow all around him, but no snow where his feet were. His third eye was open, and there was light coming from it. That, and the light from billowing columns of fire to his left and right, illuminated the scene.

We saw Mrs. Wren. She had her back to us and was facing Victor. Her shoulders hunched up as if in shock and surprise. She raised her crooked hands. "I call upon the spirits of earth and below earth! Wood! Water! Welkin! Fire and Iron! I call . . ."

Victor looked impatient. As clearly as if he had spoken it aloud, his expression said, *Inanimate elements cannot listen to you, you superstitious old woman.*

A blue-gold spark left his head and touched her. She slid and sat down in the snow, giggled, and slumped over.

He turned his head. There was Colin lying not far away. Vanity sat in the snow with Colin's head in her lap. Victor played the beam from his third eye back and forth across Colin's body once and twice. Colin blinked and sat up. "Jesus! It's cold!" He looked around. "What the hell happened here?"

Vanity said, "Everybody did stuff but me."

I said, "Fell?"

Victor closed his third eye and pointed off to the left. Fell lay like a broken doll, arms and legs spread out at odd angles.

Quentin said, "I hope you didn't kill him."

Colin said, "And I hope you did! Do you know what that horse's ass gave me on my last dom rag?"

Quentin said, "If we commit a murder, it will go very, very badly for us. The influences friendly to us will turn."

Victor said, "Don't worry. He's just stunned."

Victor explained in a few curt sentences that he had used a catalyst to precipitate out of the atmosphere the "nanites" (as he called them) that Fell had shot at him in the open thrust of the duel.

Victor said, "They just rained down on top of him. He did not notice them until it was too late. Apparently they were topically active. The nerves near his skin carried the cryptognostic signals to the motor centers of his brain, and shut him off."

Quentin pointed at the squat machine with the protruding muffler, which Victor had apparently put together out of bits and parts of the en-. gine. "And what did that thing do?"

"That gave him something to look at while invisible nanite particles settled on his skin." Victor gave one of his rare smiles. It was a small smile, just a tension of muscles in his cheeks, but I thought it made him look wonderful. "He was not expecting me to waste energy building something merely to distract him. That expectation made it not a waste. You are the one who taught me the principle, Quentin. The hand the stage magician waves in the air is not the one to look at. Fell was too much of a scientist. He should have studied stage magic."

I said, "What about her?" I nodded at Mrs. Wren.

He said, "Cryptognosis. Her body is adjusted to react to alcohol. I triggered the habitual reaction in her glands. I sent the false signal that she was drunk to her midbrain, pons, and medulla oblongata. The cells in her body will run through the cycle they learned to get rid of alcohol poisons in the bloodstream, which includes sleep and liver activity."

I said, "They'll die if we leave them asleep here in the snow."

Colin said, "Bugger 'em, if you don't mind my saying so, Dark Mistress."

I looked around at the group. "Ah, wait a minute. I want to resign as leader! Both Victor and Quentin have their powers back, and Victor seems to have his memory back."

Victor nodded. "I remember the first escape attempt. Everything up till when we were on the beach, and Miss Daw started playing."

I said, "I want to put Victor back in charge! He can decide what to do about the sleeping people in the snow."

Victor said, "Bad policy to change leaders in mid-mission. Besides, you clearly figured out more than I have. I don't know whether you talked to Daw or Boggin or where you got your information, but you still know more than I do, and I am not sure you can fill me in on all the details quickly enough."

Quentin said, "You're doing a fine job, Amelia. And we can't stop to debate. Where is Boggin? I thought you said he could fly and bend space."

"And spanks," said Colin. "Don't forget he spanks."

I said, "I want a vote. Thumbs up or down. I've messed up practically everything so far, trust me."

Quentin said, "No time. Sorry, Amelia, but the whole point of having a leader is to have someone make the decisions—even bad decisions—when there is no time to debate things. When there is time to debate, we don't need a leader, because we can form a committee."

Colin said, "Besides, Victor already said, and Quentin agrees. That's two. I vote yea, just because I like saying the phrase 'Dark Mistress.' Three is a majority. Vanity, your vote is wasted."

Vanity turned her head. She said, "He just heard us. Boggin. I don't know where he was or what he was doing before, but he's listening now."

I had wanted to see if I could get the molecular life-form to come out of Victor's body and inject itself into Fell, either to erase his memory, or make him loyal to us, or something. Now there was no time to experiment, and no piece of paper to write it on, and only fitful light to see by. However, there was enough heat coming from the twin columns of fire that I did not think Mrs. Wren would die of exposure, not in the short time it would take Boggin to get his coat off and fly here.

I said in a loud, clear voice, "Boggin! Two of your people are lying here in the snow, unconscious. I don't know how long they can keep. You can either chase us or go save them. You decide. Okay, people! We're splitting up! Pick a direction and run!"

Vanity tugged on my arm, looking like she was dying to tell me something, and she pointed at the burial mound. She made little finger-walking pantomimes, opened and shut her hands a few times, waved her arms. . . .

I tapped myself on the head and pointed at her. *There. You are in charge.*

Ho ha. Them and their policy of no votes during missions.

THE KISSING WELL

1.

Vanity pointed at Victor, made flapping bird motions with her hands, pointed at each of us in turn, and pointed left, right, here and there. Then she made a circle with her arms, flapped them again, and pointed at the mound.

I got it. I sprinted off to the East. Colin and Quentin and Victor each went other directions. Vanity ran, too.

After less than a minute, long enough to leave many clear footprints in the snow leading away from the mound, I saw Victor fall gracefully and silently out of the sky and hover a few feet off the ground before me.

I put my arms around his neck, and he hoisted me up with his hands.

Funny. He did not do even as well as Quentin had. Like I was a sack of potatoes, or something.

I flew. My hair streamed and whipped in the quick wind, and I clung close to Victor. In the nocturnal darkness, there was little to see, just the bumpy texture of snow underfoot, the barrows and hills in the moonlight. With no sense of height, it seemed curiously close and small.

Then down. Victor did not fly like Boggin had, prone, like a man doing a breaststroke. He stood in the air like a man riding an elevator, while an invisible electromagnetic force picked him up, moved him over, set him down again. As if he were a chessman being moved by an unseen hand.

Then he was up again. I was the first one here, and I looked around at the barren top of the barrow mound, wondering what was here.

Victor plunged down again. Vanity. She gave me a hug and big smile, her first time flying. She half-stepped, half-slid down the side of the barrow mound, and started touching the slabs of uncut stone that formed the base of the mound, where it met the earth. The archeologist, or someone, had spaded and cut away the turf, which otherwise would have covered it, so a snowy ditch ran in a semicircle around the base of the mound.

Victor plunged down silently from the sky, holding a disgruntled Colin. Behind him was a dark shadow shaped like wings, which fluttered and flapped but made no noise at all. The shadow touched the ground on the far side of the mound from where we were. A moment later, Quentin came into view, walking over the top of the mound and down toward us.

I pointed at him, made a flapping gesture with my hands, shrugged, tapped my forehead. Apparently he understood what I was asking. *How did you remember how to fly?* He just smiled, held up the distaff he was carrying, pointed to his ear, pantomimed listening. *I did not remember,* he was saying. *Apsu did. They didn't erase* his *memory.*

Vanity touched a stone, and it slid back without noise. There were stairs leading down to a tunnel. She gestured like a showgirl on a game show displaying a new prize the contestants have just won.

We passed through less than a hundred feet of tunnel, and emerged four miles away.

2.

The tunnel itself was five feet high, the curved roof just low enough to make a tall girl claustrophobic. The walls and roof were brown brick; the floor was leafy mold above cracked yellow concrete. There were brackets in the walls for holding torches, and dark angles of stain across the brick above these brackets. Every twenty paces, there was an oval hole in the curved roof, smaller than a woman's fist, where air and a little moonlight trickled in. There were pale ivy vines and thorny bushes growing in cracks in the stones just under these holes, as if seeds had dropped in, and enough sunlight reached there to sustain them.

At the far end of the tunnel was a tiny room like a guardroom, also made of brown brick. To the left, rusted hinges hung above a tiny niche or alcove. Three metal braces formed a crude ladder leading to a circular door at shoulder level. A hatch, I suppose. One brick at eye level was missing from that wall; this was a peephole or loophole that overlooked the door.

I could hear the ocean. Through the loophole, I could smell salt spray.

The latch for the door was just inside that missing brick. From the setup, it would take at least two people to open the door from the outside: one to stick his hand into the missing brick to reach the latch, one to pull on the door. Any defenders inside could just smash the incoming hand with a rock, or chop it off with a sword, I suppose.

Next to the door was a white stone. CLVDS IMP ET REX, L. JOV ANNO XXI. What the hell did that mean?

Vanity worked the latch. She had to put her shoulder to it, and strain. The door groaned and opened. Out she crawled.

The outer surface of the secret door was shaped like a rock, one of several rocks, which had slipped from a waist-high shelf of stone. Behind this shelf and above it was a cliff, which reached perhaps ten feet above our heads.

In the other direction was a drop to the rocks and the roaring foam. We stood among the sea cliffs. Like a giant staircase, the limestone cliffs formed shelves, one below the next, in crooked piles tumbling toward the sea.

Vanity found some handholds and footholds in a little chimney indented into the cliff behind us. She climbed up about less than a dozen. There was grass and a few stunted trees there, their branches naked of leaves.

Up we climbed.

The Kissing Well was less than a stone's throw away from us. We had traveled from the Northeastern to the Southwestern border of the estate in less than ten minutes.

Vanity announced, "It's okay to talk. We've lost him."

Colin looked to the West, staring at the moonlit waves. "Can we see a show of hands here? Who is confused besides me? Where the hell are we?"

Vanity said, "There were no prints showing Mrs. Wren going into the burial mound. No footprints. I knew there had to be a secret passage she had come in by!"

I said, "I think Vanity created the tunnel. I think she bent reality and wished it into existence."

Vanity said, "Then how did Mrs. Wren get into the burial mound? I saw her come out."

Colin said, "This is going to sound like Victor, but, how could Vanity have created a tunnel? Did she make the plants and the bushes? There was a Roman inscription on the wall, and the remains of a fire."

Victor said, "You are assuming newly created objects lack details. Since Amelia has not yet postulated a mechanism for the creation, we are not in a position to assess the likelihood of the hypothesis."

Quentin, of all people, said, "It is not an hypothesis. It is an article of faith. An hypothesis can be proved or disproved by evidence. The faith that Vanity can create a detailed object involves the assumption that she could create any evidence needed to support the object. If she can create a tunnel, why not books and blueprints showing the tunnel existed, or even people who remember building it?"

Vanity held up her hand. "Stop. I am the Dark Mistress now, and I order us all to stop jabbering about the philosophy of science! I am also turning control back over to Amelia, since I do not know what the hell to do next."

I said, "If you can turn control over to me, I can turn it back over to Victor."

Victor looked annoyed. "Fine. I order you to lead us. After you tell us what is going on, I'll be happy to serve as second-in-command, and take over if you get killed."

It was the matter-of-fact way he said that, that made us all pause and look at each other, and remember what a serious business we were involved in.

I bit my lip. "Okay, fine. Here is my thinking so far: We can't just run away. Since they have powers like Quentin's or Vanity's, they could just find us again, by magic. The moment Boggin knew we were making a break, he sent his people to guard the borders and, if he is smart, to guard the green table in his office, the big green table in a warehouse somewhere that he stole from Mestor. . . ."

Vanity said, "Who is Mestor?"

". . . Drinkwater. And Boggin would protect the safe in the Great Hall."

Colin chimed in, "Or booby-trap it."

"Since each power has one that cancels out another, he would put Mr. Glum to the South, to stop me; Dr. Fell to the North, to stop Quentin;

Mrs. Wren to the West, and Miss Daw to the East. Since Wren left her position to go help Fell when they discovered we were up North, here, West, is the safest spot. And we do not need to go East, because Victor got his powers back anyway, including some he did not have before."

Victor shook his head. "Don't overestimate me."

I said, "You beat Dr. Fell!"

"I'm sorry I didn't make this clear before. All I was doing was intercepting and copying the information packages Dr. Fell was sending out to control his nanites, and using his nanites to produce certain preprogrammed effects. During the fight, I had the creature Amelia put in my bloodstream operating to block his attempts to invade my nervous system. Since my security firewall was a living entity with free will, Fell wasn't able to come up with an attack combination. The creature was also the one who enabled me to intercept Fell's control codes, since it originally was made from him, and was tapped into his frequencies and ciphers. In effect, I had Fell's codebook in my hands during the fight. I would not be able to defeat another Cyclopes."

Vanity said, "But you remember at least as much of your powers as we had before they erased our brains, right? All Amelia meant was that we don't need to go East."

I hugged myself. It was feeling colder. "We can pause here to see if Colin can remember how to turn his powers on. Then we go straight to the Great Hall and try to break into that safe.

"I tried to blackmail ap Cymru into giving us plane tickets to Rome; it did not work, but he may have gotten them anyway. I have a key in my pocket that opens a bus locker in Waterside Street in Abertwyi. He also said he would get us passports and ID papers. We'll take the ID, but the airplane tickets are just a red herring. While they are looking for us in Rome, we take a boat out to sea. Once we are far away, we have Vanity call her magic boat, which can bring us anywhere in the world in one day. More than one world. There are other dimensions, or something."

Quentin said, "We can't steal a boat. It would make us vulnerable to a curse. We have to be careful about that."

Victor said, "I can borrow Lily's motorboat."

Vanity said, "I have a magic boat? When did I get a magic boat? What does it look like?"

Colin said, "Blackmail . . . who? Are we talking about Taffy? Boggin's henchman? The guy who hangs out here and does not seem to have a job, except for giving cigarettes and porn magazines to minors?"

I nodded. "He is actually a she, a goddess named Laverna, the queen of all fraud. She works for Lord Hermes, Trismegistus, who leads one of the factions of the Olympians, who fought a civil war, but were helping our side, except that I had a dream from your dad—I mean Morpheus—telling me we couldn't trust him. He was in our common room during the meeting of . . ."

Colin interrupted. "Does Victor, even with his normal memory back, does he know any of this backstory stuff you are telling us now?"

Victor shook his head.

Colin wagged a finger in my face, "No more talk about quitting as leader, then. Okay? If you try to resign again, I'll mutiny. Now, then! How do I get my powers back? What am I supposed to be able to do again?"

I said, "Write love letters. And I saw you jump nearly thirty feet straight up once. And maybe anything else you want. Your power works on desire. You wish it; it happens."

He closed his eyes, tilted back his head, spread his hands. "I wish I had my powers!"

We all looked at him.

He opened one eye. "Is something supposed to happen?"

I said, "I don't know!"

He closed his eye again, "I wish for a bacon, lettuce, and tomato sandwich!" He held his hand up.

He wiggled his fingers. His hand stayed empty, of course.

He opened his eyes. "Is this like one of those monkey's paw things, where my Aunt Petunia is going to die in a plane crash and leave me the money to buy a bacon, lettuce, and tomato sandwich?"

I said, "I think it has to be something you really, really want."

He closed his eyes again, spread his legs, and put his arms out as if he were ready to catch a sandbag or something about to be dropped on him. "Marilyn Monroe, as she was when she appeared in *Seven Year Itch,* naked from her bubble-bath, lonely, horny, and needing the warmth and comfort of an Irish schoolboy half her age! One, two, three . . . *go!* And she has her own birth control."

Quentin said, "You're not Irish."

Colin muttered, "I sure as hell am not English, thank God!"

"You are a monster from beyond space and time, shape-changed to look human."

"That just shows how little you know about the Irish, laddie. We're all monsters from beyond space and time. Besides, with a name like Colin . . ."

"You made that name up!"

Colin opened his eyes and put his hands on his hips. He turned away from Quentin and glowered at me. "Where's my Marilyn?"

Vanity said, "Maybe you have to throw a gold pin in the well, or something."

Victor said sardonically, "Marilyn Monroe died in 1962. Isn't that exactly the monkey's paw kind of thing you were trying to avoid?"

Colin rolled his eyes and turned toward Victor. "I said, 'as she was in *Seven Year Itch*'! That's the movie where her skirts blew up. She was alive during that scene."

I said, "Maybe it works more like psychic phenomena and less like just wishing. The desire has to come from the core of your being."

Colin said, "So . . . you're saying I should have wished for Catwoman?"

I goggled at him. "Who?"

"Supervillainess. Dresses all in skintight black leather. Wears heels. Carries a whip. Catwoman is *ichiban*. The hottest."

Vanity pointed skyward, hopping and screaming. "Colin! Put your arms out! Here she comes! It's Julie Newmar! Catch her! Catch her!"

Colin's head jerked up. Vanity leaned over, picked up a handful of snow, and dashed it into Colin's face when he brought his gaze back down.

Colin smiled a nasty smile, picked up a double handful of snow, and started forward. Vanity squealed and danced around behind me, grabbing my shoulders. "Leader! Protect me!"

I put my hand up. "Okay, children! Playtime is over. Colin, put that snowball down."

"Down her cleavage, I will."

"Drop it."

"But she started it!"

"You're a big strong Irishman, and she's English, so she gets to oppress you. Okay? We are in the middle of an escape attempt. I do not want to lose anyone this evening. Colin, I do not know how to turn on your powers. I am not even sure what they are. We only have the amount of time it will take Boggin to fly up to the North, look around, and come back. That's assuming he didn't set additional guards around the Great Hall."

Quentin said, "He's at the burial mound."

A cold sensation passed over my neck. I looked at Quentin with mingled horror and respect. "It is really eerie when you do that. How do you know?"

Quentin said, "My friend told me. Every time Boggin moves, he has to tell the spirits in the air and wind where he is, so they know where to go to bring him news of what people are saying. So, every time he moves, he has to tell them all where he is going. This wand used to belong to Mrs. Wren. She used it to keep track of Boggin. Not all of her old spells are washed out of it. When my friend moved into the stick, the house wasn't empty."

I said, "Could it be another trap? Could it be bugged, I mean? Booby-trapped? Or giving you false information?"

Quentin said, "After the oath she swore to Romus? I doubt it. But it is possible. I can throw this stick into the ocean and pick up another one right now. You want me to? You are the leader. It is your decision."

It was not an easy decision. On the one hand, knowing where Boggin was, was of utmost importance to us. On the other hand, the danger that Erichtho the Witch could still have some sort of power or mysterious connection leading back to her wand . . .

I said to Quentin, "If this were a fairy tale, and you were a prince, what would you do?"

He smiled. "I am a prince. My father is Proteus, remember?"

"And?"

"I'd pitch it into the sea."

I said, "Throw it, then. But—wait a minute. See if you can remove the curse Mrs. Wren put on Colin. You might be able to unblock his memory. The magic paradigm trumps the psychic paradigm."

Quentin nodded. "This involves a very brief demonstration."

He walked in a circle around Colin, dragging the distaff, and made a circle in the snow about him. He bowed to the West and held up the distaff in both hands.

"I call upon the guardians of the watchtowers of the West, the element of Water. I hold the power of the witch Erichtho in my hands, given to me from her, freely and without hurt. I hold here the curse she placed upon

Phobetor. Erichtho! I call you by your true name! The Guardians of the Towers of the West break your power in two! Hesperides, lave Phobetor in your wave, and let him emerge unhurt, washed clean, stainless, and forgiven! So Mote It Be!"

And he cracked the distaff in half over his knee.

He threw the two halves of the distaff spinning into the waters far below, calling out, "This gift I give to the Sons of Danu, who dwell in the waters of the West, in memory of promises kept."

He reached over with his foot and rubbed out part of the line he had drawn in the snow around Colin. "The wall around you is broken. Be free."

Colin clutched his head, rolling his eyes like a maddened horse, and doubled over, groaning.

Quentin stepped forward, looking worried. Victor said, "Did it work? Are your memories coming back?"

Colin straightened up, brushing his hands through his hair. "Naw. Just joking around. But that was a damn impressive ceremony, Big Q. Thanks for trying, at least."

Vanity said softly to me, "Permission to whack him with a snowball again, O my Queen?"

"Denied." I raised my voice. "Next step. We fly to the Great Hall. We have two fliers in the group and three walkers. Which one of you two boys can carry two people?"

Quentin, who was rather short, looked up at Victor. Quentin pointed at Victor. "Him."

Victor said, "I should take the two lightest people."

Quentin snorted and said, "I'm not carrying Colin."

Victor said, "Amelia? Colin? How much do you each weigh?"

Quentin suddenly got a funny look on his face. He said, "Amelia. I have to carry Amelia."

Vanity looked at him oddly.

He said, "There are reasons which are hard to explain. According to the signs, she flew with me before. The sympathies might be more favorable if I do not introduce any novel parameters into the demonstration."

I said, "Vanity, if you sense anyone watching us, break off. If we get scattered, we'll . . . meet back here, at the Kissing Well. Okay?"

Quentin said, "It will take me a moment to prepare."

Victor said, "Should I wait?"

Quentin looked at me. "Leader makes the call."

I said, "Let me think. If you meet Miss Daw, Colin can stop her, if he can make himself want to. Fell and Victor are at least evenly matched; so are Grendel and Colin."

Vanity said, "Who is Grendel?"

"Mr. Glum's first name. He's planning on kidnapping you and marrying you, so be careful of him. If you meet Mrs. Wren, Victor can neutralize her magic. Um. The same goes for me and Quentin running into anybody. We are either going to be equal to or be able to trump any paradigm we come across. I do not know how Olympians and Phaeacians fit into the chart, though. You guys take off; Quentin and I will join you."

Quentin said, "I have to make a preparatory lemma. I'm going uphill to that grove of trees. Follow me when I call."

He walked away from the Kissing Well to where some clumps of trees clung to the grass that broke through the rocky soil. As he approached the grove, he put out his hand.

A long stick of pale wood came falling out of the grove toward him. It was as if an unseen stagehand, hidden just beyond the tree, had tossed him a prop. He caught the stick and walked into the trees.

We waited a moment or two, until Quentin called out that he was ready. I waved at the others to take off.

Victor, without any further ado, put one arm around Colin's waist, and told him to loop his belt through the chain links of his jerkin. But Victor simply picked up Vanity and hoisted her over his shoulder, like Tarzan picking up Jane, so her head was dangling down his back and her bottom was high in the air. With no noise and no fuss, the invisible chessmaster picked up his Victor piece and swept him off the board and out of sight.

I climbed the rocky slope and entered the small grove of trees. There was no visible sign that Quentin had done anything in particular; no cut-open goats or candles floating in midair or anything like that. If he had made any scratches on the ground or the trees, it was too dim, in the moonlight, with the twigs and branches overhead, to see.

He said, "Um, Amelia, I hope you won't get mad, but . . ."

I pulled off my scarf and handed it to him. "You have to blindfold me. I've been through this before."

I had my aviatrix cap (which I take along on all my escape attempts) folded into a bulky wad in my outer coat pocket. I put it on and began tucking my hair up.

He wrapped the scarf fabric around my head, and I donned the goggles atop them.

He said, "Now open your mouth."

I hooked a thumb under the blindfold and goggles and raised one corner to turn and give him a cold, one-eyed stare.

"Why exactly am I opening my mouth?"

He said, "I thought you said we did this before . . . ?"

"Blindfold, yes. Gagged, absolutely not. I cannot go a week around here without someone trying to tie me up. Why the hell do you need me with a scarf in my mouth to fly?"

He pointed at the trees. Or maybe he was pointing at unseen things in the air around us. "The long-lived ones say you tried to talk last time. They don't trust you to keep your mouth shut."

"What if I promise?"

He cocked his head, looking thoughtful. "Um, Amelia. Rumor has been set against you. Someone has been spreading the story that you are an oath-breaker."

"Boggin."

"Well, whoever did it, the long-lived ones won't carry us without some clear sign that you won't talk. Look. I'll just tie it loosely. It's not going to hurt you, or choke you. It's a symbol. It's only symbolic. Well . . . ? The others are going to be waiting for us. We are being chased, you know."

"Okay. Okay, fine. But you don't tell anyone, *anyone,* that I let you do this."

I put the blindfold back in place. Quentin moved around behind me, reached up over my shoulders. I felt soft fabric come up toward my mouth, touch my lips.

The gag was just for show. He draped a strip of fabric—maybe it was his scarf—over my mouth and tied it in back of my head. It would not actually stop me from talking, any more than the veil of a harem girl would have. But it would remind me not to talk.

He said, "Ready? Don't talk." He stooped and swept me off my feet. He held me very close to his chest, a husband carrying a bride over the threshold. His arms were much stronger than those a boy his height should have. I had my arms around his neck.

I spoke through the so-called gag. "Uh, Quentin, can I ask you a question before we take off?"

His left hand relaxed, and he dropped my feet to the ground again. I felt the stones and leaves under my boots.

He said, "What is it?"

I said, "Why me? I thought you would have jumped at the chance to pick up Vanity and fly around with her."

He straightened his right arm, and I was standing upright again. "I did not want to have to blindfold her. She would have thought I was being kinky, or something. Here, hold still. I am going to have to make this more realistic-looking. Open wide."

This time he put a wad of silk fabric, maybe it was his pocket handkerchief, into my mouth, and tucked the scarf between my teeth. That tickled my throat, and I coughed, and I put up my hands to adjust the gag, but he grabbed my arms.

"Stop that." His voice sounded alarmed. "There is one of them standing next to me. If they think you are about to give them away, they kill me. This is serious business, Amelia! I am trying to get them to break the laws of nature for me. Those laws have police. These are like Mafia people. Do you understand? We were a mile up in the air and halfway there when you spoke before. They don't like it when you talk and attract attention. I don't like it. Now hold still. I can adjust the gag, but you can't touch it while they are watching. Put your hands behind you or something. This has to look real. Okay? Be careful."

Seething with indignation, I put my hands down while he fussed with the scarf and loosened it. I sort of had to bite down to keep the thing from falling out.

I was certainly not putting my hands anywhere but tightly around him while he picked me up through the air, though, spirits or no spirits. Did he think I was crazy?

He was probably lying about the "Mafia" spirits. Gags and blindfolds? I was lucky he didn't have a pair of handcuffs on him. I saw how much more rudely Victor had hauled Vanity than Colin when he had picked her up. Boggin had gotten all turned on and aroused after flying with me.

I think it is just a thing with men who go up in the air with women. Aren't stewardesses supposed to be really risqué and wild? That was the reason.

He muttered, "Now, remember, you are supposed to be the sensible one. *I* would not fool around with your experiments if you were trying *your* powers, Amelia."

Oho. Not exactly a fair comment. Criticize the girl when she's gagged and cannot answer back.

He picked me up again, hefted me in his arms, held me close to his chest. Beneath the blindfold, I closed my eyes. I put my head against his shoulder and tried to snuggle as close to him as I could. I did not like not being allowed to see, not being allowed to talk. It made me feel too help-less. What was odd was that even young little Quentin, when he held me, seemed in my imagination to grow into something strong, and masculine. It was so strange. I could feel my heart pounding in my chest.

Colin's voice broke the silence. "Jesus H. Christ! Quentin! Oh my God! You are the man!"

I started to kick and put my hands up toward the gag, but then I stopped. We might still be twenty feet up in the air. I could not yank off the blindfold until Quentin gave me permission.

Quentin shifted his grip. With an easy strength, he put me on my feet. I could feel a slanted surface under my boots. Was it safe to talk yet? I waved my hand behind me toward him, and made a *mmph!* noise.

Quentin plucked at the play-knot. I pushed at the gag with my tongue, but instead of falling off, it suddenly changed shape, becoming thicker, and blocked my mouth for real. The blindfold suddenly seemed snug, and more opaque.

I could feel Quentin pluck at the knot for a moment. I did not have time to start panicking, because Quentin made a slight snort of disgust, or surprise, and he tapped his staff on the ground. The gag and the blindfold relaxed. I spit out the gag and, hooking a finger through the top of my blindfold, I pulled the whole assembly, scarf, goggles, and all, down around my neck.

I said to Colin, "You did that on purpose!"

He gave me a half grin. "What? Don't I wish! I didn't talk Big Q into trussing you up like Lois Lane."

Quentin said, "It actually was part of the spell. She had to make a sac-rifice to please the spirits. A little embarrassment, I suppose, is sacrifice enough."

We were standing on the roof of the Great Hall.

Vanity was standing a few feet away from Colin and Victor, holding her nose. Victor had no expression, but there was a small greenish stain trailing down his left side.

I said, "What happened to you?"

Vanity answered, "Colin gets airsick."

Colin said, "It was the worst hour of my life."

Vanity said, "It was less than two minutes, barfy boy."

"Seemed like an hour."

Vanity jerked her head suddenly to the left, pointed her finger to a spot in the sky.

Before she could say anything, Quentin spread his arms, stepped into the middle of where we stood, and swung his stick in a wide circle. He was shorter than all of us, but he was standing on the peak of the roof a little way above us. We ducked, and the stick passed over our heads.

I could not see it with my eyes, but with my higher sense I saw a circle of light traced by the path of the staff. It hung in the air, embracing all of us, and then spread slowly out, like a single ripple in a smooth pond. A hush seemed to fall across the night sky, the estate around us.

Quentin said, "The aery ones can make the air quiet when I fly; I am using the same effect now. Vanity, is there anyone listening to us?"

Vanity shook her head. She said, "It's like a pressure. It's moving East to West across the campus. I don't think they know where we are. Going that way." She pointed. "Back the way we had come."

Victor said, "Maybe there was a bug of some sort on the stick Quentin broke. They could be going that way."

I said, "Okay. Let's go in."

8

TALISMANS OF CHAOS

1.

After all the hubbub and hoopla getting here, getting in was easy. I had Vanity touch the big metal door on the roof. She gave me a thumbs-up; no one was watching or listening to it.

It was padlocked, but Victor waved his hand over it, and the padlock jumped up and fell open. I made the door light and hauled it up and over.

Vanity went first. She said, "Jump over the third stair."

"What is it?"

She just shrugged. "It is something that watches. Just skip over it."

At the bottom of the stairs, Victor said, "Microwaves. Motion detectors, I think."

I said, "None of this was here before. I think. Can you, I don't know, interfere with the signal without setting them off?"

He said, "Maybe if I had a week to figure out the math. Can't you see through walls? Trace the wires and tell me where the switch is. If it is made of metal, I'll turn it to its 'off' setting."

I stood, eyes closed, with the building around me laid out like a blueprint. The wires were useful to someone, they glowed.

I also saw a webwork, like a spiderweb, of lines of moral force laid across the doorways and lintels.

I said, "There is a box all the wires lead to in an office on the first floor."

It took a while for Victor, blind, being led just by my voice, to direct a beam of magnetic force down through several floors to the control panel for the alarms. Vanity hopped back and forth, one foot to the other, giving out little yelps when we were about to trip something.

I could not see the circuitry go dead, since I cannot see electron flows, but I saw the system become useless.

I said to Quentin, "There is some sort of spell laid across all the doors. Can you break it?"

He looked a little uncertain. He said, "Get me to the door with the safe in it. Vanity, I hope you'll tell me if I am about to set off an alarm or something."

Victor said, "I will look for electronic signals. Amelia can look through the walls for traps."

Colin said, "And I'll look for an opportunity to drop my pants. Hey! Has anyone noticed that I'm the only completely useless person here?"

Vanity said, "Quiet, puke boy. We've noticed it for years."

Victor hushed them both.

We set off down the gloomy corridor. Our way was lit only by what moonlight there was leaking in through the windows.

Soon we were in front of the door to the second-floor corner office.

I told Victor where the wires were running to the door. He said, "I can see them." He pointed his finger, disarmed the alarms. With a click, the door unlocked.

I said, "The spell looks like a big red spiderweb to me. It is right over the door, and it goes through the walls and floor."

Quentin took a deep breath and said, "Okay. Let me try something."

He lightly touched his staff to the handle of the door, and spoke: *"Annon edhellen, edro hi ammen! Fennas nogothrim, lasto beth lammen!"*

Nothing happened.

Colin said, "Break the stick over your knee and throw it at the doors. It looked cool when you did that before."

Vanity squinted at Quentin. "Was that from a made-up language?"

"Better than most real languages," muttered Quentin under his breath. Then he said, "That would have worked if these had been dwarf doors. Well. Let me try something else." He knelt, took a piece of chalk from his pocket, and wrote some angular-looking Viking letters on the little strip of floor that showed between the edge of the carpet and the threshold of the door.

He stood, raised his wand, touched the tip to his chest, and spoke: "Nine nights I hung upon the wind-torn tree, my own spear through my own heart, myself a sacrifice to myself, high on the tree whose roots none know! None came to aid me, none gave me drink. I saw the runes below me. Crying out, I seized on them."

He pointed to one of the marks he'd made on the ground with his wand. "Three great runes burn in my hand. A fourth and greater one I know. If a man fastens chains and gyves to my limbs, I sing the song to set me free; locks spring apart, fetters jump open, my hands and feet know liberty."

He raised the wand and tapped the door.

The door trembled in the frame.

Vanity said, "Did it work? The door was listening to him."

I said, "No. I can still see the spiderweb across it."

Colin said, "Maybe Vanity can just wish a secret passage into being, and we can go into the room that way."

Quentin said over his shoulder, "That's not the problem. The door is not really locked; it is just going to let off an alarm or a curse if we open it unlawfully. The windows and floorboards are the same way. The act of going into the room is what is prohibited. If this had been a locked door, something keeping us prisoner, that last rune would have worked. Well. Maybe I can make the magic think magic is wicked. Let me try something else. . . ."

Again he tapped a chalk letter with his wand-tip. "Nine great runes burn in my hand. A tenth and greater one I know. When witch-hags ride the wild wind at night, such spell I know as to daze and confound them, that they will not find their own doorposts again, or return to don their day-shapes."

When he raised the wand to touch the door this time, the stick in his hand jumped backwards in his grip, striking Quentin a nasty knock across the elbow—he had put his arm up to guard his face—and went spinning end over end down the corridor. It clattered loudly to the carpet.

"Ow, ow, ow," muttered Quentin, holding his arm.

"Is it broken?" asked Colin.

"If it were broken, I would be crying like a girl, not saying, 'Ow, ow, ow.' "

"Well," said Colin. "Let me go fetch your wand. At least it will give me something to do."

"Don't bother. Apsu! To me!" And the invisible stagehand snatched up the stick and tossed it back to him.

"Great trick," said Colin, looking more downcast than ever.

Quentin said to the door, *"Mellon!"*

A noise came from the door, a creak of wood.

Vanity said, "What's that noise?"

Quentin said, "It is laughing at me. Apparently, I am not exactly a friend."

I asked, "What it? What is laughing?"

He said, "An undead dryad. They chopped her up and planed her into boards. I cannot break the spell, because I don't have any influences to back me up. I am a trespasser. The moral order of the universe is not on my side."

Colin said, "Tell the door that it's our stuff in there. Stolen property. Belongs to us."

"In effect, I just tried that. Whoever put up the door was not the one who stole the goods. If they are stolen."

I said, "They might have been surrendered in a war. Or they might simply belong to Boggin."

Victor said, "We are forgetting the principle of what you call the table of oppositions. Magicians don't stop spells, you said. They stop psionic effects. Materialism stops magic."

His forehead opened. His metal eye rotated into view. Azure sparks, and then a beam, lanced from his eye and played back and forth across the door.

Quentin backed away nervously.

Victor said, "There is a magnetic anomaly. But there cannot be any mind, or intention, or purpose watching this door, since only complex living mechanisms have minds, and there is insufficient complexity here for that. I see nothing but wood, and wood is carbon atoms strung together. I do not see anything that could cause the magnetic anomaly. Whatever has no cause cannot exist."

Victor put his hand out and pushed the door open.

2.

I stepped in. I said, "Quentin, do you have the disc?"

Quentin pulled out the CD.

I said, "Victor, please tell me the disc player you got from that Lilac woman is still in working order after your duel with Dr. Fell?"

Victor gave me an odd look. "Her name is Lily. I haven't checked the player. I don't know if it works. Give me the disc, Quentin."

Colin said, "What is supposed to happen?"

I said, "The last time I was here, Miss Daw played music. One of the objects in the safe reacted to the music, and sent out an energy. Call it light. That light allowed me to see in a direction I normally cannot see, and to reach a part of my body . . . God, you guys don't remember any of that, do you?"

Victor said, "I remember." To the others, he said, "She thinks she is four-dimensional. That is the model she uses to explain her supernatural effects, like psychokinesis, clairvoyance, and shape-change."

I wasn't going to argue the point. I said, "Play the music."

One of Mozart's violin concertos floated from the tiny speakers on the little square machine. I saw space shiver and flatten.

Like a crystal goblet vibrating in sympathy to a perfect note, the sphere in the safe rang. It gave off the substance of hyperspace, a material thicker than reality, which, at once, was light, music, thought, interval, time, probability, certainty. . . .

I could see the squat safe, drawn like a thick line around the other flat objects it encircled. Extending above and below it in the "red" and "blue" directions, I saw the hemispheres of the hypersphere.

Victor handed me the disc player, and I kept my hand on the button. When I stopped it, the hypersphere continued to ring and echo for a moment, and, during that moment, I could act.

I put my hand "over" the line and into the safe. I could touch the surface—one of the many surfaces of its hypersurface—of the sphere with my fingers, but I could not budge it from its location.

I pulled my hand back down into three-space.

I pushed the PLAY button again; space flattened; the flatness set the sphere to ringing; I pushed PAUSE and reached again. I tried to pick up the other objects in the safe: a book, a photo, a vial of fluid, a necklace. Nothing moved. It was as if they were frozen in ice.

Vanity said, "Gosh, that looked weird."

I glanced at her. "What did you see?"

She said, "Your hand got small. Not like it was shrinking, but like it was receding down a tunnel. You know."

"Parallax," Victor said.

"Yeah. Parallax. But the wall of that metal cabinet thing. Still looked like it was closer, even though the hand, your hand, in front of it, looked farther away. Um. And it turned red."

"Doppler shift," said Victor.

Quentin said, "Your hand turned ghostly. I saw a red light, too. But it wasn't exactly what Vanity just described."each

Victor said, "Chaos. Our brains are each programmed to interpret it according to a mutually exclusive metaphor."

Colin said, "No. I saw. Her hand woke up. This dream, this false world we are all in, it gave way. Look, you are all logical people. If the safe was real, could she put her hand through it, into it, without leaving a hole? No. The safe is an illusion. It is only there because we think it is there."

Victor said, "I cannot seem to penetrate the safe wall with my magnetics. I cannot manipulate the lock." He turned. "If your theory is correct, Colin, you could open the safe just by willing it to open."

Quentin muttered, "It is not a theory. Not disprovable. Article of faith."

Colin frowned, looked determined, strode forward with a quick and steady step, plunged his hand down as if to brush the substance of the safe aside like mist. . . .

Cracked his knuckles loudly on the steel sides of the safe, and sprang back, yelping and waving his hurt hand in the air.

Vanity said sweetly, "Illusion hurt you?"

Colin gave her a dark look. "Bugger you. Nightmares scare people, okay? They are still not real. No one dies on roller-coasters, but everyone screams on them." He wiggled his fingers gingerly. He muttered to himself, "If Catwoman had been in that safe, damn safe would have melted . . ."

I said to the group, "I can touch the sphere, but for some reason, I cannot move it. Any theories?"

Colin sat down on the desk, still nursing his hand. He said, "You know more than any of us do about what's happening here."

I said, "Wait a minute. While we are waiting, let's catch up on what we intended to do."

I looked at Victor, reached into his monad, and realigned it, so that it illuminated all the darkened sections of his nervous system.

Vanity shrieked.

"What?" I said.

"You just stuck your hand through his head!"

Colin said grumpily, "It only appeared that way!"

Victor said, "I do not know what you did, but it seems to have accelerated some of what your molecule creature was doing. Quentin? May I experiment on you?"

Quentin said, "There is something I need to do first. I don't know what you are going to do to me, but I don't want to get my memory back until I do this."

He stepped forward and, with infinite tenderness and simple strength, took Vanity by the shoulders and dipped her back.

She said in horror, "Let go of me, or I'll scream!"

He said, "Then scream."

But he kissed her, and so she didn't. She made sort of surprised noises in her throat, and waved her arms almost comically in the air, but then the throat-noises became warm and soft, and the arms twined around Quentin's neck.

Colin said, "Me next."

Victor said, "I cannot help you. You need Quentin to cast a spell to get your memory back to you."

"No, I meant I get Vanity next. Pucker up, hot stuff!"

Quentin straightened up, pushed Vanity slightly behind him with a gentle motion of his arm, as if to keep her away from Colin.

Victor opened his third eye. With my higher sense, I saw the life-force of the puppy-like helpful nanite creature stream as a series of charged particles out from Victor and embed themselves/itself into Quentin's bloodstream. Knots of moral energy that had been twisted around his heart and head went lax and slipped away.

Quentin rolled his eyes. "Oh, I am an idiot." He touched his wand to Colin's head.

Colin said, "Hold on! There is something I have to do before I get my memory back!"

And he got up off the table and came toward me with an evil gleam in his eyes.

I danced back. "Get away from me! I am not kissing some guy who just vomited! I don't even like you!"

Victor stepped between Colin and me, saying, "Colin, leave your sister alone."

That was like a bucket of cold water on me. Sister. If I was Colin's sister, then, according to Victor logic, I was Victor's sister, too.

Colin must have seen the sick look on my face, because the sort of fun-and-games grin he was wearing slipped.

He turned to Quentin. "Go ahead, Great and Powerful Oz. Zap me."

Quentin said, "I did everything right, but I did not finish the demonstration. There were other people besides Mrs. Wren who did things to you."

He tapped Colin on either shoulder, as if he were knighting him, touched him lightly with the wand on the forehead, and turned toward one of the walls (the west wall), saying in a loud voice, "Guardians of the Watchtowers of the West, it was only by Erichtho's evil that other forces and spells, potions and evils came to afflict Phobetor! You have washed him clean! He is unstained and whole! Morpheus, father of dreams, return the memories and thoughts that were lost to your son! I call upon Mnemosyne to make whole the spell! So Mote It Be!"

Colin said, "Oh my *God*!"

"What? What?" said Quentin.

"I tried to chop up Mrs. Wren with an axe! And she kicked my ass!"

Vanity rolled her eyes and made that little *ugh!* gesture she sometimes makes when Colin is around. She tucked her hand into Quentin's elbow.

Quentin said, "What about Vanity?"

Colin said to me, "Yeah. Vanity next."

Vanity looked at me hopefully. "Yes? What about me? Is it my turn?"

I felt a sickening, sinking sensation in my stomach.

"Maybe something in the safe will help," I said. "If we could get it open."

3.

We talked over several options for how to get the safe open.

Victor assumed the hypersphere was fixed in place by Mr. Glum's power, psionics, and that Quentin could release it, if he could cast a spell into the safe, which he could not. Victor said the safe was made of a durable nonmagnetic alloy, which would not let "magnetic anomalies," i.e., magic, through the surface. Maybe if I had Quentin's wand in my hand, and touched it to the ball?

I tried that. Quentin and I practiced once or twice without reaching into the safe, just to get the timing right. Only the moment or two after I turned off the music, but while the sphere was still ringing, did I have a chance to act.

I knelt before the safe, one hand on the disc player, one hand on his staff tip. He was holding the other end of the staff, standing behind me.

I clicked the button. Mozart floated into the room. The sphere rang sharply, as if the notes were hammers striking it. Click. Music stopped. The ringing started to fade. . . .

Quentin looked nervous as one end of his wand turned ghostly, reddened, and vanished into the solid surface of the safe wall. I touched the staff to one of the surfaces of the many spherical volumes of which the curved hypersurface was composed.

I said, "Quickly." Each echo was quieter than the one before.

He said quickly, "The Eloi Adonai gave to Adam dominion over all beasts of the field and birds of the air, the bugs that swarm and the fish that swim. In token of this, King Adam granted names to all living things. Force which binds; I am a son of Adam. You are a living thing of Earth. I name you, I dub, I christen you . . ."

I said, "Faster." The echoing in hyperspace was fading, fading. The hyperlight dimmed, like a candle flickering out. It was getting hard for me to "see" in that direction. Hyperspace is so very dark.

". . . You are Er, the alone one, who grips these talismans. I call you by your true name! Release the talismans! And you shall no longer be alone. . . ."

Too long. The last glint of hyperlight went dark; I lost the direction. With a spray of red sparks and the thrust of pressure, both my hand and Quentin's staff were forced out of the safe.

Quentin staggered back, looking at his staff, and at my hand. "Are you all right?"

He was talking to me, but the safe answered, with a hideous, unearthly moan, *"It hurts! It is so heavy!"*

Quentin waved his staff, and said several impressive things, but the voice did not speak again.

After a moment or two, Vanity told him to stop. "It is not listening anymore."

Victor said, "There was a magnetic flux near the point where the wand came out from the surface of the safe, but then it was smothered."

Vanity said, "I think it . . . died."

Quentin had been trying to mold the psychic energy into a living being, like drawing a face in clay. He had gotten the idea from what I had done to Dr. Fell's molecular engine, which I had given free will. His thought was that he could cast a spell on a being that had a moral nature, or at least talk to it.

Quentin looked rather pale at this point. "I wasn't expecting it to die again. I mean . . . I wasn't expecting that . . . ."

Victor said, "I have an idea, though. In your paradigm, murder is bad, right? You could argue that Boggin was responsible for that entity being killed, and . . . ."

Colin, looking at Quentin, interrupted softly, "Hey, maybe the thing is still alive, but just, you know, trapped in the safe?"

I said, "Um. No. There is nothing alive in the safe."

The face in the clay had been smoothed over and rubbed out. Unfortunately, the force was still there.

Quentin shook his head. "Why don't you guys try something else? Do it without me. I have to sit down."

He went to sit behind the desk.

Vanity said, "Quentin, I hate to say this, but we're in the middle of something right now. You have to help!"

Quentin laid his head down on the desk. He spoke without raising his head. "Okay. Fine. Here's my help. Weight is the key. The force can barely hold the talismans as it is. Have Amelia made the thing heavier. Eventually, the force will break."

Vanity looked at me and shrugged. "Go ahead and try it."

I knelt down, turned the music on, waited for a nice running glissade to get the sphere ringing really voluminously, and put my hand "past" the safe wall, and touched the hypersphere.

I could not manipulate the world-lines connecting its center of mass with the center of mass of the Earth. I was not sure why, but maybe the fact that it was a fourth-dimensional object, a perfectly regular sphere, made me unable to rotate it to alter its possible free-fall paths. Maybe my powers worked only because I had a higher dimension than the "flat" 3-D matter around me.

But Miss Daw had implied that there were higher dimensions than just the four. Maybe I could manipulate them, if I could see or imagine them.

I said half aloud, half to myself, "A five-sphere would satisfy $v^2 + w^2 + x^2 + y^2 + z^2 = r^2$. The 'surface' would be a set of hypervolumes made of hyperspheres, all equidistant from a single center-point. The 'volume' would be a superhypervolume, and . . ."

Something happened. Quietly, quickly, unexpectedly. Not what I was trying to do. But something amazing.

Under my finger, the sphere changed into a five-dimensional object. I saw it.

The ringing damped even more quickly when that happened, and I yanked my hand away even as red sparks began to tremble across the safe surface.

I said aloud, "Victor, you're good at math. What is the ratio of the surface area of a five-dimensional sphere to its volume?"

He said, "I am not good at that kind of math. But the ratio is higher than that of a hypersurface of a globe to its content, much higher than a normal sphere surface to its volume. Remember the pie plate and the goldfish bowl. The more dimensions you have, the more water you can fill in, within the same given radius."

I said, "The surface area for any number of dimensions is directly proportional to 2 pi raised to the power of $n/2$, where n is the number of dimensions. It is inversely proportional to gamma times one-half n."

Colin said, "Oh my dear lord, she is talking in equations again. Quentin! Get your gag back out! The spirits are demanding Colin be spared!"

"I'll say it simply. This will sound odd, but the hypersurface area and content reach maxima and then decrease towards zero as n increases."

Colin shook his head. He spoke in a voice of lilting sarcasm: "Odd? No. That sounds 'normal.' Why would I think that sounded odd?"

I pointed at the safe. "If I raised the number of dimensions to six, and kept the same radius, the volume would decrease, and, for a seven-D sphere, it would get even lower. So I think I cannot make it any heavier than I just did . . ."

It sounded like an explosion. The bottom crashed out of the safe with a noise like battleship armor being holed. Compared to the safe bottom, the wooden floor was matchwood. Boards and splinters flew up in a fountain. Whatever was on the floor below also exploded with noise of cracking boards, breaking glass, and screaming metal. Shocking reports like gunshots, snapping even louder than the general cacophony, stunned our ears.

Victor had his hand up. There were holes like bullet holes in the wall above us, where metal shards had flown, but he had deflected the worst of it overhead. Quentin, behind the desk, was unhurt. Colin, once again moving faster than was possible, had thrown himself in front of Vanity, with his arms out, and was bleeding from two large splinters, which had cut his cheek and shoulder. I had flinched at the noise, moved half an inch in the "blue" direction, and let the matter pass "through" me without touching me.

Victor said, "They must have heard that."

Vanity, who was looking scared, said, "I don't sense anything—"

Victor said, "Then they must be jamming your attention-detector. Leader . . . !" Victor turned to me. "I strongly urge we just grab the stuff from the safe and go. We can pause to examine it later. Which way?"

Vanity had her hankie out and was trying to wipe the blood off Colin's face. Colin was saying, "I'm fine, I'm fine. Ow, shit! These wounds are no more real than if someone painted ink on my face. Fuck! And I could get myself to believe that if it didn't hurt so damn much!"

Vanity said, "You are spouting gibberish. Hold still. You can't believe what you don't believe."

Colin muttered, "Not this me. The *real* me believes it. I wish he were here."

"Yeah," said Vanity, "Because he would not be spouting gibberish. He would also hold still."

I stepped over the wreckage of the safe, made it light, and pushed it over. There was a splintered hole in the floor. Below was a crater of what had once been a bookshelf. In the middle of the crater was a sphere. It gave off no light in three-space, but to my eyes, it was shining and pale.

I said, "Quentin, if you know any healing magic, cast a charm on Colin. If not, Victor, can you manipulate the atoms his body is made out of, and stitch up his face? Vanity, collect the stuff from the safe."

Victor said, "And you . . . ?"

"I am going down after my sphere. Everyone else start moving to the roof now. If we get split up, we meet . . ."

Damn it. I hated being leader. Leaders do not get to say things like, *meet at the house of that tawdry, grasping Jezebel, Lily Lilac.*

". . . we meet at the dock where Lily Lilac keeps her motorboat. Quentin says it will go badly for us if we steal it. If we tap on her window at—jeez, what time is it?—at four o'clock in the morning, is she a good enough . . . um . . . friend that she would lend it to you . . . ?"

Vanity stooped down at my feet and started looting the safe. There were no papers and no money, nothing but the four objects: a book, a necklace, a drug ampoule, a small brown card. Even in the dim light, the gold tracery on the cover of the book, the silver weave of the necklace, glittered and glinted. Vanity's coat had many large pockets. She zippered them carefully inside.

Except for the necklace. After staring at its fine chain for a brief moment, she smiled an impish smile, reached under her hair to clasp it around her neck. It was studded with tiny emeralds, and there was a pendant, a green stone with silver wings. It looked nice on her.

Victor said, "She said I could borrow it any time I wished."

I looked at Quentin. "Would that count? I mean, I am sure no one means it literally when they say 'any time.'"

Victor said curtly, "If she intended to convey a more precise meaning, she would have spoken more precisely."

Quentin said to me, "I'm not sure. In fairy tales, though, it is the exact wording that counts, not the intent. We can take the boat." Then he smiled and gave out a laugh.

Colin said, "I'm bleeding my face off here, and you're laughing. What's so funny?"

Victor, who had stepped over to peer at Colin's face, said over his shoulder to me, "Leader, I do not think his body is made of atoms. I cannot really do much."

Quentin was talking to Colin. He smiled a self-deprecating smile. "We should have checked the desk first . . . look here . . ."

Vanity's head jerked up. *"Wait—"*

". . . I wonder if this goes to the safe . . ." Quentin picked a small metal key out of a drawer and held it up.

"—don't touch it!"

Quentin shouted in pain and threw the key from him. The key was covered with crawling sparks, and the metal surface was red-hot. It crossed the room like a coal from a stove, like a tiny meteor, and tinkled against the far wall.

Vanity said in the shrill voice, "Leader! I regret to report that my detection sense is *not* being jammed! It just went off! Several people just became aware of us."

Quentin was clutching his hand. There were tears of pain in his eyes. "Tricky bloody bastards, aren't they?"

I said, "Roof, now! Run!"

Quentin said, "I should stay with you . . ."

I said, "No back-talk! Victor, you're second-in-command. Get everyone up."

Victor said, "How are you going to get out?"

I hesitated. I had no idea. But I was not going to leave my sphere.

Colin said, "Hey! Don't you have wings? Winged squid? Remember? I just remembered. Wings? Can't you hear me? Wings . . ."

I stared at him blankly.

He said, "Hello . . . ? Well . . . ? Do they work?"

I rotated part of my shoulder blade. Shimmering with higher-dimensional motes of music, glittering with thought-energies, pinions made of transparent blue, mingled with dapples of starlight and colors the human eye could not see, appeared around me, passing "through" the back of my coat, and yet not disturbing the fabric.

I said, "Roof. This is a direct order." I made the floor insubstantial in relation to me, and dropped from sight as if through a trapdoor.

I heard Colin mutter, "Great. Just great. Everyone can fly but me."

They ran.

WINGS

1.

The wings did not seem to operate by any principle of aerodynamics. I did not flap them. Instead, there seemed to be energy currents issuing from and rushing toward the core of the Earth, forming fast- and slow-moving streams. There was something in the wing feathers, an eye or a pressure-membrane, that sensed them. Gravity waves? Antigravity? Something else entirely? I wondered if I was detecting some abstract concept like "ownership" or "desire," because a wash of the gravity-stream ran from my heart to the hypersphere.

I dropped down to where the sphere rested among the wreckage of the bookshelf. I put out my hand.

There were other senses that opened in me when the fifth-dimensional vibration, shed by the hypersphere, traveled up my arm, throbbing. My teeth ached.

Motion was impossible in the fifth dimension, and there was nothing like vision here, but I could hear the crystal ringing of tremors and shock waves, like whale-sound or heavy drumbeats, traveling through the medium. But it was not conveying knowledge of sound to me. I was "hearing" something else, something almost incomprehensible: degrees of extension, relation, and existence.

From the degree of extension, I could sense that the medium within this dimension was even thicker and closer than the fourth; it was filled with heavy darkness, and some force or obstruction filled the area around Earth's home continuum.

The relation sense told me that, like the hypersphere, the particles here had such high volume for their surface area, that they could not be deflected from their straight-line motions by any contact with each other's surfaces. The surfaces were simply too small. Imagine if all space were filled with infinitely hard, dense points of neutronium. They could not interact.

On the existence level, I was hearing the underpinnings of the universe. The universe was somehow false: It did not "exist" as much as, it was not as real as, the void over which it was constructed.

I heard Vanity scream. The moral strands connecting me to my friends all went rigid. The moment I had spent looking into five-space had been long. How long? The time might be different between 3-D and 5-D.

First problem. How to pick up a five-dimensional hypersphere?

I said, or perhaps only thought, to the sphere, "Collapse into $x^2 + y^2 = r$." It folded from the hypersphere into a sphere, and then into a crystal disk about the size of a saucer. It was too thin to see with my eyes or touch with my hand, but I reached down with part of my manipulator-structure, and lifted the disk an inch into the "red" direction. It glowed like a lamp in my hand.

That light showed me what was around me. In the fourth dimension, I could see the wheels within wheels of Miss Daw, issuing musical concentric spheres, expanding; I saw a conical giant made of hands and arms, surrounded by waves of overbearing pressure. My other senses were confused; there were tangles of world-paths rippling and distorting from all objects in my view, blinding and blazing, as if all probabilities had gone wild, all time were bent out of joint. A tidal wave of Phaeacian space-distortion was also raging over the whole area. In the visual gibberish, I could not see where my friends were; I could not see what was happening.

I closed my higher eyes against the blazing noise and followed the jerking morality-lines coming from my heart. I spread my wings and caught an energy flow leading toward my friends. Up. Straight up I soared, passing through floors and ceilings as if they were mist.

Then I was on the roof. Victor was prone, either unconscious or dead. Colin had one arm around Victor, as if he had just caught him, and was lowering his body to the tiles. Vanity was drawing her breath to scream again, her hand protectively over the necklace around her neck. Azure blue sparks were streaming up over the side of the roof, passing through Quentin's body, and he had dropped his staff. The staff was sliding down the roof tiles, bouncing over the rain gutter and away.

In front of us were enemies. Boggin, barefoot and shirtless in the cold, wearing nothing but his purple pirate pants, was landing on the peak of the dome, not ten yards away, his red wings pumping energetically, his fists spread wide. One leg was crooked, one leg was straight, toes reaching down to the capstone of the dome.

To the east, among the moonlit clouds behind Boggin, three other winged figures flew: black Notus, whose wings were shaped like a sea-gull's, and falcon-winged Corus, armed with a bow, and an owl-winged man with streaming silver hair, who carried a rifle.

On the lawn below us, advancing with huge steps, were two giants, their heads fifty feet high. Six or ten arms sprang from the knotted muscles of their shoulders; cloaks of mist and cloud streamed from their backs, and a dozen more hands and arms reached out from the folds and billows of these clouds. Their black fingernails were the size of shields, their fingers were timber beams, their palms were courtyards.

In one of the palms of the nearer of the two giants, the one-eyed, skull-faced version of Dr. Fell stood, Telemus, his feet planted wide, one hand resting against the thumb of the giant, as if the thumb were the mast of a pitching ship. From him came the azure light that struck Quentin.

I knew Miss Daw was in the area, but I could not see her.

Behind us were enemies. Several of the hands of the giants, larger than lifeboats, were issuing from a white mist that had blotted out the roof behind us. One hand descended toward Vanity, its palm down and fingers curled like the bars of a prison gate. In the palm of another of the hands was Mr. Glum, leaning on his makeshift crutch.

The moment Glum's eyes fell on me, his face lit up with dark delight, and reality hiccuped. My wings were gone, my higher senses dimmed, and I felt the upper dimensions vanish from my memory like a dream upon waking. My winter coat and pants seemed both tighter and prettier.

Boggin was speaking as he landed. "Well, now that that little romp is over with, we can . . ."

I hit the button on the disc player. Miss Daw's lovely music floated from the tiny speaker, very quiet in the wide night.

The screams of the giants were cut off in mid-shout. The hands all vanished in blazes and explosions of red sparks. Mr. Glum toppled head-long; Dr. Fell grabbed the thumb he was clutching, and he disappeared into whatever place the hands were being yanked. The clouds of mist the giants produced erupted into red sparks, turned transparent, and were gone.

Glum struck the roof tiles, slid, and grabbed on to the rain gutter with both hands. Whatever his desires were at the moment, they did not in-clude concentrating on me. In the fourth dimension, my crystal disk shone and gave off light.

You will never be without light. . . .

And I could see my wings again. I rotated them back into this level. Shining blue-sparkling feathers fanned out to either side of me.

Colin roared. He ran forward, snatching up Mr. Glum's hoe. He moved faster than was possible, as fast as runners desire to run, which was faster than they do run.

He shouted as he sprinted past me, "Save them!"

He jumped to the peak of the dome in one leap.

My higher senses picked up Boggin's power beginning to radiate from him; morality and probability were warping, building up some sort of massive time-energy, as if fate itself were being wrenched from its moor-ings and used as a weapon in Boggin's hands.

But Colin was too quick for him. Colin clouted him over the head and shoulder with the hoe. Boggin snarled and slapped at Colin, cracking the hoe in two when Colin raised it to parry the blow.

Boggin's wings pumped furiously, and he began to rise. Colin threw himself heedlessly through the air and tackled him. Boggin began to draw in his breath, and, even from yards and yards away, I could feel the air get-ting cold. Colin, his legs dangling in midair as Boggin lifted off, drove the blunt end of the broken hoe-staff into the pit of Boggin's stomach. Boggin doubled over and coughed, but continued to rise, higher and higher.

I took a step, raised my wings, but looked back. Victor was not moving. He did not seem to be breathing. Vanity was sitting on the roof tiles, look-ing in horror at Mr. Glum's hand, which had gotten a grip on a roof orna-ment, and was lifting Mr. Glum into view. Quentin was looking hopeless and lost, his magic gone again, and he was still clutching his hand that the key had singed.

Damn, damn. A leader cannot abandon her people. But now I had to, one or the other. Either Colin, or the rest. Which? I had less time than it takes to take a breath to decide. As soon as Glum raised his head, I would be just a girl again. If I could have thrown something at Glum, or run down to him before he could raise his head, and pitched him off the roof to his death, I would have. But there was nothing to throw.

The giants were not the only ones with other hands. Mine looked like sparks and motes of energy when I rotated them into this time-space, and they swirled around Victor, Vanity, and Quentin; and perhaps my hands were not so strong as the giants' were, but I could negate the weight of my friends, so they were all feather-light.

I selected a very fast-moving energy path, caught it with my wings, and we all were swept off the roof at high speed. The path I took dipped down off the far side of the roof from Glum, putting the mass of the building between him and us for a moment.

I heard Boggin's voice crying out from above, "Stop! Stop! Stop! Or you will kill us both!"

Colin, his voice wild with glee, "No, teacher! Just you!"

I saw them outlined against the moon. They were very far away from me. There was no way I could get there, no shortcut through the fourth dimension to reach there; the distances were longer through four-space.

Boggin's three brothers were racing toward him, their wings like storms, but they were also simply too far away.

Colin was on Boggin's back, his legs around his neck. He had one hand yanking up Boggin's left wing. With the other, he flourished the broken hoe-shaft.

Colin shouted, "This is for every kid who hates wearing a tie!"

And he brained him. He struck the Headmaster forcefully enough to knock him limp. They both tumbled from the sky, down and down. . . .

There were bright moonlit clouds behind them. I saw the two tumbling silhouettes. As they fell lower, only dark horizon was behind them, tree shadows, the gloom of the earth, and I saw nothing.

Or perhaps it was tears that clouded my vision.

2.

Dawn. The sun was not yet above the sea, but the western clouds were all aflame with red, and bands of pale and distant yellow light peered through the bands of cloud. A low retaining wall of gray stone ran the length of the seafront, and above this were the shops of Waterside Street, quiet as ghosts in the dawn. There was a boardwalk on our side of the stone wall, and piers ran out on tall posts into the dark, murmuring water.

The four of us were huddled on the wide pier next to Lily Lilac's motorboat. There were crates lashed down under tarps on two sides of us, sheltering us from any view. On the fourth side was the sea. There were other boats moored here, too, but the fishermen either had not risen yet, or were taking Christmas Day off.

I had realigned Victor's monad, which had been twisted by Miss Daw to render him inert. His body had been stiff, without any heartbeat or breathing, but when I put him back to normal, the mechanical processes of breathing and circulation merely started again. It was so eerie, so inhuman, that I was having trouble remembering this was Victor, my Victor of whom I had dreamed so often. It was like seeing a computer or something, restored from a tape back-up.

Victor, in short order, had opened his third eye, and "remagnetized" as he called it, the "parts of Quentin's nervous system" which "allowed him to create magnetic anomalies." In other words, he turned Quentin's magic back on. The beam he used was more golden than blue.

Quentin poked around in the rubbish in some trash bins near the dock and found an axe-handle with no axe head, which someone had thrown away. Now he held it tucked under one arm like a baton. The first thing he had done with it was draw what he called a "circle of silence" on the planks of the dock where we hid, to allow us to talk, rather than pass notes, while Boggin's air spirits were listening for us.

The bus station was less than one hundred yards from where we huddled. It had taken me five minutes to walk up to the closed and locked door, slide "past" them, find the locker. I did not bother opening the door; I was wary of using keys. I stuck my head in, lowered the hypersphere into this space, so that its light shone on the interior of the locker. Here were papers and an envelope with money, as promised.

I would have brought Vanity, whom I now thought of as our trap-detector, but I was unwilling to experiment with what might happen if I drew her through the fourth dimension.

I drew out the papers and tickets and the envelope, and wafted through the wall. I folded my wings and assumed my secret identity as a girl again, and walked back down the street to where the others were waiting.

There were tears in my eyes by the time I got there. "Assume my secret identity" was like a phrase Colin would have used.

I stepped back into Quentin's circle, and the sea noise grew hushed and remote, as if cotton were blocking my ears.

I showed them the papers. We had visas and passports, and about £5,000 of Mr. ap Cymru's money. I was not sure if that was a little money or a lot, but I thought it was a lot. There were pictures of us, but I did not recognize the photographs; I had no idea when they had been taken.

There were papers for Colin, too, and there he was, a devilish half-smile to his face, looking out at me from his passport.

Victor said, "How long do we wait, Leader? Our chances of being spotted from the air have just gone up tremendously, because we waited till sunup."

I said, "I don't know and I don't care. You decide. This time I am quitting and for real. I resign as leader."

Victor said, "Not wise. You still have a lot of information we don't know yet."

I said stiffly, "When a leader loses one of the men under her command, she can resign."

Quentin said softly, "We do not know for sure he's dead."

Bitterness crept into my voice. "You're right. He may only be captured."

And I wondered how much of his memory they would have to erase to blot out all memories of us. All of them, I suppose. They would have to turn him back into a baby. Which, for all practical purposes, would erase him as a person. It was the same as death.

Quentin turned and looked at Victor. "It still seems like we need a leader. Someone has to decide how long we wait, whether we go back to look for his . . . to look for him, or where we go."

Vanity said, "And what about me?"

In my heart, I had to agree with Vanity. Why was Quentin automatically assuming Victor would be leader if I was not? I said, "Good point! Why can't Vanity be leader? Are we just all assuming girls can't do anything right? Is that it?"

Vanity looked embarrassed. "Um, actually, I mean, *what about getting my memory back?* You said something in the safe might help me. We haven't even looked at that stuff yet. Where do I fit in on your table of oppositions, Amelia?"

I sighed, feeling an immense weariness. I had been awake now, for how long? Two days? I lay back on the dock and tucked my hands behind my head, staring up at the sky. The zenith was mauve and dark blue, and the armies of the sunrise had not yet defeated that last rearguard of night. A star was there, faint, but not yet blotted out. One last holdout against the inevitable.

I just wanted to rest. I just wanted someone else to do the thinking for the group. I just wanted . . .

I just wanted Quartinus not to be dead. Once, at one of the irregular birthday parties Mrs. Wren used to throw for us (we had had three that year, I remember, and none the year before) Quartinus had been frightened by a party balloon. It had deflated, spitting with a rude noise, and when he ran from it, it flopped at random, here and there. Blind chance had made it seem to come after him, at least for a moment. Then he had cried, because the thing was limp, and he thought it was dead. He had been very young. I had held him in my lap and fed him a slice of birthday cake, and wiped his tears. . . .

I said dully, "Of the four powers, two of them are equal and opposite to each other. Me and Quentin; Victor and Colin. I had the hypothesis—really just a guess in the dark—that the two other powers we know exist, the Olympian and the Phaeacian, are combinations of two opposites. The Phaeacians seem to be able to bend space. I do not know by what mechanism. Dreams, or other levels of consciousness might be involved. They find shortcuts through some sort of dream-universe, where distances are meaningless. The Olympians clearly have something both in common with my paradigm and with Quentin's. They operate on moral principles. You have to break a promise to them, or break a rule, for them to get power over you."

Victor commented darkly, "That explains why religions have rules no one can follow. If everyone is a sinner, by definition, everyone is under their power."

"But they also control the fabric of time. They can bless and curse; they can create destiny. Hermes 'created' coincidences to make me visit him. I think the things Boggin can do are similar. In Victor's model, time is an absolute; it is not an object. It cannot be manipulated or affected. In my model, time is one aspect of time-space, it is relative, and certain conditions, such as proximity to event horizons, can distort time. On a quantum level, the arrow of time is ambiguous."

Vanity said, "Losing audience. Come again?"

I shook my head. "Sorry. I just think Olympians somehow combine Quentin's morality-based magic and my multidimensional time-space manipulation. If Phaeacian power is a combination of the other two—and don't ask me how pure materialism and pure mysticism can be combined!—but if it were, if the two of them worked together, they might be able to . . ."

The two of them were Victor . . . and Colin.

My voice trailed off. The one star that had been holding out against the dawn had been vanquished. I could not see it any longer.

I closed my eyes.

Vanity said softly, "Then, I'm not getting my memory back . . . ?"

Quentin said, "Is she asleep?"

I was not asleep. I just did not feel like talking at the moment.

Victor said, "We should decide how long we should keep waiting."

Quentin said, "I vote for you to be leader. Do we have any other candidates? Vanity, unless you want the job again?"

Victor said, "We have a chance to talk things out; let's not pick a leader till we need one. How long should we wait?"

Vanity: "I don't know. Is there going to be a time, you know, like noon and we know he's . . . Colin's not coming, but at eleven fifty-nine, we think he still might be coming? How do you pick a time like that?"

Quentin said, "We all have powers. Maybe I could read the cards, try to get a clue as to what is happening."

Victor said, "Does that create a signal of some sort? Is it detectable?"

Quentin sighed. "I don't know. I don't think tarot cards are radioactive or something. But I don't know. They clearly pick up influences from their environment. That is why they have to be kept in a cedarwood box."

Victor said, "Try to read Vanity's fortune. She can tell us if she feels something 'watching' her."

I heard the rustle of cards. Quentin briefly explained the positions in a cross-and-scepter spread, and started depicting a rather gloomy future, with Towers and Moons and the Seven of Swords opposing Vanity's path to happiness.

Vanity said, "Stop. I can feel it. There are some sort of creatures in the upper atmosphere that are looking at me when you do that. And you might want to redraw your magic circle. I wanted to tell you something. Amelia, are you asleep?"

Of course I was not asleep. I could hear them perfectly well.

"Guys, I think Amelia is planning on slipping away. Boggin has her bugged somehow. He can tell where she is. He's not doing it now. I assume that means Colin knocked Boggin out, if he didn't kill him dead. But if Boggin pulls through . . . well, you see what I mean? The only way the group can get away is if she's not in it. That's what she's thinking."

Damn her. Sometimes I underestimate Vanity.

Vanity said, "While she was leader, I wasn't going to say anything, because, well, you know how Churchill let Coventry get bombed, so the Axis would not figure out we'd broken their codes? I thought it was like that. But if she's not Churchill anymore, then she doesn't have the right to decide to sacrifice herself . . . well, you see what I mean?"

Victor said, "I am not sure what we can do to stop her. If Colin were here, he could stop her from walking through walls. But even for that, we'd need a wall. We don't have anything."

Quentin said, "We have the talismans from the safe. Do we have time to examine them? We still haven't decided whether to get into the motorboat now or later."

Victor said, "We ought at least to wait the amount of time it would take a man on foot to walk here from the estate. If Colin is wounded, but can still walk averaging at one mile an hour, he would get here within the next thirty minutes, assuming he set out the moment after he fell. Let's wait at least half an hour, then decide our next step."

Vanity said, "Make it an hour. You know how Colin is with directions and maps and stuff."

Quentin said, "I agree. An hour. Okay, Vanity, let's see what you've got."

"Item number one is this fine necklace. Note the alluring craftsmanship!"

Quentin: "The green stone is the same substance as the table in the Great Hall; the same one we used to summon the Head of Bran. Oh! That reminds me of a very important issue. Bran made us swear to do nothing that would hurt the British Isles. It would not bind you or Colin, but it is very important."

Victor said, "Important, why . . . ?"

"Um. Let me talk to you about that a little later."

Vanity said, "Item number two is a brown envelope. It has something written on it in Boggin's handwriting. *'Remember Next Time Not to Look.'* I can feel there is something the size and shape of a playing card. Should I look?"

Quentin said, "That could be a trick, like the burning key that scalded my hand. Why don't we leave item number two aside for the moment."

Vanity said, "Item number three is this. What is it?"

Victor said, "It is an ampoule for a syringe. Whatever the substance inside is, it gives off electronic signals."

Quentin said, "Nanites? What Amelia calls molecular engines?"

"At a guess, if it is meant for me," said Victor, "it is a library. Programs and codes stored in liquid form, which will change my brain if I inject it, and tell me how to do the things I saw Dr. Fell doing."

Vanity said, "You are not just going to inject yourself, are you?"

"Not at the moment. It might have to reorganize parts of my nervous system, and that might render me incommunicado."

Quentin said, "Or it could just be poison. If Boggin wanted to reactivate your powers, there could be a molecular key or antidote he has which he was going to feed you first."

Victor said, "Let me hang on to it. Who has that hypo we had earlier?"

Vanity said, "And last, but not least, ta da! We have a book, bound in black leather, with metal wires of gold and silver making Celtic knotwork and runes of mystic power on the cover. I have never seen something that is more obviously a grimoire in my life. Unfortunately it is locked shut."

Quentin said, "Hmm. Let me see that."

Vanity said, "Now, unless this is one of those ironic things where the instructions for molecular engine construction are in the book, and Quentin is supposed to inject himself with the nanites, which will engrave all sorts of spells into his brain, I think we know who gets what."

Quentin said, "It's not locked." I heard a rustle of paper.

A moment of silence.

Vanity said, "Well?"

Quentin said, "Unfortunately, this is written in the language of dreams. I cannot read it while I am awake. But I am pretty sure this is not molecular engineering 101. That picture is showing the Sephiroth. These diagrams are astrological charts. And that . . . I think this is the organizational table for the pre-Adamite kings and dukes, along with their telluric and mesoaetheric correspondences. Wish I could read the captions . . ."

Vanity said, "So we have four objects we either can't use right now, or aren't willing to inject or look at. And a necklace. Hey! I have a question! I wish Amelia were awake. Where is my boundary? Obviously my powers came back on, at least a little bit. And I guess this green stone is supposed to wake up more powers. But what turned on my first little bit?"

Morpheus said, "It is the boundary of dreams. The Lords of Cosmos cannot keep the powers of Night at bay. We are as close as sleep itself."

Victor said, "If that is true, Boggin could not keep Vanity's power turned off for more than one night."

Morpheus said, "It is not in the thought of the Olympians that Dream should aid the children of Phaeacia, who were, of old, our bitter foes. Yet she is beloved by you, and we work her aid. The Lords of Utmost Night shall spare her for your sake, when we uproot the world-tree, and feed creation to the final flame. She alone of all her race shall be spared."

I had the feeling I had lost track of part of the conversation. Who had just spoken?

Vanity said, "Something just became aware of Amelia . . ."

Quentin said, "Just her . . . ?"

Victor said, "How does your power work? Can you detect distance or direction?"

"Or who it is?"

Morpheus said, "It is Grendel. His desire for you maddens him. He sees you with his heart. Yet he comes alone, for he seeks you only to be his own. But there is cunning even in his madness, for he had taken a ring of Gyges from the finger of Erichtho, which will turn the curses of Eidotheia and confound his grammary; there is no power among you which can withstand his coming. Dream no more, for Dream cannot help you. My brother Death is near. I grant you shall not forget. Wake now."

"Wake up, Amelia! We think there is someone coming."

10

WATERS

1.

I sat up, rubbing my eyes. "I wasn't asleep. Who was it who spoke just now?"

Vanity said, "That was me. I sense someone is looking for you."

I said, "It's Grendel. Grendel Glum. He is all by himself, but someone just told me he had the ring of Gyges, which he took from the finger of Mrs. Wren. Quentin, you are our expert on myths. Is Gyges a name we came across in Greek literature?"

He suppressed a smile. "No, Amelia, but we read about him in philosophy. Socrates mentions the myth of Gyges in the *Republic*. A shepherd found a gold ring in the grave of some being greater than man. When he turned the collet in toward his palm, it made him invisible. He raped the queen and killed the king of Lydia. He could do whatever he wanted and no one could stop him. It is used as a symbol and example of how men act when corrupted by absolute power."

"What's a collet?" asked Victor.

Vanity answered him. "The setting. The thing that holds the stone of the ring. What do we do? Colin won't be able to find us if we run away."

Quentin said, "You said Glum was alone. If he is bound by the psionics paradigm, doesn't that mean I can automatically overcome his powers?"

I answered, "That other guy just told me the ring of Gyges will protect him from your magic, and that nothing we have can withstand his coming."

Victor said, "What guy?"

"The long-haired guy dressed in the black robes with stars circling his head. He had a silver goblet full of sand. Colin's dad."

Victor said, "You were asleep."

"He was here! I heard you talking to him."

Vanity said, "It was a dream."

I said, "I know who it was! Didn't I just say who it was?"

Vanity said to Victor, "We have to run away. Grendel is here. He is looking at us from somewhere. I think he can hear our voices."

We all looked back and forth across the waterfront. There was no one on the boardwalk, no one on the stone wall, no one in sight on the street.

Victor was saying, "We stay. I will neutralize the magnetic anomalies in the ring to kill its magic, and that will let Quentin cast a spell on him. Quentin, I assume an assault against us is enough of a moral error to let your powers work?"

I said, "There is no time to debate the issue! We have to leave. He's too strong for us. We can come back to look for Colin later."

Vanity said, "He smells us. He's that close."

There was no one on the pier. There was no noise but the wash and crash of the waves against the piles underfoot.

Victor said, "Make a circle. Stand back to back. If he's invisible . . ."

I said, "No! Get into the boat! Let's take off! Visible or not, he won't be able to get at us, unless he can outswim an outboard motor . . ."

Quentin and Victor turned so that Quentin was looking out to sea, and Victor was facing the shore. Quentin hefted his axe-handle as if to ready it. Vanity hesitated, but stepped between them and turned her back so that she was facing the motorboat.

I did not join the formation. "Wait a minute . . . !"

Quentin did not turn his head, but said to me, rather sharply, "You re-signed. Stop giving orders. We don't have time to talk."

I said, "But Victor is telling us the wrong thing to do! And who says Victor's in charge anyway? Colin's dad warned us that . . ."

Victor said in a maddeningly calm voice, "I'd be willing to abide by the outcome of a vote. Fight or flee?"

Vanity said, "Flee!" at the same time Quentin said, "Fight. If Victor can stop the ring . . ."

Vanity shrieked, "He's listening! He knows what you are planning to do! He's right here! He's here!"

Quentin said, puzzled, "We should be able to hear his wooden leg on the boards."

Victor, still in a voice of exasperating calmness, as if we had all the time in the world, said, "It's a tie. I guess we need Colin after all . . ."

I took a few steps toward the boat, saying, "Vanity, if we run for the boat, the boys will have to come." There was a note of panic in my voice, a shrill sound I did not like hearing.

Victor said patiently, "Of course, by that logic, if Quentin and I were to stand our ground, you would have to get out of the boat and come back. All that will do is split us into two bite-size pieces."

Vanity said to me in a quivering voice, "I'm not moving! He could be standing between me and the boat." Her wide green eyes rolled this way and that, seeing nothing but empty docks.

Victor said, "Does that mean you change your vote . . . ?" To me, he said, "Get in the circle and put your back to us. We have a majority."

I put my hand on the ladder to get down into the motorboat. The others were standing in a triangle, their backs to each other, about ten feet away.

I stopped. There was something wrong, all wrong.

Quentin said in a loud, clear voice, "Mr. Glum! Are you waiting for something? Why haven't you done anything yet . . . ?"

He wasn't after them.

He was after me.

He was waiting for me to get farther away from them.

I turned and ran back toward the group. I had taken two steps when the boards underneath the feet of Victor, Vanity, and Quentin exploded upward with a noise that stunned my ears.

Surrounded by flying splinters and snapping boards, a translucent column of water, a hooded cloak made of glass rose up in the midst of the explosion, with droplets like shining gems flying in each direction from it.

Not a cloak of glass. It was shivering seawater, sluicing in rivulets from an unseen form that was thrusting up through the docks. These boards were at least an inch thick, hardened by years, but they shattered like balsa before irresistible strength.

Victor did not have time to turn around. A blow tore the back of his coat and sent him stumbling over the edge of the pier. Into the waters he went. I saw the hilt of a knife sticking in the back of his coat. He rotated his head as he fell, and he opened his third eye. A blue spark flashed across the pier, and struck. Then the gray waters closed over Victor's calm face, and he was gone. He sank like a stone. He had still been wearing the chain-mail jerkin, pounds upon pounds of metal.

The blue spark struck home. Grendel Glum flickered and became visible. His face was painted, and he had a necklace of teeth rattling at his throat. A baggy gray shirt and baggy pants hung in sopping folds on his body. One pants leg had been tied off around the top of his peg leg. In one hand he held the axe-handle he had just torn from the grip of little Quentin.

Quentin had no time to cast spells or do anything but try to raise his arms. Glum clubbed him with the axe-handle. There was a sickening noise, and Quentin fell to the boards, bleeding from his face.

I tried to move into the fourth dimension. Nothing happened. I saw nothing. Even my hypersphere, my light the ghost said would not fail, was not shining.

Grendel tossed the axe-handle away, put one huge arm around Vanity's waist and, with one huge thrust of his single leg, came flying in a low tackle across the pier toward me.

I could not move. I was paralyzed with fear. Grendel didn't want me to move.

He caught me around the legs. He, Vanity, and I hung in the air for a moment as the world toppled end over end. The shockingly cold waters of the midwinter sea struck us with the force of a falling wall. It was like being stunned with a club; I could not feel my hands or feet.

I had no control. Grendel had knocked the wind out of me with his tackle. Icy salt water flooded my lungs before I could stop myself.

Swirling green-brown gloom was around us. I saw the dark pillars from the pier, reaching down to further darkness. Down we went.

Vanity was struggling and writhing, and silver bubbles came from her lips, and then stopped. Maybe Grendel had squeezed the air out of her by tightening his arm. My hands, of their own accord, clawed and struck at Grendel's face and arms. I tried to dig my fingers into his eyes; I kicked between his legs. My blows were slow and weak. Or landed wrong. Or Grendel did not desire any blows to hurt him.

The bottom was much, much farther down than I would have believed possible. My vision was turning red around the edges. Was it possible to die so quickly?

There was rubbish here, rusted barrel-hoops, a broken anchor, coral, bottles, a net weighted with balls of stone.

I saw a blue light. Victor slid into view, swift and quiet as a submarine, and the third eye in his head was sweeping through the murk of the bottom like a searchlight. He was not moving his arms or legs, and his coat was streaming back, revealing the chain-mail jerkin beneath. The knife was still hanging through the back of the fabric of his jacket, but whether the coat of rings had turned the blade or not, I could not see.

When the blue light swept over us, Grendel held Vanity overhead, where Victor could clearly see her. Then, with a huge thrust of his arm, Grendel shoved her down into the mud and sand of the bottom, and threw the net over her. Her struggles grew feebler, and then stopped.

Grendel kicked off the bottom and soared through the murk. Like Mestor, like Victor, he had some ability to propel himself through the water by thought alone. I do not know whether his method was faster or slower than Victor's. Victor dived down to haul the net off Vanity.

I lost sight of Victor as he was carrying Vanity quickly to the surface, behind us and growing farther behind, at about the same time I lost consciousness.

2.

Dimly, I sensed a sensation of warmth, of motion. My breathing was slow, heavy, and full. Someone was carrying me. Someone who loved me. Was it Victor . . . ?

I came more awake. I drew a deep breath. No, not a breath. Something heavier.

I opened my eyes and sat up. My movements were dream-slow.

I was lying in the shell of a giant clam, on a soft surface made of some sort of sea moss or red-gold seaweed. It was beautiful to the eye, but repellent to the touch, cold and rubbery. The gold weeds were half-weightless, and they floated and stirred as I sat up.

I was in a palace with a floor of gold. The ceiling was ribbed like the skeleton of a whale. Between the ribs were shingles of mother-of-pearl, nacre, and strands of hammered gold. The ribs themselves were crusted with pearl. It was more beautiful than a jewelry box, finer than a photo of a Fabergé egg I once saw. And yet it was the belly of a whale. I had been swallowed.

The walls were crusts of living coral, which had been sculpted with fantastic scenes of mermaids and storms, whales and dolphins and strange leviathans. But the carvings had a crude, rough look to them, and I realized that the coral out of which the walls were carved was still alive, rough and knobbed, so that, each month, a little bit of the carvings must be blotted out and grown over.

Even as I looked, blushes like blood appeared and disappeared across the intricately carven surface, as thousands of tiny red worms stuck their heads out into the floating dirt, or yanked them back in.

On the lintel of a distant door, there were bottles of various designs and sizes, fantasy-shapes of crystal and glass. In each one was a transparent fish, with huge blind eyes, nightmare things whose faces were clusters of teeth. Their skins glowed pale, or they held little dots of light on the end of antennae. These dim lamps lit the wide, shadowy space of the gold-floored chamber.

I sat up on the edge of the clamshell. I was floating, but for some reason, I was not actually buoyant. Were my lungs filled up with water? Why wasn't I dead?

I put one foot to the cold gold floor, and noticed that there was a slipper made of small glass beads, patterned like the scales of the snake, on my foot. A white garment like a cloud of fine mist was swirling around me, a garment from a dream.

There was a noise behind me, a small laugh of satisfaction. I turned my head, expecting to see Grendel.

There was a young and stern-looking man. Maybe he was twenty-five, maybe twenty, but there was cruelty on his handsome lips, a look of mingled dominance and pride in his dark magnetic eyes.

His eyes were sea-gray, and his hair was the color of a storm off the coast of Norway, drawn back and clasped in a pearl ring at the base of his neck. He was dressed in grand fashion, a stiff collar made bright with lace and a long coat of shining pearl buttons. The fabric swam and flickered with sea-blue colors. He wore a wide cummerbund of emerald silk, and powder blue knickerbockers clasped his legs.

No, not legs. His leg. His left stocking was a pale viridescent hue, tucked into a dark sharkskin leather shoe with a mother-of-pearl buckle.

His right leg ended at the knee, and a peg of pale whalebone held him up against the mild weight of this gloomy undersea palace. He did not have any cane or crutch in his hand. Perhaps he needed none here.

He stood with his arms crossed on his chest, looking down at me. He had been watching me sleep.

The face was so familiar. I tried to picture his cheek less lean, his hair fallen out, his face pitted and wrinkled by years of labor. And I saw, in his eyes, how that look was the same. This thin, young, hawk-faced lordling looked at me as if I were his most prized possession, the dearest of all the things he owned.

I said in soft awe, "Grendel . . . ?"

"Aye. 'Tis I." His voice was an octave lower than it had been on land. There, it had been a thin skirl of cracked pipes. Here, it was the hum of a bass viol.

"How is it possible?"

" 'Tis my true self you see, not as I am on land. In my mother's place, we are, here, and how she sees me, so I am."

When he moved, the gold floor chimed softly, like a gong, beneath his peg leg, but he moved with the grace of a moon astronaut. Underwater, the missing foot was less of a hindrance to him.

He moved forward and put out his hand, as if to help me up.

I put my hand out. I wasn't sure what else to do. Fight? Run? Scream? No option seemed very appealing. And I wasn't even sure how it was that I could be alive.

Young Grendel's lightest touch on my hand brought me floating to my feet. Only then did I see how I was dressed.

It was no fabric of Earth. It was some fairy-stuff, lighter than cobwebs and whiter than snow. There was a pinch-waist bodice set with many tiny pearls, long floating sleeves of film, a skirt of gossamer with a train of smoky dandelion fluff. A belt of translucent blue-green links hung low on my hips and came to a low V, and from there trailed down the front like a shining serpent with bright scales. On my feet were the tiny slippers made of translucent blue-green beads.

Like running smoke, the fabric of the dress changed moment to moment, growing dim and transparent, or white and translucent by turns, as it swayed and folded weightlessly around me. At no point did the fabric actually hide anything dresses are supposed to hide.

I was not even sure if the neckline was high or low. The fabric faded into existence somewhere between my neck and cleavage, becoming slightly more opaque as it curved around my bosom. The substance looked something like a spiderweb at dawn, gemmed with night dew. The strands of pearl flecks floating in the bodice fabric formed converging lines from the bustline toward the crotch, creating the optical illusion that my waist was thinner than it was.

I covered my breasts with one forearm and put my other hand between my legs, turning away from Grendel. You know the pose. Botticelli's Venus holds her hands this way when she steps from her clamshell to the shore. Of course, she is wearing a dreamy smile. I wasn't.

I caught my breath (or whatever it was I had instead of breath) when I turned. There was an antique silver mirror, something from the wreck of a Spanish galleon, propped up against the barnacle-rough side of the chamber. To either side of it stood amphorae of paper-thin ivory. Whatever phosphorescent sea monster was inside those urns could not be seen, except as moving shadows of light, but the ivory glowed and cast light from the silver mirror.

There was my reflection. I was beautiful. And yet . . .

I don't know what it was; perhaps it was a combination of many tiny changes. My lips were redder, and my hair shone, and maybe my cheeks were a trifle more pronounced. My skin seemed fairer, with no sun-freckles, bug bites, or moles. As if I had been airbrushed. I seemed almost to glow.

This was the way Grendel saw me. There was something more than flattering in this. It was almost awe-inspiring. As if I had been transformed into a goddess.

And yet I had been *altered* while I slept. The idea was a repellent one.

There was something jarring about the dress while it swirled and floated about me, shining. On the one hand, it looked like something an elf-maiden in a fairy tale could wear, glass slippers and all. Something too aetherial for Earth. At the same time, it was somehow all too Earthy, tawdry, almost tasteless, a combination of a fishnet body stocking and a wet T-shirt. A cross between what a princess and a professional harlot should wear. It confused me to see it. I didn't know what to make of it.

At my neck was a choker of glass links, matching the belt and shoes. It reminded me unpleasantly of the collar I had worn for Grendel; the one no one but he could remove.

A collar no one can remove. Now there is a thought to give a girl claustrophobia of the neck. Or what is fear of choking called? Victor would have known.

My hair was gathered into a net, finer than a silk web, set with pearls and phosphorescent dots. The dots were clustering thickly about my brows and ears, as if I wore both earrings and a tiara.

Again, it seemed both attractive and repellent. It was beautiful to have little stars caught in the net in my hair; but it also looked too much like cobwebs, over which glowing insects from some sunless mold were crawling.

"How come I'm not tied up?" I said.

In the mirror, I could see him smile, a cruel quirk of his lips on his narrow face. He put his hand gently on the top of my head, as if to pat me. The little lights webbed into the fragile snood exhaled a soft luminous twinkle at his touch. "This cap keeps you alive, allows you breath, lets your words come out, unstoppers your pretty little ears. If I yerk it from your head, you die. As long as you love life, what need have I for chain or rope to keep you by my side, princess mine?"

I reached my hand up as if to touch the cap; he slapped the wrist away. I said, "What is it?"

"Always curious? Always so bright at your lessons, eh? This cap, I'll tell the tale. This cap, it is from my mother's loom, woven of my dead father's hair, and there are so few of them left. They told you that you weren't not able to breathe water, eh? They told you the cold would kill you. That was lie. All they say is lie. This cap makes those lies have no more hold or grip on you, my pretty princess. Let it leave your head, my golden one, and you are but one more drowned maiden of all the many maidens who have drowned at sea, and only the crabs will love you then."

His eyes traveled up and down my image in the mirror, drinking in the sight. He touched my elbow gently. "Besides. I'm not going to tie up no girl in her wedding dress, not on her wedding day. What kind of man you think I am, eh?"

I jerked my hand in front to cover myself again. He tilted his head to stare in wonder and admiration at my bottom, which was about as well-clad as it would have been had a very short cigarette smoker blown a smoke ring toward my hips. He said in a sharper tone of voice, "I didn't say to move. Put down your hands. I'd like to look at you."

"I'm embarrassed," I said in a wretched tone of voice.

"That's fine. Girl should be shy on her wedding day. But once we're wed, and I am your master and your lord, you'll do just what I say, when I say, or I'll take a rod to you."

I looked over my options again. Fight. Argue. Run. Scream. Cry. Defy him. Find out if he meant a heavy bone-breaking sort of rod or a light birch-whip kind of rod. None of those options really leaped out at me.

Well, we had already established that I was not exactly Joan of Arc. I put my hands down at my side, my fingers curled into fists. In the mirror, my fists looked so small. Like a child's fists.

He touched my chin with his finger. I raised my head slightly, to get away from the touch. Once I was standing nice and straight and tall, he took his hand away.

"There we are," he said.

"If Quentin is dead, Mavors will kill you," I said.

"Och, don't worry your pretty head about that. Don't you know what he is, that one? Quentin be one of the Gray Folk. The Fallen. They can't die. They shuck off their bodies like you and I change clothes, and wear somewhat new, fat or tall, fair or foul, whatever they please."

I said, "If you marry me, Boreas will kill you."

"Maybe so, pretty one, may be so. But he has a hornet's nest around his head, once the Big Ones find out he's let you all slip through his fingers. And his power up yonder is great, for he is the captain of all the winds what served his dad. But, look you, down hither, there ain't no air here, eh? Here's the water, black water and deep. What need have I to fear the wind down here?"

He stepped behind me and reached his hand over my shoulders to take my cheeks, one in each palm. It was an odd yet intimate gesture, and very gentle. This made me stand slightly straighter, on tiptoe, and something about how lovingly he spoke frightened me. "But lookit yourself in the glass. I look, and I see you're worth dying for. I ain't afraid of nothing when I look at you, if I make you be mine."

He took his hands away, but I kept standing at attention.

He did make me seem so pretty; so very pretty.

After a moment, he added, "I gave up my Vanity for you, even though she's prettier and girlier than you. I wanted you more. You saw me put her aside and take you."

"What do you mean, 'girlier'?" I asked. The moment the comment left my mouth, I realized how bad it sounded. As if I were jealous, and competing for Grendel's affections.

He laughed and put his hand around my elbow, a gentleman taking a milkmaid to a country fair. He gestured toward the door. We began walking across the shining gloom of the golden floor toward it.

As we walked, young Grendel seemed to absorb me with his eyes, drunk on the sight of me. His prize. His possession. He said, "Well, she ain't much one for all that running around with sticks and balls and what-not."

"Sports," I said. "They're called sports."

"Well," he said, "they'll be no more of that."

That grim little comment brought home to me what was happening. A sea monster was about to marry me. And then he would be in control of my life until I escaped him, or died. If he wanted me to wear my hair up, I'd wear it up. If he wanted it loose, it would be loose. If he didn't like the way I talked, or walked, or thought, he'd whip me till I changed to please him. And then when he tired of me, I'd be left alone in some cell buried under the sea. Or he'd strangle me and throw my body to the crabs.

Unless he needed me alive to nurse the baby. Our baby. Sea monster junior.

There was a pressure in my eyes. I blinked, but nothing happened. I started to raise my hand to my face, but then he took my hand with grave and polite grace, raised it to his lips, and kissed it.

He said softly, "You're trying to cry. You cannot do it down here. This is all tears, all this salty ocean. Your folk wept when they was driven out by Saturn, and all the seas turned salt. That's how sad they was. But you have no cause to be sad, darling. Darling girl. My darling. Undersea is a happy place, see? There's no crying here, so it must be happy, get it? My mother told me that when she used to whup me. Heh."

And then he said, "Come along," and he turned and stepped out from the golden doors.

I followed him. His palace was gloomy, a place of massive shadows and slow whale-like noises. I saw corridors and arches, and, dimly, jars and fences behind which luminous fish and glowing worms trembled and flickered.

When I saw myself shining in the panel of some polished wall of silver, or cut marble, I saw how filmy trails and tails of the dress swept over the darkly sparkling floor and remained all white and unstained. The slippers shone brightly.

I said, "So much wealth . . ."

"Hmph. 'Tis of no worth to me, golden one. All the treasure of all the ships that ever sunk is gathered here, and when my mom wants for more, she sinks some ships and drowns some sailors more. But what's to buy with it, eh? There is no beam of golden sunlight here, nothing bright nor fair . . . till you."

Great gates like the baleen of a whale, set with gold and pearls, drew aside at our approach. We were outside.

The palace behind us was formed into the great shape of a dome, half-covered over with coral and slaked with mud. Pearls and ribs of gold and other shapes of great beauty reared up from the gates out from which I stepped, but the beauty was half-shrouded in the murky mud and twitching sea insects that formed dun clouds to every side.

The heavy water was black overhead. There was no sun.

We stood on a hillside, or, I suppose, one should call it the slope of a sea trough. The greatest light in the area came from a mound of coral and seashell cemented into a rough dome. There were joints and parallel strands of some phosphorescent material set into that coral as well, and round lumps of it. It seemed a fairy castle, laced with light. And yet, something in the shapes of those lights was odd. It looked like rib cages, skeletons, skulls, all the ivory of the dead lit up with Saint Elmo's fire.

In that dim light, I could see a few other scattered mounds, much smaller than the main dome. These were palaces like the one from which I had come, going away down slope. They were beautiful, but the lifeless light in them made them seem like graveyard things.

To my left was a cliff, rising sheer into the gloom. In the cliff was a crack. Gathered about the lower lip of the crack, and spilling down to the mud below, were heaps of gold and silver coins, the wreckage of a chariot, the skeletons of two horses, and the rusted remains of once-bright helmets. The loot of sunken ships, I supposed, left lying in the mud.

I turned to him. "Who promised Vanity to you?"

"Just a voice in the wood."

But there was something in the way he said it.

I said, "You recognized that voice, didn't you? You told Dr. Fell you did not, but why would you have heeded a voice you didn't know?"

He squinted at me, and frowned. "Sneaking and peeking, were we? Hiding and listening? I recall what I told Fell. He knew what I meaned, even if you didn't. I spoke of the voice, to make him know, in case he wanted to get in on it. To get in on divvying up the loot. Boggin were a sinking boat, see; and I was telling Fell it were time to jump ship. But did he listen? Gar! He says to me, he says, 'Go tell Boggin when you hear this voice, eh?' You listened, little princess, but you didn't hear what was being said."

"What was being said?"

"I was telling him Boggin is done for, and that I was going to get Vanity for my own, when my new friend came to step on Boggin and take his stuff. I were asking Fell if he wanted to get on the right side, and I were telling him he could get stuff, too. Sweet stuff, very sweet. I was offering you. He said no. Now, of course, I'm glad he turned me down."

"Who was this new friend?"

Young Grendel grinned. "I ain't saying. But it were one of the Big Ones, one of the Olympians. One of them what could make be so, what he said be so."

"Then it was not Boggin?"

Grendel laughed at that idea. "Har! Boggin? Offer to give me Vanity? Not no how. Wants her himself, that one does. He's all stiff in the trousers when she walks by, swaying her hips and with her shirt all open. But he ain't going to marry her, him. He ain't honest."

I pointed. "What's that?" I gestured toward the pile of gold coins and pins below the crack in the cliff wall.

Grendel said, "Folk throw coins and pins down. Half is Mother's; half is for the Fair Ones what built this well. They ain't never coming for it, but we daren't touch their half of it. The Fair Ones, they gets all the nice things. They are so fine and high and mighty, or they was. Like you. Fine and fair."

I said, "Is that the bottom of the Kissing Well?"

"Full of questions, aren't you? Aye, that it is."

"But I thought this was the sea. You said it was salt water. Well water is fresh."

"It gets fresher as you go up."

"How is that possible?"

He shrugged, clearly uninterested. "The Fair Folk do it. Dunno how it works. Come along."

I did not move. "Where are we going?"

He pointed to the huge rough dome made of glowing bones on the hillside. "Ma. That's her place. She's the one what dressed you."

I said, "She dressed me?"

Grendel's mouth gawped, and then he looked embarrassed. "You don't think it were me? Undressing a girl naked without someone there? An unmarried girl?"

He was flabbergasted at the concept.

He squinted at me and looked me in the eye, and that squint made him look so much more like the old, grizzled Mr. Glum I knew. He said, "Look'ee here, Melia! I'm a bad man, there's no denying it. A bad, bad man! I've stove in skulls of those who done me no harm, and bit off ears, too. I've drowned folk and eat their flesh cold, and drank their blood like soup. I've pinched things what weren't mine and lied about it after. I've promised to be a place, and then weren't nowhere near when the time came. But I ain't never cheated at no game of cards, and I never give no sass to my mom, and I ain't never diddled with no unwed girl, or brought no shame to her name."

He straightened up and pointed at the dome made of seashells, coral crusts, and luminous bones. "My mom lives just over yonder. You think she'd let me carry on like Boggin does? You'll find out what she's like."

I did not move from the spot where I stood, and he did not seem to be in a hurry. The fact that the crack in the cliffside led up to a place I knew made me reluctant to lose sight of it. It was like seeing blue sky through prison bars.

"Who is your mother? I thought Beowulf killed Grendel's mother."

"Him? Yellow-haired bastard sticking his oar in where it weren't none of his quarrel. Them that bragged Hereot were a finer house than Arima! Fairest house in middle-earth, they said! It weren't so fair once we had done some dirty work on it, though. Heh. No, they didn't have no joy in their fine house with its roof of gold for many a day, and it was only wailing, not singing, their poets did.

"Anyhow, blondie comes in for no reason, and killt my older brother, from who I got his name second-hand. But Mom weren't killed. Can't.

Mighty wounded, though, hurt bad. She had to go to the Destroyer what to get herself fixed up, and that one, he made her change sides and swear up and down to serve the Big Ones on the Mountain. We used to be part of you lot. That whelp Quentin, he's my mom's nephew. My grand-dame is Ceto, what gave birth to the Gray Witches, what gave birth to Quentin.

"Anyway, the Destroyer kept his part of things, and sent a dragon to go take care of that blond guy. Showed him. But, no, she didn't die."

He looked at me sidelong, and added: "*You* know she can't die. I heard you talking about her once."

"Me?"

"Yeah! In classroom. I were outside the window, listening. You were doing your lessons, and talking about her. I came right on down here afters, and told her what you said, and it made her smile. She don't smile much, and it does a heart good to see it."

"What did I say . . . ?"

He looked hurt. "You mean you don't remember?"

I said blankly, "I . . . I do a lot of lessons. I don't remember them all."

"You were talking about that poet. I ain't got much book learning, but when Mom found out that guy wrote her up in a poem and all, she were wild about it. Made me go up and rememberize it, so as I could come down here and tell it her. Not the whole poem; just the part about her. I wanted to steal the damn book, but Mom ain't so good with her letters, and the pages would have got wetted and spoilt anyhow. It's funny, I know and you forget. You think I'm stupider than you, but I didn't forget my lessons. You want to hear . . . ?"

Without waiting for an answer, he tucked his hands behind his back, and squared his shoulders, and cleared his throat, and recited: "*And in a hollow cave, she was born, a monster irresistible, and there are none, mortal or immortal, like unto her. She is the goddess fierce Echidna, who is half a nymph with glancing eyes and fair cheeks, and half again a huge serpent, great and awful, with speckled skin, eating raw flesh beneath the secret parts of the holy earth. And there she has a cave deep down under a hollow rock far from the deathless gods and mortal men. There, then, did the gods appoint her a glorious house to dwell in: and she keeps guard in Arima beneath the earth, grim Echidna, a nymph who dies not nor grows old all her days.*"

He grinned. "Hear that? Even your poet feller said her house was glorious. Better than that damn Hereot place, anyhow. Ma liked that a lot. She used to have me say it out for her like that, especially when she was eating, 'cause sometimes the people she had for dinner was making lots of noise, screaming and carrying on. You know what her favorite part was? 'Irresistible!' She liked being called irresistible, on account of she is a mighty fine looker.

"She said you was quite a looker, too. *Better than was fit for me,* she says. She was really tickled when she saw how you fit into her dress. Didn't even have to take it in at the chest or nothing, not like some we've had down here. Good stock, she said you were. That's a joke, see? Get it? Good stock?"

"I don't get it," I said.

"Soup stock. Never mind. You'll get used to her little jokes. It's always a lot better when she's kidding around than when she gets in her black moods." He shook his head sorrowfully.

"Black moods . . . ?" I asked.

"They killt my brothers, you know. Hercules and Bellerophon and folks like that. Oedipus shoved my sister off a cliff. They say she jumped, but that's a lie. She was the smart one in the family, the only one was all loved and got along with.

"My mom, she's got like a little pile of bones out back, one pile for each of the departed, and she keeps 'em to remind herself how much she misses them. When she misses them too much, she goes out hunting to get more bones to pile on. I tell her to go up the surface, so as she can cry and let it all out, but she don't listen to me, even though I'm the only one of her kids what still sticks by her. But she surely misses her babies, sometimes. The pile for my sister is the biggest of all, on account of she misses her the most. Such a pretty thing, too! Took after Mom, at least from the waist up.

"You'd think those puny folk couldn't do folk like us much hurt, but they had it out for my brothers. Especially Hercules. Five of them are dead. No, six, if you count Orthus. Mom ain't got no memento for him. He were the eldest, and weren't too bright, and we always called him the 'Shy One Brain,' on account of he only had two heads instead of three. I'm kind of sorry I made fun of him, now he's dead, but he was a bit of a bully, really, and he was married to Mom for a while, which sort of turns your stomach, if you think about it. That was after the Thunderer killt

Dad, and Orthus was kind of the man of the family, but he didn't really ask Mom or nothing. He just did it.

"He turned over a new leaf, and tried to straighten up. Got himself a job guarding the Cattle of Geryon. Good work, steady. And he were fierce, but Hercules laid him low.

"My second biggest brother, though, he's safe. Ain't no one ever going to kill him, not ever. He got himself a good job, watchman sort of thing, working for the Unseen One. Mom is always ragging and worrying us, why we can't get no good jobs like he got. I reckon he just got that job to make the rest of us look bad. Anyway. Mom's real proud of him, though he never comes back to visit. I just saw him in a dream the other day, though. He weren't too friendly, and me his brother and all.

"I guess 'cause his boss were looking on. Normally, he's kind of easy-tempered and funny like Mom is, you know: 'And you think your work is Hell!' That's something he says. It's a joke. You get it? You don't get it.

"Well, anyway, there is just me now, and Ladon comes by when he can, and gives her some of the apples he's supposed to be guarding. He's the young one, runt of the litter, but he got a pretty good job himself.

"You'll meet him in time, I guess. If you don't cross Mom and she don't eat you like she did the last one. Hey, and if you butter him up, maybe he'll filch an apple for you, so as you can be immortal, too.

"We can be your family, now. You ain't had no family, had you? No one to look out for you." He patted me on the shoulder. "I'll look after you now, me and Mom, and my two brothers. You ain't never going to be lonesome again."

As he spoke about his dead brothers, a sense of pity welled up in me, but also a sensation of cold horror.

"But you are monsters," I said. "You kill and eat people like wolves kill rabbits."

"Yeah, but people don't mind. They used to, but these days? They're always going on and on about overpopulation and the balance of Nature and stuff. We gotta dress up different these days, o' course, serial murders and axe murders and so on. Jack the Ripper—heard of him? One of my nephews. He only killt whores, though, and everyone knows they're too many of them; all the preachers say so. No, you ain't worried about human beans, are you? It's Mom. Who would not be nervous meeting her, what with her being famous and written up in a poem and all?"

He reached out and took my hand in his. He stared down at it for a moment, as if impressed at how slim and white it looked, fingers slender and well-shaped, so unlike his own. Then he bowed his head over it, as if he meant to kiss it, but he did not.

He straightened, but did not let go of my hand. Instead he raised his other hand and stroked my knuckles with caresses as gentle as he could manage.

"Don't worry about a thing. I gave up a lot for you. I gave up Vanity; I cut my own foot off for you. Mother's not going to eat you. She likes you. I told you that's her dress."

"Dress . . . ?"

"Her wedding dress. My mom's wedding dress. She wore that dress when she was hitched up with Typhon. She saved it in a box for the Sphinx, but Sphinx got killt by Oedipus. That cap is hers, too, last one I got. That's why I could not keep you and Vanity both."

I reached up my hand to touch the web of pearls and lights around my hair.

"Don't touch that, I said! You don't want to die by drowning. It's a foul, foul death," he said in a matter-of-fact voice. "I know the word to break the charm on that there cap. You are thinking how far you can run? Not far enough. You try to run off, and I say the word. You stab me in my sleep, and Mother says the word.

"Now, come along! We tarried enough, jawing. Mother wants to talk to you and give her blessing. She keeps her blessings in a jar next to her high seat. She's going to say about how not to be afraid of having babies, and how you'll love the ones with two heads as much as the ones with three. It's a thing matrons say to virgins, you know? And she's going to say some stupid stuff about how it hurts the first time, so liquor up good after the ceremony, but after that you learn not to mind. The kind of garbage womenfolk think men don't know you talk about. Besides, I wouldn't hurt you for all the world."

I drew a deep not-breath. Suddenly, I was calm and unafraid. It was simple. It was like a math puzzle. There were certain known factors I could control, and certain factors he controlled; some were known and some were unknown. I could solve for the known factors.

Actually, it was more like a chess puzzle. Math puzzles do not require one to sacrifice pieces.

I said, "No, Grendel."

He said, "What's that?"

"No. You shall not marry me. I will not stay here. You shall take me back up to the surface in the next five minutes."

He said, "You want me to go fetch the rod, is that it? It's an ill thing to beat a woman on her wedding day. I'd rather wait till after the preacher were done, to make it proper and legal-like."

I looked at him. I don't know what he saw in my face, but he quailed and stepped back, even though he was immensely stronger than me, and possessed of a power I could not oppose.

My words marched out of my mouth like soldiers: "Hear me, Grendel. I pity you, for you are wretched, but I will not be yours. You wish to possess me, and I do not wish to be possessed. My wishes will be granted, and yours will be thwarted."

He stepped forward again, beginning to smile. "I'll get my way."

"You will do what I wish you to do. You will take me to the surface."

"And why will I do that, little golden princess?"

"Because my will is stronger than yours, Grendel."

He may have had some intimation of what I was about to do, because he grabbed for my wrists. Too late.

The net I wore on my head, the mermaid's cap, came up easily off my hair, and tore in half very easily. There was a flash of green sparks as the fabric parted.

The sounds grew rubbery and thick, and the icy water shocked every inch of my flesh, every cubic inch of my lungs. Oddly enough, there was no sensation of choking, because my lungs were already entirely filled with water.

And it was cold, so cold, that it felt, paradoxically, as if all the water around me had turned to lava. As if my arms and legs were burned to stubs immediately, I could not tell whether I could move them or not. My vision went dark.

Pnigerophobia. That was the word. Fear of choking is called pnigero-phobia.

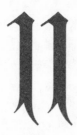

TALON, TOOTH, AND NAIL

1.

For a time, I lay between waking and not-waking, troubled by memories of dark nightmares of cold, endless cold, and of choking and vomiting black water. I remembered rough lips trying to breathe life back into my lungs, and being unable to breathe and unable to see or feel. And reality had somehow . . . snapped into place . . . and in the new version of reality, the lips came again, and breathed into me, and I breathed in and out. In and out.

There is no sensation more wonderful. How pleasant, how wonderful life is, which allows us to enjoy this pleasure, life's best pleasure, ten or five times a minute, when we relax, fifteen when we are filled with excitement.

Except . . . why was I only breathing in through my nose? What was blocking my mouth?

I came fully awake. I opened my eyes.

There were two large campfires burning left and right. I was wrapped snugly in a bearskin rug, folded over me and under me like a sleeping bag. It might have been the same bearskin rug Grendel wore as a robe.

I was lying, rolled up in the rug, on snow. Around me were a few scraggly trees, naked and powdered with snow. Every twig bore a little icicle. Not twenty feet away was the rocky soil the Kissing Well stood on, its little witch-hat roof layered with a second hat of snow. Beyond it was the cliff. I could see and smell the sea.

Even with the bearskin and the fires, I was still cold, although, perhaps, I was not near death. Grendel had not removed the wedding dress, and I could feel its sopping wet fabric clinging tightly to me, freezing. Little puddles had collected from the garments and gathered under my stomach.

Yes, I was lying on my stomach. And yes, I had a gag in my mouth, the second one today, if I hadn't lost count. And, yes, I was tied hand and foot, and from what I could tell from a little wiggling, probably elbows, knees, upper thighs, around the waist, etc., etc. You get the idea. Grendel had gone at least a week without seeing me trussed up like a turkey; his favorite spectator sport. I was surprised he hadn't roped me down like a landing zeppelin to tent stakes in the ground.

And there he was, Old Grendel was back, bald and crooked, dressed in a wet gray shirt and sagging patched trousers. His peg leg was made of wood again, not ivory.

He leaned close and whispered, "Sush! Sush! If you make any noise at all, Boggin might hear. The winds do his sneaking and eavesdropping for him. Got me?"

Have you ever had something really, really important to say, when a magic sea monster had you gagged, so that you could not even make very much noise out of your nose? Very frustrating. It helps to have expressive eyes.

Thunking a bit with your bound legs can help, if you do it regularly enough to make him think you've got a signal you are trying to send. If he just thinks you are struggling, it would just turn him on. Pervert.

He took the gag out. "No carrying on. You're already due for a licking when we get back home, scaring me like that. Don't add to the account."

I said through chattering teeth, "I am going to freeze. I am going to die. My clothes are still wet. It's turning to ice on me . . ."

He looked up, worry plain on his face. "Yeah," he muttered. "Weather always turns fierce cold when *he* gets mad . . ."

I said, more loudly, "You have to dry me off, get me someplace warm! Get me out of these things!"

Without getting up, he reached over and picked up a broken tree branch he was using as a crutch. He whispered, uncertainty in his voice: "I were going to get Mom, seeing if she wouldn't change her mind, get me another cap. I'll bring her up here . . ."

I wondered if my powers would come back on if he went away. I did not think so; Miss Daw had implied there was no range limitation.

"Look!" I said, my voice shivering and choking with cold. "If we are engaged, it's legal to look at me naked, see? It's not like this dress actually covers me anyway! Are you an idiot? I thought this was your sick daydream come true: a half-naked girl begging you to strip her clothes off. Are you going to marry my corpse? Is that the plan?"

I should mention that Grendel did not seem to be doing too well, temperature-wise, either. His soaking wet pants and ragged gray shirt were stiff with frost. But it wasn't killing him. Maybe he had blood like an arctic walrus or something, or natural antifreeze.

Well, that little speech got me untied and got me out of that dress. Both the ropes and the fabric just parted under his hands. I spent a moment, for the second time this month, if I hadn't lost count, stark naked in the snow.

I hopped from foot to foot, while he shook the cold water out of the bearskin; then he wrapped the huge skin over my shoulders and all around me.

I was sure he was aroused by the sight of me dancing and shaking, goosebumps on my goosebumps, blue lips and all. Me, I just felt as if the nadir of misery was not far away. Where was that brave feeling, that I-am-not-afraid-to-die recklessness that had possessed me just a minute ago? Maybe people can only be brave when they are warm.

But Grendel did not look aroused by the sight; he looked concerned. When he folded the bearskin around me once more, I felt like a child at the beach being wrapped in a fluffy towel by a worried mother. The skin was voluminous enough that I could stand on one flap of it and have another flap wound around my sopping hair like a turban. Where in the world did they make bears this big? I wondered if Grendel had killed it during the previous ice age.

He leaned on his tree branch, watching me huddle close to the bigger fire. Every now and again he threw a worried glance at the sky, as if fearing the fires would be seen.

Grendel whispered, "Hurry it up. I'm going to have to gag you and bind you, so as you don't cry out for Boggin."

I whispered back, "I am not going to call out for Boggin, you moron! I am getting away from here in a minute. Turn my powers back on."

He blinked. Still in whispers, he said, "Lost your wits, is it? Mother said you might go mad, once you saw her. Didn't think it would happen before."

I whispered, "You've already lost, Glum. Lost. You are a card player? I called your bluff. You folded."

"Listen here, girl: You are my property. You're mine. I took you 'cause I wanted you, and no force under heaven can stop me. I never had nothing so fine as you. I never saw no one as fine as you. Except maybe Vanity, and I had to give her up to get that Telchine off my tail; and even her, to my thinking, ain't not so pretty as you are now. You're the only thing I have in my life."

I said quietly, "You can have my dead body. You want it? You can keep it. I'm not going to miss it once I drown."

He squinted, looking uncertain.

I said, "Or were you thinking of keeping me ashore? In the air? Boggin will find you. He'll make you cut your own penis off and eat it like a sausage. Or am I wrong about him?"

The look on his face told me I was not wrong. I had read about all the color leaving a man's face, but I never saw it happen before.

I whispered, "Do you have something else besides those fragile little mermaid caps for keeping a girl able to breathe down there? I don't think you do, or you would have used it. You wished me back to health when I was dying, and I thank you for that. But you couldn't wish air into my lungs, or you would have done it."

He stared at me, his face a little slack.

And then he grinned, a big grin, showing all his teeth. He tucked his branch under one arm, and pantomimed clapping his hands together, making the motion, but not making the noise.

"That were good," he said quietly, his eyes sparkling with admiration. "You talk a good fight. Let's see how it works out."

He flicked the branch back into his hand and struck the blunt end solidly into the bearskin, just at the point where my midriff was.

I doubled over, suddenly out of breath. He dropped the branch and caught me up in his arms, arms as tough as old tree roots. One arm wrapped around me, pinning my arms to my sides. With the thick folds of the bearskin draped over, I could not even raise my elbows.

His other hand he clapped over my mouth.

He breathed in my ear. "You're a quick one, a clever one. I like that. Lots of book-learning. Suppose to give a girl polish, book-learning. Refined. But you ain't never been one of my people. Everything we can do, we do with our feelings. The world is a big lie, and we are the biggest liars in it. And sometimes the world believes us, if we are sincere enough. Sincerity; that's the thing, the very thing. You see, I can't just stop wanting you, desiring you, needing you, just 'cause I want to. My feeling is too strong. Now you come and say your feeling that you'd rather die than be with me is stronger than my feeling to the contrary. Well, maybe you caught me in a weak moment. But I know all about feelings. I studies 'em. All my folk do. We know what makes a man go, and a man stop. Some feelings, they blaze bright enough, but they are like fire in autumn leaves, see? Poof, and they are gone. Now, you think you can keep your feeling up forever? No matter what I do? What if I was to burn off your foot, slow-like, so you'd be matched with me, eh? Then you wouldn't be so sad I couldn't go dancing with you."

He picked me up as if my weight were nothing, and hopped a one-footed hop closer to the fire. With one hand still over my mouth, and one around my arms and waist, he thrust my feet toward the fire.

I kicked and lifted my legs as high as I could, writhing beneath his arm. I could not get free; I could not bite his hand; I could barely make any noise through my nose. The bottom of the bearskin fell in the flames, and started smoking and crawling upward.

"Now, then," he whispered. "That looked bad, didn't it? Here you are all willing and ready to die, but not to get a little singed? I'll make you a promise. You stick your foot into the hot coals, and let your foot get burnt black, without flinching, without being afraid, and—hey!—I'll let you go and with my blessing. Mucius Scaevola did it. You can do it."

I did not do it. I kicked once or twice more, trying to get my legs higher up.

"Such pretty, pretty legs," he whispered. "I make it simpler. One toe. You burn off one toe without flinching or making a face, and I'll let you go. It will convince me you mean what you say. No? Come on. Even a bunny will gnaw off its legs if'n it's caught in a trap. And I ain't even asking your whole leg. Just a toe. It won't hurt after the nerves burn off; it'll smell like roast pork."

That did not make the prospect any more appealing. I gathered my every ounce of strength and strained against his arm, making a shrill noise through my nostrils. It was the same as if iron bands were wrapped around me.

He was standing on one goddamn leg, and all my kicking could not knock him over.

"Naw. Time's up. I changed my mind. Your legs are so long and fine. Trim ankles, just like a naiad." He made a little hop, and took me away from the flame. The bearskin was still smoking, and I jumped and kicked where little flecks of ash touched me.

"And besides, you can dance for me, even if I can't dance no more. Belly dancing like those houri girls do. But I'll give you one more test."

He moved his thumb less than an inch, and pinched my nostrils shut with his hand.

"Maybe I hold you this way till you pass out. Maybe I kill you dead. You don't know, do you? But I tell you what. You hold still and look real brave, and I'll know, I'll really know, you don't mind smothering to death. Maybe I'll do this over and over and over again, while you faint each time, till I am really convinced."

Wherever that feeling of calmness, that chess-match feeling, was, which had made me so sure I had all the answers, that feeling wasn't here. I really tried to hold still. But when your lungs are empty, your body starts jerking.

And you start thinking about books you started reading that you want to finish. Things you wanted to say to friends.

He hissed, "You see, it's one thing to close your eyes and jump down into a pit. It's another to take a spade and dig that pit, and lay down in it, and then pull the dirt atop you, one spadeful at a time. Plenty of time to think, when you dig your own grave. Are you going to hold still? I'll be impressed."

I rolled my eyes and looked up at him. I was ready to surrender. But now, I could not even tell him I was ready to give up.

He must have seen it. But he held his hand there, choking me.

Then he moved his thumb. Less than half an inch. That is how much space separated me from not-me. Half an inch.

And yes, I was weeping. Quentin had done so well when it was his turn to face this kind of thing.

Grendel said, "I take my hand off your mouth, if you're willing to do one little thing for me. You say, 'Thank you, sir,' when I let you talk again."

I nodded. It was Boggin and his making me count, all over again.

He took his hand away.

I said, "Thank you, sir."

"That's better."

"I'm not talking to you."

"What?"

"I see something you don't see." I was draped over his arm at the moment, remember, and my face was turned toward the sky.

He turned his head and looked up.

It was perfect timing. He could not get his hand up to save his face.

Like a thunderbolt, a huge black eagle with white-tipped feathers struck, claws like knives digging deep into his cheeks. The sharp beak rose and fell like a hammer, or rather, like a pickaxe.

Thank you, sir. Oh, thank you, whoever you are.

When the eagle's head yanked back, there was something long and bloody in his beak. A tongue?

Grendel let me fall, and he sprang back, toppling, batting at the wings that were batting at him. Reality quivered, and when the quivering stopped, Grendel was gone. In his place stood an enormous three-pawed bear. Tatters of his torn shirt fell from the bear's shoulders. There was that much concession to reality, but the fact that an extra seven hundred pounds of matter just popped into existence out of nowhere evidently did not annoy the Grendel paradigm of the universe.

The bear swept out with a paw and delivered the kind of blow that can decapitate a full-grown bull. Boom.

But the eagle, instead of collapsing into a bloody mess, bounced away and flew back in the bear's face. It thrust its beak into the white muzzle and tore a swatch of tissue out of the bear's nose.

I shrieked and winced. Very girlish. Grendel would have approved. But seeing the nose ripped off a bear, all that delicate tissue come out, is almost too gross for words.

This time the bear got his claws into the eagle, and it was time to feel sorry for the eagle. Blood and feathers flew up—I do not know from where—and another sweep of that terrible paw sent the bird rolling across the snow, leaving a swath of red drops on the white snow.

The rolling mass of feathers would have seemed funny, if this had been a cartoon. But as it was, I think it was one of the most horrible things I ever saw. No, wait. Seeing the bird flop to a standstill, and wiggle its wings, was worse. Both wings flopped. Both were broken.

Then, somehow, it was even worse again to see the eagle stretch out its neck, drive its beak through the snow to the hard soil, and jerk its neck and shoulders. It pulled itself forward an inch. Two inches. Three.

The bear, dripping bloody gore from its face, and bellowing in pain, rose up, teetering on one leg, clawing at the sky and screaming; and even the bear stopped in astonishment, and watched. Four inches. Five.

The bird kept coming. It did not give up. It wanted to keep fighting.

The bear dropped to three legs, loped in one huge rolling wave of muscles and fur over to where the eagle was crawling toward him, stepped on the bird with one huge paw. The eagle was driven down into snow. I wondered why all its hollow bones were not cracked.

The eagle craned its neck around at an impossible angle and bit the bear in the foot.

The bear had had just about enough from this eagle. Taking the eagle by the neck in its jaws, the bear lashed to the right and left, smashing the eagle's body over and over and over again into the snowy, rocky soil, until there were splatters of blood to the left and right.

I cried out, "Grendel! Don't kill him!"

My shout was loud enough to draw an echo from the Kissing Well. The voice sounded like a man's voice. ". . . don't kill him . . ." Unlike my voice, the echo was calm and soldierlike. A voice giving an order.

A second bird fell from the sky. This one was a vulture. It was more enormous than any vulture of Earth. It had black wings and a white head.

The vulture struck, driving claws like sabers into the shoulder and chest of the great bear. It drove its beak into one eye socket and pulled out the eye in a gush of blood and vitreous humor.

The bear dropped the eagle and raised its claws to defend itself, knocking the vulture away from it. In a flurry of wings like the snap of gale winds, the vulture returned.

The bear was battering the vulture, and was winning. But the eagle, still somehow alive, even with two broken wings, and while being trampled underfoot, raised his beak and his shivering claws.

The eagle clawed at the stump of the severed bear paw, and opened the seam that held it shut. At the same time, I saw something not almost too gross for words, but really too gross, even though I cheered and hurrahed at the time. The eagle drove his beak straight into . . . Well, never mind. Why don't we just say it was the upper thigh, or near there.

The bear began lumbering away. It was blinded, noseless, bleeding from jowls and groin and leg. The bear ran toward the sea cliffs with the wounded vulture in pursuit, its wings like a storm.

At the edge of the cliff, the bear tried to rise up on its one hind leg. The vulture landed on its face again. I saw the vulture tear at the bear's throat, and a splash of blood shot out. It looked like a death blow. The bear went limp but caught the vulture in its paws as it fell. They both went over. If there was a sound of a splash, I did not hear it.

Clutching the bearskin tight around me, I went closer to the wounded eagle, my bare feet sloshing through the snow. I was afraid to touch a wounded animal, but I knew this was something supernatural, something that had come to save me. Eagles were the symbols of Jove in myth. Maybe this was one of Boggin's servants?

I looked at it. It looked terrible.

What could I do? What was I supposed to do? I wasn't a veterinarian. Maybe I could move it closer to a fire, but I was afraid to try to pick it up. It had just bitten through a bear. What could it do to my little hand?

I tried to look into the fourth dimension, now that Grendel was . . . dead? In the sea? I could see the tiniest glimmer of light from my hypersphere, but then darkness closed over it again. The Grendel effect was fading, it seemed, but it seemed it might take a while to fade. How long? A minute? A day? Six months?

The wind blew by, and I shivered. Once I started shivering, I could not stop.

This will sound selfish, but suddenly I was worrying about more than just the wounded bird. Where was I going to go? How was I going to get away, if my powers did not come back on in time?

I could stand near the fire, I supposed, wrapped in the bearskin. Until the fire died out. Then what? Gather wood? Wait till Boggin found me? I was sure that a fight to the death between two supernatural birds and a shape-changing bear monster was something Erichtho's mirror or tarot cards could pick up, even if Boggin's winds hadn't heard the noise and weren't coming to investigate. I was still on the grounds of the estate.

I reached out and touched the bird gently. It flinched when I touched it, as if my hand had hit a sore spot, and the beak snapped in my direction.

The eagle seemed to have a cross expression on its features, even though it did not really have expressions.

"Sorry!" I said. "Oh, I am so sorry!"

The eagle looked at me as if I were an idiot. It had a sarcastic look.

"Is—is there anything I can do?"

The eagle dropped its head back into the snow, eyes sinking shut, too weary to continue withering me with its contempt.

"Please get better. I don't know if you are magic or anything, or if you can grant wishes, but—please get better! I'll do anything if you get better!"

One yellow eye rolled open, and the beak snapped. A hissing croak came from the throat. Was that a yes? I know that in fairy stories you are not supposed to make wishes or say things like "I'll do anything," but I didn't want the poor creature to die on my account.

I said, "Are you going to get better?"

Then the eye stopped moving; the lid drooped. It looked dead. Maybe it was just resting. But it looked dead.

The wind blew again. Cold, cold, cold.

I hopped and danced (a little dance I like to call the frostbite toe dance) over to the fires.

It was painful to get a dozen feet across the snow back to the fires. I could not even imagine trying to make the two miles or more to the village. Assuming the group would be waiting for me still at the same dock.

Think, Amelia, think. Review options. What would Victor do? Use logic. What did logic say?

Look over all raw materials. Okay. One wounded eagle. One bearskin. My wedding dress, hanging on a branch not far from the fire . . . Hm. Probably dry by now. Little glass slippers at the foot of the tree. Lots of rope on the ground, in case I wanted to tie myself up again and wait for Grendel to come back.

Wait. Rope.

Where had Grendel gotten the rope from? Or the bearskin? For that matter, where were the materials he used to start the two campfires? He might have just ripped the branches off trees with his bear claws, but then what? Any matches or anything he might have been carrying in the undersea kingdom would have been soaked through.

I remembered how Boggin had kept his man-clothes in the bell tower, where he could reach them from the air. Grendel said he visited his mother on a regular basis. Where did he keep his man-clothes? It had to be near the Kissing Well. . . .

Think, Amelia. You are standing in snow. Look at the ground.

And there they were. Bear tracks going from the well into the little stand of trees not far away, a footprint and a peg-print coming out.

I hopped over to the slippers, hoping they might have some magic to enable them to resist the cold. Well, they didn't. It was the same as being barefoot. I took the dress, too. Don't ask me why. It was still a pretty dress, sort of.

One girl in a bear rug (me) went running as fast as she could into the woods.

Here was a little shed, no bigger than a closet, with a round roof made of sod patches, buried up to its neck in the ground. You had to step down into a waist-deep pit to get at the doorflap, which was made of deerskin heavy with ice.

Inside the hut were two chests, and a circle of ash on a flat stone beneath a smokehole. Sitting in the ashes were three right boots. The place was too small to step all the way inside. I knelt, and reached in.

And there were clothes. I stole two pairs of his pants and put them on, one atop the other. I took up a shirt, but it was so scratchy and disgusting that I put on the wedding dress first. It did have some magic for repelling dirt or something, because when I put three shirts on over top, this time they did not scratch or feel greasy.

Was there anything else worth stealing? I found a heavy knife in a sheath. Girl can always use a knife when she is out walking. The boots? One was burnt through and through, but the other two were in so-so shape. They were large enough that left or right did not matter to me, and I could slip my feet into them, glass slippers and all.

Anything that might help the wounded bird? One chest had a compartment with some white handkerchiefs in it. I wondered why Grendel would carry gentlemen's pocket handkerchiefs. He did not seem the type to use so many.

Oh. I should have recognized them. Except I knew them better by taste, not by sight. Handkerchiefs? Not quite. This was what he used to gag his prospective brides with.

I pulled out a handful. Maybe I could bind up the bird's wounds with them.

Beneath the hankies was a book: Hesiod's *Theogony.*

That brought tears to my eyes. I know Grendel was an enemy, and a rapist, and he was going to kill me, and torture me, and . . . and . . .

And I felt sorry for his mother. There would be another pile of bones out back.

When I got back out to the bird, it was sitting up, preening. The wings seemed better. They did not look broken. Every time it drove its beak through the layer of bloody feathers, more red drops fell to the snow, leaving the wing clean and unwounded.

I crept closer. It did not smell like blood. It was a smell I knew. I had smelled it every day in my life. All students did.

I put my hand to the snow, touched a drop, raised it to my nose, touched it to my tongue.

Ink? It was red ink.

Wait a minute. Who had just been saying that wounds were nothing but red ink . . . ? And the vulture. I knew who sent the vulture. Lord Mavors. It was part of his curse. Whoever threatened to kill one of us would die. And the vulture . . .

The vulture had not been coming to save me. Grendel had no intention of killing me. The vulture had been coming to save . . .

I looked at the eagle.

"Colin . . . ? Is that you . . . ?"

12

NORTH BY NORTHWEST

1.

I walked south, parallel to the sea cliffs, my feet wiggling a bit inside Grendel's big boots. Snow whitened the ragged boots and the burnt hem of the bearskin. I wore the bearskin over my head like an Indian squaw in a blanket. My hair was still wet, and it hung in icy snarls down my back.

I had lost my leather aviatrix cap somewhere along the way. It was true that I also had lost my shoes and underwear and clothes and every other worldly possession. But I missed my cap.

At first, I walked with the eagle held close to my chest, with a flap of the bearskin over him, trying to warm his cold feathers with my body heat. His wounds were mostly healed, but not all. I do not know why the turn-the-blood-to-red-ink trick worked on some wounds and not on others.

For that matter, if Colin could cure two broken wings, why was Grendel unable to wish his severed leg back on? Surely there was no desire stronger or more profound than that of a one-legged man to get his foot back. I wondered if Boggin had interfered with Grendel's wishing-ability in some way.

There was still blood seeping from his feathers, but I did not see any red spurts, as you would get if a major artery were pierced. I kept him wrapped in a handkerchief, until it got brown; then I would change bandages by throwing that hankie away, and wrapping another one around the shivering bird.

For the first mile, I had talked with the bird, trying to get him to clack his beak to count out numbers, or respond to signals, or do something to demonstrate that he was something smarter than a bird. Maybe he was too sick and cold to try to communicate. Maybe it wasn't Colin at all. I didn't know.

My ability to fret was eroding. I was still grateful to the bird, even though the idea that it was not Colin grew on me. I did not drop the creature in the snow, but I stopped thinking of him as my wounded comrade-in-arms. I held him to my chest under Grendel's shirts, so that his head was under my chin, his beak peeking out from my collar, yellow eyes peering at the pathless path ahead.

2.

After the first mile, I was too cold and weary to keep trying to talk. I just gritted my teeth and trudged. Little white clouds puffed from my lips; sogginess sloshed in my boots. Every hundred paces, I would try to look into the fourth dimension. The light from the hypersphere was a distant ember, then a dull spark, then a not-so-dull flicker. It was still too dim and far-off to see with; my hyper-body and higher senses were blind and numb still; but the fact that Grendel's curse seemed to be wearing off comforted me.

And I admit, I had to use one of the handkerchiefs to wipe away tears that, to my surprise, I kept finding on my cheeks. By rights, I should have cheered when Grendel got his throat ripped out and fell to his death. He had boasted about murdering people and "biting ears off," and I suspected I was not the first virgin girl he had dragged down to his lair for a quick wedding and a brief life as a sex toy.

I could not even think of another person so horrible as Grendel had been, except maybe for some of the oriental tyrants described in Herodotus, or Torquemada, or Adolf Hitler or something.

Those sailors he killed had wives and sweethearts and children back home. No doubt, they had stared out windows at the gray sea on cold nights, wondering; and no doubt, years passed, and no news ever came of the boyfriends, husbands, and fathers who had been the central pillars of their lives.

But pity is not something that fits in an either–or matrix. Just because I felt sorry for his victims did not mean I was not also sorry for him.

It would have been simpler if I could have just hated him and laughed when he died, or made some cruel wisecrack, like a good British spy in the movies when he pushes the bad Chinese spy into a nuclear reactor coolant tank. ("Have a nice *trip*, Grendel! See you next *fall*! Har, har, har!")

When I was young, I thought the act of getting older meant, year by year, getting more sophisticated, more hard, cool, and unpitying. Less innocent.

Maybe that was a childish idea of what getting older was about. Maybe adults, mature adults, get more innocent with time, not less. Because the word "innocent" does not mean "naïve," it means "not guilty."

Children do small evils to each other, schoolyard fights and insults, not because their hearts are pure, but because their powers are small. Grown-ups have more power. Some of them do great evils with that power. But what about the ones who don't? Aren't they more innocent than children, not less?

So I trudged in the snow, weeping slow tears for a dead monster who had wanted to marry me, and wishing I were like a child, cruel and unpitying, again.

3.

I topped the rise. Below me was a narrow slope of hill, then the brink of the upper cliffs, the ragged limestone juts of lower and lesser cliffs, and the inlet, where the docks of Abertwyi are. The village curves around the mouth of the inlet, separated by a low stone retaining wall from the water. Across the water could be seen the looming silhouette of Worm's Head, a steep-sided island, which rises sheer from the waves.

On the slopes north of the village, climbing up toward my vantage point, were derricks and ropes used by stone miners. To the south was the fish cannery that had made the Lilac family rich. On a hill in the middle of the village were the church and the courthouse, and to the east were the tenant estates of some of the influential local families, the Penrice and Mansel Halls. To the northeast was the extension of the highway, easily visible through the nude trees of wintertime, a marching line of telephone poles and power lines to either side . . .

Except it was not there.

Gone. Vanished.

The physical features were the same. There was the inlet, the cliffs of limestone, and, across the water, the brooding rock of Worm's Head.

There was a village there. It looked enough like Abertwyi that a moment passed before I noticed how small it was. During the day, it is hard to tell whether a town has suffered a power blackout, but after a moment, I noticed no lights were burning anywhere.

The fish cannery was gone. The highway was gone. There were no power lines or telephone poles. The streets were narrower, unpaved, and there were no signal lamps. There was no traffic. On the slopes closer to me, there were a few crudely made wooden derricks, and only a small part of the cliff had been mined for limestone. At the mouth of one of the cuttings, I saw, not a diesel engine, but a steam engine from a museum, next to a coal bin. Both were coated with snow and ice at the moment, white and motionless.

The boats. Nothing seemed that different about them, except that there were far more, even though the docks were fewer. Then I noticed the lack of motorboats. Then I saw the side-wheeler, with a crooked black smokestack above it.

I tried to look into the fourth dimension again. For a moment, I got a clearer view, then a dimmer, and I could see the utility and inner nature of the things around me. The moment I looked, a strand of the morality substance touching me jerked rigidly, and glittered as some energy or signal passed along it.

That jerk frightened me; it looked too much like a trip wire being sprung. I closed my eyes tightly for a moment. When I opened them again, the fourth dimension was dim again, my hypersphere only a candle flame, illuminating nothing.

I admit I was scared. It is much easier to be scared when you are cold, tired, and footsore. And hungry. When was the last time I had eaten? Holiday pie and hors d'oeuvres at Lily Lilac's house, I think.

Why had my upper senses failed just now? Maybe I had strained them by trying too hard. Maybe fear hindered their operation. Maybe it was part of a trap, or an attack. Or . . .

I said aloud, "Colin, this is creeping me out. What was your motto: 'When in doubt, bug out'?"

Time to run away.

4.

I turned east and began to jog. In ten minutes, I had trees around me. By fifteen minutes, I was getting tired and beginning to wonder what time it was. Near noon? In the afternoon? Where was I going to sleep tonight?

Twenty minutes, and I came to a break in the trees.

And there was the highway. I walked across the empty lanes, staring left and right in wonder.

Power lines were dripping with icicles like Christmas ornaments. The telephone poles stood as stiff, regular, and proper as Beefeater guards before the palace of the Queen, with no expression to show that they had been gone from their posts when I last looked for them, half an hour ago.

One lane of the highway was paved in black slush and puddles of blue-gray water. In the distance there came one truck on the road, rolling cautiously down the lane, little wings of filthy water dashing from its tires as it came.

I put up my thumb. I cannot recall if they ever taught me not to hitchhike at school. Maybe they thought I would never leave the estate. But, unless the guy driving the truck was Grendel Glum's twin brother, I thought I would be in less danger than I had been anytime that morning.

I danced back to avoid getting sloshed, tripped on the snow, and landed on my bottom by the roadside, my bearskin flopping open, my hair tangles spilling every which way. My bird flapped and shrieked in annoyance, a high-pitched whine like a steam whistle, cold and lonely.

And shockingly loud. No ghost, no banshee could utter a wail as penetrating as a prince of chaos, trapped in the form of a brainless, blood-stained bird, lost in the snow.

The truck went on by. I understand it is customary in these situations to make rude finger-gestures in the rearview mirrors. I was too well brought up. I stood up, bird in one hand, and tried to shake the snow off my bearskin with the other.

Maybe the bearskin flapping did it. The truck slowed, stopped. Its reverse lights came on, and it backed up. It made a little *beep-beep* noise as it came.

A man leaned from the driver's side and pushed open the passenger's door. He was a rough-looking fellow in a gray knit cap and a heavy woolen sweater. He had a pipe in his teeth, and the cab of the truck was thick and wet with pipe smoke. I stared in disbelief. Who smoked a pipe in a cab without opening a window?

He had a thick Cornish accent when he spoke. "Merry Christmas, little lady. What might yew be doing out in the wet, on a day like this day?"

"You would not believe me," I said.

"Oh, I hear a lot of things."

"Today was supposed to be my wedding day and someone stole all my clothes, and I'm lost, and I was supposed to meet some friends at the docks in the village, but that was this morning, and they may have left. . . ."

He looked at my face, which was probably all tearstained and red-eyed; at my clothes, which obviously were not mine; and at my bird, which was wrapped in a bloodstained handkerchief. The collar or choker made of green glass was still around my neck, and the matching bracelets shimmered and twinkled on my wrists. Maybe he thought they were real jewelry.

The pipe, as if by itself, slid from one corner of his mouth to the other. He pushed the door wider. "Get in. I can give yew a ride to the dock. 'Tis nought but five minutes awa'."

I climbed in gratefully. The cab was so high that I had to climb a little ladder thing set along the wheel guard.

It was hot to the point of stifling in the cab, and I coughed on the smoke.

He reached across me to grab the handle and rolled down my window. I must have had a worse morning than I thought, because when he reached out his arm, I fully expected him to grab me and tie me to the seat, or something.

He leaned back, giving me a cocked eye. "Jumpy, are we, missy? Yew've had a bad time, no doubt." He pronounced it *doowt*.

I said, "I can't believe you believe my story."

He shrugged. "Yew dinnae know me. Why would y' lie? If yew are to lie, why not say something like to be believed, such as yer car broke down? Or that yer a traveling bird salesman who carries a big black bearskin rug

around on her head? Besides, it's Christmas Day, it is. So I'll pretend to believe yer tale, and yull pretend yew fooled me, and 'twill be our little Christmas gifties to each other, hnn? 'Tis a day of faith, ye know."

The truck trundled over the rise and came down again into the village.
The lanes narrowed, and he began maneuvering the massive lorry down
crooked little cobblestone streets to the dock area.

I looked in relief at the red and green traffic lights.

I said, "Ever had one of those days where you are not sure what year
you are in?"

He grunted. "Every Saturday morning, if my Friday night goes as big as
planned. If I remember not a thing, I know I had a real damn fine good
time."

Then he extended one big hand in my direction, not taking his eyes
from the lanes. "Name's Sam."

"I am Miss Windrose." I shifted the eagle to one hand and took his
handshake gingerly.

"Howdjadoo." (He pronounced it as one word.) "Yer thinking 'tis un-
chancy that there is no one about?" ("aboowt") "They're all at church.
Driving on holy days . . ." (This was two words) ". . . 'tis always quiet and
graveyardlike, hn? But they give me triple wages, any hauling I do today.
How's that for a life? But I won't tell you my base wage, either. It's a pretty
penny, too. We got the whole country by the throat, and they pay what we
say. It's grand."

I looked at him sidelong. There he sat, working his clutch and gearshift
with unselfconscious grace, puffing away like six chimneys, half-hidden in
clouds of tobacco, boasting of the highway robbery he enjoyed. Was this
what real human beings were like?

I said, "What would you do if you had magic powers?"

"Hn? Join the circus, I guess. Do tricks."

"No, I mean real magic powers. If you could grant wishes . . . ?"

"Travel the countryside on holy days, disguised as a beautiful motion
picture star in baggy clothes, wearing a rug and carrying a bird. Then I
would ask folks strange questions. What would you do, missy?"

"I'm serious!"

"Of course you are. Anyone who carries around a hawk covered with
blood on her wedding day is serious."

He slowed the truck, stopped, engaged the brake. We were on Water-side Street. I could see the boardwalk and the piers. Empty. I could see the slip where Lily Lilac's boat used to be. Empty.

5.

Sam was looking at my face. He said, "You need some food in you?"

I stirred. I said, "What . . . ?"

He pointed at a little shop across the way. "I always eat there. The owner is a Hindoo, and he is only closed on Hindoo holy days. Ramandan, or something."

"Ramadan is Islam," I said.

"Well, whatever may be. He's open now, and the first cup of coffee is always free."

"I don't have any money," I said.

"I'd throw it back in yer face if yew did. Christmas gift. Coming?" And he opened his door and began striking his pipe against his boot to throw hot ashes out into the snow.

Not five minutes later we were both eating potato bread and butter pancakes and breakfast ham; not what I expected a Hindu to serve. (I had never seen pancakes before; I thought only Americans ate them.) Of course, the place was called "Jerry's Fine Café," and Jerry (whose name was probably Ramarjuna or Sajeeve) was a dark-skinned man who came out and exchanged pleasantries with Sam.

Jerry looked disapprovingly at my eagle, but Sam told him it was my Seeing Eye bird, and the law required shop owners to allow it on the premises. Sam and I were the only customers in the place, so Jerry let the matter rest.

I leaned and whispered, "Is it okay to take these boots off? My feet are all wet and sore."

Sam leaned and whispered back, "Go on. Jerry comes back, I'll tell him yer Japanese."

He stared, not without curiosity, at my beaded slippers, glittering with translucent green beads and lines of crystal. I dried my feet off with a paper napkin, and put my feet back into the slippers, but left the boots on the seat of the chair next to me.

"Yew need something warm in you," he said.

I sipped my first ever cup of coffee. Bleh. Did people actually drink this stuff?

We ate without speaking for a time. I was very hungry.

Then, with no preamble, Sam pointed at me with a fork, which had a piece of pancake on it, dripping syrup. "I been thinking! Here are my wishes. First, I got a nephew who's wrong in the head. They have him in this place near Edgestow. He's fifteen, but he thinks he's five. Bright, for a five-year-old, but . . . Well, I'd wish his head back straight. I'd wish my wife, second wife, be up in heaven with the angels. She died of tuberculosis, oh, four years back. About this time of year. First wife, I'd wish her straight to hell, her and her lawyers, too. That's three. Course, Annie probably didn't need any help from me getting to heaven, so let me change my second wish to curing everyone who's got tuberculosis. Filthy disease. Aside from that, I don't have much I need. Wouldn't wish for money, though. Ruins people. How 'bout yew?"

"Well, I actually have magic powers, and I am trying to decide how to use them."

"Hn. Use 'em for good rather than for evil, I'd say. Create world peace, that'd be a good one. So they let yew out of the institution on Christmas, do they? I don't suppose yew know my nephew. Mortie Finklestein."

I goggled at him. "Your name is Finklestein?"

"My sis, she married a Jew. What's so bad about that! Is it a crime to marry out of the faith? Benjamin Disraeli was a Jew, and he was the finest PM this island ever had, says I, bar none. Einstein was a Jew and smartest man ever lived, wasn't he?" He waved the bit of pancake to make his point, and chomped into it aggressively.

He poured himself another cup of coffee, and poured some more in my cup, even though I didn't ask. I felt I had to try another sip, since he had poured for me. I stirred in five little plastic containers of cream, to make it as white as possible, and endless spoonfuls of sugar. Bleh. Who invented this stuff?

I looked at him, and said in an accusing voice, "You stopped because you saw my hair, didn't you? Had I been a man, you would have kept going."

Now it was his turn to goggle at me. "What? Yew think it rude to be polite?"

"Maybe I don't like being condescended to."

"Well, hn! When yoor done eating up, I can give yer a lift back and putcha in the snow, if yew like." He snorted and laughed, pleased at his own wit.

Then he put his fork down and pointed his finger toward my face, very rudely, I thought: "Lookee here, life is more cruel to women than it is to men, and there is no use saying it's not! Here yew are, a woman stood up at the altar, or one who says she is, and yoor telling me women and men got dealt the same hand of cards?"

I felt I had to stand up for my sex: "The equality between men and women requires that they be treated the same."

"Yeah? Well, I don't know what kind of men you know, but the ones I know always feel a little hurt when yew give 'em a hand. Y'know? I'm not saying it's right or wrong, I'm just saying women make it easier for yew to help them. And being pretty as a Sunday morning doesn't hurt matters either.

"Besides, no girl ever tried to hijack my load. You think it don't happen, but it does. In Liverpool, I was once.

"But, listen here! Don't turn down help when someone reaches out his hand, hn? It's the only thing that keeps human beings alive on the Earth, and I am right about that!"

He picked up his fork and stabbed it back into the pile of pancakes. He chewed for a moment, and then spoke with his mouth full, mumbling. I had never seen someone talk with food in their mouth before, and I stared in amazement. But I suppose there was no Mrs. Wren in his life to slap him with a ruler for bad table manners.

This is what he said: "Little missy, I stopped when yew fell, cause I hear'd a cry, a high cry, and I thought yew were holding a baby in yoor arms. And yew fell down."

He swallowed a bit; then he continued: "Maybe I shouldna stopped for a woman with a baby on Christmas Day, issat what yew think? But I hear'd the cry and I stopped. Didn't expect it was yer pet screeching."

We ate in silence for a while. I felt a bit like a wretch. This man was the only person who had rescued me with whom I had argued. (How many times had I been rescued . . . ? Just the Grendel menace: once by Boggin, once by Telegonus, once by the eagle . . . was there one I had forgotten? Romus had rescued me from Erichtho . . .)

I started to apologize, but he waved my words away, and changed the subject. Sam said, "What can yew do with your magic powers? Talk to the departed, tip tables, tell fortunes, that sort of thing?"

I said, "Well, maybe I can show you . . ."

I looked into the fourth dimension again. I saw two things at once. The rooms of the little restaurant were laid out like a blueprint. I could see Jerry in the back room. He was on the telephone, saying, "Yes, Constable, I am not very likely to be mistaken! It is one of the five strange children from the Branshead estate. How is it possible I could not know one of them? The ones who never get any older . . ."

At the same time, I saw the moral strand running to me jerk, and flicker with light. This time, I used one of the other senses to look at the first sense, and sought its internal nature. Magic. I was seeing a magic spell. A finding spell.

I jumped to my feet. I pulled and pushed on the higher parts of my body, but it was mostly still numb. I could not deploy my wings or move into hyperspace.

Sam dropped his fork. "Um. Don't get excited. . . . Is, ah, is everything . . . ?"

"Sam!" I leaned across the table and kissed him.

He looked, at once, startled, pleased, surprised, and worried. "Hold on . . ."

"Thanks for saving me! You're my second rescuer today, fourth one this week. I must run. I have enemies. Bad, bad people. Actually, um, gods. Old gods from the pagan days. They are beyond your strength. Don't follow me!"

I stepped toward the door and he grabbed at my arm. My "pet bird" snapped at his fingers with the razor-edged bolt-cutters of his beak, but I yanked the bird back with one hand before he drew blood. The snapping bird made Sam flinch, and I was away.

Even had Sam been faster than me in the sprint (which I doubt), he was not faster than me in the steeplechase. I leaped from table to table in a straight line toward the door, and cleared one or two chairs in my way with a good takeoff, slightly wobbly landing. I lost the bearskin rug behind me during one jump.

The little bell tinkled, and I was out the door.

On the street, Waterside Street. Still deserted. Maybe everyone was at church; I could hear bells tolling solemnly in the distance. Which way? Would any direction do? Away from the docks, though: I might have to come back here, and it would not do to lead any pursuit that direction.

I turned and sprinted up Main Street, which was more or less straight, heading toward the hill where the church and the courthouse were. I tucked the bird under my arm like a ball.

And Sam came pounding down the street after me. He still had a napkin tucked in his collar, and was carrying a fork in one fist. He had left his coat behind. His form was not bad, for an old guy. Maybe he did rugby when he was younger.

Up the street. About one hundred yards ahead of me was a carriage circle, with a circle of grass in the middle, and a pillar bearing the names of local townsmen who died in the Great War. They had put a statue of an angel up recently; at least I did not remember seeing it there before, tall atop the pillar. They had painted it for Christmas, blue and white. I was still at least a quarter mile from the church . . .

Wait a minute. Why was I going toward the church? If that was where all the townspeople were, (*a*) I might be putting them in danger, (*b*) they might call the coppers on me, just as Jerry had done. This was the worst direction of all to be going.

I stopped at the carriage circle, blowing puffs of white and looking left and right. There were lanes running north and south.

The angel on the pillar turned its head, spread its peacock-blue wings, raised his bow. There was an arrow in the string.

"Phaethusa, Helion's daughter, I make it fated that you will be struck by this shaft if you do not surrender to me. I am Corus. I am the North by Northwest Wind, a humble god, perhaps, for only one-sixteenth part of the infinite sky is mine; but I am great enough to wound you."

I stood with one hand on my knee, bird in the other, blowing white puffs. I shook my head. "No. No, thanks. I'm sick and tired of surrendering."

He said, "Do you toy with me, Chaoticist?"

"Lord Mavors said you can't kill us! How are you going to stop me if you don't risk killing me!"

"I make it fated that you shall not die when my arrow strikes. With such a fate, I may strike your eye with no fear the shaft will enter your brainpan, or hit your thigh, hand, bosom, marring and maiming, as I will."

I straightened up, and held up the wounded eagle in both hands. "Look out! I've got a magic bird . . . this bird will save me! And I am not a monster or anything. I'm just a girl with a monster's powers, and I've never done anything wrong, so I don't want you to shoot me."

Sam came trotting into the carriage circle, slowed down, and walked up. His mouth and eyes were wide. "Hey! Are yew an angel? Don't point that thing at the girl here. She's touched in the head!"

Corus said, "Creature of Prometheus, go, and I will spare you. I make it fated that when you wake after you have slept, this will fade like a strange dream. If you speak of it this day, you will not be believed, even by those that love you . . ."

"Is my wife up there with yew all? Second wife, Annie, I mean . . ."

"Go!"

He turned the arrow toward Sam.

Sam set his jaw and looked stubborn.

I said, "Um, Sam, maybe you should . . ."

The bowstring sang.

I jumped in front of Sam and threw out my arms. The eagle, released, flapped and jumped in front of me. The eagle moved faster than was possible, as if it were trying to bat the speeding arrow out of midair with its wing. The arrow passed through the one wing, lost all velocity, turned sideways, and slapped against me before it clattered to the pavement.

The eagle screamed, loud, shrill, and piercing. There was an answering scream from far away. I am not an expert on bird screams, but I am pretty sure that second scream was one I had heard earlier today.

The eagle flapped to the ground and began poking at its newly re-wounded wing.

Corus looked down, frowning. Then he put his foot to the bowstaff, bent, and unstrung his bow. "I release you," he said.

"What?" Had I heard that right?

Corus spoke quietly, his eyes downcast, "Little softhearted girl with the powers of a monster, who steps in front of our cattle, the frail and foolish mortal men, go and be free. On one condition, I release you."

"What's the condition?"

"That you tell no one of my dereliction."

"I want to be able to tell my friends."

"Only on their oath likewise, not to reveal this act."

"Won't Boggin just hear what you are saying now? He can hear the wind."

"I am the wind."

"I will agree. . . . But! But I have one condition . . ."

That made him smile. He put his hands atop the bowstaff and leaned on it. "You are just as bold as brass, aren't you, little foe of all creation?"

"You have to tell me why. Why you are doing it?"

Corus frowned again.

Sam pointed upward with his fork, and said to me, "Yew know him, do yew?"

Corus glowered at Sam and waved his hand. "I make it fated that you will sleep before I speak this word."

Sam sat down on the cobblestones, blinked, slumped slowly over, snoring. His fork clattered to the pavement with a tiny tinkle.

"You didn't hurt him, did you? Is he going to be all right?"

The eagle twisted around its head and squawked at me angrily. Well, maybe the bird had a point. He had been hit with an arrow, and I was fretting over a sleeping guy. I picked up the bird and brought out another handkerchief to wrap around him.

There was another small tinkling noise when I did that, and something bright lay on the pavement. I put one slippered foot casually atop it.

Corus said, "I do not prey on the cattle of Mulciber. This world is his. I make it fated that this man shall be found by kind strangers, who will see to his care. I accept your final condition, O monster who pities even such low creatures as this man. Here is my reason: Thelxiepia begged me, that if by chance I were the first one to find you, that I be slow to carry out my duties. She is the finest, most beautiful, and most ill-used of women. I wanted to use the bounty Boreas placed on your head to buy her freedom, and I did not hear her plea, although my heart was torn. She said you would not destroy the world, and I did not believe she knew whereof she spoke. Now I know that she is also wise, and kind, and good . . ."

I said, "Oh my gosh! You are the one! At the party! You and Miss Daw. The Lady said someone was going to fall in love at that party! True love! She said it would be true love."

His grin was like the summer sun breaking through clouds, and his face lit up with happiness and embarrassment. He turned his head away, and put his hand on his mouth to still his involuntary smile.

Corus spoke again without turning his head. "I have fulfilled my condition, and now I lay my fate upon you: should my Brother or any who might tell him of my treason to him, learn of it from you, your suffering and pain will be greater than mine, and last nine times the span of time."

He turned his back to me and spread his wings. "Your companions, who also seek you, await you in the harbor. Warn them that each time Nausicaa calls her silvery ship, or bids it sail, Mestor's lodestone is drawn.

"Do not mistake this act of mine for kindness. You and your kin I hold in hatred and contempt, for your life is the death of the earth and sky; and you wounded my great brother Boreas, who now lies in his sickbed, caught in dreams with no waking, for he is under attack by Morpheus the Lord of Night."

I said softly, "I am sorry for that. I like Boreas, even though he was so mean to me."

He did not turn his head, but he snorted. Perhaps he was amused at the idea of the softhearted monster, as he called me. He said in a gentler tone: "And do not envy me my true love. The Lady Cyprian did not warn me how it would stain my honor, sever my kinship, and make all my roads as hard as iron swords to cross. Yet I regret nothing."

And he stepped from the pillar and rose into the sky.

When he was gone, I moved my slipper and looked down.

The ring of Gyges lay under my toe.

13

FREEDOM AND FLIGHT

1.

The church bells rang again, and down the street, the tall doors opened. A little crowd began to form on the stairs of the church, little figures in the distance in their best formal clothes.

I trusted the "fate" Corus had put upon Sam, that someone would find and help him. I would have called out, but I feared they would call the police on me.

Bird in hand, I walked quickly down Main Street. No one was following. When the slope cut off the view of the church behind me, I ran.

I had the ring in my fist as I ran, but I was too wary of the unknown to put it on my finger.

How had it come to be in my pocket? At a guess, when Grendel came out of the Kissing Well with me freezing to death in his arms, he stepped over to his little buried shed, saw it was too small to get me inside, but grabbed up his cloak and fire-making tools. And took the time to take off the ring, wrap it in a hankie, and put it in his trunk? Maybe. He had that trunk open because he was getting a gag out for yours truly; he was terrified that I would make a noise and call down the vengeance of Boreas on his head.

But the fact that I had it, seemed like a coincidence. From Corus, it was clear that arranging coincidences was the especial province of the Olympians. But why? Maybe it had a tracking device in it, or the magical equivalent to one. Even so, several clues implied the Olympian power could only work on someone who broke a law, went back on a promise, or was indebted. I had not stolen this ring. Did that make it safe to use?

I came out onto Waterside Street.

I heard Vanity's voice before I saw them, a cheery voice ringing with relief and joy: "Oh! Look! It worked! There she is!"

I turned my head, and there they were. Quentin had his huge black cape on over his school uniform, a staff of white wood in his hand; Victor was wearing a brand-new buff-colored jacket that fell to his knees, with a chain-mail jerkin dangling and clinking underneath; Vanity was dressed in a plush red winter coat with white mink fur trim about the hood and wrists, with matching gloves, with little black booties below. It was an outfit I had never seen before. She looked like a glamour model doing a "Santa's little elf" theme.

I ran up and threw my arms—one arm, anyway—around the smiling Vanity and gave her the biggest hug circumstances allowed. She flinched and giggled when the huge bird of prey fluttered his wings across her head.

We were standing, of all places, right in front of Jerry's Fine Café. Victor had his back to me and was helping a police constable sit down on the bench that was there. A second police constable was already seated, slumped over the bench arm, ear on his shoulder, eyes closed and mouth open. There was a teardrop of drool dangling from his lip. I would have thought he was dead, but dead men don't snore so loudly.

Quentin's eyes were also closed. He had his left hand held out at shoulder level, with rosary beads twined through his fingers. A cross was hanging from it, like the bob of a pendulum. The pendulum was not swinging. The rosary was motionless, suspended at the apex of its arc or swing, and the cross was pointed at me.

Quentin relaxed and muttered, *"Ave et vale. Abi!"* Whereupon, the rosary in his hand also relaxed. He opened his eyes, casually looping the rosary around his hand to tuck it into an inner pocket, and he said, "I was looking for Colin, that time."

I said, "I sensed someone looking for me. Was that you?" And without waiting for an answer, I held up the bird. "This is Colin, I think."

Vanity stepped away and blinked at the bloody eagle. "Colin was taller, last time I saw him, wasn't he?"

Quentin said, "Found this on the bed of the sea, when I was dowsing for you. Like attracts to like. You wouldn't believe how often Victor went diving for you."

He handed me my lucky cap.

I was angry with Victor, of course.

If he had been thoughtful enough to be the one to return my aviatrix cap to me, I would have had the perfect excuse to kiss him. But he didn't. How rude.

Victor straightened up. "I have stimulated the narcoleptic reflex in their brains, but they are not actually asleep. That would require brainwave alterations to delta states, which are controlled by more complex sections of the medulla oblongata. In the meanwhile, they can hear us, so we should not discuss anything in front of them we do not want the enemy to know."

I said, "The gods erase the memories of people who learn about them; it just happened to a guy who helped me. Funny guy, real nice to me. Thelxiepia told me gods kill people who find out too much."

Victor nodded, looking entirely unsurprised by this news, and said to the sleeping policemen: "Your planet is being secretly controlled by a group of entities who need or enjoy the admiration and worship of human beings. They control a highly advanced technology which can affect thought processes. If you reveal what you have overheard to anyone, you run the risk of being destroyed by them. Nevertheless, you may wish to take that risk in order to organize a resistance to them, if you find that their rulership is unacceptable to you."

To me, Victor said, "Let us go back before more people come. These officers were sent for you."

I said, "Back?"

He pointed.

Out in the harbor was the silvery ship. She rested on the waves, bright as a naked sword blade, slim as a swan. The eyes to either side of the prow did not seem as blind as painted eyes should be; the long bronze ram extending sloping into the waterline gave the ship a friendly, almost comical look, like the nose of Cyrano. There was a crystal lantern shining (pale as the moon seen by day) on the mast, but no sails.

There was something so odd and so dreamlike about the silvery ship, that I looked again with my upper senses. The ship was not actually floating on the waters of Earth, not fully. The waters below her keel were an ocean that extended in another direction, becoming ever more mystical, haunting, and phantasmagorical in the distance. The two oceans overlapped when the silver ship met the sea, so that she was actually afloat in the ocean of dream, but her deck was exposed to the airs of Earth.

Quentin took the bird gently from my hand and frowned at him, scratching his head gently and muttering over him.

We all started to walk toward the pier. I put one hand through Victor's arm, and Vanity took my other hand. Quentin walked behind, stroking the bird.

The boardwalk boomed under our footsteps. Vanity said, "So this is a new look for you, isn't it, Amelia? The sort of grungy, baggy, two-pairs-of-pants look?"

"Look who is talking! Where did you get those clothes?"

"Paris. We sailed up the Seine. Humans can't see *Argent Nautilus*. That's her name. We spent some of the money you got us."

I felt as if I had been kicked in the stomach. "You went—to France—? Without me? You went shopping! In another country! In Paris! And I missed it!"

It was one of the worst moments of my life. Imagine if your friends got married, had a party, went to Alpha Centauri, discovered an alien civilization, and got to name all the planets in the new solar system with new names, but they did not invite you. You were off being burnt and choked by a one-legged sex maniac. The boat sailed without me. One of the worst moments of my life.

Vanity said, "I would have invited you, but you were drowned by Grendel."

Victor said calmly, "They were buying scuba gear to help me look for you. Vanity's boat ignores distance considerations. Timewise, Paris was just as close as Oxwich Green or Swansea."

"I am not blaming you—I'd like to, but I'm not. Oh! Before I forget! Her boat is detectable. Each time she calls her or sails her, Mestor's lodestone points at it."

Victor said, "We already have a plan for that. We are going to have the *Argent Nautilus* tow Lily's motorboat into the sea lanes somewhere near Australia or America, or some other English-speaking country, and then lead them away on a goose chase. We'll flag down a passing ship and say we're lost at sea."

"You really went and bought clothes without me . . . ?"

Vanity said, "Victor took his drug. Quentin read his book. I waved the necklace around my head and shouted at it, but nothing happened. We all looked at the card."

The second most horrible moment in my life. My friends were doing experiments, fascinating scientific experiments, and getting new super-powers, all without me!

I said, "A vulture swooped from the sky and killed Grendel. Tore out his throat and he fell off a cliff! I felt bad about it before, but now I feel like celebrating. Did you guys buy any champagne? That's what made me think this was Colin; the curse of Mavors is protecting him."

Vanity said, "Why would we buy champagne? We were outfitting a rescue expedition!"

"You bought new clothes, didn't you?" I admit I was green with envy. After a whole life of school uniforms, I could not even imagine choosing your own clothes. From a store! With your own money! Not asking anyone's permission!

Vanity said, "We got some for you, too."

Quentin said, "Are you sure this is Colin . . . ? He is not reacting to my charms."

"Oh!" I said, "And I've got this! Grendel dropped it."

And I pulled out the ring.

Vanity looked impressed; Quentin whistled. Victor said only, "Is there a way to tell if it is booby-trapped, or carries a location signal?"

2.

The *Argent Nautilus* breasted the waves as swiftly as an arrow flies. The waters under her keel, however, were unruffled. The passage was silent, with only the most graceful of sea-motions to impart a sense of travel, mystery, and delight to the sailor. The winds of the world we passed through were surely supersonic, but only a stiff sea breeze, a token of that wind, passed within the rail of the ship, enough to bring a brisk chill, not enough to blind or stun us. Magic. It was the way folks sail in dreams of flight, faster than was reasonable, without seasickness or strenuous effort.

I stood at the stern, watching the island of Worm's Head sink away behind us. I had never seen the far side of that rock before, though I had seen its hither face many times. It was like seeing the dark side of the moon, or the strange constellations of the antipodes.

Victor was standing next to me, also looking astern, concentrating.

I stepped close to him, till my shoulder almost touched his. He did not seem to notice. I told myself that his task must have absorbed his concentration.

Astern of us, bouncing and sending up wild spray, like a drunken water-skier, was Lily's motorboat, which we towed on the end of a long rope. The motorboat was in water that retained the properties of Earthly water, mass, resistance, and so on, and so the boat made noise, a great deal of noise, as it was yanked through the water at blinding speed. As fast as the speed of sound? I could not estimate. But the poor motorboat was leaping from wave crest to wave crest in sheets of exploding foam, and it spent half the time in the air, tumbling and careening.

It was Victor who was keeping the motorboat from capsizing, using magnetic force-beams to try to stabilize the worst of the turbulence.

Vanity was seated on the bench, facing forward, smiling into the sun, which was now declining into the afternoon. This bench was of ivory, curiously carved, and fair to the eye. I stood next to it. The bench was fixed to the deck in the place where a steersman would sit on a boat that had a steering board. Quentin was seated at her feet, drawing circles on the deck in chalk around the bored-looking eagle.

Quentin was looking fretful.

The eagle was looking (you guessed it) bored.

3.

The first thing I wanted to know was how much money was left. It looked to me as if Vanity and the others had bought several department stores' worth of material. The boys had bought Aqua Lungs and fish-spears, camping equipment, food, chemicals. Victor had bought half a dozen textbooks on advanced neurological psychology, which he (before injecting himself) had memorized, flipping pages as quickly as he could, and then thrown aside.

Quentin had bought a knapsack full of crystals and rune-stones and candles and other litter from a fortune-teller's shop. Quentin commented that he now knew not to be a fool when he shopped: none of the things he bought did what the fortune-teller said, and they were made of impure substances. None of it worked; none of it was real magic.

Apparently the amount of money ap Cymru had given us was enormous, or maybe the exchange rate between the pound sterling and franc was good for England at the moment, or something.

4.

The next thing we did was have a birthday party. It was a very strange birthday party, because I was the only one opening presents.

Vanity insisted on showing me everything she had gotten for me in the Paris shops, and as we opened dress-boxes and hat-boxes and shoe-boxes, the sea wind caught the crepe paper some of the goods were wrapped in, and blew it off the stern. Like confetti.

Everything was beautiful and wonderful. Things I had only seen in magazines, or only heard described, were there, and Vanity has exquisite taste. Or maybe her taste is bad, but at least it matches mine.

I realize that to people who have things, mere material possessions seem tawdry and unimportant. But to a girl who has only ever worn the uniforms assigned to her, the ability to pick whether to put on a pale blue blouse or a black dress with pearls was the doorstep of paradise. It is what freedom is for, being able to pick, in little matters as well as in great ones.

Vanity also knows me. Guess what else she got for me! Running shoes. The things were as light as feathers, made of god-knows-what space-age materials. They were gorgeous.

After spending an endless time selecting an outfit and accessories, shoes and stockings, I suddenly looked up and looked around.

I said, "There is no cabin on this boat. There is no place to change."

It was true. There was a little deck in the stern, and there were lines of rowing benches (I have no idea what for, on a ship without oars) and a tiny gangway that ran from the bow to the stern.

Quentin said, "Vanity is very proud of her ship. But, because she is so swift, *Argent Nautilus* was not designed to be at sea for more than a few hours, or a day at most. So, no cabin, no galley. There is a sail, apparently for times when you go into nonliving waters."

Vanity said, "I think there is a rain tent in the storage locker we can set up on deck. You could change in there. Or the boys could just close their eyes."

I started putting stuff back in boxes. "No. Let me keep on this filthy stuff, at least until we are out of danger. There might be a fight if we are overtaken, and I won't care if Grendel's ratty stuff gets ripped."

That comment ended the party atmosphere. We started exchanging histories.

I was still wearing the baggy dungarees and flannel shirts of Grendel. But I did put on the running shoes, and, because the wind was still slightly chill here, I put on the new coat Vanity had bought for me: a long black affair of silky fur, with gold buttons to match my hair.

I sat sideways on the stern bench while Vanity brushed out my tangles with her new silver brush, and we talked.

5.

Vanity had shrieked and commiserated while I told her of Grendel's various depredations. She is simply a wonderful person to tell stories to, because she hangs on every word, her eyes glowing with sympathy for the heroine, her lips pouting with boos and catcalls for the villain.

And Victor patted me on the hand, and told me he was proud of me for how bravely I had endured the ordeal. I thought that was a funny thing to say, because the worst part of my adventures had been that I had not been anywhere as brave as I would have liked.

I told them about what Grendel had said about Echidna and Beowulf, and his several dead brothers. I described the ripping of the mermaid's cap, choking, being healed by Grendel and then waking up all tied up in his bearskin rug. I glossed over the parts where he was threatening me with conflagration and strangulation, and I described the fight in gory enough detail that it made Vanity queasy and she begged me to stop.

I told them about the mysterious town I saw, resting where Abertwyi is in our world. A different time? A different time line? We wasted some time discussing theories.

Quentin recalled that the enemy had mentioned multiple worlds during the meeting of the Board of Visitors and Governors.

I even gave them a brief précis of my conversation with Sam the dray-driver. My encounter with Corus I repeated word for word.

Vanity was enormously upset about Sam the dray-driver, for reasons I did not quite understand. She shook her hair with anger, so that red strands the color of fire stood up from her furry hood and whipped in the wind. "I've been thinking of nothing else for two days except how I was going to tell the newspapers! Maybe get a book deal out of it! You know, 'I was a teenage love slave of a pagan god.' Good title, eh? And now your Sam—the entire Sam you met, as far as I'm concerned, is dead, or as good as. What's the point?! What's the point of knowing the secret truth about the world if you cannot tell anybody!"

Quentin did not really understand her anger either. He said, half to himself, in a voice as if he were quoting a poem: "An eighteenth I know, which to none I will tell, not to maiden nor another man's wife—what is known to oneself and oneself alone is warded best. Only to my sister, would I say it, or the wife I hold in my arms . . ."

Victor summed up their adventures in a few terse lines, to which Vanity added comments, examples, descriptions, and digressions. Vanity had called her Swift Silver Ship; they had sailed to Paris. Their passports and visas did not seem to be needed; they changed some of the pound notes to francs, and bought gear. At sea again, Quentin slept on the boat, and read the first three chapters of his book, the *Arcanum Oneirocritica*. Victor took his drug. Vanity fretted. After, they circled spots Quentin divined I might be. Victor dove.

Victor was now about three inches taller than when I had last seen him. He explained: "I've been modifying myself. I rearranged some clumsy joint structures and muscle tissue connections. My muscle pressure has increased, and I have increased the rate of nerve firings per second, to give myself finer motor control.

"The extra height? I created spare abdominal spaces, and I compressed other organs, to make room for certain amplifiers and storage cells I am in the process of growing; also focusing elements and sensory adaptations. The blueprints were coded into my memory by the ampoule.

"I have made additional ganglia connections between various sections of my cortex and lower brain functions, to give myself more direct access to involuntary activity.

"The library has a wide listing of coded commands to impose into other people's nervous systems to trigger their reaction cycles. The system is called cryptognosis.

"Certain of the molecular chains take much longer to put together than others, and I have to build step-by-step certain molecular-construction tools and processes which the library-compiler evidently thought would be already installed in me, or automatic.

"However, the work proceeds very slowly. Whoever put together the coded molecules of memory-stuff that was in the syringe seemed to have no understanding of biology, or terrestrial conditions. I have instructions and reflexes set up in my nervous system now, which, if I set into motion, would turn me into something that could not exist on Earth. There were also no safety features in this library, no warnings for what nerve cells are needed for other functions or not.

"Quentin keeps telling me it is dangerous for a scientist to experiment on his own brain, but I tell him that a magician's credo is to know, to dare, to will, and to be silent. Obviously, to know all, the magician must dare all, and be silent about the risks."

Victor smiled one of his rare smiles. I listened with surprise. Was Victor actually telling a joke?

Quentin, despite that he was fussing over the bird, had a much more relaxed and confident poise to him than I had seen before. There was a glint in his eye, and he talked back to Victor in a way which, when he was younger, he never would have done: "And I keep telling him that the principle of empirical experiment requires the experimenter to remain objective, a scientist who monkeys with his own mental hardware compromises his ability to observe.

"Victor!" Quentin spoke firmly. "I've warned you that my science, the true science, cannot fix you once you render the humors in your brain impure; your disbelief in magic casts a negative ward around you. You are a soul who has convinced himself he has no soul; damage your brain, and that silly belief may turn out to have a self-fulfilling character, my friend."

Victor, still smiling his small smile, said to me confidentially, "Quentin now is convinced he knows everything, because he has read the first three chapters of his book. I tell him the book is just gibberish, and he is only reading it in his dreams, and he agrees with me. Perhaps I have not drawn out the implications of my comment with sufficient clarity."

Vanity was probably also not used to the idea of Victor kidding around.

She reacted as if he were serious, saying hotly, "The book is just great! The first chapter tells about the creation of the world; chapter two is the hierarchies of eternity and those ions and emissions . . ."

Quentin said gently, "Aeons and Emanations. Gnostic words referring to angelic reflections or subdivisions of the divine."

She turned to him. "Chapter three was the bestiary, right?"

Quentin said, "The names Adam gave to beast and bird, crawling things and swimming things. But each name is a true name, and contains the tale of the beast, the history of the first two of each of their kind, and how long they stayed in the garden in Eden after the departure of Man. The hour and the gate of their departure defined their roles in the world. The hound and the horse, the swine and the kine, left with him, through the gate called Peace, but the cat actually left before him, sniffing out the ground, which is why those domesticated beasts, the sons of Cadwal and Rahal, Ghiuor and Muor, retain their loyalty to humanity, whereas the sire of all cats, Greymalkin, was granted a degree of independence, a reward for his curiosity. The serpent, Issrashah, most wise of beasts, was the last to depart. There are several references and tales about creatures of great beauty and power, who I am assuming were wiped out during the deluge of Noah."

Quentin smiled, looking young and handsome and eager, and he continued: "I am looking forward to chapter four tonight. I hope it contains the original language of Enoch, who built the first of the cities of man on Earth. I will also have to learn the lore of Tubalcaine, to be able to cast influences on things man-made of metal and brass; and likewise for Jubalcaine, in order to influence the doings of poets and singers."

I wondered if Quentin's newfound boldness came from his memory, now restored, of nerving himself and defeating his shyness to kiss sweet Vanity for the first time. I think he did it three times, and he got me, too. Not to mention, he now recalled spitting in the eye of the Lamia bent over him to kill him. All those bold memories were part of him now, back where they belonged, and it was forming part of his character.

6.

Victor said, "Enough about the past. Let's discuss the immediate future. First, which way do we go? A point is approaching where Vanity will have to decide whether to head for Australia or America, straight across the Atlantic or south to the Horn. Second, Vanity's memory. Third, Colin's body. And apparently his brain, too, because he does not seem any smarter than a bird in that shape."

Vanity said, "Colin's body before my brain. I am only missing a few days. I can function. If we get assaulted by—which one is it, sirens?—if we get assaulted by sirens, we have no defense."

Quentin said, "Besides, we need Colin to do Vanity."

Vanity and I both giggled, while Quentin looked puzzled. "What did I say?"

I said, "Nothing, ah—nothing. So Colin is going to *do* Vanity, right?"

Quentin looked at Victor, who shrugged. Victor said, "Colin, then Vanity. When we got aboard the ship just now, we all used what powers we had to check for bugs and spies and seeking spells, and Vanity said we were clean, at the moment. What happens the moment we are not clean? Remember in Amelia's story, how certain ap Cymru was that we would be found again. Why? Why so certain? We need to prepare for the next attack. An addendum to point four, the ring of Gyges. What do we do with it? Vanity also says it is clean, and Quentin detects no spells. I can see it is not giving off any radio signals on any wavelength."

I said, "Can we do point two first? Colin might want a say as to where he is going to be living next."

Quentin said, "Point five. What about our parents? Our families? Our homelands? Vanity's ship could take us there right now, couldn't she? They are experts at all this stuff we are just learning. But—there is a problem. A big problem. It is that important matter I was starting to discuss earlier, having to do with the oath I swore to Bran."

Victor said, "We are out of England now. You swore not to hurt England. I do not see the application."

Quentin drew a deep breath, and actually looked scared for a moment. Scared of Victor? But he was also looking at me. That was more than a little surprising. Even though, according to Boggin, I was the "dangerous one," I did not see how anyone could be scared of me.

Vanity saw his expression. She laid her hand gently on his back and said, "Dear, maybe now is not the time. Let's wait till Colin is whole again, you know? Otherwise, we have to tell them twice, and stuff."

For a moment I felt annoyed. It was obvious Vanity and Quentin had discussed something that they were keeping from the rest of us. Weren't we the Three Musketeers Plus Two? Why was there suddenly this barrier of silence splitting the group?

Then I put my hand in front of my lips and suppressed a smile. I am sure my eyes were shining. What in the world was I thinking! And me, still wearing a wedding dress under my stolen clothes! What else could it be? What other secret surprise would two young lovers have to announce to their friends, that they wanted to keep hush until everyone could hear it at once?

I smiled and patted Quentin on the shoulder, leaned in and gave Vanity a hug, "Oh, congratulations!" I said. "And I am sure you are making the right decision!"

When I let go of Vanity, the look on her face told me I'd guessed wrong.

Quentin was not so observant, and so he was saying: "It *is* a very tough decision, but I do think it is indeed the right one. I did not know you would be so happy about it, though, all things considered. Well! This is a relief . . ." Vanity touched his arm and gave him a little shake of the head.

She said, "Later. After we fix Colin."

7.

Victor did not seem interested in talking about things not on the topic, and he was clearly not curious about what was up between Vanity and Quentin. All he said was, "Destinations? Remember, we can also pick unknown worlds. I'd recommend against it, because they are unknown."

I said, "I can speak for Colin. Ireland. It's English-speaking. He thinks of himself as Irish."

Quentin said, "But he's not Irish."

I said, in a tone sharper than I wanted to use (okay, maybe I was still smarting about being left out of whatever secret Vanity and Quentin were sharing): "He picked Irish! That's the nationality he picked."

Vanity said, "Do we all get to pick nationalities? I'll be Spanish."

Her tone of voice was so light and gay that I had to laugh. So, I can't stay mad at her. I said playfully, "A Spanish redhead?"

"Everyone knows the Spaniards are the most romantic people on

Earth. Spanish women get to knife their unfaithful lovers." She said to Quentin, "Nemo is Latin. I guess that makes you an Italian."

Quentin said, "Don't I get to pick, myself? The Romani, whom you call the gypsies, retain the remnants of the Egyptian lore. All the true practitioners of the Art these days are Romani."

Vanity looked at me. "What about you, Amelia?"

"Easy," I said. "American. Neil Armstrong, Chuck Yeager, the Wright Brothers, and Sally Ride. What do they all have in common? Americans."

"Yuri Gagarin was Russian," said Vanity.

"Women in America carry guns and own businesses. They kick ass and they use rough language like 'kick ass' and nobody looks cross-eyed at them. American women are the greatest."

Vanity said, "Victor . . . ?"

Victor said, "We are picking a destination, not choosing nationalities. This conversation is irrelevant."

Vanity said, "Wherever we pick, we might be there for a long time. We may have to become natives. So which nationality would you pick, if you had to?"

Victor decided to play along. He did seem more easy and relaxed than the Victor I knew. Of course, the Victor I knew had spent every minute of his life inside what he thought of as a prison. Maybe this Victor was new.

He said, "Logically, from the way the question is asked, given that wording, only Amelia's answer is correct."

"Thanks!" I said. "But how can there be a right or wrong answer to a question of opinion?"

"The question was asked, which nationality would I choose? The question contains a false-to-facts assumption. Every nationality—with one exception—is something you are born into. It is not a matter of choice. One must be born Spanish to be Spanish, born Gypsy to be Gypsy. Americans are a self-selected group. Americans are people dedicated to a proposition that all men are created equal. It's a matter of choice."

Vanity said, "Can I be Spanish-American, then?"

I said, "If we are really going to pick a destination . . . ?"

Victor said, "I don't mind being back on topic. Yes?"

"I do not want to go to Australia."

Quentin smiled, and said, "It is not really peopled entirely with criminals, any more than Cornwall is all smugglers."

"A woman cannot own a gun there," I said.

"Why is that important?" said Quentin. "I hope we're not planning to shoot someone."

I said only: "The next Grendel gets it."

There was a moment of dull silence after that.

Victor said calmly, "I vote with Amelia. Only an armed man is free; anyone else is the ward or dependent of such a man. Besides, America is richer than Australia, bigger. Easier to blend in. We can hide."

Vanity said, "Hollywood. Everyone in the world watches the movies made in America. We can be famous."

Quentin just laughed, and spread his hands. "The only people on Earth with no tradition and no lore, a people utterly cut off from the ancient masters. A land famed only for its materialism and lack of high culture. Fine. Not only am I outvoted, but we all are going to go wherever Vanity wants, because she is the only one who can steer the boat."

Vanity sat down on the bench, closed her eyes, took a deep breath. She meditated for a moment, or maybe she slept, or maybe she entered another state of consciousness for which I have no name.

The *Argent Nautilus* leaped about, and sped like an arrow in another direction.

A ship—as huge as a city floating on the water—was spotted off the bow, came abreast of us, and was far astern in a matter of moments. I saw the giant ocean liner astern, a shadow on the bright horizon behind us, only a dot.

Vanity smiled, opening her eyes. "I asked for the biggest ship I could find, heading for New York. The *Queen Elizabeth II*. Do you think they'll pick up four kids and a bird in a stranded motorboat? They might make us work, but maybe we have enough money to pay for tickets. Ap Cymru gave us a lot. A whole lot. I wonder why he gave us so much?"

14

THE CROSSING

1.

It was a palace.

I found it hard to believe that mortal men, the same race that lived in such humble circumstances in the fishing village of Abertwyi, could construct something so fair, and yet so mighty in size. If someone told me later that it was the handiwork of immortal elves, or the proud sons of Atlantis, I would have been less surprised. Of course, it was made by Englishmen, who probably have more than a touch of the blood of magical races in them. How many a sailor out of Bristol brought back a mermaid as his wife, whose fishtail dropped off, replaced by legs when the church bells rang on her wedding day?

Since the gods destroy the memories of men, we can be certain of no answer.

And do not tell me the sea people don't lust for their air-breathing cousins ashore! I came so narrowly close to being Mrs. Grendel Glum I nearly choked.

2.

Our suite was gigantic, at least five hundred square feet. Was that normal for cabins, or did other people have smaller ones? It was done all in a

tan-and-gold color scheme, with two marble bathrooms and a salon separate from the two bedrooms. There was a staircase. We had our own staircase in the suite.

Aboard ship, there were at least three restaurants, a bar and grill, a dis-
cotheque, the most enormous swimming pool I had ever seen occupying
deck after deck. My mind boggled at the idea of carrying, aboard a ship, a
body of water large enough to row a boat across.

And there was a beautiful, beautiful gymnasium. The spa occupied at
least a third of the deck, and I would estimate the deck area to be at least
a thousand feet stem-to-stern and one hundred feet wide.

The vessel carried its own row of shops, and not just any shops. There
was a Harrods on the promenade deck.

A library. Did I mention that the floating palace had its own library? A
theater. Both a film theater and a Broadway show production, as if we
had already arrived in New York, and were carrying part of that metrop-
olis with us.

There was a statue made of gold in the middle of the restaurant dining
room.

There was a series of lectures being given by authors. I attended one,
but it was strange to think of an author being alive, and not being Greek
or Latin. The author talked about things I did not understand, and the
other people in the audience laughed at his witty comments, which made
no sense to me. I assume they all knew about things, famous people or
events, I had not been told about.

There was a parking garage for people who wanted to carry their cars
across the Atlantic. I counted at least fifteen elevators, for people who did
not want to walk up and down the ten decks. This vessel was taller than
the Great Hall on the estate, taller than the church steeple in Abertwyi,
taller than any building I had ever seen.

And there was television! There was no one to stop you from watching
it if you went over the one-hour-a-week limit. There were over one hundred channels. The television in the room had a little box you could hold
in your hand and make it change channels and control the volume. Victor
could lie on his bed, and did not need to hold the little box in his hand to
switch channels; he could emit the signals from his nervous system.

There was another television, just as large, with another little box, in our room. There was a telephone, so Vanity or I could telephone to the boys in the other bedroom, if we did not feel like shouting across the suite.

I had read many plays in school, but I had never actually seen a play until the night Vanity and I went down to watch the show. There was dancing and music along with it, and the people sang to each other; I did not know whether that was normal for plays or not.

Victor said our rate of speed was twenty-five knots. There was no chop, no sensation of motion, even when the seas got rough. You could lie on your bed, your enormous, enormous bed, and look out the porthole in the morning, and watch the rising sun come up red and gold over the sea, and watch the restless waves flow by, minute by minute and hour by hour, always changing, never changing.

And as far as the eye could see, there were no obstructions, no obstacles, no one to block us or hem us in. The horizon was so far away, so very far away.

I was in love with that horizon, and I never tired of looking at it.

3.

To get from the *Argent Nautilus* to the motorboat, Victor carried Quentin, who said his "friends" were made nervous by the sea, and would not come to his call. I carried Vanity piggy-back, because I could manifest my wings without touching her, even though she was occupying what seemed to be the same space.

Vanity then closed her eyes and napped (or something) and told the silvery ship to go circle Antarctica. I waved good-bye as the ship sped away, swift as a seabird skimming the waves.

We had a while to wait while the rescuing cruise ship traveled from the horizon to our position, and I filled up the time talking. I did almost all the talking, because they wanted to hear the details of everything that had happened to me that I had not had a chance to tell them before. I had a million questions myself, but kept putting off asking them, thinking I would have time later.

As it turned out, I only had time for one question. "What happened to you all after Colin was flung by Miss Daw off the cliff? Where were you kept in jail for that week?"

Quentin said, "Boggin breathed on Colin as he was falling and floated him to the ground. Rather nice of the old fellow, actually, considering that Colin was a would-be axe murderer."

Victor said, "None of us were in jail for a week, or even a day. We all had our powers neutralized by Fell and Wren and Daw, and were subjected to one or more memory-blocking techniques."

"Why was I singled out?"

Victor: "They needed your keeper, Mr. Glum, and he was not available."

Quentin: "Glum wasn't exactly inspired to help Boggin. Other things on his mind, you know."

Vanity: "And later, he was in hospital, recovering from leg amputation."

I wanted to ask them how they discovered this, but by that time, a motor launch from the ship was coming abreast of us, and we had to wave and shout and look lost.

4.

Our first chance to be alone did not come until sunset. We said good-bye to Miguel, who was very kind to us and did us favors. He wore a white jacket, and I am not sure what you call a butler or waiter at sea. A steward? A cabin boy? Whatever his rank, both he and everyone had been so very kind to us, it was hard to believe.

In fact, I did not believe it. As soon as Miguel was out the door (and I looked "past" the door to see that he was moving away down the plushly carpeted corridor), I put my back to the door, and turned accusingly to Quentin.

"You hypnotized them, didn't you? Captain Warwick and the others? The bursar."

Quentin, Victor, and Vanity had finished their initial inspections of the suite. Vanity had ooh'd and ahh'd over the luxury, hopping and clapping her hands, while Victor had probed the walls with rays, looking for electronic bugs. Now they were all seated in an impromptu picnic in the middle of the carpet, pulling open the savory packages Miguel had brought us from the galley. There was food of a kind I had not seen before, with meat or fish salad rolled up into a flat unleavened bread. At least, I think it was bread. Vanity had already dropped crumbs on the carpet, crumbs someone else (not us!) was going to clean up. Victor was inspecting a bottle of soda pop, a brand he had not seen before, something with an Italian label in a green glass bottle.

Quentin was also seated cross-legged on the carpet. He carefully brought his hands out from beneath his voluminous cloak, and twisted them in midair. One moment, his hands were empty; the next, he had the ring of Gyges in one hand and an exasperated-looking eagle in the other. The eagle was no longer seeping any blood. As far as I could tell from a one-glance inspection, it seemed entirely recovered from wounds which should have killed it nine times over.

The eagle hopped from Quentin's hands and drove its beak into a sandwich, which was lying on a napkin on the floor.

Quentin looked up. "It wasn't me. I don't have that art. I think chapter seven might tell me about the vapors and humors affecting the intellectual and passionate psyches, but even that would only influence moods, not control minds."

I said, "Well, someone did something. Why wouldn't they just radio for a coast guard or something? Or call back to England and tell Boggin?"

Vanity said, "There are a lot of people in England. I don't think they all know each other's names yet. Maybe after Christmas. Hey! Try these potato things. They have some sort of spicy stuff baked into them."

Quentin said, "We did pay a great deal of money for a cabin that otherwise he had not rented out for this crossing. Besides, isn't it a law of the sea that one must rescue stranded blondes and redheads?"

Vanity said, "They would have been quicker to pick us up if Amelia and I had been in bathing suits, like I suggested."

I sat down and tried the potato things. They really were quite good.

Victor said, "I did it. I used a cryptognostic technique on the captain. Every time his nervous tension levels started to trigger a glandular reaction, I interrupted the stimulus cycle in his hypothalamus. Whenever one of us spoke, or he looked closely at us, I lightly stimulated the pleasure center of the brain. I did not have long enough to establish a true operant conditioning cycle, but apparently it was enough to influence his judgment in our favor."

I was upset by this news. "That's terrible! You can't go around tinkering with people's inner thoughts that way! What makes you any different than Corus, the brain-eraser? Or Dr. Fell?!"

Victor said in a dismissive tone, "The process would not affect the judgment of people who did not make decisions on an emotional basis."

I said hotly, "I think we need to discuss how we are going to use our powers, and whether normal people should be off-limits!"

"Fine," said Victor, taking a bite of the wrapped-up food roll-thing. (Maybe it was a Mexican food?) He chewed and swallowed, and said, "Let us add it to the agenda right after point five, which I believe is tabled until we restore Colin. Restoring Colin is the topic that has the floor at the moment. Any theories as to why Quentin's true-shape charm is not working? Amelia . . . ? Anyone . . . ?"

Vanity said, "Colin is not a witch flying on a rafter. Don't look at me like that! That was in the poem he said."

Quentin said, half to himself, "That 'little poem' is the words of the High One."

"Besides, the little poem Quentin said is meant to *prevent* witches from returning to their day-shapes, isn't it?"

Quentin just sighed, and said to Victor, "I am sure that someone versed in the true science could restore Colin swiftly. I am an apprentice without a master, working from a book."

Victor said, "Do you have anything else you could try?"

Quentin sighed, and looked at the cabin ceiling for a moment. "I could ask Marbas, who is a great president, and governs thirty-six legions of spirits, and who also can change men into other shapes—but that demonstration would require that I accomplish the figure of memory first, which I can only do on the new moon . . .

"There are a number of basic steps, amulets, and phylacteries I should have been using since long ago, and certain consecrations I ought to do before attempting anything more. Like you, I don't have some basic tools my book talks about. I've been using a butter knife for my athame. I do not have any sort of athanor or any way to make one. It is all going to take time I do not think we have.

"And if I did something wrong, as Vanity says I did, I might have trapped Colin in that shape by mistake."

Vanity said, "You said chapter two had the bestiary in it."

"It was chapter three. Chapter two is the celestial hierarchy . . ."

"Whatever! You know the true names of the lord of eagles, and the true name of Colin, so why can't you just zap him?"

"Well, watch . . ." Quentin put out his hand. We had not yet unpacked, so all the Paris clothes boxes and scuba gear and stuff were simply lying piled on the divan. The white birch wand jumped across the room from the pile into Quentin's hand.

He touched the wand to the bird first with one end, then with the other. "Ter! Remove this false shape from one who is not your son. Phobetor! Return to your own human shape, without hurt or pain, and stand before us. I charge and compel you in the name of the Third of Choirs: Eliphamasai, Gelomiros, Gedobonai, Saranana, and Elomnia!"

Vanity looked at the bird curiously. "Was something supposed to happen?"

"There is a thing called the Almadel I am supposed to make, but I haven't gotten the chance yet. A square of wax written with holy names and bearing the Seal of Solomon. So, I guess I am not doing it right. But even without that, if there was a curse keeping him in this shape, I should have just revoked it." Quentin put his white stick down beside him and reached into the food again. "Hey! This is soup in this container. Smells wonderful. Did they give us spoons? Oh, and before I forget . . ."

He tossed the ring of Gyges across to me. I caught it, but I said, "Don't give it to me! I am the only one here who doesn't need it. I can step half an inch into four-space, so that photons slide past me without touching. I can do better than invisibility."

Victor was pouring ketchup on some potato things, which (in my opinion) defeated the whole purpose of having them baked with spices. "Not me," he said, "I might demagnetize it by mistake. I think all that thing really does is interfere with the visual centers of the brain, anyway."

I tossed it to Vanity, who caught it. "What!" she said. "Am I the cripple in the group or something, the only person not from Chaos, so I need to be able to turn invisible? It is obvious that Colin has to get this ring, and for the same reason Grendel wanted it. If Colin wears it, he can stop Miss Daw, but Mrs. Wren cannot stop him. If Grendel is dead, they can't mount an effective attack on us. Amelia is now our trump card. No one can neutralize her. She neutralizes Dr. Fell, and with Fell out of the way, Quentin can blast them with magic."

Quentin murmured, "Not exactly 'blast.' I can tell them the true name of the first Salmon."

I said, "Maybe I was wrong about who stops whom. If someone other than Quentin tried to unstick Colin . . ."

Victor said, "You are not wrong, Amelia. Quentin, show her the diagram."

Quentin said, "I cannot believe they did not give us spoons. Does anyone mind if I just drink this straight out of the container? I mean, if no one else wants any . . ."

Victor said, "Quentin, the diagram, if you please."

"Oh, sorry. Here." And he took his grimoire out from an inner pocket of his long cloak, waved his hand over it in a mystic gesture, while unlocking it with his other hand (I saw him do it), and opened it to the frontispiece.

"There it is, right in the beginning," Quentin said. "Your table of oppositions. The four houses of Chaos and their relationship to each other."

I saw a diamond, whose opposite corners were connected by the arms of a cross. There were heraldic signs surrounding each corner, and writing along the lines in some sort of crooked, cursive script. The script did not actually change when I was looking at it, but I kept getting the strange feeling that it just had changed.

I said, "I cannot read the faerie letters."

Quentin said, "Don't worry about that. It correlates the houses with the four elements, the four seasons, and so on. You can still look at the pictures. The apple blossom symbol at the top is your people. The pomegranate at the bottom is mine. The poppy flower to the left is Colin, and the mistletoe to the right is Victor's group, the Telchine. Here is what is interesting. The horizontal line connecting poppy to mistletoe, marked with a white lily, represents the Phaeacians; the vertical line connecting pomegranate to apple blossom, marked with a red rose, represents the Olympians, although you can see a thyme leaf where the Olympians touch you, and a sage herb where it rests on me . . ."

All these flowers were confusing me. Apple blossom? Why was I an apple blossom?

I interrupted, "So what is the deal with all this? What's it mean?"

Quentin said, "We think it means your table of opposition was a correct theory, and that you guessed right about the two non-Chaotic powers. This chart implies that the Olympian power is a mean between multidimensionalism and the True Art, your paradigm and mine. A second implication is

that the Phaeacian power is a mean between or combination of materialism and mysticism, Victor and Colin."

Vanity said, "It was Miss Daw and Mrs. Wren who were tending me
when I had pneumonia. The so-called pneumonia."

Victor said, "Which means we need Colin to fix Vanity."

Vanity said, "Maybe Colin is stuck because he still wants to be stuck. I
mean, did he really enjoy himself when he was a boy? Sometimes, I do not
think he was very happy. It's hard on a fellow who is stupider than everyone around them."

Quentin frowned at her, his face dark, and real anger in his eye. "Don't
say such things again. You were brought up better than that!"

Vanity said, "Why are you standing up for him? You were the one he always picked on!"

Quentin said, "Colin? He never picked on me. Where do you get these
ideas? I won't have you speaking such ill of him, especially as you are the
one he is going to save, once we get him back. Don't let such words pass
your lips again!"

5.

The scene of mild-mannered Quentin browbeating the bubbly Vanity
over what was obviously just a lighthearted joke made me uncomfortable.
(Besides, Colin *did* pick on Quentin, all the time. How could Quentin not
see it?) I stood up. "Listen—I am going to go to my room and change out
of these Grendel things. I cannot believe I have been wearing them all
day. You guys keep talking. Figure something out."

I gathered an armful of dress boxes and the things I wanted to put on.

Vanity leaped to her feet, all smiles. "I have the answer! I have an idea!
I've got it!"

I had my hand on the door to my cabin, and I turned to see Vanity, the
Colin eagle resting in her hands, come skipping after me. "Come on!" she
said to me.

"What?" I said.

Bird in one hand, she urged me into the bedroom. She paused to stick
her tongue out at the boys, and danced into the room, closing the door behind. The lights had a dimmer switch, and she turned them only to a dim,

golden half-light. Everything was touched with soft shadows and rich textures in that light.

Vanity put the eagle on the headboard of the bed. "This is *such* a good idea. I *know* it is going to work!"

I put the boxes and stuff on the foot of the bed, and started to unbutton the first of the two shirts I was wearing.

Vanity came dancing back, grinning, and put one arm around my waist. She turned and smiled at the eagle.

She said through her teeth, "You're not smiling!" This came out sounding like: *Iour nn't sn'lingk!*

"I am entirely convinced you have lost your mind, Vanity," I said. "What are we doing, here, exactly? And move your hand so I can take off this smelly shirt."

She skipped a step back, still grinning. "Okay! But do it more slowly! And look like you are enjoying yourself."

She started to unbutton the top buttons of her blouse, too, but she was swaying her hips and rolling her shoulders, as if dancing to music I could not hear. I wondered if she were under some sort of spell or hex cast by the enemy.

"Do—what? What are you going on about?"

But now her eyes fell upon the transparent misty top of the fairy dress I was wearing, which became visible as I shrugged off my second shirt.

Vanity said, "You are going too fast! And— Wow! What is that?"

I bent to push the two pairs of pants off my hips. They were so large and baggy that I thought I could just slip them off without unzippering them, once the belt was gone. It was a little tight, but I wiggled and slid them down my legs.

"Now, that was really good!" said Vanity. "But you should be the other way around . . ."

I straightened up and put my hands on my hips. Vanity had her shirt off and was standing there in just her skirt and stockings. The bra she had bought in Paris was a lacy black thing with the tiniest little red bow deep in her cleavage. I don't think I had ever seen black underwear before, not in real life, and the bra must have been a padded support bra, because her breasts looked even larger and perkier than normal in it. I thought it looked very pretty, though maybe peach would have gone better with her light complexion.

"Vanity, what the heck is going on?"

Vanity bent down, pouting seductively, and with little, teasing tugs, tugged her skirt off with a slow, very sensuous motion, and it clung for a moment to her hips and buttocks, and dropped gently to the floor. She was now posed with one hand on her knee, one hand caressing her own hip, and the shining curve of her slip exposed to the soft, sepia-toned light.

Why was Vanity smiling over her shoulder at me? Why were her eyes half-lidded, as if she were aroused by some deep romantic passion?

We undressed in front of each other naked every single night of our lives. Why was she making such a big production number out of it tonight? But there was no mistaking her attitude and gestures. She was doing a striptease. She . . .

She was not smiling at me. She was smiling at the bird. At Colin.

I turned my head. The bird was staring at me with bright, bright yellow eyes.

Vanity pouted and said softly, "Are you sure you don't want to be a man, Colin? There are *soooo* many things men can enjoy that birds can't! We'll both give you a kiss if you turn back into a man . . ."

I was wearing a floating cloud of fairy vapor, which exposed my nipples. My pubic hair was visible as a faint bluish triangle, at which all the pearl strands running through the wasp-waisted corselette pointed. The bodice of this dress was webbed with something like a fishnet body stocking, exposing every curve and making them curvier. This dress left nothing to the imagination, except where it hid just enough to make the imagination of an aroused man more aroused.

And I was standing in it, naked, worse than naked, in front of Colin mac FirBolg.

I shrieked and yanked up the skirt Vanity had discarded, trying to hold it over me, yanking it high to cover my top, yanking it low to cover my bottom, and probably not covering very much.

Victor's voice came from the other room: "Is everything all right in there?"

Vanity called out gaily, "Yes! We are all fine here! Just fine!" She reached over and pinched me.

"Ow!" I said. "Stop that!"

Vanity said, "You've got to help! Why aren't you helping?"

"This was your plan? To wiggle and strip in front of Colin mac FirBolg?

The world's only walking bag of hormones, the guy who uses testosterone rather than neural fluid to convey charge across his brain cells?"

"You know how much he wants to fly. We have to offer him something he wants more. Something he can't get when he is a bird! You are the one who told me his powers are based on desire. So!" and she took the skirt out of my hands and tossed it on the bed. "Start acting desirable!"

I stood there, my mind a complete blank. "How do I do that?"

Vanity said, "I don't know. Dance around a bit. Flirt. Make eye contact."

I tried striking a few poses. I tried folding my arms behind my head and arching my back. I wiggled my bottom at the bird. I gave it my best smile. The eagle stared at me with its yellow eyes.

I put my arms down. "I feel silly."

Vanity said, "Just do what comes instinctively. Girls know what turns boys on!"

She leaned over the footboard, pouting and making kisses toward the eagle, drawing her elbows into her abdomen so as to squeeze her breasts dangerously close to popping out of her black bra.

Looking at her sidelong, I imitated the same pose. "Is this instinctive?"

She tilted her head to one shoulder, then to the other, pouting and batting her eyelashes. And she was straightening one leg and relaxing the other, and then reversed, so that her hips cocked from one side to the other, over and over, a little sort of dance rhythm. It did not look particularly sexy or unsexy, one way or the other. More like the kind of thing a person did on an exercise bike.

She answered me: "You should know instinct girl stuff instinctively!"

"Remember, I am actually a squid with wings. I don't think I have those instincts."

"Well, he's staring at you. Project sincerity. Look at him sort of sideways and lower your lashes. Hmm. More sincerity. Tell him you want him to rip your clothes off."

"Colin, please rip my clothes off, if it's not too much trouble . . ."

"No! No! No! Tell him with your eyes!"

"What? Blink in Morse code?"

She straightened up and put her hands on her hips, and her eyes flashed and her nostrils flared. "Amelia! You're being obstreperous! He's trapped that same way you were trapped by Grendel! He rescued you, even though he got hurt! You can at least try to rescue him!"

That comment struck home. Here was Colin, my comrade-in-arms, who had jumped on Boreas the Wind god with nothing but a stick in his hands, risking his life so that we could get away. And he lost his life, his human life, at least, his ability to think and reason.

And when he was left with nothing but the miserable life of a bird in the wild, he risked that, too, and let himself get mauled by a bear in order to save me. The first feat had been to save the group. The second had been just for me, Colin's personal gift to me. My freedom and my life were from him.

Vanity was saying with angry passion, "Think of Colin! What would he do if you were stuck? If he thought stripping half-nude and wiggling his fanny at you would save you, he'd do it!"

What's funny is, I thought she looked prettier when she was angry. That stuff she was doing before looked silly and fake to me. But, if she knew what she was doing . . .

"Okay! Okay!" I pouted. "Just tell me what to do. I'll do anything you say."

"Well . . . it's clear we have to pull out all the stops. . . . hmm . . ." She slipped out of her slip, so she was only standing there in her garter belt and panties.

"Hey, is that a garter belt? Why didn't you get normal stockings?"

She held out her leg, showing off her stockings, and looking pleased. "I thought Quentin might like it. Feel the fabric. Look at how sheer!"

I caressed her upper thigh. "That's nice. I'm sure he'll like it. Pretty color, too. I wished you had bought some for me." For the moment, we had both forgotten about the Peeping Tom with feathers.

Vanity glanced at the eagle, and I saw her face light up. "Oh! I've got it! I've got an idea! Here! Kiss me!"

I leaned down and gave her a peck on the cheek.

"No, no, a real kiss!"

I straightened up, "Vanity, I am not going to give you a kiss on the lips."

She rolled her eyes in angry exasperation, stood on tiptoe, and threw her arms around me, holding me tightly. "This will work! Guys think this stuff is kinky!"

"How do you know what stuff guys think is kinky?"

"Colin told me! Come on! You promised!"

Well, I had promised.

Vanity stood on tiptoe with her hands on my shoulders, her head tilted back, eyes closed.

Kissing a girl was odd. Her lips were cool, and I could taste a hint of the lip gloss she used. There was nothing particularly interesting about it.

Of course, maybe that was the way kisses were supposed to go; my only experience was Quentin trying to shut me up in midair, and Grendel giving me mouth-to-mouth resuscitation.

When I pulled my head back, Vanity looked up at me in surprise. "You don't close your eyes when you kiss."

I said crossly, "Quentin got to kiss me before Victor did, and now you. I'm kissing everyone I don't want to! Life stinks." And I turned my head to scowl at the bird. "Change back!" I snapped.

But he didn't. Colin was being stubborn.

Then, to Vanity, I said, "Arrgh! He's faking. He could change back any time he wanted! He's probably watching and enjoying all this."

"We're getting close! I can feel it! Here! Try this!"

Vanity kept one hand on my shoulder and put her other arm around my waist. She raised her left knee to the level of my hip, struck a pose, and said to the bird in husky whisper: "Oh, Colin . . . ? Amelia and I have been lesbian lovers for years! In bed, at night, she forces me to pretend I'm you, and has me spank her bottom . . . ! Turn back, and we'll show you . . . ?"

Exasperated, I shrugged her grip away. "Oh, stop it. Spanking isn't kinky, or sexy, or anything. It just hurts and it's humiliating. Like getting your foot caught in a slamming door. Vanity, this is really not working. Let's get dressed."

Vanity said, "One last idea. And this one I know is going to work! Please? You did promise."

"Okay, what is it?"

"Here. Turn toward the door. Let me put my arms around you again . . ."

"Okay, fine. Now what?"

Vanity suddenly seized my wrists and pushed them behind my back, crossing them and extending them toward Colin. "Quick, Colin! Amelia wants you to tie her up! She's *into* that sort of thing!"

I threw my arms up, so that she stepped back, off-balance. "Oh! That's the last straw!" I said. My face felt hot. I was blushing with anger or embarrassment, or both. "What a terrible thing to say! You owe me a big . . ."

But Vanity's face was slack with shock; her eyes were round as saucers. I heard a noise behind me. A rustle. Something larger than a bird was on the bed.

Vanity screamed.

I turned. I don't know what I expected to see, a monster or something. It was Colin. He was standing on the same bed where we had thrown our clothes, so we could not exactly get to them. There he was, large as life. And naked as a jaybird.

And erect. I didn't know they could turn purple colored. Like a big, sort of, tree, I guess, coming out of a fuzzy black bush.

I screamed, too. It seemed the thing to do at the time. I suspect my brain had sprung a leak at the sight of a naked Colin.

We both ran out the door, shrieking with the shock of it, the unadulterated embarrassment.

Victor and Quentin had just got done leaping to their feet by the time we nigh-unto-naked girls came running into the room, jiggling, I am sure, and wiggling all sorts of exposed surfaces we normally keep covered.

Even Victor, the unflappable, looked flapped at that moment. Quentin had his mouth open as the two-girl train of unclad beauty drove toward him, and I could see he did not know whether to laugh or cry or just drool.

We hopped behind the boys. I got behind Victor, and Vanity was behind Quentin, which, in hindsight, was good, because had it been the other way around, my chin would have been on Quentin's head (making him feel not very protective) and Vanity would have been unable to see what happened next, with Victor's shoulder blades blocking the view.

Victor, his eyes on the door, put his hand back in that cliché protective male gesture to make sure your woman is behind you. Whether by accident or design, the hand touched my nude hip (or maybe there was a wisp of mist draped over it), and I could feel all my little goose flesh hairs stand up. His fingers were warm.

Quentin was having trouble swallowing. He, too, kept his eyes on the door, but Vanity was huddling much closer to him than I was to Victor, had her arms around his waist and chest, and her breasts were mashed up into his back. I don't know much about men, but I knew enough to know that every one of Quentin's nerve signals was concentrating on increasing the sensitivity and reception from that area of his upper back.

Victor said sharply, "What happened?"

Vanity could not talk. She had just realized (I could see it on her face) that she was standing in her panties and bra, with her risqué French garter belt, silky stockings and high heels, in a position where, if either boy moved, they would see her. Again. She could not get back to her clothes without being put on display. Again.

So she was blushing. It was almost fun to watch, because her whole face glowed red, and her neck, and shoulders, and even the tops of her breasts. That is the price you pay for having such a clear complexion. We girls with tans, at least during the summer, can hide shame better.

I said, "It worked as planned."

Colin, from the other room, called out, "Don't shoot me! It's me, Colin. Or maybe it's some horror from the pit who learned to impersonate Colin's voice."

Quentin asked (quite reasonably, I thought), "Shoot you with what?"

Colin shouted back: "Where the hell am I?"

Victor said, "You are in the Caledonia suite on deck four of the cruise ship *Queen Elizabeth II,* one day out of Bristol, bound for New York. What happened in there? Why are the girls wearing costumes?"

"I think it is part of an important master plan. Send the naked girls back in, and I will investigate, and then report back. What happened to Boggin?"

Quentin shouted, "We don't know. What happened to you?"

"Ah! I put myself in a situation where I really, really wanted to fly. My thoughts became, how to put it—? Focused. Very focused. You should try it some time. How long has it been?"

I said, "Tell him it's been twenty years. It'll be funnier that way."

Colin shouted, "Is that Amelia? Nice dress, Amelia. I think your dress-maker just saved me from the doom of eternal birdhood. Thank you."

I was trying really, really hard to see the humor in this situation, but there are certain things that are just too embarrassing. I put my head down and pressed my closed eyes into the fabric of Victor's shoulder. I could feel hot tears beneath my lids.

Colin shouted, "And your breasts, of course. They saved me, too. I did not realize how large your aureoles were. I would like to thank your breasts more personally, later."

Colin appeared in the doorway. We all gawped at him. He was wearing

Vanity's skirt, with the frilly top of one of my outfits from the dress box over him like a shirt. The top was too small for him to button.

He looked down at the clothes, and squinted.

Quentin said, "Colin, this will sound like an odd question, and I want you to think it over before answering. Why are you in drag?"

Colin was red-faced when he looked up. "Ah. Hum. I thought that the bird thing was so successful, you know. The key to my powers. If you just want something hard enough, right? So I thought I could turn this into my clothes, if I . . . you know . . . I really, really do not want you to be seeing me dressed this way . . . And I thought . . . well, I'd rather die than have my friends see me this way, so . . . and, there weren't any clothes in the drawers in there. . . . Whose room is this? Are we on a ship?"

Victor shrugged out of the long buff jacket he was wearing and, without turning his head, passed it over his shoulder to me. His chain mail glinted and gleamed in the light from the cabin fixtures.

Victor said, in the exact same tone of voice as before: "You are in the Caledonia suite on deck four of the cruise ship *Queen Elizabeth II,* one day out of Bristol, bound for New York."

Colin said, "Nice room. Do you guys have any spare, um, boy clothes?"

I said from over Victor's shoulder, "We thought you were dead."

Vanity had recovered a little, and she dug her fingers into Quentin's ribs, "Hey! What about me! Get me something to wear."

Quentin said, "Well, I mean, you are wearing something."

She poked him again, and stamped her foot.

Colin craned his head to one side, trying to catch a glimpse of more of Vanity's bestockinged legs. Quentin's normal "mine not yours" guy-instincts turned on, and he swirled the huge black cloak from his back and gathered up Vanity in it.

Quentin escorted Vanity past Colin back toward our room. Vanity said over her shoulder, "Colin, I got you some things. When we were in Paris. I bought you clothes."

"You went to Paris? Without me? And you thought I was dead? You thought I was dead so you went to Paris to buy me clothes, without me? You bought clothes for a guy you thought was dead, so you went to Paris?"

Vanity waved her hand toward some of our boxes on the couch. "Just because you were dead doesn't mean I wouldn't get you anything! What kind of person do you think I am?"

BLIND SPOTS

1.

I tried to get Victor to escort me back to my room, but he just pointed at that door and inclined his head slightly.

Once we were both back inside, I turned to Vanity angrily, intending to claw her eyes out for embarrassing me so thoroughly. Or at least give her a severe tongue-lashing. But at the same time, through the closed door, came Colin's voice, soft and young with wonder: "You mean . . . we're *free* . . . ? We made it . . . ?"

Victor's voice, calm and measured: "Amelia arranged the escape and got us this money, passports, and once we were at sea, Vanity called her ship . . ."

Colin interrupted with a huge long howl of triumph, like something from an Old West movie: *"Yeeeeeaaaaa-haahhhh!"*

All three boys started singing a Christmas carol, something full of sound and joy, peace on Earth, goodwill to men. It was a happy thing to hear, and it made me smile. And I admit being pleased with Victor's comment: *Amelia* arranged the escape.

After that, I did not have the heart to stay mad at Vanity.

2.

I was sure that the "wedding dress" from Grendel would be hexed, or impossible to take off, or something, so it came as a pleasant surprise that it just unlaced in the back and slipped off over my head. I folded it carefully and packed it in tissue paper, and put it in one of the empty dress boxes.

Vanity donned her blouse and skirt and was back into the other room. At one point, I heard Colin's voice suddenly get louder: "You bought scuba gear? You thought I was dead, so you went to Paris without me and bought scuba gear? Without me? To Paris? So this scuba gear is . . . French?"

I selected a slim black dress with a necklace of pearls, black shoes with silver clasps. Once again, examining myself in the mirror, I was puzzled as to how much money we had spent, how much things cost, how much Vanity had bought.

I came back out into the salon; Colin, seated at ease on the divan, with his feet up on the chair facing him, was staring at the pamphlet that came with the room, which explained how the television worked, listed the ship's computer-use fees, gave the menus, and so on. He had the rebreather of the scuba unit in his mouth, which he puffed like a hookah.

He was wearing a white loose shirt with puffed sleeves gathered at the wrist, and cream-colored whipcord riding breeches that showed off the muscles in his legs. He looked like something between a flower child and a king's musketeer. I was surprised Vanity had not also bought him a hat with a plume.

Colin looked up when I entered, tried to wolf-whistle but could not, and tried to applaud, but could not, his mouth blocked by the rebreather, his hands by the menu.

Quentin was picking up some of the litter off our carpet from the impromptu picnic, and was staring in puzzlement at a clearly labeled box of spoons.

Vanity was sitting in a chair with her eyes half-closed; Victor had one hand on her wrist and was looking at his new watch, like a doctor taking her pulse.

Colin spat out his rebreather. It hissed at him. He said, "Don't you clean up pretty, Amelia? Nice dress."

Quentin glanced up from his spoon-frowning activity. "Yes. Very attractive, Amelia."

I said thank you and turned around with my arms out, giving them a little catwalk spin.

Colin said, "The other one was nice, too. The breast-exposer dress, I mean. Very Minoan."

I made that noise one tends to make in one's throat when Colin talks, a sort of half-gargle, half-sigh, as if one is preparing to spit out a bad taste. "Well! Enough about me! Let's see to item number two on our agenda. Vanity's memory. What do we do?" I said.

Colin emitted a short, high laugh, and put his rebreather back in, bending his head over the entertainment listings.

I gave Colin a sharp look. "What? What?"

Quentin answered. "It's done. We're done. Victor and Colin performed the operation while you were getting dressed. It didn't take long."

Victor looked up at me. "Colin impressed his view of Vanity onto her while I sent a cryptognostic probe into her long-term memory areas. The enemy could not seem to actually destroy the memories, but they misfiled them."

Colin spat the rebreather out again. "He's telling it wrong. Miss Daw increased the amount of time surrounding each memory, so it happened a million years ago, instead of last week. No wonder Freckle Fox couldn't remember anything! And Mrs. Wren cast an enchantment on her, so it seemed like a dream, and faded."

I was still blinking, "So . . . you already did it? It's over?"

Quentin said, "Our part is over. Vanity is on a spirit quest. She may be gone all night."

Missing something because I had been kidnapped, that was one thing. Missing something because I had paused to get dressed, that seemed downright rude, somehow.

I said, "Well? Are you going to tell me what happened? What did you do to her?"

Victor said, "There was almost nothing to do. Quentin's book, the chapter on the Ancient Art of Memory, described a method of approach. Vanity was subconsciously hypnotized into believing in 'magic,' and so she was the one actually suppressing her own memories, due to her faith in Mrs. Wren's so-called spell. Once nerve paths were opened between her cortex and the hypnagogic areas of her brain, she became aware of the deception."

Colin said, "I will translate from Victor-babble into the common tongue of Westron. Miss Daw thrust a million years of time-energy into Vanity's brain. Once Vanity realized that time is an illusion, the million years went away. There was also some sort of spell, too, but Victor neutralized it with his magical anti-magic ray that magically pops out of his head and magically shoots out magic beams of blue magic."

Quentin said, "There is no such thing as magic. Victor does not believe in magic."

Colin said, "Victor does not believe in magic because that mind-set is one of the ingredients in the magic spell he uses to throw magic blue beams from his magic third eye. It's just an ingredient, like having eye of newt or toe of frog."

"It's not magic," insisted Quentin.

"Guess I was fooled by the big blue extra eyeball! Extra eyeball! Or didn't you notice he has an extra eyeball? Count them. I get at least to *three* before I get confused. Isn't that one more than you or me, and two more than Popeye the sailor? Check my math here."

Victor spoke without looking up from his watch: "Your dispute is terminological. Check your definitions."

3.

We all sat or stood, watching Vanity breathing. She breathed deeply and slowly. It did not look to me as if she were asleep.

I spent more than an hour trying to catch up Colin on some of the things he'd missed while he was a bird, including hordes upon hordes of information I had already told the others while we all were waiting in the motorboat.

He seemed disinterested after a while, and I let the conversation lag. Eventually things trailed into silence, and we sat watching Vanity. In, out. In, out. I assume the guys got more fun out of seeing her chest rise and fall than I did.

4.

Quentin looked up from his grimoire (where, I assume, he was only looking at the pictures) and he said to Victor, "I notice that three of the paradigms, Vanity's, Colin's, and Amelia's, do not seem intellectual in nature."

I stirred from my lethargy and said, "*It is so* intellectual in nature! What I do? It's geometry."

Quentin said to me, "How did you give the molecular engine living in my bloodstream free will?"

I blinked. "Um. I turned the moral energy strands back on themselves to form an infinitely recursive fractal loop. Once the awareness was self-reflexive, it was self-aware. See? That was a very intellectual-in-nature thing to do."

Quentin said, "And how did you know to do that? How were you able to 'turn' this moral energy? Manipulate it?"

I said, "That's not really a fair question. An eyeball cannot see itself. No mind, by definition, can be aware of the subconscious foundation of its own thought; nor can any mind exist without such a foundation. How can I describe a process when I am part of that process, and the act of making up a description changes the process? I have limbs and organs and energy-manipulation systems in the fourth dimension. They do things. I am not a biologist; I cannot tell you the mechanism."

Victor said, "I am a biologist. It takes a child months or years to learn to develop nerve paths to control a limb or organ. If you discovered a new hand grafted to you tomorrow, it would take you months or years to learn how to use it, because you would have to develop the nerve structures and reflexes one at a time, like a child."

I said, "So what are you saying?"

Victor said, "Those nerve paths must have been impressed upon you without your knowledge."

Quentin said, "Or you have always had them, you and every member of your race. Or maybe I should say, everyone who follows your metaphor of the universe." To Victor, he said, "Amelia is basically agnostic; she has theories about the limitations of human knowledge, she believes in the uncertainty principle. All knowledge is relative to a frame of reference.

For her, 'Chaos' is that which by definition is unknown and unknowable. The fourth dimension is her metaphor for it."

I said, "It's not a metaphor. I've seen the fourth dimension."

Quentin spread his hands. "And I have seen aetheric spirits dancing in palest raiment by the light of the moon around a mushroom ring, and I've heard the harps the Four Living Beings play who ward the dancers sacred to Endymion. Where those light feet had passed, I drew up a residuum through a wand of willow-wood, into an alembic, and sealed those vapors there by virtue of the key of Solomon. Explain my experience."

I said, "I can't. What cannot be explained is a given, like a premise."

Victor said to Quentin, "Undeveloped sections of your nervous system were reacting to energies around you, and presenting childlike images to your cortex in response. A sufficiently detailed examination of the motions of the atoms in your brain would reveal what causes these images to arise."

Colin said, "Examinate, exschmaminate. You saw what you wanted to see, Big Q. It was magic."

Quentin raised his finger. "And that is my point! Amelia, Vanity, and Colin operate without conscious thought . . ."

I sat on the divan, murmuring, "I could have told you that about Colin years ago . . ."

"But what you and I do, Victor, requires specific knowledge and liberal arts. Natural sciences, knowledge of the correspondences between herb and constellation, phases of the moon, and their angelic governors and principles. And these molecules and atoms and void and what-not you believe in. Specific knowledge."

Victor said, "Is this comment leading to something?"

"Note the symmetry in the table of oppositions. The Phaeacians tie together you and Colin: one intellectual with one nonintellectual paradigm. The Olympians, likewise, with me and Amelia. But the Phaeacians, or at least Vanity, operates without conscious knowledge. She does not know how she creates secret passages. She does not even believe it is she herself doing it!"

"So?"

"So, assuming the symmetry is maintained throughout the whole table, the Olympians must operate by a specific science or body of law. Once we know the law, the specifics, we can stop them. A technology can be foundered on the rocks of detail, in a way that emanations from a nonintellectual force cannot be."

Colin stretched his arms and yawned. "I prefer the terms *esprit de finesse* and *esprit de geometrie.* I'll just wish our foes into oblivion! I really, really want that. By the way, has a busty cat burglar in skintight black with a whip shown up yet, or *Seven Year Itch* girl? Amelia and Vanity in their underwear don't count."

Quentin said, "According to the book, your power doesn't work that way."

Colin straightened up. "Since when? Amelia said . . ."

Quentin came across the salon from where he had been sitting and settled in the chair opposite me, saying, "Ah! Listening to Amelia in this one case was a mistake."

"Hey!" I said, feeling a little put out.

"Oh, don't misunderstand me, Amelia!" Quentin said. "But what is going on is— Ah, wait, I will show you. Colin! Ready for a question?"

Colin shrugged, looking curious. "Ask away."

"Do you understand what it is I do? My 'magic,' as you call it?"

"Sure. You wish for things to happen, and they do. You go through a lot of rigmarole with wands and chalk and candles and junk because it impresses the ladies. Or maybe you need it as a crutch."

"What could I do to do it better?"

"That's obvious, Big Q. If I were you, I'd throw all that mumbo-jumbo away and just do it by concentrating. I mean, it is obvious you already have the power, but you are wasting energy by putting power—putting belief—into things like wands."

Quentin grinned and turned toward me. "Did Colin give me good advice?"

I said, "I don't think he knows what it is you do. Not that I do, either . . ."

"He gave me the worst advice imaginable. Do you know what they call a practitioner of the Art without his wand?"

"What?"

"Unemployed." Quentin turned and hooked one arm back over the chair. "Just out of curiosity, Victor, what would your advice be?"

Victor said, "To do what?"

"Be better at what I do?"

"Define 'better.'"

"Oh, come now. More able. You know what 'better' means."

Victor said, "You are the victim of a complex cryptognostic trick. A set of nerve paths has been instilled in you, each one of which creates a distinct reaction in your environment when they are triggered. Each nerve path runs through your hypothalamus and reticular formations, and affects and is affected by reaction-complexes from symbols embedded there. Your specific pseudoscience relates to discovering which symbols create which reactions. So, first advice: learn all the symbols and their correlated reactions."

Quentin said, "That is basically what's in the *Oneirocritia.* What else?"

Victor said, "The things you call 'spirits' are electromagnetic entities of specific voltage, wavelength, and properties, who have been programmed to react to certain commands given in certain ways, gestures and so on. They are made of matter just as everything else is.

"Also, the molecular combinations which make up this world— Mulciber's world—have been impregnated with command and control codes to react to signals passed through the electromagnetic entities.

"Were I you, I would use your symbol codes to condition certain selected bundles of entities to react to a separate and simpler set of symbols, a set specific to your personal nerve structure, rather than taken from general mythological themes. This will make your commands simpler and more flexible, and prevent interference from other practitioners of your art."

Quentin looked considerably impressed. He turned to me. "And his advice? Was it good or bad?"

I spread my hands. "I can't tell. You'd have to try it and see."

"No, I do not have to try it. He just revealed, in his own quaint metaphor, of course, what it is each practitioner does when he becomes a master of the One True Art. All knowing is reflected in all other knowing. He just told me to find and construct my own mythology, my own special runes and tools, which expresses my personal relationship to the infinite, and to have a cadre of cacodemons and eudemons swear personal fealty to me."

I looked skeptical. "Victor, is that what you said?"

Victor looked up. His answer surprised me. "Yes. Of course, I said it in precise terms, and Quentin is speaking in the sloppy metaphors he uses to express himself, but his symbols were fact-to-fact associations."

Victor looked down again, but continued talking. "Also, Quentin, the other thing you should do is discover the programming language for the electromagnetic entities. Since they react to a word-and-gesture code, they must each have a listing of their codes embedded in each entity."

Quentin looked very impressed. "You refer to the Enochian language in which the Creator's Word spoke the universe into being?"

I snapped my fingers in front of Quentin's face. "Hey! Hello! You were going through this big long digression to tell me why Colin should not listen to me, when I told him how his powers work."

Quentin smiled. "Because you have no idea how his powers work, you told him all the wrong things, and, what's more, you will never understand how his powers work any more than Colin will understand mine, or I will understand Victor's. Our paradigms each have a blind spot. It influences our psychology."

I pointed at Colin. "So you tell me. How does Colin's power work? What can he do and can he not do?"

"He is a shaman, what Victor would call a psychic. He comes from an earlier tradition than mine, before the boundaries between man and angel were established."

I said to Colin, "Can you translate that from Quentin-speak into the common tongue of Westron?"

Quentin answered me. "Colin is psychic. Telekinesis, telepathy, mind-over-matter, metamorphosis."

Colin said, "I can't make things fly through the air like Victor can. I've tried."

"But you can metamorphosize objects at a distance. Turn a knot into something no one can untie, for example. Grendel could turn cold iron into a lightweight metal."

"And I can't read minds."

"Not when they are awake. You are Phobetor, Prince of Nightmares. I suspect those starlets in Hollywood went to sleep before they were influenced to write back to you."

Colin: "Okay. How's it work?"

Quentin: "Not by desire. Not by willpower."

Colin said, "But *it is so* by willpower! It worked! When I was falling from the sky, boy oh boy, did I desire to fly. And Amelia was—well, you are too young and innocent to know what she agreed to let me do to her. It turned me back into a man, though."

"Colin, I room with you. No one stays young and innocent who talks to you every night after lights out. But you don't know what you are talking about. It's not desire. Or, I should say, it is not *just* desire."

I said, "Okay. So what is it?"

"It's inspiration."

I looked at Colin. "Translate. Inspiration is a type of desire, right? It's a driving passion from your subconscious mind."

Colin looked like an idea was forming in his head. He said, "I think Big Q is using the word literally. Inspiration. Spirits come in."

Quentin nodded at Colin. "The reason why Amelia misidentified what she saw is that there is no category for this in her paradigm. To her, a genius is a man who is particularly brilliant. To me, a genius is a spirit who inspires a man to brilliance.

"Look at the cases we saw," Quentin continued. "Just now, Vanity and Amelia tried to inspire, ahem, manly feelings in you. I suspect what they actually did was summon a cupid into the room. Invisible lust energy, if you will. The energy passed through your soul, and it wanted you to turn into a man.

"Your soul acts like a conduit between the physical and the spiritual realm. Normally spirits cannot affect matter, not directly. But any spirit that passes into and through your soul, can, and does.

"Second case: falling. I remind you that you were riding the back of the master of the gods of the winds, with other wind gods coming to save him. Every spirit in the area was thinking about flying."

I said, "What about the time I tricked Grendel? When his desire to have me remember being kidnapped by him outweighed his desire to erase my memory, his attempt failed. Only Dr. Fell's medicine had any effect, and it did not affect me very much."

Quentin said, "I suspect it was your pity for Grendel, and not the lust you tried to instill in him, which drove away the spirits which otherwise would have given him power over you."

I said, "You are trying to interpret it in terms of good and bad. Pity is a finer emotion than lust, so it wins, is that your idea? But that is not the way psychological reactions work. The mind is a self-referencing infinitely regressive set of meanings; there are any number of possible relations within that set."

Colin said, "And what about my getting better? Amelia said Grendel kicked my ass, but here I am fit as a fiddle!" He raised his arms and tensed his muscles, our own private Charles Atlas.

Quentin said, "Good point. Third case: rapid healing. You tried to heal the splinters that struck you when Amelia blew up the safe. Nothing happened. Not ten minutes later, you are riding Boreas down to destruction, like Ahab clinging to Moby Dick. Actually, you were doing a little better than Ahab, but not by much.

"You had broken the wing of Boreas. Maybe there was some healing power in the area, being thrown on him by his friends to fix his wings. When you changed into a bird, your wings seemed to be healed first. I am thinking Boreas' allies released essential potentates of Aesculapius into the area, what you would call healing energy."

I said, "No. That was something else. The rapid healing."

"What was it?" asked Quentin.

"I, um, I did that. I really, really did not want Colin to die when he was a bird, and I asked him to get better."

Quentin squinted at me. "That, by itself, would not do it. Just asking."

"I kind of, um, promised him that I would do something for him, if he got better. Would that summon a spirit? Build up this energy you say passes through his body?"

Quentin said, "I do not think he has a body. He is made of aery substance, not matter. That's why he can bridge the veil. What did you promise him?"

"I'd do him a favor . . ."

"What kind of favor?"

Colin was looking on with great interest. "You were not wearing that little white number during this promise-making, were you?"

I blenched. Actually, I had been wearing that dress, hadn't I? Or had Grendel stripped it off me by then? "I think I was naked under a bearskin rug."

"Oh, this gets better." Colin smiled. "And your promise was, what, again, exactly . . . ?"

"Oh. I, um, don't feel like talking about this now. I need to go stick my finger down my throat or something right now." I jumped to my feet.

Colin said, "While you're up—is there anything to drink in this stateroom?"

I said, "There's an automatic bar thingie. I think it charges room service when you open the little door."

"Well, I'd ask you to get me some liquor—but . . ." He grinned at me wickedly. "I don't want it to count as this 'favor' you still owe me. We are talking about sexual favors, aren't we? Was Vanity telling the truth about you in there? You know . . ."

My face was turning red; I could feel the heat in my cheeks. "The part about she and I being lesbian lovers is true, of course. But I don't make her pretend to be you before the nightly spanking sessions. She pretends to be Quentin, I play you, and we act out what everyone knows you English schoolboys do at night in your dorm rooms!" And I stomped off toward the wet bar.

Colin said, "Actually, I'm Irish."

Quentin said softly, "What does she think we do at night? I mean, aside from listening to Victor tell you to shut up and go to bed."

"I don't know, loverboy. Maybe she noticed the missing hamsters."

"The missing what?"

"Never mind. I told you how to improve. According to your theory, you understand my power better than I do—hey—!"

"What?"

"I should understand Amelia better than she does. I mean, if this all goes in a circle around the diagram."

"Try doing what you do when you shut her powers off, but do it in reverse."

"What about me, Big Q, my guru, mojo macho master of the mystic arts, necromancer of naughty gnosticism?"

"What about you? You are a babbling dunderhead. The great Oz has spoken."

"Thank you, mystic master. Seriously, did you have a real idea how to improve my powers? I do not want to have to jump on Boggin's face every time I want to turn back into a bird."

"Amelia told you exactly the wrong thing to do. One hundred eighty degrees wrong. You have to learn to meditate, to relax, and to let the spiritual energy flow through you and inspire you. You must be like a crystal window. Your own thoughts and desires cloud the window. The real you, your oversoul, stands in the light beyond it."

This little bit of nonsense seemed to impress Colin deeply. He looked at Quentin with awe and wonder on his face. Since I had never seen that expression on Colin's face before, I assumed he was just suffering from a bit of upset stomach.

5.

Vanity was still sitting. She breathed more. Victor was still monitoring her pulse. He did not look bored. I do not think he has any circuits in his brain that do the "bored" function. Maybe he had them removed.

I drew up a chair and sat down. I had three bottles of beer in hand, which had come out of the automatic wet bar that came as part of the room. Colin looked interested, and I passed them around.

I called across the salon. "Victor? I couldn't find the fork screw. Whatever that thingie is called . . . bottle opener. Would you . . . ?"

Quentin said, "I think these twist off."

But it was too late. Victor, without looking up, waved his hand in our direction. Bottle caps sprang away from bottle necks with a loud noise and hovered in the air.

"Never tried this before," said Colin. He and Quentin clinked bottles, and both quaffed.

"Blech," said Colin. "It's gone bad."

Quentin was puckering and licking his lips. "Is it supposed to taste that way?"

I also took a sip, and put the beer in the same category as the coffee I had had earlier that day. Why do adults drink foul-tasting stuff? I said, "It's not champagne, that's for sure."

Colin said, "This is our first night of freedom. Let's get some champagne!"

"There's the phone," Quentin said, reaching up to pluck the three hovering bottle caps, one after another, from the air. "You just call, a guy named Miguel brings it. Oh, and you hide in the closet, because you're not supposed to be in here. We did not buy a ticket for you."

Colin said, "Oh, come on. Hide in the closet?"

"Aha!" I said. "You will be the master of hiding! I have a present for you, Colin! Victor? Where did Vanity put it? The ring?"

Victor plucked the ring out of Vanity's pocket and tossed it across the room to me.

I held it out to Colin. "This is for you," I said.

"This is all so sudden," he said, sniffing. "I—I don't know what to say. Of course I will marry you, but you will have to give up other women . . ."

"No, you moron!"

"Shouldn't you be kneeling?"

I proffered the ring to Quentin. "You give it to him."

Quentin waved it away. "And run the risk of another round of English schoolboy jokes? Not me. No. No, thank you."

I said in anger to Colin, "It's a magic ring!"

"Of course. I expected that. What's it do?"

"Turns you invisible!"

"I expected that. Of course. Does it inevitably corrupt the ring-bearer?"

Quentin said, "It's from Plato. It's a symbol of absolute power corrupting absolutely."

"And I am getting this fine, fine gift of corruption, why, again, exactly?"

Quentin said, "Dwarfs make less noise when they fall than giants. You know, less distance to the muck. So when the word 'corruption' popped up in conversation, the name 'Colin' sprang up on our lips almost of its own accord!"

I said, "It will protect you from Miss Daw's magic. No more being flung off cliffs. You'll be the strongest person in our group. It won't really corrupt you."

"I'll be the strongest person in the group . . . ?"

"Yes," I said.

"And it won't corrupt me . . . ?"

"One never knows."

"Will I be able to command the Nibelungs with it?"

"Do you want it, or not?"

"You are sure about the 'no corruption' thing, right?"

"Do you want me to stuff this up your nose?"

"No. Give it here! It already seems very precious to me, yessss. . . . Precioussss . . . Is anyone hungry for fisssssh or is it jusssst me?"

"Will you stop fooling around?"

"Ach! They hates us, my precious! Nasty elfish blondes!"

16

REMEMBER NEXT TIME NOT TO LOOK

1.

Colin slipped the ring on his finger. "Well? Am I invisible yet? I want to know when I can start taking off my clothes."

Quentin said, "The clothes turn invisible, too."

"Yeah, but I get to walk around in the buff, with no one staring. I can pick my nose, scratch my bum, you know . . ."

"Um, well. In cold weather, you can put on clothes, and your socks will no longer need to match," Quentin said.

"What about things I pick up? What if I just lean against something, and pretend I am picking it up? If I turn a laser beam invisible, can I make it harmless? What about radio waves? Am I also stealthed to radar? Can I blind an enemy by making his retinas invisible?"

I looked impressed. Actually, I thought they were good questions. Smarter than I expected Colin to ask. Maybe he had been hanging out with Victor more than I noticed.

Quentin said, "I would guess it relates to objects directly related to identifying you, such as clothing or footprints. When you turn the collet of the ring toward your hand, you see, that acts as a symbol of the hiding of your seal, or, in other words, your public or outer self."

"Ah! I see! It is all clear! . . . Except . . ."

"Except . . ."

"What the heck is a collet?"

"That thing there."

"Aha! On—! Off—! On—! Off—!" Colin twisted the ring on his finger, round and round. He vanished and reappeared, vanished and reappeared.

I noticed that something other than being permeable to photons must be creating the effect. Not only did his clothing vanish, but the seat cushion where he sat was not depressed, or did not look depressed, when he was unseen.

Colin flickered and reappeared. "I am trying to get it exactly halfway between turned in and turned out, to see if I can make only my left disappear. Here! Watch this." He vanished. "Tell me when you see the beer turn into urine. Ready?"

When he picked up the beer bottle, I was expecting to see a floating beer bottle, like in every version of the movie *The Invisible Man* I had ever seen. Instead, I saw the bottle, I knew it could not float by itself, saw the fingers, and traced the line of his arm back up to his face. His features were dark and clouded with shadows, as if light were avoiding him.

I stuck out my tongue and waved at him. "There is a limit on what you can do," I said. "If you attract attention, people can see through the illusion you're casting."

He looked at Quentin. "Can you see me, Quentin?"

Quentin had his face turned toward Colin's chair, but his eyes were unfocused, like a blind man's. "Not at the moment. I cannot see the beer bottle either. It was there a moment ago, but I do not remember seeing it fade out or wink out, or anything. I must have blinked just when you picked it up."

I said, "How many people do you think you could lift, Colin? I mean, if you can pick up a beer bottle, you can pick up Vanity. Maybe the whole group could vanish, if need be."

He said, "In my elephant form, or as a human?"

"Do you have an elephant form? When did you get an elephant form?"

Colin twisted the ring. A sort of pressure in my sinuses and eyes relaxed and faded. It was a small thing, and I was not aware of it until it went away, but something, some hypnotic compulsion, had been trying to get me to look away, or blink.

Colin said to Quentin, "Okay, great and powerful Oz, how do I get an elephant spirit to come and flow through my crystal window?"

"The true name of the father of elephants is Tantor."

"Great! What good does that do me? I am not a necromancer. I cannot summon up spirits by calling on their names."

Quentin said mildly, "Are you sure?"

"Okay!" Colin put the beer bottle aside and stood up, making a dramatic gesture with his hands, "Sim-sala-bim! *Size of . . . an eleph—*"

"*No!*" Quentin and I shouted together. I jumped up and grabbed Colin's arm. "If you turn into an elephant in the cabin, you'll crush the deck up and smash everything! Are you crazy?"

Colin sat down again. "Doing a Quentin-type spell would not work for me, anyway. I do not believe in that stuff, so it wouldn't work."

Quentin said, "Actually, what I do works whether I believe in it or not."

Colin picked up the beer bottle and gestured with it: "Aha! You *believe* that, don't you? So it's true for you."

Quentin turned to me. "Amelia, help me out . . ."

I said, "Don't look at me! I believe every statement has truth-value only in relation to its frame of reference. An Englishman and a Chinaman pointing 'up' both point away from the center of the Earth, but if you extend the lines from their fingers indefinitely, they get farther and farther apart . . ."

"No, that wasn't the help I was asking for. Look at the ring of Gyges. What does the ring look like to you? I am curious as to how you see it."

I opened my higher senses and looked.

2.

The ring was the center of a webwork of morality strands, which extended throughout the entire nearby area of time-space. Major arms of the strands extended to some place I could not see with merely four-dimensional senses.

I "lifted" my hand out of Earth's continuum and plucked my hypersphere from where it rested in my wings, and I rotated it from circle to sphere, and then to four-sphere, and then to a five-sphere.

It grew immensely heavy in my hand as "hemispheres" of crystalline energy popped up into existence "below" and "above" the (now flat-seeming) plane of hyperspace. It began issuing concentric pressure waves into the solid neutronium medium of five-space.

The range of echo response in five-space was very short, so I had to touch the ring with my other hand to be able to "sense" it. The sense was more like hearing than sight. Sort of.

Even though my hand was five-dimensional, and Colin's was only three-dimensional, he closed his fingers around my hand when I touched his ring. The fingers felt normal to me, not flat. They were round, warm, strong. I could feel my sense perceptions beginning to slip, as if I were about to collapse back into three-space, but I used an energy-balancing technique to let the ring affect my lower vision centers. If I did not "look" at the impossible hand-clasp Colin had me in, the uncertainty wave would not collapse, and he would not collapse me out of my shape back into 3-D girldom.

Instead, I looked at the ring.

I could no longer see the morality webs—they were too thin and insubstantial to be seen, since they were merely made of flimsy four-dimensional material—but I could sense the extensional, relational, and existential measurements of the ring of Gyges.

The ring's extension degree was congruent with the light-cone it gave off, and it reached to all observers.

The relation degree was a moral one. Apparently the ring imposed an obligation onto any onlookers not to look at the wearer. Anyone who violated that prohibition was penalized by being forced to obey the imperative to look away; but, logically, also had to "look away" from the fact that he was being forced to look away. By definition, a person is always unaware of what he is unaware of.

The existence degree was metaphorical rather than literal. Although I could no longer see them, I now knew where those longer arms of the morality strands were leading. They were going into the place behind the walls of the tunnels Vanity created. They were going into the dream continuum. But whether they were reaching in the dreamlands surrounding Earth, or the dreamlands of some unknown sphere or region of matter–energy outside the star-filled universe of Earth, that I could not say.

I tried to explain this as best I could to the boys. My explanation seemed to confuse more than it illuminated. I said, "The ring may have a weak spot. Innocent eyes will not be deceived by it. A person who bears you no ill will, or a child perhaps. Someone without sin. Eye unclouded by hate."

"Oh, great!" said Colin. "Now I know what my friends think of me."

I folded up my sphere and pulled my hand back "down" into three dimensions.

3.

Colin held my hand for a moment longer than he should have. I tried to yank it "up" into the red or "down" into the blue continuum. That would have worked on anyone else in the universe, but his fingers still seemed real and solid, no matter what.

I looked at him, "Let go of my hand, and I'll tell you the answer."

He said, "Tell me the answer, and I'll let go."

I said, "Music."

Both the boys looked at each other, saw their mutual confusion, and looked at me. Colin said, "Great. Now tell me the question."

"How do you get Tantor to come? How do you attract spirits, since you are not a warlock, and cannot call them by ritual? Music."

"You mean, I play 'Elephant Walk' for elephants, and 'Flight of the Bumblebee' to turn into a bug, and maybe theme from 'Batman' to change into a bat . . ."

"I'm serious. Quentin, tell him to let go of my hand."

Quentin said, "Be nice, Colin, or I will have the girls do another striptease for you."

Colin said, "What is the downside of that, again, exactly?"

"They will have to do it to return you to human form," Quentin said darkly. "Remember, don't make promises you don't intend to keep. It makes you vulnerable to certain operations."

Quentin's stick flew from across the room and into Quentin's grasp.

Quentin reached the quivering wand toward Colin's hand, and the look on Quentin's face was so grim and so unpitying, that even I said, "Quentin! Wait a minute! We can't just use our powers on each other—! Quentin! Stop! Stop!"

Quentin did not stop. The wand drew closer.

I shouted, "Victor, do something!"

Victor, across the room, did not look up. "Check your premises."

Quentin touched Colin on the knuckle with the wand. Quentin's lips did not move, but we heard a voice, a thin version of Quentin's voice, begin to mutter and chant: *"Gallia est omnis divisa in partes tres! Arma virumque cano! Res ipsa loquitur. . . ."*

Colin's nerve broke. He dropped my hand and jumped back as far as his chair would allow. "Keep off! Keep off! Damn! He's gone mad with power!"

Quentin smiled and put his stick aside. "Yeah. Be careful, or I'll tell you the name of the Father of Salmons."

"Hey! I've got this ring! I am supposed to be immune to magic powers now!"

"Yes, Colin, but I have said before I do not do magic. I only seem to. It's a trick done with mirrors. Your ring cannot stop me from pulling a rabbit out of my hat."

"You . . . tricked me!"

"Ah, grasshopper! You have learned everything there is to know about magic! Now you shall be the master! Go, and rule the world in my name!"

"Don't single me out for your magic curses. I am not the only one! Amelia made some sort of promise to me, she's not saying. What about that promise?"

"I can tell her the name of the Father of Salmons, too. It's Gwion. Now listen to what she has to say."

" 'Music' . . . ?" Colin looked at me.

"The Lamia said it. Remember, Quentin?"

Quentin said, "I would say, there are some things you just don't forget, but I think I forgot that scene twice." He shivered and looked unhappy. "I remember."

"In the story you told us? The Lamia was complaining that right under everyone's noses, Boggin had been teaching us the paradigms we needed to control our powers. They taught me Einstein, and Newton to Victor, Aristotle to you, and to Colin . . ."

Quentin muttered, " 'He taught music to the wild prince of Night and Dreams. . . .' "

Colin said, "That doesn't make sense. Not only do I hate music, but Miss Daw is the music teacher, and she's the one who uses Amelia's paradigm. Daw is a four-dimensional squid with wings, right?"

"Actually, she looks like wheels within wheels with eyes on every rim,"

I said. "But, you are wrong about one thing. She used her music to stop me. That's not part of my paradigm. That's against my paradigm."

I turned to Quentin. "Could she be something, I don't know, sort of halfway between my position and Colin's?"

Colin said, "Glum did not use music."

Quentin said, "But he did use a bearskin to turn into a bear. That was his beast-shape-cloak, his bear-sark. He was doing a shamanistic thing. It also sounds like he had a fetish."

I rolled my eyes. "I'll say!"

"No, I mean a real fetish."

"It was a real fetish," I said.

Quentin gave up on me and turned to Colin. "It sounds like Grendel used some shaman props to work his art. That would put Grendel halfway between you and me, sharing some of the properties of both."

Colin said, "Who else fits where? And why does everything have to be so complicated?"

I said, "If things were simple, everything would have been solved long ago."

Quentin said, "At a guess . . . ? And this is just a blind guess, I'd say the Hecatonchire are a cross between Victor's people and Amelia's. And who knows? I can't think of anything that could possibly fit between me and Victor. He and I have nothing in common, really. No overlap."

I said, "Maybe the Cyclopes. I've been assuming Dr. Fell is just like Victor, but maybe he actually does semi-magical stuff like potions and alchemy as well as molecular engineering. Some of the enemy called his stuff 'potions.' We don't have any evidence either way."

I leaned back in the divan, wondering if, all this time, Vanity had gotten the best catch out of the three. Victor was unapproachable; Colin was crude. But Quentin . . .

I said, "When did you become the Answer Man, Quentin? Why do you know all these things all of a sudden?"

He picked up his gold-and-silver grimoire, and pointed to it. "*Nam et Ipsa Scientia Potestas Est.* Colin's Dad told me. He wrote this book. You know, this might have been the talisman meant for Colin, except . . . Happy birthday, Colin! More powers for you."

He took out the little brown envelope, on which was written in Boggin's crisp, wide-looped penmanship, *Remember Next Time Not to Look.*

"My talisman! You and Victor got instruction books on how to use your powers. I guess my instruction booklet can be written on the three-by-five card." Colin opened the envelope and took out something about the size of a playing card. The back was embossed with a design of a poppy blossom. "Oh, great," said Colin, looking terrifically unimpressed. "What's it supposed to mean?"

"I don't know what it means," said Quentin. "I don't know what is on the face of the card."

"What do you mean? Look." Colin held the card toward him facefirst.

Quentin flinched and put up a hand to block his vision. "No, no, no! Don't show me. We all played around with looking at that card. Thanks, but no thanks."

I said, "Why? Does something terrible happen when you look at the card?"

"Amelia, can you hear me now?" asked Colin.

I said, "Of course, why shouldn't I be able to hear you?"

Colin looked at Quentin and whistled. "Wow."

Quentin said, "Same thing happens to me and to Vanity. Victor is unaffected. That doesn't make any sense on our table of oppositions, because I should be able to trump your powers."

I said, "What's going on? Is there something on that card I can't look at?"

Colin said, "You want to see it again?"

"What do you mean 'again'?"

"Here, look."

"I am looking. Hold up the card." I turned my head. Quentin was now sitting on the divan beside me, and Colin was in the chair Quentin had been in.

"Good trick," I said to Quentin.

"Here is a better one," said Quentin, handing me a piece of paper.

On the piece of paper were words in a flowing, delicate handwriting:

Picture shows a man standing in black robes, stars in robe, cup of sparks in hand. Crowned w/ crescent moon. Cup tilted, sparks fall into pool at feet. V. pretty woman kneels by pool. Crowned w/ poppies. Crying. Tears fall in pool. Basket in pool. Baby in basket.

Behind them dark forest, tall tower of wh spiral. Unicorn horn?
Heraldic emblem top of card. Winged horse w/ head dragon, ram-
pant, propre.

It was my handwriting.

I looked up. "What does it mean?"

Victor from the across the room, said, "The card is an artifact from Quentin's paradigm, not from Colin's. It interferes with the time-binding function of the cortex."

I said, "I assume I was not asleep . . . I wrote this?"

Quentin said, "The thing that happens when one wakes in the morning, to make one forget one's dreams, is in that card. It does not affect Colin, because he is entirely made of dream stuff. It does not affect Victor, because, well, not to sound mean about it, Victor is a robot. No offense meant, Victor."

Victor replied, "None taken, puny flesh-slug."

I said, "He's not really a robot."

Quentin said, "But I don't think he has any part of his being made of dream stuff. I mean, that sums up all the differences and similarities between our four paradigms, doesn't it? Colin is all spirit, and Victor is all matter. I am both, an immortal spirit trapped for a time in a mortal body made of clay. You . . . Gee, Amelia, I do not know about you. Both? Neither?"

I said, "It's actually pretty simple. I have a controlling monad which is the final-to-mechanical causality nexus for governing other lesser nexuses, each of which has its own meaning axis and the non-meaning axis. What you call matter is an extension of non-meaningful relationships. They are objective and devoid of self-awareness or purposeful behavior. The other axis informs meaningfulness. Meaningful things are subjective. The meaning axis forms the context, the frame of reference, in which the non-meaning axis operates. Perception presupposes a perceiver and a perceived. The final cause of our perceptions, the reason why we have them, is to render matter meaningful; the mechanical causes of perception are the sense-impressions which arise from matter."

Quentin turned to Colin, "Can you translate Amelia glossolalia into the Common Speech of Westron?"

"She thinks matter and spirit are two parts of one underlying thing, I think," Colin said.

"No," I said. "I think questions like that are, by their nature, unanswerable and ultimately, unaskable. Life requires us to adopt dualism, at least in our actions. We move thoughts by thinking, we move matter with other bits of matter. Matter is what we call those things we cannot control with our thought alone. If everything was matter, everything would be inanimate, and there would be no deliberate action. If everything were thought, everything would be omnipotent, perfectly tranquil, and at rest, for there would be no need for action.

"Logic says there must be one underlying reality, a nexus of cause and effect, by which final causes relate to mechanical causes. This is called a monad. It cannot be investigated by introspection alone, because it is not made of thought alone. It cannot be investigated by material science alone, because it is not made only of matter. Therefore, we cannot investigate it at all. We know it must be able to influence and be influenced by thought; we know it must be able to influence and be influenced by matter. That is all we can ever know about it."

Colin said, "I said that. I said what she just said. She thinks mind and body are part of one underlying thing. How come no one listens to me?"

Victor said, "Everything is inanimate, if by that you mean things that operate according to cause and effect. Free will is an epiphenomenon, a misjudgment impressed upon us and sustained by the actions of brain molecules in motion."

Colin said, "Are we going to do philosophy? Everything is animate. Cause and effect is illusionary. We are all omnipotent, perfectly tranquil, and at rest. Our real selves. But we are dreaming. In our omnipotency, one of us or all of us conceived the desire to meet a challenge equal to our strength. Since we could have everything we wanted, voilà! One of the things we must have wanted was not to be able to have everything we wanted. We got trapped in the illusion. Be careful what you wish for."

Quentin said, "You folks know what I think. The pituitary gland is the point where the spirit is connected to the flesh."

Colin said, "Since it is my birthday—I am the one getting presents here—I officially ban all further philosophy until further notice. Amelia is going to start talking in equations if we don't cut this off.

"And we are never going to agree," Colin continued. "In fact, I think, if any two of us *did* agree, one of the two would lose all his powers. Okay? Instead of figuring out the nature of the universe, let's figure out the nature of this card. It is smaller than the universe, and should be simpler to figure out, and we are all bright guys with big brains, so what the hell does it do? Do I eat it? Rub it on my head? Sleep with it under my pillow? Burn it? It seems like pretty much of a dud, to me. I got gypped."

I said, with some surprise, "Colin? Didn't I tell you who is on that card when I was under its amnesia spell?"

Colin shook his head.

"Ohh . . ." I did not say it aloud, but I knew why my earlier (and now lost) version of me had not said anything. I wanted to see and remember his reaction when I told him.

"You know something about the card?"

I said, "I recognize the man. He is your father. That's Morpheus. The beautiful woman lowering the cradle into the water must be your mother. I don't know her name. The baby is you. This is your family. This is what it looked like when your parents lost you. They were forced under threat of death to turn you over. That landscape in the background is your homeland, where you were supposed to grow up and be happy. That white spiral tower is your home."

Colin took out the card and stared deeply into it. A haunted, lost look came into his eyes. The look of a baby who lost its mother, a toddler whose parents never saw his first step, the child who spoke his first words to strangers, the youth who was robbed of his life and his loved ones, the man who was robbed of his true identity. And then the expression stiffened, and it became the look of the prince who was robbed of his kingdom, his fatherland, his people.

Tears came next.

The tears flowed down his stiff cheeks like water trickling over iron. He did not bother raising a hand to wipe them away. It was strange and horrible to look on Colin and see him as a man so grim and fell. Now that I had done it, I was sorry I waited to tell him. I would have preferred that this scene be blotted from my memory after all.

"What's happened to you, Colin?" I said softly.

"I am still the same Colin," he said in a voice like ice. "But now I'm . . . inspired."

I did not want to ask him, *Inspired with what?*

He must have sensed the unspoken question, because he answered anyway. "I feel like I'm turning into your crystal window, Quentin. My real self is on the other side. He is fire and the firelight is shining through him. He has a question for the group. When is the enemy going to show up next?"

It was Vanity who spoke next: "They are going to try to kill us, the next group that finds us."

We all turned to look, some with surprise, some slowly. There she sat on the chair with her eyes open.

"How'd it go?" asked Quentin.

She said, "I had to travel back a million years to find my memories. Boggin hid them a long way away. He let something slip in front of me, and I figured it out."

Victor said, "Tell us."

"Boggin wants to find out which group sent the Lamia. So we are being left to dangle out here in the wide outside world until the Lamia feels safe to strike again. We have our powers now, so she is going to have to get someone very strong—in other words, her boss—to come kill us. Boggin wants to find out who that boss is. Boggin has some way of finding us again, or driving us back to him. We are not free. We were let go. We're bait."

17

THE IRE OF THE HEAVENS

1.

Vanity told us her tale.

She had been sitting in Boggin's office while the Headmaster, peering down at her from behind his huge desk, with jovial threats and smiling intimidations, was trying to get her to agree to promise not to attempt escape again. Vanity sat and nodded, agreeing to nothing, and saying, "Go on," each time he came to a full stop.

Mr. Sprat had called on the intercom, an urgent voice warning Boggin that he had a guest, who could neither be delayed nor denied.

Boggin had evidently not wanted Vanity to be seen by the guest. A switch in his desk had opened a panel behind the portrait of Odysseus.

Boggin took Vanity by the elbow and roughly hustled her in through the secret panel. In she went. The door slammed shut behind her and locked with a click.

Inside was a narrow room lit by an even narrower window. There was a cot, a washbasin, several locked cabinets, a locked rolltop desk.

If this was the inner sanctum of the Headmaster, he certainly did not coddle himself. The room was Spartan. There was no fireplace, no heat; the cot was hard.

The only ornament in the room was a cabinet containing a miniature shrine. Behind the cabinet doors was a nine-inch-high statue of a stern and kingly figure on a throne, an eagle on his shoulder and a crooked lightning bolt made of brass in his marble hand. There was a cutting board and knife rack before it. The cutting board was bloodstained, and there were tiny bits of down and feather littering the surface.

Vanity was certain that an evil mastermind like Boggin must have an escape exit from his inner lair, but the only thing she found was a hidden hatch leading to a defunct dumbwaiter shaft. She stuck her head into the hatch. There was a skylight high above, and the shaft below fell sheer into darkness. No one without wings would be able to use this route.

She also was curious about the conversation she was not able to overhear, and wondered at the identity of the guest Mr. Sprat dared not to stop nor delay. Evil masterminds simply had to have methods of listening in on what happened in rooms adjacent to them. They had to! It was an article of faith with her.

Sure enough, when she looked for a peephole hidden in the panel behind the Odysseus portrait, there one was. There was a mechanism for listening, basically a bell with an earpiece, sort of a crude stethoscope.

2.

The visitor was standing. Boggin was kneeling on one knee before it, with his mortarboard in his hand, his long red braid of hair, normally hidden, now trailing down his back.

The visitor was thin and tall, like a leopard or a jaguar might look if standing on hind legs. Parts of its skin were made of bronze, or perhaps metal plates had been fused to its chest and back, metal scales along its upper arms and metal greaves on its lower legs. Because its neck was long and flexible, its head looked small. It had long hair like a woman, but its teeth were sharp like a lion's teeth. Its lips and cheeks were so plastic that it could flex its mouth from a tiny pink rosebud to a white grin whose corners touched the spot where, on a human, there were visible ears.

It wore a scarlet cloak. In one hand it gripped a short stabbing-spear with a metal head and a wooden shaft, a weighted spike at the butt end; in the opposite elbow it held a narrow-cheeked bronze helmet with a drooping red plume. As a gratuitous anachronism, the warrior-creature also carried a stub-nosed submachine gun of squat design at its hip, a bandolier of magazines looped over its shoulder.

Vanity did not hear the beginning of the conversation.

The creature was saying, ". . . Uranians have demonstrated that they could escape your confinement. A second escape is likely to be believed. The Lamia will no doubt make a second attempt at that time. Our military intelligence department estimates the chance of Lamia making a second attempt while the Uranians are still in custody to be a small one."

Boggin spoke in his normally hearty and self-interrupting fashion. He did not speak as a kneeling man should. "Ah . . . ! I am certain, my dear Centurion Infantophage (and a fine name you have chosen for yourself!), that the military intelligence department of the Laestrygonians—are you familiar with the word 'oxymoron'? No? I thought not—a department that enjoys such fame, or, one is tempted to say, such notoriety for the accuracy and timeliness of its predictions and warnings, well, such an august institution is one with which it is certainly, ah, futile, if not to say, pointless, to remonstrate."

The creature's eyes glittered with hate. "You are mocking us, airblower?"

Boggin lowered his head, but his voice was still rich with good humor: "Oh, my dear Centurion Infantophage (a most excellent name, have I said how well it fits you?), certainly I would not wish to be understood by you if I were mocking you to your, ah, shall we call it a face? To your face. No, indeed. I hold the Laestrygonians in the greatest possible respect! The greatest, indeed, possible to grant to Laestrygonians. Your fine military intelligence department was charged, I believe, with the duty of bodyguarding the Lord Terminus, was it not? During the battle of Phlegra. The late Lord Terminus, I should say. The late, departed, once-alive but now-dead, which is to say, no-longer-alive, Lord Terminus. No doubt the sincere grief of your master, the Lord Mavors, at the departure of his father Lord Terminus was modified, if not ameliorated, by his joy on discovering (no doubt, to his complete surprise) that he stood to inherit the throne of heaven. The rulership of the entire sidereal universe must be a heavy burden."

"My master does not care for the throne. He assumes it as a matter of duty, no more and no less."

"What an unlucky day that was for him, then, when the Laestrygonians failed to protect his father from Typhon of Chaos! I am certain that the punishments visited upon the Laestrygonians by Lord Mavors when they fail at their duties are as great as the generous rewards he heaps upon them when they succeed!"

"Lord Mavors is harsh to those who fail him, but just. He is a good leader."

"And may I also take this opportunity to congratulate you and your department for its recent elevation to the status of the Praetorians? The halls and palaces that you now occupy on the lower slopes of Olympos are indeed splendid, as well I know, since I and my brethren inhabited a very similar station of rank under the rulership of Lord Terminus."

"I do not see how that comment is relevant to this conversation."

"Of course not, Centurion. Of course you would not see. Forgive my digression. What in the world could I have been thinking?"

"You will arrange the release of the Uranians. Lord Mavors has laid a malediction upon whoever should kill one or more of them. The nature of Olympian curse allows the maledictator to become aware of opposition or resistance to the malediction . . ."

"Ah, indeed?" muttered Boggin. "I am grateful, certainly grateful for your instruction upon this obscure point. You will tell me more about the operation of the Olympian art of destiny-manipulation when you have opportunity, I hope, Laestrygonian."

"Enough! Why do you speak with such insolence?"

"Every teacher learns lessons from his own students, Centurion."

"You are insubordinate."

"As the term is usually used, Centurion, in fact, I am not. I am not under the orders of Lord Mavors, nor does he have authority to command me.

"Indeed," continued Boggin in that same hearty tone, "Lord Mavors is asking me to go directly against the last orders I received—one might, without undue exaggeration, almost call it the dying wish—of Lord Terminus. 'Protect those infants!' Those were his last words to me, Centurion: 'Your life, and the life of Cosmos itself, is forfeit, if they are harmed.' Actually, his very last words to me were: 'We shall impart further instructions by Our next messenger.'

"Well, that never eventuated, did it, my dear Centurion? His last messenger, Lord Trismegistus, had (so to speak) turned in his two weeks' notice, and was busy showing the Phaeacians where to go to ship the hulking mass of Lord Typhon of Chaos to the foot of Mount Olympos at the time, and Lady Iris was busy trying to run his errands for him.

"I do not recall receiving any message from Lord Terminus saying, 'Obey Mavors, he is Our royal heir,' or anything like that. The present situation might be more, how shall I say, unambiguous, had a message of that nature been received by any party."

The Laestrygonian smiled, which was a truly alarming sight. (Vanity was reminded of a shark opening its mouth.) "Lord Mavors says this is the only method to arrange for the safety of the hostages. Until the traitor is identified and rooted out, they are not safe here, or anywhere. It will reduce rather than increase the danger. Lord Mavors is not contradicting your previous orders."

Boggin said, "The traitor could be anyone, could he not?"

The Laestrygonian nodded his graceful head. "You are above suspicion, Boreas. You have had too ample an opportunity to kill the hostages in the past, if that were your scheme. But the traitor must be someone who wishes to break the present truce with Chaos."

Boggin might have been tired of kneeling. Or perhaps he felt there were some things that one must stand on one's feet to say.

He rose up, and said, still in a pleasant and good-natured voice, "Well, well, who could it be? If war broke out, to whom would everyone turn to lead us in war against our mutual foes? I do not think it would be the god of the toy-makers, would it? It is surprising how quiet fraternal discord becomes, when an enemy none of us can resist separately marches against us, burning planets as it comes."

The Laestrygonian's eyes glittered like the eyes of a cat in the dark, and its shark grin dwindled to an amazingly small pucker of disapproval.

"You suspect Lord Mavors of favoring war?"

"Well, they do say it is the quickest time to rise up through the ranks, wartime. Success in war carries many a general on the shoulders of clamoring crowds to Caesar's purple."

"And failure in war leads to bonds, stripes, imprisonment, crucifixion, and the death of one's baby sons and lady wives. Mavors knows we cannot prevail against the Chaoticists, divided as we are, if the foe makes a coordinated and intelligent attack. Even a victory would make the Cosmos suffer losses in men and territory we cannot spare. You are said to be quick-witted, lord of the snowy winds, a lover of intrigue: Does your crooked mind find no more likely candidate than Lord Mavors for the power that sent Lamia to attack young Eidotheia, child of the Gray Sisters?"

"You are, as the expression goes, too kind for belief, Centurion. Were I a real master of intrigue, I would not have the reputation for being a master of intrigue. As for who it is? The person I least suspect would be Lord Mulciber. He has a smooth pathway leading him to the purple; why should he shoot arrows into his own shoe?"

The Laestrygonian sneered, "You overestimate the chances of the god of toil and stench. Which one of us prefers to have the horseshoe-maker lead us in glorious war, rather than the horse-master?"

"Who prefers to have the master of creating be the master of creation, rather than the master of destroying? Not everyone savors the smell of burning villages, or prefers the clash of iron to the clink of gold."

The Laestrygonian made a dismissive gesture. "Let us agree the Lame God is beyond suspicion."

"As if our agreement mattered, my dear Centurion . . ."

"I do not bother suspecting the Unseen One. If he wished for the throne of heaven, he could take it by force of his terror. Even my master, Lord Mavors, admits that no one can stand against the Cold Lord of the House of Woe; every soldier slain on either side during the fray awakens on the next day, marching beneath the black and unadorned banners of the God of Eternal Torments."

"Let us, as they say, work down the list from oldest to youngest. Lord Pelagaeus is next in age after the Lord Who Wept But Once. Pelagaeus, or the Earthshaker, if I may so call His Lordship, has always opposed the rule of Lord Terminus, and always sought to increase his own kingdom. Remember the deluge of Deucalion?"

"He is a candidate. And yet one of his principal grievances against Lord Terminus was that the quarrelsome and short-lived humans were given dominion over the fertile and beautiful dry land, while the peaceful and long-lived nymphs, naiads, nereids, and sea elves were forced to live amid the muck and filth of the sea bottom, exposed on several borders to attacks from Pontus. Ever since the petrification of Phaeacia, however, Atlantis has grown in wealth, power, and prestige. Neptune's continent now covers an area equal in extent to all the lands of all the worlds; and all his peaceful sea folk enjoy pastures of surpassing splendor. But notice that it lies between Olympos and the likely attack routes from Pontus and Chaos beyond. Lord Pelagaeus would be the most to suffer, and the greatest to suffer, should the truce between Cosmos and Chaos fail."

"Ah ... really ... ? I suppose you are right. What a funny coincidence ..."

"You are the one who recommended to Lord Terminus the grant of the fair continent of Atlantis to Lord Pelagaeus, and who suggested the position. Are you still dismayed at how little the intelligence branch of the Laestrygonians discovers? You can rely on us to remind you of things you have forgotten."

Boggin said, "Pelagaeus is still a suspect. Suppose the Chaoticists offered to let him keep the living sea and the island of Atlantis, if he would help them tear down the sky and sink the lands and mountains occupied by human beings into the brine? The offer would tempt him."

"He is not the only suspect. Of course, the Vine God would welcome war between Cosmos and Chaos; he is a creature of madness, drunkenness, revelry, disorder."

Boggin said, "And yet he also presides over public festivals and feasts, and soothes the weary toil of man with the refreshments and pleasures of the vine. Some say there is none who delights more in the happiness of mortal man aside from Dionysus. He is a strange fellow, but I would not head my list of warmongers with his name."

"He was one of the three who conspired with Chaos against Heaven."

"I did not say he was off the list. I just would not put him at the top of it."

"Who would you put?"

"That remains to be seen. On the one hand, Lord Trismegistus, the Swift God, the Father of Lies. He has no hope of gaining the purple by any peaceful means. He was the second of the Three."

"If he were not in Tartarus, I would suspect him. The fact that he is dead excuses him."

Boggin said, "Did you see his dead body with your own eyes, fingerprint it, check its retinal eye patterns, put your hands into its wounds?"

"Of course not. Lord Trismegistus fell into the Abyss, with the silver arrows of the Huntress sticking into him."

"Then do not count him dead. That could have been an actor, or a wax mannequin. Or the Huntress could have conspired with him, and shot him with blunt trick arrows into bladders full of pig's blood he had beneath his robe."

"Put him on the list then, if you fear the work of those who no longer exist." The Laestrygonian sneered again.

"No. I still put Trismegistus at the bottom of the list. He had concourse with Chaos before any other of the Triad; he knew the royal families in Chaos, he loved their people, and adopted their ways. They say he had a wife among them. Would he kill the children of his friends just to start a war where more of his friends would die? A war that, I should add, would put him no closer to the purple. Does he want to rule the wreckage of creation, once all created things are dead? It does not sound like him."

"Who else is on your list, then? So far the Vine God is the only suspect."

"Good Infantophage, you have not mentioned the third leg of the Triad. Dionysus and Trismegistus are but two. What of the Gray-Eyed Lady, the Wise One? What of the Lady Tritogenia?"

"She is a woman."

"Does the word 'Queen' or 'Empress' not exist in your limited vocabulary, my dear Centurion? Lady Athena Tritogenia would make a better ruler than your master. She loses battles less often."

"She is a virgin. How would she establish a dynasty? The Huntress is crippled in the same way. I suspect they are sterile, or lesbians. Why else would they don armor, and fight and hunt? Besides, if a woman could take the purple, why has not the Queen of Heaven taken the throne? Both Mulciber and Mavors would support the claim of the Queen Mother, Lady Hera."

"So are you putting all three ladies on the list of suspects, good Centurion?"

"No. The Huntress has no following worth mention; she slays Chaoticists when she finds them and skins them like beasts. She would not welcome war. The Gray-Eyed Lady I think is too wise to let war loose upon the universe, for any cause. She wins more often than my master because she fights like a woman, timidly, and only when she knows victory is with her. No son of Uranus would cooperate with Lady Hera Basilissa for any reason whatsoever. From the first moment of time, they had no greater foe than the Queen. Rule, Law, Good Order are her watchwords. Even Lord Terminus was wild and chaotic, compared to her."

Boggin smiled. "I see you share your master's good opinion of the Queen of Heaven."

"There would be neither grain nor roads nor laws without her. Do you dispute this?"

"I was one of the ones she sent to harass Aeneas, who, as far as I could see, had broken none of her precious rules. But no matter! The Queen and two virgins are not on the list. Do we need to discuss the Goddess of Households, or the Goddess of Love?"

"Lady Hestia is the eldest of all of them, older even than the Unseen One. What she did in the before-times, or what she learned from Rhea, no one knows. There is a power in her she keeps hidden. My master Mavors respects her."

"And he shows his respect for the institution of marriage by getting together with the wife of his brother, no doubt to sing hymns to the Lady Hestia, while holding hands chastely."

"Do not mock the Lord Mavors!"

"Me? Why should I? When the very existence of Archer, the young Love God, advertises the virtue of Lord Mavors for all the world to see? What need have I to add to that mockery? I would plunge my manhood between the silky thighs of the Lady Cyprian if she wanted me to plug up the hole of loneliness she feels in her life, and I would never fear the consequences. Mock him? I envy him! Indeed, I will not put the Love Goddess on any list, or even speak ill of her in a whisper; she is the one who made me fall in love with Orithyia, and look at how that turned out. She wants her son on the throne, and she wants all wars to stop, forever, so everyone can get on with their mooning and sobbing and waiting and mating. I would suspect myself before I would suspect the doe-eyed Aphrodite. Of the women goddesses, who is left?"

"The Queen of Grain."

"Unimaginable."

"Agreed," said the Laestrygonian softly. "Even I (and I am as loyal as his own right hand is to Lord Mavors), I would embrace my own spear before I would raise a weapon against the Lady Mother Demeter. The only one left is the limp-wristed poet."

"I thought we were listing goddesses."

"We are."

"We are speaking of the Bright God, the one they call the Destroyer?"

"The Flaming Solar Faggot, I call him. His hand is on the harp-string these days, not the bow-string."

"You amaze me, Centurion, in the breadth, or shall I say, the depth, of your wisdom. It is like a hole without a bottom. You must have studied for years to learn the art of forgetting every lesson in history. The Destroyer is the greatest god of us all, invincible in war, a master of all arts and sciences, a philosopher, learned in letters, a prophet who sees the secrets of the future. . . . Do you recall that he shot one million arrows at the Telchine demon called Phython, when that monster was nigh to destroying all of the established Earth? Alone and without aid, the Destroyer fought him on the sea and in the air, burned him with arrows of fire, and broke his back over his shining knee. So great was that battle that some of those arrows are still in flight through the upper heavens. When they fall to Earth, they make a streak that men call falling stars, and they are held to be a sign of good luck."

"A million, you said? How many missed? In my company, we get a stroke of the rod for every arrow that misses the target."

"The Destroyer is not on my list at all. He does not want the throne; he does not want for there to be a throne at all, but prefers we had the demos vote, as they did in Athens."

"He is also not on my list. The boy-kisser does not have the balls it would take to conspire against my lord Mavors."

"Well, then, who is left?"

"The young Love God. The Archer. Remember? Our Emperor. The one the Three Queens assigned to rule over us now that Lord Terminus is gone."

"You mean Lord Eros, son of Mavors and Cyprian. I recall him well. We endured the rule of Love in Heaven for all of thirteen years, during which time he disbanded the army, emptied the treasury, trampled on all of our ancient rights and privileges, turned the tablets of the laws on their heads, so that the innocent were punished and the guilty were spared. They say the English who lived in this land, during their years of darkness, prayed to their god to spare them from the fury of the Norsemen. Were their god a real one, I would pray: 'Spare me, O Lord, from the Compassion of Reformers!' "

"You think the Archer would kill the hostages?"

Boggin said, "I do not know what Lord Eros is capable of. He may have been in the pay of Chaos all this while. If he had been setting out to do as much damage as possible to the strength and dignity of the Sovereignty of Heaven, I do not see how he could have done more. If he was not in the pay of Chaos, then I congratulate their wisdom: they saved money."

The Laestrygonian said, "You said you would not put the Vine God at the top of your list, but you have removed nearly everyone else from the list. That puts him at the top, does it not?"

"So it seems."

"We will assign watchers to keep eyes on the Vine God; your task is to arrange a likely-seeming escape for the Chaos pups you have here. Do you understand?"

"I think there is very little chance that I would misunderstand the situation to the degree and in the way that other people in this room might have done, my dear Centurion."

"When will the escape be carried out?"

"Oh, but my good Infantophage, such things require great delicacy! We do not want the children harmed, do we? That would defeat the purpose. I will keep you informed as events progress."

"Do not toy with the idea of disobeying the Lord Mavors."

"Oh, I would never toy with that idea, my dear Centurion. Not toy with it. Oh, no. I greet the orders (albeit, the word 'suggestions' comes to mind as one that may be more apt in that context) of the Lord Mavors with the most grave, and, shall I say, sober deliberation. I daresay I put as much thought into obeying his instructions as he put into formulating them, or, since any finite sum exceeds zero, I am tempted to say, more. He certainly knows how children should be treated! What a fine job he did raising the Lord Eros from a spoilt, immature, mewling baby to a spoilt, immature, mewling tyrant . . . well, to someone who was occupying, that is to say, taking up space on, the very throne of Heaven itself! Mavors must stay awake nights thinking about what a fine job he did raising Lord Eros."

"Lord Mavors did not raise Lord Eros. The child was born a bastard out of wedlock. What in the world are you talking about?"

"Ahh . . . ? Hm . . . ? Well, perhaps I was thinking about someone else. I understand your orders. There may be delays in carrying them out. . . . We cannot be too careful in these matters, eh?"

The moment the Laestrygonian had gone, Boggin turned and smiled at the peephole, sucking through his teeth a great, hissing indrawn breath. A gale-force wind sucked the panel door open and pulled Vanity flopping headlong into the room.

Boggin seized her about the shoulders and drew her up. Her legs kicked, unable to touch the floor. "As one of the few people endowed (may I say blessed?) blessed with the power of the Phaeacians, I find it unduly, even absurdly, useful to be able to tell when people are spying on me, my little Miss Fair. My fair Miss Fair. No harm shall come to you, however, my pretty little sneak-mouse. But when you intrude your perky little nose into business of your elders, it is regrettable, and I do regret, that certain steps must be taken, to preserve your life and, indeed, the lives of all the other young women in the universe, women not so very attractive as yourself, of course. I will not ask you to forgive me—My! You do wiggle quite a bit when you struggle, don't you?—no, I will not ask, not because I do you no wrong—I fear it is a great, one is tempted to say, a calamitous wrong—but, rather because, in the future, I hope that, in the kindness of your heart, you will put this whole incident from your memory. To help you with this process, we will go inquire after our good Dr. Fell, perhaps with some help from our own dear Miss Daw and our own not-so-dear Mrs. Wren, if she is not stinking drunk today. Shall we?"

And he tucked her over his shoulder, Tarzan-carrying-Jane style, and walked out of the office with her.

3.

Because Vanity had just been stimulated in her memory by a molecular engine of Victor's, aided by a psychic energy by Colin, her memory of this event was crystal clear. She was able to report it word for word, in perfect detail.

She stood in the room, pacing back and forth, showing us the expression and mannerisms of Boggin and his thin guest. She did such a lifelike impersonation of Boggin's hemming and hawing that we all laughed, until Victor shushed us to hear the grim words Vanity was repeating.

Miguel arrived with the champagne about then, and Colin twisted his ring for the moments while the steward was in the room.

We passed around the shining and bubbling wine and drank toasts, led by Colin, who stood atop the table in the center of the cabin, one after another, to every class Colin had been behind in, every upcoming test he had been dreading.

We talked over Vanity's story for what seemed like a long time, though perhaps I was merely sleepy and thickheaded with champagne.

Victor believed that Boggin was cooperating with the Laestrygonian, and had arranged our escape, merely by picking certain coincidences and placing them in our future. Perhaps the Olympian power of destiny control allowed for this. Perhaps not.

I argued the other hand. If Vanity were accurate in her portrayal of Boggin's tone of voice, his supercilious expressions, and lilting sarcasm, it was clear to me that Boggin had no intention whatsoever to cooperate with Mavors. The Laestrygonian had expressly said that the Lamia would not attack us while we were still on the estate grounds; Boggin said his mission was to prevent us from being attacked. All he had to do was continue to make one excuse after another to Mavors, saying, whenever he was asked, that the escape attempt was not quite ready yet. He could play such delays interminably. I thought we had escaped all on our own, and everyone but Victor seemed willing to believe me.

My main argument was this: If Boggin had helped us escape, he would have put some sort of tracking device on us.

Vanity said slowly, "But he did. He has one on you. Your promise to him acts as a consent to be found by him."

I put my hand toward her. We held hands. I asked, "Is he tracking me now?"

Vanity closed her eyes. For a moment, I thought perhaps the champagne had sent her to sleep, but then she stirred and said, "Maybe he is still in the hospital, or maybe he's not thinking of you. He's not aware of you. Not right now."

Victor handed Vanity the little box that controlled the television. He turned his back to her and asked her to point the little box at him. She did, giggling, and we all joked she was raising and lowering Victor's volume and so on.

He turned and came back. "Could I sense you when you were not sending a beam toward me?"

Vanity pouted. She said, "He's right. If they have a bug on us, or on our clothes, and it's not broadcasting at the moment, I would not sense that we were being watched. If they were tape-recording our conversations, and they hadn't gotten around to playing the tapes back yet, I do not think I would sense that either."

Victor said coldly, "We would be fools to assume, after a warning such as this—a warning which, by the way, we can assume Boreas could arrange fate to make us stumble upon—we would be fools to assume we are safe. The next attack is going to be lethal. We don't know when it will come, or where. We are like the farmers who lived on the slopes of Vesuvius: We know the eruption is coming. I suggest we stand watches tonight and that we do not go out of this cabin for the remainder of the voyage. Furthermore . . ."

But the rest of us were not as worried as Victor. Colin, for example, had already nodded off; Quentin was yawning, and Vanity had put her head on his knee and had her eyes delicately closed, her soft lips parted, her own red tresses a thick pillow beneath her ear.

I leaned over and tugged Vanity's shoulder till she stood up, blinking. I said, "Okay, Victor. You boys stand watch over us helpless girls. If anyone comes into our bedroom, we'll both scream. How's that?"

18

FESTIVE DAYS ON
THE SLOPES OF VESUVIUS

1.

Three days of sailing passed without incident. Surrounded by the luxuries and entertainment of what was certainly the finest ship afloat, we simply could not take Victor's worries seriously. We tried to keep watches at night, and the boys did not mind taking turns staying up late, watching the miraculous television.

There were two or three channels that had nothing but rock-and-roll, to which half-nude starlets jumped up and down to truly primitive jungle-drum music. Colin was fascinated, and spent hours absorbed in music television.

Quentin thought the act of casting his circle of silence might attract more attention than it deflected, and he asked us to rely on Vanity to tell us if the wind were listening to us. And yet he also seemed relaxed; he dreamt he read his book at night, and his book hinted that, over the sea, the gods of land had less authority, less power.

At Victor's insistence, we always traveled in pairs, or stayed within shouting distance. More or less. I mean, a person can really shout a long way, right? This was not really a burden, either; Vanity and I did not want to be alone when we explored the ship, and we sort of needed each other's protection to ward off the gallantries of passengers and crew, all of whom seemed old, so very old to me.

It was our own fault. Vanity had bought us both bathing suits in Paris. Hers was a peach bikini the hue of her skin, that made her seem nude at five paces; mine was a black one-piece, but hardly demure, for it had lace panels down the sides, with a neckline that opened almost to the belly button. And it tied up the back and front with such a thorough web of laces that I am sure Grendel's opposite number among human bathing suit designers had drawn up the plans.

We went swimming the first day in a nearly empty pool. By the afternoon, the pool was crowded with onlookers and men and boys splashing near us and trying to show off. The handsome young lifeguard came by every few minutes to make sure I hadn't drowned. I also caused a sensation just by swimming laps. I do not know what I did wrong or did differently from anyone else, but if I could swim faster than a human being, or hold the pace longer, or hold my breath longer, it might have been obvious to them and not to me.

I jogged on the deck and played some games they had there; I visited the spa; I played racquetball with a handsome young man named Klaus, who owned his own business doing something with computers or telephones, or both, which he tried to explain to me while he was trying to get Vanity to go away so he could molest me.

I saw a movie in a real movie theater, and found out I could borrow movies on tape from the ship's library and watch them in the stateroom.

There was one, a black-and-white Western starring Gary Cooper and Grace Kelly, about a man who has to save an ungrateful town from four bad guys coming to kill him. Everyone tries to talk him out of it, his friends, his newlywed wife, everyone. She leaves him. In the end, when he does away with the bandits, they don't even thank him. It made me cry. I don't remember the name of the film, but I hope it won an Academy Award for its year. Marshal Kane was the character's name. I told Vanity that this was the way I wanted to act: to do what was right without fear of failure, without expectation of reward. The wife came back, in the end, Grace Kelly's character.

We rang in the New Year that night. The ballroom was splendid with decorations. I found the images of Father Time with his scythe a bit sinister, though. We went dancing, both swing-time dancing and formal ballroom dancing. Victor is always fun to waltz with because he never loses the beat and never makes mistakes, but Colin was fun to waltz with, too, and he seemed almost polished and polite when he spoke.

Colin and I spun around the dance floor to the lilting strains of "The Blue Danube" by Strauss, and I said, "Have you been replaced by a Colin-shaped robot duplicate?"

"What's the matter, Amelia?" He smiled down at me. His eyes were blue and warm.

"A whole hour has gone by, and you haven't used the word 'breast' or even 'nipple' once in the conversation. You said 'Please' earlier this evening. I heard it. It's like seeing a wild boar use a litter box. Has someone domesticated you?"

He grinned his normal the-devil-may-care-but-Colin-does-not-care grin and said, "Well, Amy, being poked by Dr. Fell and sneered at by Boggin and ear-pulled by the porcelain Daw, and ruler-whipped by baggy Mrs. Wren gets to a fellow after a while. I was never the teacher's pet like you were, and I couldn't be the iceman like Victor. And I couldn't even shut up and keep my head down like Big Q. Vanity could hypnotize the male teachers and staff with her industrial-strength, king-sized breasts, of course, or threaten to hose down rioters with milk from her nipples. What did I have? I could take the heat for you guys. So I took it."

"Took what?"

"You know. When you guys got in trouble, I would throw myself on the hand grenade for you. When you broke some small rule, I'd break some huge rule, and you'd get off with a little delicate slap on your little delicate wrist while I went into the hotbox."

"Hotbox" was Colin's word for solitary detention in the library, which, in summer, was quite hot.

"Then when I got out of the hotbox, you guys would be finishing up some game I was too late to get into, or you'd be playing tennis doubles and there was no room for me. If I didn't make a fuss, you guys ignored me. And if I did make a fuss, Amelia the Great Blond Valkyrie would kick my ass. That was back in the days when your arms were longer than mine."

"You must be from a parallel universe, Colin. None of it happened that way."

"You think I made trouble for myself because I like trouble? You think I enjoyed having Mr. Glum threaten me with an awl?"

"When did Mr. Glum ever threaten you with an awl?"

"The time he thought I stole his pornography magazines he had hidden in his tool shed."

"You did what?"

"Now you are doing it again, Amy. Instead of, 'Thank you, Colin, for deflecting trouble from me,' now you are trying to change the subject to Mr. Glum's pornography. Anyway, that is why. Every day before today, I've been under someone's boot. Now the boot is gone. I'm a new man. Want to feel my new manhood, Amy-doll?"

I said, "Don't call me Amy."

"Melly?"

"No."

"Melanomia."

"No."

"Melon breasts. Megamammary."

"You just turned back into the boar. The dance is over."

"The music is still playing!"

"The dance is over for you and me. Take me back to my chair."

He walked me back, frowning.

But then, at the chair, I turned and I kissed his cheek, and said, "Thank you, Colin, for deflecting trouble from me."

He said, "You're welcome. Oh, and, Amelia . . ."

He kissed me on the lips. Before I could decide whether to pull away or not, he just kissed me, just like that. He was certainly a better kisser than Quentin in midair, or Vanity. It was warm and nice, and I felt my limbs go soft, so he put his arms around me to hold me.

He pulled his head back.

"Damn you," I said. I had been trying to save at least one of my first few kisses for Victor.

He just grinned his little half-grin. "You are welcome, too. Thanks for breaking us out of Devil's Island."

"Let go of me."

He put me back on my feet. "About that favor you owe me . . . ?"

I looked at him. "Yes?"

"What did you promise exactly? And did it involve a can of chilled whipped cream, warm fudge, and a lot of licking?"

A girl can only take a finite amount of Colin at a time.

2.

There were more wonders aboard the finest ship afloat on the second day. One of the meals (breakfast or luncheon, I do not recall which) was served buffet style, so that I could eat what I chose, as much as I chose, and go back for seconds without asking anyone's leave. They had slabs of peach pie with ice cream for breakfast (or perhaps it was lunch). I ate my dessert before I ate my meal, and was certain that Caesar's concubines in all their pampered luxury did not know such a sheer decadence as that.

More swimming; more sporting; more time in the spa. I discovered the delight known as the Jacuzzi, which is a heated tub where warm, warm water bubbles and massages your limbs. I had been cold, so cold, for so long, shivering in my dorm room at night, plunged in icy waters, naked in the snow, that I determined now that the goal and pinnacle of my life, indeed, my purpose on Earth, was to luxuriate in the Jacuzzi till the end of time. If Grendel had only had a Jacuzzi, I would have stayed with him. I know a girl should have her standards, true, but on the other hand, in life, there seem to be certain temptations that a girl cannot resist.

Vanity finally saved me from my circle of admirers, oglers, and onlookers. She had picked a rather flattering bathing suit for me, hadn't she?

Dinner was a formal affair, and she and I wore our nicest dresses from Paris, and nice polite young men in long white coats saw to our every need and pleasure. They poured us wine when we asked, and we did not need to speak in any sort of pass-the-whathaveyou code.

Quentin still did not talk of any serious matters when the waiters were too near. He saw no reason to involve the human beings in our affairs. And if any Olympian had made it "fated" for men to be kept in ignorance of immortal matters, he might detect the event, even an unwitting one, which sought to undo his decree.

When the waiters were not near, Quentin said, "I spent today in the library. I tried to look myself up. I am sad to report that, according to what I found, Proteus had two sons and one daughter. Both sons were killed by Hercules in wrestling matches; the daughter was named Eidotheia. She is the one who betrayed her father's secrets and taught Menelaus how to capture him. Apparently I am a girl."

Colin looked up from his food. "The mold of clay into which your soul was poured may have had a different shape back then. The poet says so."

Quentin said, "I beg your pardon . . . ? What poet?"

Colin surprised me (and, I think, surprised us all) by saying, "Milton. Book I. Lucifer marshals his forces on the fiery plain. The poet recites the names by which the Damned were known in times after, as pagan gods and goddesses. Some are male and some are female. He says:

For Spirits, when they please
Can either sex assume, or both; so soft
And uncompounded is their essence pure
Not tied or manacled with joint or limb
Nor founded on the brittle strength of bones
Like cumbrous flesh; but in what shape they choose,
Dilated or condensed, bright or obscure,
Can execute their airy purposes,
And works of love or enmity fulfil.

Vanity gaped in astonishment. "Is that Colin? Reciting poetry . . . ?"

He quirked an eyebrow at her. "You are the one who helped me study for my examination on that one, Freckle Fox. You know I knew it."

Vanity gaped in astonishment still greater: "Colin remembered something he crammed for a test?"

I said to Quentin, "I do not think you are Eidotheia. We have undone all the memory-erasing tricks done to us, but no memory of former lives has come back. I don't think there was anything to bring back. I think we were children when we were taken."

Vanity said, "But we overheard Lelaps also calling me a 'daughter of Alcinuous.' "

I said, "He was speaking in poetry at the time. He may have meant it the way Quentin called human beings the 'sons of Adam,' or Greeks are called the 'Helenes,' you see?"

Colin said, "I like the theory that Quentin was a girl better, personally. It explains why I had such trouble turning him into a man."

Vanity said, "Quiet! Or you will set off another round of English schoolboy comments."

Colin said, "Has anyone got a flaming fag to smoke? I'd like to put one between my lips and suck."

Quentin said, "If you like the girl theory, you'll love this. Victor is supposed to have flippers for hands and the head of a dog. That's what myth says the Telchines are."

Victor looked interested. "Anything else about the Telchines?"

"They forged the adamantine sickle with jagged teeth Saturn used to castrate his father Uranus."

Colin said, "I love old myths. So very graphic, you know? Just the thing for small impressionable children to hear."

Quentin said, "One myth says they reared Poseidon. They discovered iron and the art of working metals by fire, and were the first to cast bronze statues of the gods. When they slowly turned into vicious magicians, and took up the practice of pouring the water of the infernal river Styx mixed with sulfur upon animals and plants with the purpose of destroying them, the Telchines were cursed and scattered. Their city of Ialysus was destroyed by Zeus and flooded; another version says Poseidon, out of tender regard for the good they did to him once, despite their present crimes, took the city underwater, but the people were preserved as fishmen."

Colin said, "And how about you, robot-man? What have you been doing all day, Victor?"

Vanity said, "I saw him. He was napping."

Victor smiled, an event I no longer thought of as rare. "Not quite. I went up to their business call center here on ship. They have mechanisms for allowing computer uplinks through satellite systems to ashore-based stations. So that businessmen can send electronic mail, I suppose, or encrypted phone calls. I studied the wave-forms and the 'handshake' procedure, till I thought I could imitate it just with the neurocircuitry in my head."

Colin said, "Oh my God! Victor was surfing the Net! He was downloading porn! Go, Victor!"

Victor said, "Not quite. I did not have an account. I only had limited access. But there were still other channels of radio traffic being used by the satellites, and my signals were traveling faster than the pulses they use to talk to each other, so I was able to dither them and break in. I was listening in on military satellites talking to each other."

I said, "What do you mean, faster?"

"Their broadcasts were only moving at 186,000 miles per second. I simply added more velocity to my return signals."

I said, "But nothing moves faster than that."

"Of course it does. Light is only made of atoms, like everything else. Little hard pellets. Any object, no matter how fast, if you add speed, moves faster. I do not know why they all limited themselves to that one speed. It allowed me to intercept their lock-and-key signals, so I could hear what password they wanted me to give back before they could call down to their synchronous command center to get confirmation."

Colin saw I was about to start arguing physics, and he waved his hand to me to shush me up, saying to Victor, "You believed in your ability to break in more firmly than they believed in your ability to keep you out. What did you find out?"

"Branshead estate does not exist. I saw reconnaissance photographs, and examined electronic maps. Everything is mapped on this planet, down to the meter. There is no village called Abertwyi. There is a town called Rhossily in about the position our village is supposed to be. But there are no huge burial mounds to the north, no tall hills to the west, no forest to the south. Arthur's Table is in a place called Tefn Mawr, which is about fifteen miles away. The highways are there, but in the wrong positions. There is an Oxwich Green, a Swansea, and a Bristol, however."

Colin looked very smug and leaned back in his seat, and said, "I am the only one who has a right not to be surprised by the news. Didn't I always say the Earth we were learning about was not the Earth on which the estate stood? And I knew that a village with a dumb name like Abertwyi was something made up by Boggin. And I bet he let Mr. Glum make up that dumb island called Worm's Head. That cannot be a real name."

Victor said, "Worm's Head is real."

Quentin said, "It is the skull of the dragon whose spine forms the land throughout the peninsula." Then he muttered to himself. "I wonder on what world I stood when I opened the old mound at midnight? Or what king he was, who rose up before me, pale and glimmering in the moon?"

3.

I made a new discovery on the third day; there was a place to rent something like a roller skate, but the wheels were lined up in a line, like the blade of an ice skate, and the whole affair was encased in this huge plastic

boot with snaps and clasps going halfway up one's thigh. Helmets and elbow pads and knee pads and thick gloves completed the kit, so the skater
looked like some crazed warrior who had thrown away his breastplate,
but kept his gauntlets and greaves.

There were only certain places and times where one was supposed to
skate. Being released from so many arbitrary rules in my life, and not being Colin, I obeyed the traffic laws and stayed on the track and certain
areas of deck set aside for this sport.

It was my turn to buddy up with Victor that day. I provoked him into
racing me on skates. I won the first lap, but he figured out an energy-
conserving glide step to use, and he had more mass to throw into the
sharp turns. Awkward at first, he mastered the skill with effortless grace,
as he did everything he put his mind to.

Afterwards, over lemonade, I brought up a topic that had been gnaw-
ing at me.

I began with an apology. He just looked puzzled. We sat at a small café
table, which was set along a balcony overlooking the indoor swimming
pool (or "the great lake" as it should have been called). Sharp echoes reflected from the roof. Below us, there were sedate old men and women
moving with timid pleasure through the water.

Victor had a towel around his neck, and he glowed from the sweat of our
skate-race. A thin shirt of skintight stuff showed off the sculpted planes of
his shoulders and chest. He was muscled like a swimmer, built for stream-
lined endurance, not for bulk. Yellow sunlight slanted through polarized
windows and gave his contours a hard look, as if he were a statue of cast
gold, or fine copper, machine-lathed to a perfect shape and hand-polished.

I said, "I'll never question your leadership again. If it hadn't been for
me—"

He said, "Is this about the thing on the dock? Glum's attack?"

"If we had all gotten in a circle like you said, he would not have been
able to carry off both me and Vanity. If he had only gotten one of us, you
could have stopped him. I saw him turn visible when you demagnetized
the ring of Gyges . . ."

"I'd like to point out that you are merely speculating about might-
have-beens. Were we in a circle with our backs to the spot where he
smashed up through the boards. It might have gone better or worse if you
had been closer; I don't see that your conclusion is at all clear."

"If we had all been in the boat as I said, he would have capsized us and maybe killed us all."

"Possibly. On the other hand, we don't know what his swimming speed was. Again, you are speculating. Since the situation is unlikely to rise again, the speculation does not seem to be one to lead to a provable theory one way or the other. Is there some experiment you can think of that would settle the question as to whether things would have gone better or worse had we acted otherwise?"

"Quentin was right, and I should have listened to him! I should not have been arguing with the leader!"

"I am not sure, legally, I was the leader at that moment in time. We attempted to settle the question of leadership by vote, and came to a tie. As far as that goes, everything was done by proper Robert's rules. My only criticism against you is that you resigned leadership before an unambiguous next leader was chosen." He looked thoughtful, saying, half to himself, "Although, since you had appointed me second-in-command previously, I do not know if resigning your commission would have elevated me to leader or would have acted as my resignation, as well . . ."

I broke in on his ruminations: "You are our leader! Our chief. Only you; you always have been. There was no ambiguity."

He smiled and sipped his lemonade. "Amelia, when we were young, you and I had to be the ones leading the others, just because we were older. We had the self-control they lacked; we knew things they didn't. I don't think those conditions obtain anymore. If anyone, Quentin is the natural leader at this point; the information in his book is giving him insights the rest of us don't have. I have made several suggestions as to how to defend ourselves against the next attack, which we have reason to believe will be a lethal one. Mostly, I have been ignored." His eyes twinkled, and he threw back his head to drain the sour and sweet dregs of the lemonade.

He stood, as if preparing to have us depart. I put my hand out and took his hand. It was still warm and sweat-touched by the exertion of skating.

I said, "Wait. There's something I want to ask you."

He looked down at me, his gaze level and patient.

"It's about—oh! Can't you sit down?"

"You wanted to ask me whether I can sit down?"

"Please sit."

He resumed his seat.

"Victor, I have an important question to ask you."

He looked attentive.

"I—I—"

"You . . . ? You . . . ?"

"It is about us."

"Define 'us.' "

" 'Us' means 'us'!"

"The whole group, all five, or just you and me? English is ambiguous when it comes to inclusive versus exclusive first person plural."

I said crossly, "This would be easier if you would at least try to guess what I am about to say!"

He leaned back in his chair and regarded me with what I can only call a Boggin-like expression. "What wavelengths can your brain generate? If you have a way of broadcasting a signal I can pick up, it would be very useful to secure communications practice."

I sat in miserable silence for a few moments. "Well—"

I could not ask him. I groped for some different question to ask.

I finally said in the most lame and insincere tone that has ever come out of a girl's mouth, "I was wondering if you knew what Vanity and Quentin were keeping from us . . . ?"

"Of course," he said in a tone as bland and certain as could be. "It's obvious."

"What?"

He seemed a little surprised. "Quentin does not want to tell us that we ought not go home."

4.

I blinked. "Not . . . home . . . ?"

He favored me with that Victor-raising-an-eyebrow look I knew so well from my youth. "Back to Chaos. Myriagon. Ialysus. Cimmeria. Phaeacia. And wherever Quentin's people hail from. We ought not go back."

"Why can't we go back? We don't even know what's there. It's unexplored terrain!"

"I did not say we *could* not. Obviously, we could jump on Vanity's boat as soon as she can summon it here, and, if the *Argent Nautilus* functions as promised, and nothing stops us, we could be in those places within a day. I said we *ought* not, not if we want to preserve the human race and the organized universe from attack. Our enemies, even when talking among themselves (in a situation we have every reason to believe was not arranged for our ears) seemed honestly to think this was the most likely outcome of our escape back to Chaos. I think we cannot ignore that opinion without some clear proof that is it false."

"But what about seeing our parents? Our families?"

"Good question. The people whom the war would kill have parents and families, too. Now then, they are just mortal men, or, as Corus would say, 'cattle.' But since you seemed to think it inadvisable for me even to influence the captain's glands while he was thinking, I assume you do not share the view of Corus on this matter."

I said, "I certainly do not share Corus' view on the matter. How dare you think that of me?"

"Well, there is also the matter of the promise you and Quentin and Vanity made to the Head of Bran. Quentin takes such promises very seriously; broken promises directly interfere with his abilities to manipulate his magnetic entities he calls 'spirits.' Need I say that, if the universe is destroyed, it is unlikely that the British Isles will be preserved? You at least would need to exact a promise from our relatives to spare England from general and universal destruction before we went home and triggered the general attack from Chaos."

I sat there, a sinking sensation in my stomach. I had been hoping to see my parents, whom I had never seen. Helion and Neaera. I am sure Quentin felt the same way: people who would understand us, for once; people who would be on our side, for once; people around whom we would be the normal ones. Our people.

People who would be glad to see us.

Loved ones.

Colin did not even know the name of his mother. I don't think we knew the name of either of Victor's parents.

I said in an empty voice: "But—what else can we do . . . ? We cannot go back to the school."

Victor shook his head. "As long as we put a higher priority on freedom than on staying alive, no one can imprison us again."

He meant that we should kill ourselves rather than be captured again.

Sometimes I love how calmly he puts things. A "higher priority," he calls it.

5.

He continued, "Besides, I am not certain you have exhausted all the cases. We could remain at liberty on Earth. We could return to Chaos in disguise. We are alleged to be shape-changers, although I have not noticed Quentin or Colin practicing to see what new shapes they could form themselves into. We could hire actors and actresses to impersonate us, and have them go back to the school in our stead, so that the Chaoticists will continue to be reluctant to attack."

I said, "I don't know how likely any of those options are."

Victor said, "The most likely scenario is one that has several severe disadvantages. As I see it, the enemy obviously thinks our aid, given to one side or the other, could allow a clear victory in the coming civil war. I am not sure why they are so optimistic; myself, I do not see how I can do anything Dr. Fell cannot do, for example. I think, by the way, there is still a mystery here as to what they so fear from us. I have been assuming they were afraid of something personal we could do that they could not. Although, the more I think about it, it is more reasonable to assume that they are simply afraid that we can summon aid from the various armies of Chaos."

"What about your 'most likely' scenario? You didn't say what it was."

"Sorry. I thought it was obvious from context."

"Make it more obvious."

"We could select which faction among the Olympians to help, and use our powers or position to set one of them on the throne of Heaven. Once there is a strong leader, an army, and whatever else the Olympians need to fend off an attack from Chaos, we are no longer an issue in any way. Then we can go home."

"And if we are not willing to help the Olympians maim and murder each other? That is what we are talking about. War is murder, king-sized."

"If we are not willing to help the Olympian civil war, there is always life. Life on Earth. We may have more than one Earth to choose from, if

Vanity's boat does what she says it does. There is also the possibility that Vanity can go home; her situation is not exactly parallel to ours (if my understanding of the situation is accurate, which, I admit, it may not be)."

I looked around at the wide swimming pool below our balcony, at the windows and balconies around us, the tastefully appointed corridors I could see, the chambers and shops beyond that. I smiled and said, "Life on Earth does not sound that bad to me, considering. . . ."

I turned to him and leaned forward on the table, and said, "What are your dreams, Victor? What do you want to do with your life on Earth?"

He looked a little surprised at the change of topic, but he answered, "I think I want what all young men want: a wife, a home, and a family."

I had to smile at that. "The average young man wants a harem, a beer, and a pot of gold, or maybe a race car."

"And how would you know what the average young man wants?"

"I've never heard any young man say he wants a home."

"And you've met so very, very many young men . . ."

"I know. I know what the average young man wants."

"And what does he want?"

"He wants the egg of the Roc. He wants to find the lost city of El Dorado in the Amazon. He wants to ride the decks of a man-o'-war and give the pirates blast for blast, even while the scuppers fill with blood. He wants to plant the flag upon the desert sands of Mars, and leave the first footsteps of Man upon that frigid, rust-red world. He wants to cross blades with Cyrano de Bergerac and match him rhyme for rhyme, blow for blow, parry, riposte, and counterparry! He wants to slay the dragon. He wants the Most Holy Grail."

"So I take it all men are unhappy and frustrated, except for Sir Percival, Saint George, and maybe John Carter of Barsoom and Captain Horatio Hornblower, right? Is there anything else men want?"

I looked at him from under my lashes. "There are other things a man wants. He wants Sophia Loren and the Queen of Sheba and Helen of Troy and Marilyn Monroe in a little white dress, her skirts blown up around her knees."

"I would add Joe DiMaggio and Menelaus to my list of non-unhappy men, except that, as I recall, things did not turn out so well for either of them. Once these men have Helen of Troy, do you know what they expect to do with her? Even Paris took her back home to live with him. I think you are describing what Amelia Windrose wants in life, not most men. How would you know what anyone else in the world wants, but you?"

"I've read books."

"The books we read in school? I am not sure they are a representative sample. The young men in those books divide into three camps: those who want to defeat Napoleon at the battle of Borodino; those who want to defeat the Persians at Marathon; and those who wish to live lives of temperate virtue, untroubled by the clamor of the senate and left in peace by the spies of Caesar. Unless you want to talk about the plays we read, also? All the Shakespeare comedies end in mass marriages. So don't tell me men don't think about marriage. What is the first thing Romeo and Juliet did?"

"Achilles chose a short and glorious life rather than a long one. He was a hero."

Victor said in a saturnine voice, "Among all your heroes and demigods, Amelia, you seem to forget that Odysseus was doing nothing but trying to get home to his wife and kid, and Aeneas was trying to find a new home for himself and his people. And they were men, heroes, some would say, more heroic than Achilles, by a long shot. The whole poem was about nothing but his lack of self-control."

"So what is your goal in life, really, Victor?"

"All living organisms desire to reproduce. It is programmed into us at a fundamental level. Likewise, thoughts form 'memes' or self-replicating mental viruses. They desire to be passed on also. A stable environment, a family, in fact, is the only way to pass one's memes and genes along."

"That sounds *sooo* romantic. A robot factory manufacturing another robot factory."

"What is your goal?"

"I have found my calling in life. It is to spend as much time in a Jacuzzi as possible. Like Socrates, I want to live a life of reflection and virtue. I just want to be warm and wet while I am doing it."

"Very Epicurean of you. You have another two days of such a life. I assume you have thought beyond that point?"

Actually, I hadn't. Why does Victor always make me feel so stupid?

"Two days . . . ?" I said.

"Well," he said sardonically, "this trip is a reckless expense, and we are almost drained of the absurd amount of money Mr. ap Cymru gave you. I did not know it at the time when Vanity picked this boat to hitch a hike on; I would have objected. We should have found a tramp steamer."

"What's wrong with this boat?"

"Nothing, were we not paupers. I am sure our enemies have not found us simply because their brains would not accept the idea that the first thing we would do with the only real money we have ever had in our lives is blow it all on one pleasure cruise."

"Are we out of money? Nearly out or all out?"

Victor let out a loud laugh when I asked that. He actually slapped his knee and laughed.

I said, "What is so funny!"

Victor pressed his lips together to smother his laugh, but his eyes still twinkled. "Yes, Amelia, we are nearly out of money."

"Was I supposed to know that? You are the one keeping the envelope in your jacket!"

"Actually, I altered my skin to make a watertight pocket, like a marsupial. I am keeping the envelope in my pouch. And yes, you were supposed to know that. I assumed you could do math."

"What are we going to do?" I asked, eyes wide.

He smiled. "Get jobs."

"Jobs?"

"I am afraid that something as glamorous as the film actress career Vanity has her heart set on might attract the attention of the enemy. It is, of course, her risk to take. I was experimenting last night with using a molecular sieve method to collect gold out of seawater. That might tide us over until I can find a more promising career."

I said, "I don't think you can own gold in America. Franklin Roosevelt took it all away, or something."

"Hmph. And it advertises itself as a free country. It is supposed to be this great paragon of the free market. The subjects there cannot own money?"

"They have paper money."

"An oxymoron. Paper is IOUs never intended to be repaid. Only metal is money. Well, I will have to find something else to do."

"Like what?"

"Dig ditches. Draw water. Chop wood. Tote barges. Lift bales. You know: work. The capacity to move mass over distance. Work."

"Hmmm . . . Doesn't sound very appealing. Is there any job I can get that does not require moving out of the Jacuzzi?"

"I can think of two, playwright and Playboy model, depending on whether you are willing to have people photograph you in the water as you bathe. Come on, Amelia. We are not really British. We do not have to look down our noses at honest labor."

"Digging ditches is not my idea of a bright future."

"Those who work are free. There are only three categories of nonproductive people: babies, beggars, robbers."

"I still do not want to dig ditches."

"What do you want, then?"

"I want to be the first girl on Mars."

"Without moving out of the Jacuzzi? That will be a feat."

"How much money is left?"

"Why do you ask?"

"I want to spend some of it before it is gone."

He laughed. I was beginning to think I liked Victor better before he was so happy and at ease.

I said crossly, "I have not ever seen it! I have not spent a dime. Vanity was in Paris; I haven't bought anything in the shops here on the ship. I didn't even rent the skates we are wearing; you did! Don't I get a cut of the money?"

His flesh rippled, and a pair of lips formed near his belly button. He stuck his hand into the lips and pulled out an envelope.

He passed it to me. "It's all yours."

I said, "What? Only one fifth of this is mine."

Victor said, "How do you figure that? You got it from ap Cymru. None of us did anything to get it. As far as I am concerned, that is your property. I was only holding it because you handed it to me to count when we were standing on the dock, and then Mr. Glum attacked." Victor could count faster than any of us.

I said, "Well, I'm ceding it to the group. Four fifths of it. No, I don't even need that much. I guess we'll have to rent a room in New York when we get there, won't we?"

Victor jumped to his feet, slamming his hand down atop the envelope. He stood, looming over the table.

I shrieked and flinched backwards in my chair, shouting, "What? What? What is it?"

But he was not looking at me. Face blank, his eyes were scanning left and right, right and left.

He said, "There is something invisible in the immediate area. I hope it is Colin. Colin . . . ?"

No answer.

Victor opened his third eye. The metal orb, shining, came out of a seam on his forehead. Blue sparks began to glow in his depth, brighter and brighter as the nested spheres began to align their irises, one after another. . . .

I looked in the fourth dimension. A web of spider-lines? No; it wasn't there. But had I seen it for a moment?

Colin appeared, right hand curled around his left index finger, twisting the ring collet-out. "Okay, okay, smart guy. You got me. Put your eyeball away before someone sees it."

Victor closed his third eye. "Don't play tricks. We are about to be attacked by people who want to kill us rather than capture us."

"Sorry. But you guys are the ones who told me not to go around attracting attention. On account of I don't have a ticket, see?"

"By not attracting attention, I meant stop pulling the ice sculptures of mermaids off the buffet tables and waltzing with them."

"My date walked out on me. Are we going to divvy up the loot?"

"If Amelia says it is okay. Myself, I think we should pool our resources. I doubt if this is enough to rent a room, even a poor one."

"Oh, come on!" said Colin. "America is a rich country. They are not going to let people starve there! I mean, Margaret Thatcher's not running the place, is she?"

I put my hand on Victor's hand, saying, "I'll be happy to dig ditches with you, if you want, Victor. Anything is better than being a baby, a bum, or a robber." I favored Colin with a dark look.

Victor said, "How long were you listening, Colin?"

Colin said, "Keeping secrets from me? I heard you guys talking about not being able to go back home." Colin returned my dark look and made it darker. "Or was this one of those mixed doubles things, where the fifth guy from the hotbox doesn't get to play?"

I said, "Maybe absolute power does corrupt absolutely. What are you going to do for a living when we get to the States? Be the world's greatest pickpocket? Walk through girls' shower rooms? Strangle the president?"

"With great power comes great responsibility," said Colin earnestly. "I will dedicate myself to ridding the world of evil! I will use my great powers of invisibility to fight crime! Maybe I can catch the Catwoman. I sure as hell am not going to end up waiting tables for tips. That is your future, you know, Dark Mistress. Or should I say: Dark Waitress."

"I don't think so," I said haughtily.

Colin grinned one of his slimier grins. "Yeah? What marketable skills did Boggin teach you in that fine school we just fled from?"

I stared at him in silence, unable to think of anything to say.

Colin said, "Maybe you can recite the *Iliad* in Greek on a street corner and leave a hat out for people to drop dimes into. 'Of wrath sing, oh goddess . . . !' "

"We learned other things . . . ," I said, pouting.

"Astronomy? There is big money in calculating the orbit of Jupiter using Ptolemy's *Almagest* these days. Philosophy? Get yourself a cardboard sign: *Will think for food.* You'll be on the dole with me in no time. Then we can have our argument about Margey Thatcher again."

Victor put the envelope of money into my hand. "Don't starve yet. I still say this is yours, not ours. If you want to split it up once we are all together, fine."

Colin said, "That should be in about one minute. Quentin sent me to go get you. He was playing around with calculating the orbit of Jupiter in hexadecimals, and he was using a system in that book of his. Apparently there are four more planets in the dream world than there are here, and he can get better results if he takes their motions into account, too. Anyway, tonight is the night."

Victor said, "In what way? The night for what?"

Argh! Victor is so slow sometimes. I said, "Vesuvius erupts tonight."

Colin gave me an odd look. "No. Not at all. The attack is coming tonight. We are going to be attacked. What is all this about Vesuvius?"

Colin is slower.

19

THE FURY OF THE DEEP

1.

Vanity was with Quentin in the cabin when we arrived. Quentin was seated cross-legged on the floor, wearing a dark opera cape of rich material. It was an article of clothing I had not seen before; I assume it was a Paris acquisition. He had his tarot cards spread out in a half-circle before him, along with two candles, his white staff, a wineglass, a steak knife.

Vanity was seated on the couch. She had gathered some of her clothes and mine, and was moving things from a pile on her left to a pile on her right. Some of the boys' clothes were there, too, as well as some of the camping gear, scuba gear, and climbing gear we had brought along, or bought along the way.

The first thing she said was, "I'll bet it's the ring. Hand it over, Colin."

Colin, at the door, said, "The precious? Our birthday present!? I gave it to this German chick I found sleeping in the middle of a circle of fire. . . . Kidding! Just kidding! Here it is. I knew the damn thing was bugged when you gave it to me. Good old expendable Colin!"

He pulled it off his finger and tossed it across the air to Vanity.

Victor followed Colin into the room. "Why did you think the ring was bugged?"

Colin said, "Because I was listening when Quentin explained how magic works. In order for the Olympians to curse someone, that someone has to do something wrong. Well, stealing a ring is wrong. Mr. Glum stole it from Mrs. Wren; he said that to Amelia, right?"

Quentin looked up from his cards. "Right and wrong have nothing to do with it. It has to do with obligations being kept or violated. It has to do with rules being broken or not broken. Being in debt. Owing a favor. Any rule. The rules don't have to be fair; they just have to be rules. For example: in Amelia's story, Sam the Drayman got cursed with amnesia by Corus. I assume the rule Sam broke is that mortals are not supposed to look at gods."

Vanity (who was, I assume, still annoyed at how Sam had been treated) said sharply, "When was that a rule? Who made that a rule? Where are these rules written?"

Quentin looked a little puzzled, as if he had never thought of those questions before. "I don't know. But the sanctity of the gods is well established in literature. Paris, by asking the three goddesses to strip for him, committed an offense that cursed and destroyed his home city of Troy. Actaeon was turned into a stag and eaten by his own hounds for gazing at Artemis bathing. Moses could only look at the rear of God. There are other examples."

Colin flopped down on the divan next to Vanity and picked up a peach-colored satin bra from the pile, and looked at it speculatively. "Maybe God just had a real nice butt, and wasn't too happy about his face. You know."

Quentin put the ring on a piece of paper on the floor in front of him, and began inscribing, with compass and straightedge, a pentacle around the ring on the paper. I saw his tongue protruding a little from the corner of his mouth.

Quentin said to Colin in a mild tone, "Maybe you should not talk about things you know nothing about, Colin."

"Yeah, well, then I'd never get to say anything, would I?" Colin said.

Vanity snatched the bra out of his hands. "That's what we all pray for."

Colin dropped his voice into an intimate tone: "At night? In your nighties? On your knees? You're praying for me to do what again?"

Victor stiffly sat in the chair opposite them. "I know what she was praying for, Colin. If I could have prayed and gotten God to come walk into the dorm and shut you up at lights out, I might not be the atheist I am today."

Quentin looked up from his diagram. "Is that all it would take to turn you from a skeptic into a pious man, Victor? I agree that it would have been a miracle of Biblical proportions to get Colin to settle after dark. But I always thought you would not believe in any superior beings, even if you saw them."

Victor said, "Define 'believe.' If the Martians of Mr. H. G. Wells landed in their tripods tonight, and started wiping out things with their heat ray, I would believe in superior nonhuman beings. They would exist. But I would not bend knee to them, nor to any other creature, superior or not, no matter what his threats."

"What if he were morally superior?"

"Then he would not be the bloodthirsty maniac described in the Jewish folk tales, would he?"

Colin gestured at Quentin with a flap of the bra. "Well, well, when did Big Q become a Christian? Is this the same fellow who woke me up at four thirty in the morning last May Day to go comb dew off of a hawthorn tree with a sickle he had me steal from Mr. Glum's shed? I don't remember that from the Common Book."

Quentin was frowning down at his piece of paper, tracing a line along a ruler. He spoke absentmindedly, without looking up: "I am not one or the other. I go where the True Science leads me. I doubt either neopagan or Christian would admit this, but the two traditions are the same, one growing from the other. The myth of Christ is the same as the fable of Adonis, except that the Christian tales have the stern moral flavor and intellectual depth that the Neoplatonists, Stoics, and the late Roman writers added to them. All tales are one grand tale."

He straightened up from where he had been hunched over the ring. "Let me attempt a demonstration. Amelia, if you will shut off the lights . . . ? No one talk; the spirits and aery humors released by your breath, not to mention the ambient charge on any names, words, or symbols you might express, will disturb the pattern of influences I am trying to establish. If Amelia starts to talk, somebody kiss her."

"I am on it!" said Colin, beginning to get up.

"Never you mind," said Victor.

I had walked in the front door with the rest of them, and had not yet taken a seat. As it chanced, I was standing near where Victor sat at his ease.

I stood there, blinking, caught between hope and wonder, doubting my ears. What had Victor just said?

Victor reached up from where he sat and, without asking, without even the slightest qualm, took me by the hand and steered me over in front of him. He put both his hands on my hips and pulled me down to sit on his knee.

I think Victor said something like, "Carry on," or maybe Colin made a wry comment, but I could not hear anything clearly. My heart was pounding in my ears, and I was afraid to turn around, as if maybe Victor would vanish if I turned to look at him, or it would all fade into a dream. Or, worse, he'd look at me as if I were his sister.

But he kept his hands on my hips. Firm, strong hands. I could feel how warm they were.

I sat there feeling pleased and foolish, wondering if I should lean back against him, if I dared. I missed what happened next, because I wasn't paying attention.

There was a noise like the chime of a bell, and I was not sure where it came from. Vanity waved her hand at Quentin and slapped herself on the neck. Bugs. Something was listening.

I had the impression that Quentin had just asked a question. Something or someone in the room answered him, because a shy, unearthly voice murmured very softly: "I am the hate of the voiceless wound; I am the blood which is not allayed; I am the silence of the broken word; I am the trust betrayed. Erichtho laid her curse on Echidna's son, and took the ghost of his leg away; all other wounds of his knew how to close; the knowledge was lost; what was marred was to be marred for forever and a day."

Vanity slapped herself on the neck again, looking worried.

I looked into the higher dimensions and saw bundles of moral energy issuing to and from the ring. At right angles to all other right angles was a figure surrounded by the laws of nature of the dream continuum. It seemed to be a corpse, taller than a human being, clad all in bronze armor, and resting in a strange coffin, which was shaped in the form of a hollow brass horse.

Quentin said, *"Ave et Vale."*

The figure in the armor turned and looked at me, as if he could see my eyes, despite that I was looking from another dimension; he started to raise a gauntlet toward me, as if to speak, but at that same moment, the hollow brass horse came to life, and galloped away, with the corpse rattling

and banging back and forth in the hollow vessel of its chest. It sounds perhaps comical to think of a man rattling around in a horse's hollow chest,
but there was something so horrible, and so helpless, and so sad about it
all, that I turned my higher eyes away before I could see more.

Quentin said, "Demonstration over. You guys can talk again."

I was aware only of a sinking sensation. I had missed my opportunity.
Why hadn't I started to talk out of turn?

2.

There was a brief discussion. I described the spirit I saw, and Quentin
gave the opinion that this was the ghost of the original owner of the ring.
Who or what it was, he could not guess.

Vanity confirmed that the ghost had been the only thing looking at or
aware of us—except when he said the name Echidna. Vanity said, "At the
moment that name was spoken, something very old and very powerful
turned and looked at us. It is coming now."

Even as she said those words, fat drops of rain began to spatter against
the portholes of our cabin. In the distance, a swollen red sun, balanced
between low clouds and the dark western horizon of the sea, was being
blotted up by thunderheads.

Quentin looked worried, and ashamed. "Maybe there were more pre-
cautions I should have taken. Is this officially an emergency? I'd like Victor to be in charge."

There were four votes for aye. Colin had not raised his hand.

I said to him sharply, "Is there some other candidate you'd like to
propose?" My tone, I suppose, was less polite than it should have been,
because I thought he was angling for the position of leader himself.

Colin, slouched like a panther at rest over the arm of the divan, regarded me with a lazy, mocking stare: "I just thought the Dark Mistress
had done such a fine job before. . . . Are you canvassing for a vote for Vic,
Amelia? What are you offering? I'll make it unanimous, if I get to have the
blonde in my lap next time around. . . . No? Fine. Who am I to break with
tradition, though . . . ?" He raised his hand anyway.

Quentin said, "Leader, I'd like to do a reading on the influences from
the middle air and the upper aether. Unfortunately, I already know from

Vanity that there are actually spirits of some sort, princes of the air and darkness, who react when I read, and go somewhere and do something to fetch the answers to my questions."

Victor said, "You are thinking it might attract more attention?"

"Well, if I were Boggin, and I had the winds at my command, I'd have them watching the princes of the middle air. Why should it be impossible for spirits to spy on each other?"

Victor said, "This is your area of expertise. Make a suggestion."

Quentin started gathering his cards up off the floor. "Leader, two days of reading one book does not make me an expert."

"But you have an idea."

"But I have an idea. We take Colin's ring; we have Amelia look along these ropes or webs she seems to be able to see, we have you denature them—demagnitize them, as you call it, not the whole ring, but just one after another—to isolate which strands represent which obligations or which sense impressions. Colin can add back in any influences you drive out—adding 'energy,' as he calls it. With each strand, as we turn it off and turn it back on, Vanity tells us if anyone is watching us. I do a reading with my cards meanwhile. We see if we can fine-tune it. Fine-tune the ring. If we are really clever about it, we may be able to have the invisibility cast its influence all the way around me doing a reading. You see my idea?"

Colin said, "Whoever the people are you are getting your information from, turn them invisible, so that Boggin's spies can't see them doing whatever it is they do when they answer your questions. Right?"

"Right."

"What if I cannot turn on what Victor turns off?"

"Then the ring is broken and worthless to us, and we have destroyed a great treasure for no purpose."

Colin shrugged and nodded, and said to Victor, "Is there a downside to this, leader-man?"

Victor said, "If we attract the attention of Boggin or the other Olympians, the worst that will happen is they might send some force to protect us from the lethal attack which is coming. And, by hypothesis, they already have such a force in place, and already have us under some sort of observation that Vanity cannot detect; therefore we lose nothing by this. No. There is no downside, aside from the value of the ring itself, and the general risks, if any, associated with Quentin showing command-symbols to the electromagnetic entities he calls spirits."

Vanity said, "I don't see why it can work at all. Only the ring-bearer turns invisible. How do you project it onto someone else?"

Colin said, "Step on them."

"I'm serious."

Colin said, "So am I. That ring is thorough. When you wear it, nobody sees footprints you make in the water puddles in the girls' locker room, or sees the shower water deflected from your body. Nobody sees the water displacement when you slip naked into a crowded Jacuzzi. No one hears the noises you make when you bump into something. Now, if you pick something up, like an envelope full of money, a person who notices details, like Victor, or whose brain is hard to fool, will spot you."

Vanity said, "Were you really in the girls' locker room?"

Colin rolled his eyes, "What? Do you think I was staring at all the old wrinkled hags they have here on this trip—yeech! But you understand what the logic of the ring has to be? If the ring-bearer can make it so that you do not notice sound waves coming out of my mouth, I don't see (if you'll pardon that expression) why it can't mask someone who talks back to me. If you hear them, you'll know I'm around. How is that different from all the other clues that I am around it is erasing, such as light photons bouncing off me? I don't go blind when I put this thing on, you know. I must be casting a shadow."

Victor said, "Let us try Quentin's experiment, then. He may be able to generate additional information, which may enable us to survive the coming attack."

I said, "But they are not bugging the ring, then? I wasn't sure I understood what the ghost of the first owner said."

Quentin held up the ring. "Mr. Glum had a right to this ring. It was a wergild. Mrs. Wren cursed his leg so that he could not fix it—haven't you seen Colin simply shrug off mortal wounds, broken wings, things like that? But her enchantments trumped his psionics. She did him wrong by doing that. In retaliation, Glum stole this. At a guess, it would seem, that in the spirit world, two wrongs do make a right. Shall we try my experiments? Ladies? Gentlemen?"

Unfortunately, that meant I had to get up off of Victor's lap.

3.

The storm grew. The *Queen Elizabeth II* was so mighty a ship, her draft so huge, that she did not even slacken her speed when fifty-meter waves began to pound against her side, and gale-force winds blew nearly solid sheets of screaming rain across her decks. The captain informed the passengers that the hatches to the deck were being chocked, and no one would be permitted up on deck till the storm blew over. But within our stately cabin, there was no roll, no pitch, no sensation of motion. The vessel was simply too large for any storm to disturb her serenity.

But it was loud. Even through the decks and bulkheads, we could hear the sound, the outrageous sound of it, as if a voice of infinite strength and endless hate screamed and roared and yelled one long insane yell, never pausing for breath.

Our cabin portals were black circles. They might have been windows looking into an airless coffin, for all the light they shed. There was no sign of my far horizon, my horizon as wide as the sea. It was as if the portholes had been bricked over.

4.

We spent two hours investigating what turned out to be a dead end. After about forty tries, we knew twoscore ways to cast a spell to read the stars which could easily be detected by someone with Vanity's power.

At the end of that time, Quentin had covered about threescore sheets of paper with pentacles and hexagrams and septagons and octograms, and had burnt out his last wax candle. He looked up at Victor and said, "That is about all I can do. If there was anyone bugging the stars, they heard us talking to them, and they know what we asked."

You would think, after all that, we would have gotten forty astrological charts' worth of information. But apparently, for real magicians, consulting the stars was a business as complex as the radar, radar-beam deception and counterdeception, radar-jamming, jam-breaking, and anti-jam breaking techniques of the electronic espionage of World War II.

"Here is what we now know," Quentin summarized his results: "The attacker is coming by sea, coming from a dark place where the stars never shine, and of which the stars know nothing. It is not the Olympians. It is someone who intends to kill one or more of us. It is not a Maenad—which might be significant, if Lamia is no longer traveling with the Maenads. It is definitely a female or females."

Colin said, "Or a guy in drag."

"Well, yes. Or an effete male. It is someone older than the established universe, or, at least, older than the stars, since the stars know no birth-date or nativity constellation for the attacker or attackers. She intends to kill many people, including any humans around us. She or they is carrying a talisman of great power with her. I should say 'she or they,' I suppose, since it could be a band of women, for example, amazons or something."

Quentin had written this all out on a little steno notebook he was using to write down lessons from his dream grimoire. Now he flipped the pages shut with a sigh. "And, if our stars are being bugged, they know we know. The stars are also betting on the other side, and they give us about sixteen-to-one odds."

Colin looked up when he said that. "You are kidding about that last part, right? The stars don't really bet, do they?"

Quentin said, "Not the stars per se, but the mesoaetherians do—the princes of the middle air. They also cheat on their bets, and send omens and signs to people to change the odds of one fate winning out over another. That's why most omens are so vague—if the mesoaetherians are caught, they can always claim they were not really trying to tell the humans things humans are not supposed to know. What's the word from your spy novels, Colin?"

"Plausible deniability."

"Anyway, among the many other illegal things my friends do, they gamble on human suffering and the outcomes of wars and natural disasters. I told you they were like Mafia people."

I raised my hand.

Quentin pointed at me. "Yes? A question?"

"No," I said, feeling tired. "I was only indicating that it was me. I was the one you said that to."

"Oh. I told Amelia. Mafia people."

Victor said to Vanity, "Vanity, call your boat. How long will it take to get here from Antarctica?"

Vanity looked surprised, as if she had been caught unprepared for a pop quiz. "I—I don't—how would I know that? She might be on the far side of the Antarctic. I don't know her top speed. You do know Corus warned Amelia that they can tell when I call my boat?"

Victor nodded. "But the people watching the boat, Mestor and Boggin and his crew, want to keep us alive at all costs, and the people coming for us now want us dead."

Quentin looked down at his diagrams. "They want everybody dead."

Victor said, "What's that?"

Quentin passed him a sheet of paper covered with zodiacal symbols and crabbed mathematical calculations. "Not just us. Everyone. They want everyone dead."

Colin said, "Everyone on the ship?"

I spoke up. "I think he means everyone everyone. The whole enchilada. All living things that breathe. Lamia told Quentin her master wants to start the last war, the Armageddon, between Cosmos and Chaos, remember? They want the stars torn down and the dome of the sky to collapse." And, before Victor could object that the sky was not literally a dome, I added, "They want to crack the planet like an egg and make an omelet, trigger a nova in Sol. That sort of thing."

Quentin sighed again.

Vanity leaped to her feet. "Oh my goodness!"

Colin said, "What is it?"

Victor said, "Is someone watching us?"

Vanity said, "I didn't get a chance to finish checking all our stuff! There might be a bug, just a physical bug somewhere, planted on us. I never finished looking!"

Victor had a stiff look to his face. I would not have recognized that look even a little while ago, but in my heart I knew what it was. Leaders who make bad decisions get that look. Leaders who think they may have endangered the lives entrusted to them. But what could he have done differently? We had needed Vanity in here to help with Quentin's experiment, which, had it worked, might have told us the nature of, or how to escape from, the coming danger.

Victor said, "Go look through our possessions. Prioritize your investigation. Check the things we got from Paris last. Anything that the enemy touched or handled is suspect. Anything we took from their hands, or . . ."

Colin said, "Passports. Money. The things Amelia got from ap Cymru."

Vanity said, "I checked mine . . ."

We all passed our papers over to Vanity, and I included the envelope of money. Vanity closed her eyes and began shuffling through the passports slowly.

I jumped up. It was obvious. So obvious. I said, "It can't be the passports. Those came from ap Cymru. He is with the Olympians! It's not the Olympians attacking—Quentin just found that out! It's the dress! My wedding dress!"

Colin said, "What wedding dress? Did you guys hear some story no one bothered to tell me?"

I was running toward my room. Over my shoulder, I shouted back to them, "It's not Lamia attacking. It's not Lamia! It's—"

At that moment, even over the mindless roar of the storm, we heard the hideous, tormented, long-drawn-out shriek and rumble of metal plates, vast and heavy metal plates, grinding and twisting, being torn, buckling under unimaginable, titanic pressure.

The deck heeled over at a forty-five degree angle. I slipped and fell to the carpet. The divan was bolted to the deck, but the pile of clothes boxes atop it was not; fabric and cardboard and scented crepe paper fell over my face. I heard crashes behind me as the bottles slid out of the wet bar and clattered to the floor. Our television, our luxurious television, toppled from its stand and fell with a noise of shattering glass.

"I'm not paying for that," said Colin, who was facedown on the deck.

An alarm hooted through the ship. I heard tumbling crashes, shouts, and screams of alarm and panic ringing from the other cabins and staterooms.

"That felt like we hit an iceberg," said Quentin, from somewhere behind me.

The lights in the cabin flickered and went dark. It was black as pitch. There were no lights anywhere.

"No," I said, raising my voice to be overheard above the rising wail of mixed people's voices crying out from the cabins around us, the hoots and klaxons or various alarms. "It's Echidna. Grendel's mom. She's pulled the ship off course."

5.

Yellow emergency lights spluttered and came on. As soon as the ship was done with her sharp-angled turn, the deck went flat again. The captain's voice, immensely amplified, rang from loudspeakers, telling the passengers that the ship was still afloat, urging them to be calm. "We may have caught up against an obstruction. We are investigating the cause . . ."

I was looking through, or, rather, "past" the decks and bulkheads and hull of the ship.

Victor said, "Do you see what's happening?"

I said: "The water is dark, but, when she grabbed the keel of the ship, there was a flash like emerald-green lightning igniting the water in the sea for a moment. She has transparent flukes like an eel and a sting in her tail like a scorpion sting. I can see the shape of her arms and hands, and the cloud of her long hair as it streams back. She had just ripped away the rudders and propeller of the ship; they were tumbling in the water around her. Her face is very beautiful, but pale and terrible.

"There is something else: ahead of us, at right angles to this normal continuum, is another time-space, intersecting. The intersection takes place along a tubelike zone of discontinuity. Where the tube meets the water, there is a circle of ocean whose inner nature is slightly different than that of our world. Directly below this circle of water is an undersea mountain with a flat top; there is a courtyard and a temple atop this flat area, and lights shining in the windows of the temple. In the courtyard is a sailor, tied upside down to a post, with his eyes torn out. The remains of a sailor. It is about fifty fathoms down. That is where she is taking us. We are going to be passing over that position."

There was a moment of silence while Victor absorbed this information. Everyone looked blanched and strange in the harsh glare of the emergency lights.

Colin said, "Orders, Leader? And let me just take this moment to say, I hope the words 'run away' appear somewhere in the commands you are about to bark out. And I think I speak for all the parts of my presently un-killed body when I say this."

Victor said slowly, "There may be complicating factors. This isn't Lamia. Grendel's mother may be here simply to kill the human beings aboard. If we are obligated to risk or sacrifice our lives to save the mortals, we cannot run away."

Colin quirked his mouth to one side. "Hmph. Sacrifice lives. I did notice the words 'run away' did appear in the orders, but not exactly in the word order I would have wanted . . ."

"Enough chatter. The question may be moot," Victor said, frowning. He looked at Vanity.

She said, "I can't tell how far away my boat is! She heard me when I called; I can tell she can tell where I am and she is coming, but I don't know any more than that."

Victor turned to Quentin. "If this is Grendel's mother, and she operates on his paradigm—that is the psionic paradigm, right? The inspiration paradigm? Quentin, you are supposed to be able to trump that paradigm. Can you summon up or banish the inspiration energies, the power source, she is using?"

I said softly, "I know what it is. The inspiration. She is coming to build another pile of skulls in her garden behind her house."

Quentin said, "Let me see what I can do. *Incanto sanctum circumque.*" He tapped his wand on the ground and a soft, pearly light issued from one tip. He held it out at arm's length and waved it around his head. The pearly light drew a clearly visible line of light into a perfect circle around him. A ring of pure light hung, floating, in the air at about the level of his shoulders, serene, luminous, wonderful. It was one of the coolest things I had ever seen.

Quentin took out a hand mirror and placed it on the carpet between his feet. He lowered his head and stared down at it, muttering: *"Sator Arepo Tenet Opera Rotas . . ."*

Victor turned to Vanity. "Either to fight, or to flee, or to find your vessel, we will have to get up on deck. All the normal passageways and hatches were locked after the storm reached hurricane proportions. Look for another way out."

Vanity said doubtfully, "I don't think people build secret passageways on boats."

"Look for one nonetheless."

There was noise from the corridor. I could hear voices, calm, loud, authoritative. It sounded as if a gang of the ship's staff were going from door to door, reassuring people and asking if anyone needed help.

Victor said, "Amelia, keep an eye on Echidna."

Vanity yelped. "She can hear it. When you say her name!"

Victor said calmly to the rest of us, "No one say her name again. Say 'fishmonger.'"

Victor stepped over to the door. When the officers knocked, he called out that everything was fine in here. I did not see whatever energy or particle-beam left his body and flashed through the door at them, but I sensed its utility to Victor, and its internal nature. Glassy-eyed, the men turned and continued on down the corridor.

Victor looked over his shoulder. "Progress?"

Colin said, "I am doing a whole fat lot of nothing here."

Vanity said, "Found it. The air duct. For some reason, they built it large enough to crawl through. You would think they'd only make it wide enough to let air pass, wouldn't you? But here it is."

Vanity had her head halfway into a square hole which had opened in the wall above the wet bar. With a click, electric lights came on in the hole, and shone around her body. "There is a switch," she said.

I said, "Something is distorting space-time. That undersea mountain is no longer far away. Now it is almost directly underfoot. We are about to pass into the intersection zone."

Colin looked at the porthole, as if to see outside. Blackness pressed up against the glass. The roaring waves of rain beat a tattoo on the glass.

A whisper came from the light-encircled Quentin. It sounded like his voice, as if he were doing ventriloquism. His voice seemed to be coming from the mirror at his feet. I could sense it was useful to someone other than Quentin, that voice, and its internal nature was alien to this time-space.

"Death, painful death, is all fate holds in store; some will die for want of air, some for terror, hunger and despair. Death if you approach her, one or many, of your four. And yet among your number there are five. Let her return what she has stolen, and she may yet return a . . ."

Colin cried out and put his hands up as if to ward off a blow. The mirror at Quentin's feet cracked. The mirror above the wet bar turned into a spiderweb of shatter lines with a noise like a gunshot. From the bathroom, I also heard tinkling glass and the clatter of falling shards.

The stone on Vanity's necklace gave off a lancing green dazzle, like a flash of summer lightning. And she shouted. Her shout was a shout of joy, however.

I turned to look at the bathroom, expecting to see the mirror broken there. But instead, walls and surfaces blocked my view. For a moment, I was confused. How could a merely three-dimensional surface prevent me from seeing "over" it? Then I squinted, letting out a low moan of fear and annoyance. I had been girlified again. Three-dimensionalized. Amelio-rated, so to speak.

Victor said, "Report."

Everyone started to talk at once.

Victor said, "Oldest first."

I said, "Powers shut off." Keep it brief.

Vanity said, "I sensed what she did. We just passed over a boundary. It is so obvious! I should have figured it out before! This necklace has a boundary stone in it, just like the green table, just like Boggin's ring on his toe. All you are doing is attracting or deflecting the attention of whatever enforces the laws of nature. That is why I can sense when people are pay-ing attention to me, you see? It is so I can do what I do. That is the prin-ciple the ships are built on; that is why they can read minds! I know how to do it now! The trick I did with Bran's Head to turn people's powers off and on! I know how to do it!"

Victor said, "Do so. Do it now."

Vanity said, "Well, I can't do it now. My power is off. But if my power got turned back on, I could turn it off. Other people's, too. You have to be near a boundary for this to work. Something decides where boundaries are . . ."

Victor said, "Later, please. Colin?"

Colin said, "I had a dream while the voice was talking. Knowledge just came into my head out of nowhere. Were you guys wondering what I am supposed to be able to do, like Amelia seeing through walls and Victor seeing molecules and magnetic fields? I saw something with my heart. I saw the future. Fishmonger is going to capsize the ship and trap an amount of air in it. She is going to push it to the bottom. She is going to eat the people a few at a time. She is going to keep them alive, keep the air fresh, for a long, long time. Like a crab tank in the restaurant. I saw an old couple, lying in bed in an upside-down room. I thought they were hug-ging each other. At first, I thought they were kissing. You know, saying good-bye because they both knew they were both about to die. The old gal was already dead. The guy must have been very hungry because he was eating her face . . ."

Vanity said, "Ugh! Stop! No descriptions of cannibal face-eating! No! Ugh!"

Colin said, "A lot more will kill themselves, or each other. It's going to be pretty bad. You know that scene I never translated right in the *Odyssey*? The one where Odysseus and his men are trapped in a cave by a man-eating Cyclopes? Okay. The fishmonger here is from that same background story, see? It will be pretty bad for the people."

Quentin said, "The fishmonger must have pushed us over a ward, in addition to pushing the ship into another sphere of reality, because my friends all fled. The one who was talking was one of the Dukes of Hell, a fairly influential fellow, and the largest spirit I had yet called up. I was going to use him to drive away the influences controlling the fishmonger's powers. I waited too long. We could have won, and been free. I wasn't expecting this. I didn't think our powers could just be shut down like that. The undersea shelf we are passing over must be an area like the school grounds back home. Kind of clever of her, actually."

Colin bent, picked up one of the shards of the broken mirror, and, before anyone could stop him, he drew the sharp point along one arm, making a scratch and drawing blood.

"Gross!" said Vanity.

Colin then dropped the shard, passed his hand over the cut, and wiped the blood away. The scratch was wiped away as well, and his arm was whole.

Colin looked up. "Leader, I can report my powers are still on."

Victor sat down in a chair, and bowed and put his face in his hands.

We were all silent, staring at him.

I had never seen Victor hesitate before. I had never seen him afraid.

The noises in the background, the stir of the wind, the shouts of alarm from other cabins, grew dim. Perhaps the storm was dying down, now that we were overtop the undersea mountain.

Victor raised his head, and his face was pale and stern. He spoke in an even-toned and level voice: "Either we have an obligation to save the human beings, or not. If not, we should run away. If we have an obligation, then we cannot risk ourselves fighting a monster, because good evidence suggests our death would immediately trigger an attack on Cosmos by Chaos, and entail the destruction of the Earth. There are more people aboard Earth than are on this ship. The people here aboard ship, if they viewed the matter objectively, would agree that their sacrifice, in order to preserve the Earth, is a reasonable exchange. Logically, of course, these people aboard ship will perish in any case if Chaos destroys Cosmos. In either situation, whether we are obligated to defend the humans or not, logic suggests that we should run and leave them to their fate."

I could feel the blood draining out of my face. The others had strange, strained looks on their faces, too. Colin was looking particularly annoyed.

Victor continued, "A second factor, though, is the fact that they rescued us. They did not know we were not in any real danger, but, nonetheless, the crew of this ship rescued, to the best of their ability, a group of us stranded in a motorboat. As a general principle, in order to encourage the rescues of ships at sea, there must be an incentive rather than a disincentive attached. One incentive is that the rescued party should operate according to a reciprocal standard, and perform such rescues as may be needed when called upon to do so."

His voice trailed off.

Colin said, "What does all that goobledygook mean, Mein Führer?"

Victor said, "We must see if there is anything we can do without getting ourselves killed, since getting killed, so it seems, might entail the destruction of the Earth by Chaos. We have Colin turn into something large enough to hold us all, something that swims or flies. If we cross back over the boundary we just crossed, our powers may simply turn back on again; Quentin may be able to vanquish the fishmonger in short order."

I said, "In case I wasn't clear on how big she was, let me say again; Grendel's mother is twice as long as this boat; there is no way to get into the water without being right next to her. As for a flying thing, I'd be surprised if Colin could take off in this weather."

Quentin said, "If we cross the ward, and my friends return, I will not be able to send anything back across the ward to where she is wrapped around this ship. We will be able to save ourselves, but not this ship. That is assuming Colin is able to change shape, carry us all, and get us across the ward—which remains to be seen."

Colin said, "What if Colin quits the group?"

As what he meant sank in, I felt as if I had been slapped. Quit the group?

Vanity looked too outraged to speak; I saw the feeling of betrayal and treason written on her features. Quentin bowed his head slightly, turned to one side, hiding his reaction.

Victor remained calm. "I hope you would do us the courtesy of waiting till we are no longer in the middle of an emergency."

Colin said, "I am not sure I want to be in a group that is going to run off and leave this whole ship's complement to die horrible, horrible deaths. What kind of people would that make us? I'd rather be dead than be that kind of person."

Quentin said softly, "And rather have the Earth destroyed in the process, too, I suppose."

Colin barked at him, "Yes! Why not? I am not responsible for what the folks in Chaos do! I didn't start this war!"

The deck tilted slightly underfoot. We all felt it. After a moment, the deck righted itself.

The sensation would not have been strange for someone in a smaller boat. Boats always rock when someone climbs over the side. A ship this size, as steady as a fortress even in the heaviest waves, would not rock if any lesser creature climbed aboard. But Echidna was not one of the lesser ones.

Victor said, "We have no time to debate, no time to come to a consensus. At the moment, you cannot quit the group, since we are in the middle of an emergency. Is it possible, I admit, that my orders are ill-advised, or even wrong. Nonetheless, you will all obey them, promptly and without question, while the emergency lasts."

Colin said, "And what if I just say, stuff it, and go off and fight the monster myself, since no one else seems to be able to?"

Victor spread his hands: "It would be somewhat out of character for you."

Colin's face turned red: "Are you calling me a coward?"

Victor said calmly, "I mean, before now, you displayed great strength of character. You have been, till now, entirely devoted to the group, even to the extent that you committed acts of vandalism and extraordinary disobedience in order to attract attention and pull punishments onto yourself which would have otherwise fallen on other members of the group, especially Amelia, who seemed not to notice your self-sacrifice. I thought it was obvious what you were doing. It showed that you were serious. Serious about the group. Are you not serious anymore?"

Colin said, "We can't just let all these people get killed! They rescued us! You said it yourself!"

"Nor can we all go shooting off any which way we like," said Victor.

For some reason, Colin looked at me when Victor said that. I realized that I had not told Colin about the episode when I would not obey orders during Grendel's attack. That did not mean someone had not told him about that event. And he might have heard a version much less flattering to me than what I might have said.

Colin compressed his lips and said nothing.

Victor was saying, "We are losing time by this talk. I will point out that the fishmonger has already climbed aboard the deck. It is only a matter of moments before she begins tearing up hull plates and killing people. Since this matter is serious, however, I would be willing to have a vote of no-confidence right now, if someone will propose another candidate for group leader. I will ask for a straight vote with no debate. Pausing to debate might cut off any possibility of escape. Fishmonger may be sitting on the hatch that this vent leads to. Candidates?"

Colin said, "Me. I want to lead. And I do not think we can run away. If I am elected, I am going to go fight her."

Victor said, "No speechmaking, please. Any other candidates?"

Quentin said, "I nominate Victor. And I vote for him, too."

Colin said, "I vote for me. Two to one."

Victor said, "I have not voted yet. It is one to one."

Vanity looked at me. She said, "What do we do, Amelia?"

That really surprised me. I suppose Vanity still thought of me as the wise older sister, the person to turn to when the boys were fighting. And although no one had raised a voice, or raised a fist, this was a fight, a fight to the death, really. Colin was challenging Victor's supremacy as the king stallion of the herd.

And it was my fault. It was all my fault. I was the one they were really fighting over.

And the fact that Echidna was here was my fault, too. If I had not taken the wedding dress, she would not be here. It had been hanging on a branch, and I had paused to take it and put it on. My four friends would not be doomed.

Because if Colin fought her, he would die. The voice from Quentin's mirror, the Duke of Hell, had said so. If any of the four of us approached her, either singly or as a group, we would die. The voice said so. But there were five of us.

Let her return what she has stolen, and she may yet return a—

A what? Return a book to the library archive? Return around five? Return all roasted like a pig, apple in her mouth, spiced with garlic and chive?

Alive.

I said, "Alive."

Vanity said, "Amelia . . ."

"Rhymes with five. Alive."

Victor said, "If you would please pay attention to our present political crises, Amelia, we . . ."

"Me," I said, "I am the one he was talking about . . ."

Vanity said, "I second the nomination and cast my vote for Amelia."

I blinked, "What? I wasn't nominating myself for leader—"

Victor said, "I also vote for Amelia." He laughed and looked quite relaxed.

I said, "Wait a minute—"

Victor said, "The leader has ordered us to wait a minute. Everyone please wait."

I said, "How am I leader? Not everyone voted."

Victor said, "If you vote for Colin or for me, that will tie it up one to two to two. But since you nominated yourself, the vote tally now stands at three to one to one, doesn't it?"

The deck shivered underfoot. In the distance, we heard the scream of metal as some huge amount of deck plate was ripped up from its moorings.

Quentin raised his hand to his brow, and gave me a snappy salute. "I change my vote. She knows what we have to do. I see it in her face. Four to one."

Colin raised his hand and gave me a stiff-armed Nazi salute. "Who am I to stand in the way of progress? Five to naught. Hail, Dark Mistress! I yearn for your whip! What are your orders? Do we fight or do we flee?"

More snapping of metal overhead. Echidna was tearing the hatches open.

I said, "Neither. You flee. The four of you. Colin, turn into something. I have to go face Echidna alone . . ."

Colin blenched. "Fuck, no! You cannot just sacrifice yourself to—"

"Quiet! No back-talk! No debate! Everyone in the crawlspace! Snappy! Double-time! Go, go, go!"

I ran into the other room and shoved aside boxes. There it was. I lifted the lid to make certain I had the right box. Soft fabric lighter than smoke, with glints of pearl and shivering dew drops shone back at me: the wedding dress.

20

DIES NOT, NOR GROWS OLD
ALL HER DAYS

1.

Vanity's crawlway led only a dozen feet. There was a set of grilles through which rain was blowing, and a cylindrical housing for some sort of pump or turbine. Unfortunately, the metal cylinder of the turbine occupied all but the merest sliver of the crawlway, and was between us and the grilles which opened out onto the deck.

Colin was in front, and I was in the rear, behind Victor. Vanity and Quentin were in the middle. We heard Colin grunting and straining for a moment or two.

Vanity called to him (shouting over the storm noise), "Use your powers on it!"

He shouted back, "Inspire me!"

Vanity shouted, "Amelia and I will do another striptease act for you if you get that vent off!"

"Ho ho. That would be nice, if I believed you," said Colin.

Well, on the one hand, I did not want to be embarrassed. I should say, I did not want to be crucified with embarrassment. On the other hand, being stuck in an airshaft on a ship about to be pulled underwater by the eldest mother of all monsters who ever preyed on humanity, was not such a great option either.

I wished I could have just whispered this in his ear.

I said to Victor, "Tell Vanity to tell Colin that I promised him anything."

Victor, over the storm noise, said back, "I beg your pardon?"

"Pass the message forward. The promise I made to Colin. Anything. I
said, I'll do anything."

Victor spoke to Quentin; Quentin spoke to Vanity. I heard the mur-
murs of their voices up ahead.

Vanity shouted back to me: "He doesn't believe me! You have to tell
him yourself!"

Oh, God. I put my head down on the cool metal surface on which I was
kneeling. Was I going to have to say this in front of all my friends? In front
of Victor? Oh please, no.

I waited a moment for some miracle to occur, to spare me from this humiliation. But Providence was obviously busy somewhere else today, or
maybe this was one of the things that is supposed to build character.

I shouted, "I said I'll do anything you want, Colin!"

He shouted back, "Anything, anything?"

I shouted, "Yes!"

He shouted back, "Just so we are clear on this, we are talking about
sexual favors, are we not?"

I was really not sure what kind of character this was supposed to be
building.

"Yes!" I shouted back.

"Yes, what?" he shouted in return.

"Yes, we are talking about sexual favors! I want you to cover me with
hot fudge and lick it off!"

2.

There was a noise like the end of the world. Over the shoulders of everyone else in the way, I saw the huge engine-cylinder get crushed like an
empty tin can, and smashed out through the broken grilles. Part of the
wall had been exploded outward, also.

Colin called happily over the noise of the storm, "Well! I guess I am
feeling kind of inspired tonight!"

Soon we were all on deck, being lashed and drenched by the storm.

I could not face any of them. I kept my head turned to the wall, and I clutched the box containing the wedding dress to my chest with both hands.

Someone put a hand on my shoulder. I thought it might be Victor, and the thought that Victor would understand, and would come to comfort me, was comforting.

But Colin's voice came into my ear, "Hey, uh—Amelia. We were just kidding around, okay? I mean—don't be mad at me—okay?"

I shrugged his hand off. It was not Victor. Victor no doubt made his judgment based on the words he heard coming out of my mouth; and no doubt it was a harsh judgment. Not that I blamed him.

I said, "Go to the stern. Change shape. Save the others. Try to get back over the boundary, the ward. No talking. Go."

The hand was removed from my shoulder. In the midst of the storm noise, I heard no sound of footsteps, no final words, well-wishing, or good-byes. Maybe there were none. Maybe they expected me to live through this.

3.

The winds buffeted me as I moved forward. When I came to the main deck, I took shelter underneath an overhang of the deck above. Originally, there had been deck chairs and café tables here. Now the space was empty, and metal grates had been pulled down across the windows.

You might wonder where I found the strength, the courage, to go forward. Any reasonable person would have run away.

But I was upset about Colin and Victor.

Upset? Upset is not the word. I was choking on tears. My life had been ruined, and there was nothing I could do about it. It wasn't bravery. I wasn't sure I had a life worth worrying over. Maybe that is what saved me.

But I was crying, and sobs made it hard for me to breathe, and my eyes felt raw.

I sat in the rain-shadow of the deck for a time, weeping. I hope it was a short time.

When I looked up, I saw that there were lights shining from upper windows, but the ship seemed strangely silent. I could not hear the alarms or klaxons. Had they been shut off? Or was the wind merely drowning all noise?

Lightning flashed. I saw that part of the deck before me, the beautiful deck with the handsome appointments and polished rails, had been driven in, and the bulkhead smashed inward as if a freight train had plowed through the steel and glass.

I picked my way across scattered rubbish and litter. Metal fragments screeched and hissed as they were pushed along the deck surface by the winds, scraping.

There was light to my left. Three decks of balcony and bulkhead were crumpled and staved-in as if a tree had fallen on them. It would have had to have been a redwood tree, I suppose, and made of iron. Perhaps dropped from orbit. Never mind the tree; it looked like a bomb had gone off.

The covered pool was now open to the sky for at least half its length. I walked forward, and was standing on tiles. Not long ago, this had been indoors. There were lights burning on the balconies to the left; those on the right had been extinguished. The balconies, deck upon deck of them, were cracked and leaning, and tables and chairs had been flung each way like leaves in a hurricane. There were metal shards and crumpled wreckage to my left, where tons of steel had fallen as the roof and upper deck had collapsed. To my right was the deep end of the pool. The diving board was still intact. There were tables undisturbed and pretty, sitting beyond, and doorways and storefronts of certain shops built along that deck. It all seemed so normal, that little corner. The shallow end of the pool was beaten to froth by the rain. The deep end was tranquil.

I saw headless corpses floating in the water. One of them wore a white jacket. Was it Miguel? Another had a green-and-gold jacket I had last seen on Klaus, the man who had wanted to take a Jacuzzi bath with me.

I heard a slithering sound behind me. Glass and metal snapped and groaned.

I turned.

4.

Fathom upon fathom and yard upon yard of snaky folds were draped across the deck. Some sort of phosphorescent crusts or barnacles were clinging here and there in scattered scales along her belly. Her scales were gray and green, but with spots and dapples of rich purple, vermilion, poisonous yellow, blood-red. Every few yards along the coils of bunched muscle, translucent flukes of singular delicacy waved like the fans of an angelfish.

Up from the mass of knotting and unknotting coils, rose two swaying columns of scaly flesh. One was her tail, which was fluked like an eel, and bore an enormous swollen sting, lolling like the sting of a scorpion, and the stinger was going in and out, wet with shivering venom. The other blended into her curving hips, narrowed to a sudden waist, above which was an ample bosom, delicate shoulders, graceful arms with slim fingers. She had them over her head at the moment, like a ballerina caught in mid-gesture.

Atop a slender neck was a girlish face, but of a classical beauty: a firm chin, perfect cupid's-bow lips, a straight nose, deep and large eyes beneath level brows. Her hair hung in dark ringlets across her shoulders and down her back, curled like ivy vines, but black as night, and shining with water. Imagine the Statue of Liberty if she were younger. Her eyes were turned upward at the moment. I don't know what she was looking at.

Between her naked breasts, on a necklace that glinted with mingled silver fire and starlight, hung a green stone, a tear of polished marble. It was not the twin of Vanity's necklace, but it was at least a cousin, the work of the same craftsman.

There was darkness overhead, and she stood framed in a great panel of wreckage where she had pulled loose the bulkhead and several balconies. Rain fell all around her.

I do not know how she was able to shrink from something twice the size of a ocean liner to something merely twenty yards long. But it should have occurred to me before this that she could change, or ignore, her mass and length and dimension. After all, the dress I was carrying in my arms fit a girl my size.

She caressed one arm with the other, in a gesture that at first seemed very odd. But then I recognized it. I did it in the shower. She was washing.

She rubbed her hands together, and then, sliding forward in a tremendous rush and rustle of scales, knots of coil opening and folds unfolding, she bowed her head a bit, and dipped her hands into the water of the indoor pool. She shook pink stains off from her delicate fingers. Her profile seemed so serene, so pretty.

Echidna was washing blood off her hands.

It was only then she seemed to notice me. Her head was no higher than mine off the ground at the moment, for her snaky body had dipped to let her touch the pool water. She turned her classic profile, and I looked into her eyes. It was like looking into the eyes of a glacier. Her face was drawn and pallid with anger and grief. Her lips were drawn and bloodless.

Her face was so cold. So pretty, and so very stiff and cold. Imagine a fury and a sorrow too deep to leave any trace of expression.

I didn't know what to say. I didn't say anything.

She stared at me, frozen in surprise, a lioness seeing a bunny sitting fat before her, not running.

I opened the box and shook out the dress. The fairy garment shone and shimmered like smoke.

I held it out.

Echidna stared at the dress, and her eyebrows drew together. A slightest wrinkle of frown creased her ivory brow. There was no other change of expression.

I took one step forward, then another. I held the dress up.

She cocked her head to one side, perhaps puzzled, or perhaps feeling a greater anger beginning to build.

She did not reach for the dress. With one white finger, she reached toward my face. I closed my eyes when she touched me. I don't know what I expected. I expected pain. I expected her to poke an eye out.

She caressed my cheek very gently with a fingertip. I opened my eyes. She lifted a drop of water from my cheek with a fingertip, brought the finger to her lip, and kissed it. No, she did not kiss her finger. She was tasting the drop from my face.

I do not know how she could pick one teardrop out of all the rainwater on my face, and I do not know how I knew that was what she had done. But I was sure.

Gently, she lifted the dress from my arms with her other hand. She smoothed the fabric with her hands, and smiled at it, a smile of long-lost memory, wistful and sad.

Still moving with slow gentleness, she reached out with her hand again and took my shoulder. Her fingers dug into my shoulder cruelly. I winced, but did not cry out.

Like a second head of a two-headed giant, her scorpion tail now rose over her shoulder, pointed its stinger blade at my heart, and drew back.

I said, "I am sorry for your son. I am sorry I didn't love him. I am sorry that he died for me. But I did not kill him. None of these people on this boat killed him."

There was a blur of motion as the scorpion tail shot forward. I closed my eyes, expecting death. I felt the breeze of rapid motion near my face. Her hand was still digging into my shoulder.

I opened my eyes again, and wished I hadn't. The sting was now hanging four inches in front of my eyes. I could see every little detail in the way the sting was constructed. The barb had many little backwards-pointing hairs epoxied together into a single shaft. I saw the mucous membranes surrounding the orifice where the sting retracted and extended from the poison sac. I could smell the heady smell of the venom. It smelled a bit like turpentine, or almonds.

I heard a voice. I am not sure if I heard it in my ears, or in my heart. *Who, daughter, who?*

I said aloud, "Will you promise to spare the people aboard this ship?" *Who killed your bridegroom, daughter?*

The fingers dug more deeply into my shoulder. The long red nails drew blood from my flesh.

I said, "Ow! Promise me. Uh—Mother . . . ? Promise me, please—ouch! *Ow!*"

A look of impatience came over her face. I could see the tension in the tail rise to a peak, and . . .

"Mavors! Mavors sent his bird. But it wasn't his fault. Grendel was about to kill Colin, and he . . ."

She took her hand from my shoulder, raised one finger, and laid it softly across my lips.

Hush, daughter.

With another great surge and rustle of snaky folds, her head went swooping away from me, and train upon train of serpent-mass rose and slithered and folded after her. She did not move like a sidewinder, but, rather, she undulated in an up-and-down sine wave, hypnotic.

Echidna moved away. Chairs and tables, pillars and posts, were torn up and thrown aside in the wake of her passage.

She sine-waved out into the storm, and crossed the wreckage of the deck.

Now she was at the rail of the ship, and her size had increased by ten-fold. She seemed also to be surrounded with a shadow that grew and grew darker as she grew.

Echidna turned and looked over her shoulder at me. Her hair lifted up in a weightless cloud, as if she were already underwater again, and drew a veil across her chins and lips.

Over top of that veil, I could see her eyes, her cold, mad, crazed eyes. In those eyes there was a look of softness.

None of the other women wept for him.

Like an avalanche falling from a sea cliff into the sea, with her graceful hands sweeping back in a swan dive behind her, Echidna fell into the sea. The train of her body surged up in a writhing mass and unwound in midair to follow her into the waters.

After she was gone, I fell to my knees and put my face in my hands, and wept, and wept. These were merely tears of fear, coming now, senseless, now that the cause for fear had passed.

5.

The rain hammered down, less and less.

I looked up when I heard a noise. The rain was getting weaker. I saw a silvery ship in the waters below me, shining.

I heard quick footsteps behind me. I turned just as Vanity, her red hair all plastered down by rain, and sopping wet, threw her arms around me and gave me a hug.

Colin was a few steps behind her.

Vanity sobbed into my shoulder, "You're alive!"

I said, "Where are Victor and Quentin?"

Colin said, "Victor is lowering a lifeboat. Quentin is with him."

I said, "And what the hell are you doing here? My orders were for you to change shape and run away."

Colin spread his hands, raising his eyebrows and looking innocent. "I tried, Dark Mistress, really I did. I just wasn't inspired. I couldn't fly with you left behind—my heart wasn't in it."

"That is the same tone of voice you used to use on Dr. Fell when you hadn't done your assignments."

"It's my paradigm . . ."

"The making-up-excuses paradigm! You are going to get us all killed if
you don't learn to obey orders! We are going to have a court-martial, and
you are going to be punished for this. Don't tell me I can't punish you; I
can have Quentin turn you into a newt!"

Vanity said, "It's my fault. My powers just came back on. I felt . . ."

"If it's your fault, then you will be punished, too! We can't survive if
the group doesn't follow orders!"

Vanity looked shocked, and her lower lip trembled a bit.

Colin stiffened into a proper beefeater's attention and snapped out a
salute. "Leader! Ma'am, yes, ma'am! We thought you were dead! We
thought you were committing suicide to let us get away! You forgot to appoint a second-in-command! Ma'am! There was no way to vote in a new
leader, ma'am! It was a two-to-two tie! Ma'am! So actually, it's your fault,
ma'am, if you don't mind my saying so, ma'am! Private First Class Fair reports that someone is watching us now! We may be under attack!"

I said to Vanity, "What's going on?"

I could see that she really didn't want to talk to me, because she
thought I was being unreasonable and cruel, but she straightened her
spine and stiffened her trembling lip and spat out in a voice as calm and
controlled as anything Victor could do: "The moment you were killed—
we thought you were killed—something far away turned and looked at us.
Like an alarm bell ringing. I thought it might be Mavors. Ma'am."

I opened my mouth to say she didn't have to call me "ma'am," but
then I closed it again. Maybe she did have to. It might be good for her.
Build character.

Vanity forgot about being angry with me in the very next second. "Oh
my God! There she is! It's my ship! Yoo-hoo! Hullo!" And she pointed
toward the waters behind me.

There was a flash of lightning at that moment, and all the sea was lit up.

In that single, suspended split-instant of dazzle, I saw the fleet surrounding us.

These were warships of ancient make, like Vanity's ship, but black as
night.

The gods of Olympos had come.

Here Ends *Fugitives of Chaos,*
Volume Two of the
Chronicles of Chaos
to Be Concluded in

TITANS *of*